This Must Be the Place

THIS MUST BE THE PLACE

Maggie O'Farrell

ALFRED A. KNOPF   NEW YORK   2016

THIS IS A BORZOI BOOK
PUBLISHED BY ALFRED A. KNOPF

www.aaknopf.com

Grateful acknowledgment is made to David Higham Associates
for permission to reprint an excerpt from "Snow" by Louis MacNeice,
published by Faber and Faber.

Library of Congress Cataloging-in-Publication Data
Names: O'Farrell, Maggie, [date] author.
Title: This must be the place / by Maggie O'Farrell.
Description: First American Edition. | New York : Alfred A. Knopf, 2016.
Identifiers: LCCN 2015044361 (print) | LCCN 2015048955 (ebook) |
ISBN 9780385349420 (hardcover) | ISBN 9780385349437 (ebook)
Subjects: | BISAC: FICTION / Historical. | FICTION / Urban Life. | FICTION / Sagas.
Classification: LCC PR6065.F36 T48 2016 (print) | LCC PR6065.F36 (ebook) |
DDC 823/.914–dc23
LC record available at http://lccn.loc.gov/2015044361

Jacket images: (clouds) by Brian Stablyk/Getty Images;
(lighthouse) by Zoe Barker/Millennium Images/U.K.
Jacket design by Kelly Blair

Manufactured in the United States of America
First United States Edition

for Vilmos

World is crazier and more of it than we think,
Incorrigibly plural.

—LOUIS MACNEICE, "Snow"

Contents

CONTENTS

This Must Be the Place

The Strangest Feeling in My Legs

DANIEL

Donegal, 2010

There is a man.

He's standing on the back step, rolling a cigarette. The day is typi-cally unstable, the garden lush and shining, the branches weighty with still-falling rain.

There is a man and the man is me.

I am at the back door, tobacco tin in hand, and I am watching some-thing in the trees, a figure, standing at the perimeter of the garden, where the aspens crowd in at the fence. Another man.

He's carrying a pair of binoculars and a camera.

A bird-watcher, I am telling myself as I pull the frail paper along my tongue, you get them in these parts. But at the same time I'm thinking, Really? Bird-watching, this far up the valley? I'm also thinking, Where is my daughter, the baby, my wife? How quickly could I reach them, if I needed to?

My heart cranks into high gear, thud-thudding against my ribs. I squint into the white sky. I am about to step out into the garden. I want the guy to know I've seen him, to see me seeing him. I want him to register my size, my former track-and-field-star physique (slackening and loosening a little, these days, admittedly). I want him to run the odds, me versus him, through his head. He's not to know I've never been in a fight in my life and intend it to stay that way. I want him to feel what I used to feel before my father disciplined me: I am on to you, he would say, with a pointing finger, directed first at his chest, then mine.

I am on to you, I want to yell while I fumble to pocket my cigarette and lighter.

The guy is looking in the direction of the house. I see the tinder spark of sun on a lens and a movement of his arm that could be the brushing away of a hair across the forehead or the depression of a camera shutter.

Two things happen very fast. The dog—a whiskery, leggy, slightly arthritic wolfhound, usually given to sleeping by the stove—streaks out of the door, past my legs, and into the garden, emitting a volley of low barks, and a woman comes around the side of the house.

She has the baby on her back, she is wearing the kind of sou'wester hood usually sported by North Sea fishermen, and she is holding a shotgun.

She is also my wife.

The latter fact I still have trouble adjusting to, not only because the idea of this creature ever agreeing to marry me is highly improbable, but also because she pulls unexpected shit like this all the time.

"Jesus, honey," I gasp, and I am momentarily distracted by how shrill my voice is. "Unmanly" doesn't cover it. I sound as if I'm admonishing her for an ill-judged choice in soft furnishings or for wearing pumps that clash with her purse.

She ignores my high-pitched intervention—who can blame her?— and fires into the air. Once, twice.

If, like me, you've never heard a gun report at close range, let me tell you the noise is an ear-shattering explosion. Magnesium-hued lights go off inside your head; your ears ring with the three-bar high note of an aria; your sinuses fill with tar.

The sound ricochets off the side of the house, off the flank of the mountain, then back again: a huge aural tennis ball bouncing about the valley. I realize that while I'm ducking, cringing, covering my head, the baby is strangely unmoved. He's still sucking his thumb, head leaning against the spread of his mother's hair. Almost as if he's used to this. Almost as if he's heard it all before.

I straighten up. I take my hands off my ears. Far away, a figure is sprinting through the undergrowth. My wife turns around. She cracks the gun in the crook of her arm. She whistles for the dog. "Ha," she says to me before she vanishes back around the side of the house. "That'll show him."

My wife, I should tell you, is crazy. Not in a requiring-medication-and-wards-and-men-in-white-coats sense—although I sometimes wonder if there may have been times in her past—but in a subtle, more socially acceptable, less ostentatious way. She doesn't think like other people. She believes that to pull a gun on someone lurking, in all likelihood entirely innocently, at our perimeter fence is not only permissible but indeed the right thing to do.

Here are the bare facts about the woman I married:

—She's crazy, as I might have mentioned.
—She's a recluse.
—She's apparently willing to pull a gun on anyone threatening to uncover her hiding place.

I dart, insomuch as a man of my size can dart, through the house to catch her. I'm going to have this out with her. She can't keep a gun in a house where there are small children. She just can't.

I'm repeating this to myself as I pass through the house, planning to begin my protestations with it. But as I come through the front door, it's as if I'm entering another world. Instead of the gray drizzle at the back, a dazzling, primrose-tinted sun fills the front garden, which gleams and sparks as if hewn from jewels. My daughter is leaping over a rope that her mother is turning. My wife who, just a moment ago, was a dark, forbidding figure with a gun, a long gray coat, and a hat like Death's hood, she has shucked off the sou'wester and transmogrified back to her usual incarnation. The baby is crawling on the grass, knees wet with rain, the bloom of an iris clutched in his fist, chattering to himself in a satisfied, guttural growl.

It's as if I've stepped into another time frame entirely, as if I'm in one of those folktales where you think you've been asleep for an hour or so, but you wake to find you've been away a lifetime, that all your loved ones and everything you've ever known are dead and gone. Did I really just walk in from the other side of the house, or did I fall asleep for a hundred years?

I shake off this notion. The gun business needs to be dealt with right now. "Since when," I demand, "do we own a firearm?"

My wife raises her head and meets my eye with a challenging, flinty look, the skipping rope coming to a stop in her hand. "*We* don't," she says. "It's mine."

A typical parry from her. She appears to answer the question without answering it at all. She picks on the element that isn't the subject of the question. The essence of sidestepping.

I rally. I've had more than enough practice. "Since when do *you* own a firearm?"

She shrugs a shoulder, bare, I notice, and tanned to a soft gold, bisected by a thin white strap. I feel a momentary automatic mobilization deep inside my underwear—strange how this doesn't change with age for men, that we're all of us but a membrane away from our inner teenage selves—but I pull my attention back to the discussion. She's not going to get away with this.

"Since now," she says.

"What's a fire arm?" my daughter asks, splitting the word in two, her small, heart-shaped face tilted up to look at her mother.

"It's an Americanism," my wife says. "It means 'gun.' "

"Oh, the gun," says my sweet Marithe, six years old, equal parts pixie, angel, and sylph. She turns to me. "Father Christmas brought Donal a new one, so he said Maman could have his old one."

This utterance renders me, for a moment, speechless. Donal is an ill-scented homunculus who farms the land farther down the valley. He—and his wife, I'd imagine—have what you might call a problem with anger management. Somewhat trigger-happy, Donal. He shoots everything on sight: squirrels, rabbits, foxes, hill walkers (just kidding).

"What is going on?" I say. "You're keeping a firearm in the house and—"

" 'Gun,' Daddy. Say 'gun.' "

"—a gun, without telling me? Without discussing it with me? Don't you see how dangerous that is? What if one of the children—"

My wife turns, her hem swishing through the wet grass. "Isn't it nearly time to leave for your train?"

I sit behind the wheel of the car, one hand on the ignition, the cigarette from earlier gripped between my lips. I am searching my pocket for an elusive lighter or box of matches. I'm determined to smoke this cigarette at some point, before the strike of noon. I limit myself to three a day and, boy, do I need them.

I am also shouting at the top of my voice. There's something about living in the middle of nowhere that invites this indulgence.

"Come on!" I yell, secretly admiring the volume I can produce, the way it echoes around the mountain's lower reaches. "I'm going to miss my train!"

Marithe appears unaware of the commotion, which is commendable in one way and irksome in another. She has a tennis ball or similar in a sock and is standing with her back against the wall of the house, counting (in Irish, I notice, with a ripple of surprise). With each number—*aon, dó, trí, ceathair*—she thwacks the socked ball off the wall, dangerously close to her body. I watch while shouting some more: she's pretty good at it. I catch myself wondering where she learned this game. Not to mention the Irish. She is homeschooled by her mother, as was her elder brother, until he rebelled and enlisted himself (with my clandestine help) at a boarding school in England.

My schedule is such that I often spend the workweek in Belfast, coming back to this corner of Donegal on weekends. I teach a course in linguistics at the university, coaching undergraduates to break up what they hear around them, to question the way sentences are constructed, the manner in which words are used, and to make a stab at guessing why. I've always concentrated my research on the way languages evolve.

I'm not one of those traditionalists who lament and breast-beat about how grammar is deteriorating, how semantic standards are slipping. No, I like to embrace the idea of change.

Because of this, within the extremely narrow field of academic linguistics, I retain an aura of the maverick. Not much of an accolade, but there you are. If you've ever listened to a radio program about neologisms or grammatical shifts or the way teenagers usurp and appropriate terms for their own, often subversive use, it probably was me who was wheeled in to say that change is good, elasticity is to be embraced.

I once said this in passing to my mother-in-law and she held me for a moment in her imperious, mascaraed gaze and said, in her flawless Parisian English, "Ah, but no, I would not have heard you because I always switch off the radio if I hear an American. I simply cannot listen to that accent."

Accent aside, I am due, in several hours, to deliver a lecture on pidgins and creoles, based around a single sentence. If I miss this train, there isn't another that will get me there in time. There will be no lecture, no pidgins, no creoles, but instead a group of undergraduates who will never be enlightened as to the fascinating, complex linguistic genealogy of the sentence: "Him thief she mango."

I am also, after the lecture, due to catch a flight to the States. After extensive transatlantic pressure from my sisters, and against my better judgment, I am going over for my father's ninetieth birthday party. What kind of a party may be had at the age of ninety remains to be seen, but I'm anticipating a lot of paper plates, potato salad, tepid beer, and everyone trying to ignore the fact that the celebrant himself is scowling and grumbling in a corner. My sisters have been saying that our father could shuffle off his mortal coil at any time, and they know that he and I haven't always seen eye to eye (to put it mildly), but if I don't come soon I will regret it for the rest of my life, blah, blah. Listen, I tell them, the man walks two miles every day, eats enough pulled pork to depopulate New York State of pigs, and he certainly doesn't sound infirm if you get him on the phone: never does he find himself at a loss when pointing out my shortcomings and misjudgments. Plus, with regard to his much-vaunted potential death, if you ask me, the man never had a pulse in the first place.

This visit—my first in over five years—is not, I am telling myself, the reason for my stress, the explanation for my brain-bending craving for nicotine or for the jittery twitch of my eyelid as I sit waiting. It has nothing to do with it, nothing at all. I'm just a little edgy today. That's all. I will go to Brooklyn, I will visit with the old man, I will make nice, I will go to the party, I will give him the birthday gift my wife has purchased and wrapped, I will chat with my nieces and nephews, I will stick it out for the requisite number of days—and then I will get the hell out.

I crack open the car door and scream "Where are you? I'm going to miss my lecture" into the damp air, then spy a crumpled book of matches in the footwell of the car. I disappear down for it, like a pearl diver, resurfacing triumphant with it in my hand.

At this moment, my wife yanks open the door and commences strapping the baby into his car seat.

I exhale as I strike a match. If we leave now, we should make it.

Marithe scrambles into her place, the dog squeezes in, then over the seat and into the back; the passenger door opens, and my wife slides into the car. She is, I notice, wearing a pair of man's trousers, cinched around the waist with what looks suspiciously like one of my silk neckties. Over the top of this is a coat that I know for a fact once cost more than my monthly salary—a great ugly thing of leather and tweed, straps and loops   and on her head is a rabbit-fur hat with elaborate earflaps. Another gift from Donal? I want to inquire, but don't because Marithe is in the car.

"Phew," my wife says. "It's filthy out there."

Into the backseat, she tosses a wicker basket, a burlap sack, something that looks like a brass candelabra, and, finally, an ancient, tarnished egg whisk.

I say nothing.

I slide the car into first gear and let off the brake, with a perverse feeling of accomplishment, as if getting my family to leave ten minutes late is a major achievement, and I draw the first smoke of the day down into my lungs, where it curls up like a cat.

My wife reaches out, plucks the cigarette from my lips, and stubs it out.

"Hey!" I protest.

"Not with the children in the car," she says, tipping her head toward the backseat.

I am about to pick up the argument and run with it—I have a whole defense that questions the relative dangers to minors of firearms and cigarettes—but my wife turns her face toward mine, fixes me with her jade stare, and gives me a smile of such tenderness and intimacy that the words of my prepared speech drain away, like water down a plughole.

She puts her hand on my leg, just within the bounds of decency, and whispers, "I'll miss you."

As a linguist, it's a revelation to me the number of ways two adults can find to discuss sex without small children having the faintest idea what is being said. It is a testament to, a celebration of, semantic adaptability. My wife smiling like this and saying, I'll miss you, translates in essence to: I'm not going to be getting any while you're away but as soon as you're back I'm going to lead you into the bedroom and remove all your clothes and get down to it. Me clearing my throat and replying "I'll miss you too" says, Yep, I'll be looking forward to that moment all week.

"Are you feeling OK about the trip?"

"To Brooklyn?" I say, in an attempt to sound casual, but the words come out slightly strangled.

"To your dad," she clarifies.

"Oh," I say, circling my hand in the air. "Yeah. It'll be fine. He's . . . er, it'll be fine. It's not for long, is it?"

"Well," she begins, "I think that he—"

Marithe might be picking up on something because suddenly she shouts, a little louder than necessary, "Gate! Gate, Maman!"

I stop the car. My wife snaps off her seat belt, shoves open her door, steps out, and slams the door, exiting the small rhombus of the rain-glazed passenger window. A moment later, she reappears in the panorama of the windshield: she is walking away from the car. This triggers some preverbal synapse in the baby: his neurology tells him that the sight of his mother's retreating back is bad news, that she may never return, that he will be left here to perish, that the company of his somewhat-scatterbrained and only occasionally present father is not sufficient to ensure his survival (he has a point). He lets out a howl of despair, a signal to the mothership: Abort mission, request immediate return.

"Calvin," I say, using the time to retrieve my cigarette from the back of the dashboard, "have a little faith."

My wife is unlatching a gate and swinging it open. I ease up on the clutch, down on the gas, and the car slides through the gate, my wife shutting it after us.

There are, I should explain, twelve gates between the house and the road. Twelve. That's one whole dozen times she'll have to get out of the car, open and shut the damn things, then get back in again. The road is a half mile away, as the crow flies, but to get there takes a small age. And if you're doing it alone, the whole thing is a laborious toil, usually in the rain. There are times when I need something from the village—a pint of milk, toothpaste, the normal run of household requirements—and rise from my chair, only to realize that I'll have to open no fewer than twenty-four gates, in a round-trip, and I sink back down, thinking, hell, who needs to clean their teeth?

The word "remote" doesn't even come close to describing the house. It's in one of the least-populated valleys of Ireland, at an altitude even the sheep eschew, let alone the people. And my wife chooses to live in the highest, most distant corner of this place, reached only by a track that passes through numerous livestock fences. Hence the gates. To get here, you have to really want to get here.

The car door is wrenched open and my wife slides back into the passenger seat. Eleven more to go. The baby bursts into tears of relief. Marithe yells, "One! One gate! One, Daddy, that's one!" She is alone in her love of the Gates. The dashboard immediately starts up a hysterical bleeping, signaling that my wife needs to fasten her seat belt. I should warn you that she won't. The bleeping and flashing will continue until we get to the road. It's a bone of contention in our marriage: I think the hassle of fastening and unfastening the seat belt is outweighed by the cessation of that infernal noise; she disagrees.

"So, your dad," my wife continues. She has, among her many other talents, an amazing ability to remember and pick up half-finished conversations. "I really think—"

"Can you not just put the seat belt on?" I snap. I can't help it. I have a low threshold for repetitive electronic noises.

She turns her head with infinite, luxurious slowness to look at me. "I beg your pardon?" she says.

"The seat belt. Can't you just this once—"

I am silenced by another gate, which looms out of the mist. She gets out, she walks toward the gate, the baby cries, Marithé yells out a number, et cetera, et cetera. By the penultimate gate, there is a dull pressure in my temples that threatens to blossom into persistent dents of pain.

As my wife returns to the car, the radio fizzes, subsides, crackles into life. We keep it permanently switched on because reception is mostly a notion in these parts, and any snatch of music or dialogue is greeted with cheers.

"Oh, Brendan! Brendan!" an actress in a studio somewhere earnestly emotes. "Be careful!" The connection dissolves in a crackle of static.

"Oh, Brendan, Brendan!" Marithe shrieks, in delight, drumming her feet into the back of my seat. The baby, quick to catch the general mood, gives a crowing inhale, gripping the edges of his chair, and the sun chooses that moment to make an unexpected appearance. Ireland looks green and pleasant and blessed as we skim along the track, splashing through puddles, toward the final gate.

My wife and Marithe are debating what Brendan may have needed to be careful of, the baby is repeating an *n* sound, and I am thinking it's early for him to be using his palate in such a way as I idly turn the dial to see what else we can find.

I pull up at the last and final gate. A Glaswegian accent filters through the white noise, filling the car, speaking in the self-consciously serious tones of the newscaster. There is some geographical blip that means we can, on occasion, pick up the Scottish news. Something about an upcoming local election, a politician caught speeding, a school without textbooks. I twirl the dial through waves of nothingness, searching for speech, panning for a human voice.

My wife gets out of the car; she walks toward the gate. I watch the breeze snatch and toy with hanks of her hair, the upright, ballet dancer's gait of her, her hand in its half mitten as she grips the gate lock.

The radio aerial strains and picks up a female voice: calm but hesitant. It's something about gender and the workplace, one of those issue-led magazine programs you get in the middle of the morning on the BBC. A West Country octogenarian is speaking about being one of the first women employed as an engineer, and I'm about to turn the dial farther, as it's the kind of thing my wife will be avid to hear and I am really in the mood for some decent music. Then a different voice comes out of the little perforated speakers near my knee: the dipping, vowel-lengthened accent of the educated English.

"And I thought to myself, my God," the woman on the radio says, into my car, into the ears of my children, "this must be the glass ceiling I've heard so much about. Should it really be so hard to crack it with my cranium?"

These words produce within me a deep chime of recognition. Without warning, my mind is engaged with a series of flash cards: a cobbled pavement indistinct with fog, a bicycle chained to a railing, trees dense with the scent of pine, a giving pelt of fallen needles underfoot, a telephone receiver pressed to the soft cartilage of an ear.

I know that woman, I want to exclaim, I knew her. I almost turn and say this to the kids in the back: I knew that person, once.

I am remembering the black cape thing she used to wear and her penchant for unwalkable shoes, weird, articulated jewelry, outdoor sex, when the voice fades out and the presenter comes on air to tell us that was Nicola Janks, speaking in the mid-1980s.

I slap my palm on the wheel. Nicola Janks, of all people. Never have I otherwise come across that surname. She remains the only Janks I ever knew. She had, I seem to recall, some crazy middle name, something Grecian or Roman that bespoke parents with mythological proclivities. What was it now? I am recalling, ruefully, that it's no real surprise that things from that time might seem a little hazy, given the amount of—

And then I am thinking nothing.

The presenter is intoning, in the straitened, delicate way that can mean only one thing, that Nicola Janks died not long after the interview was recorded.

My brain performs a series of jolts, like an engine about to stall. I look instinctively for my wife. She has swung the gate open and is waiting for me to drive through.

There is the sensation that a window somewhere has blown open or a single domino has fallen against another, causing a cascade. A tide has rushed forward, then pulled back out, and whatever was beneath it is altered forever.

I gaze back at my wife. She is holding the gate. She leans her weight against it so that it doesn't blow back against the car. She is holding it, trusting that I will drive the car through, the car that contains her children, her offspring, her beloveds. Her hair fills with the Irish wind, like a sail. She is searching the windshield now for my face, wondering why I am not moving forward, but from where she is standing, the glass is opaque with the reflections of clouds. From where she is standing, I might not even be here at all.

The train pulls over the border, in an easterly direction, in and out of rain showers. I sit with the newspaper my wife bought me rolled in my hand like a baton, as if I am on the brink of guiding an invisible orchestra through a symphony.

It's been ten years since I did the reverse journey, on a pilgrimage of sorts. I'd never been to Ireland then: it had simply never occurred to me to come. I am not one of those Irish Americans coshed by a sense of Eiresatz nostalgia, filled with backward-looking whimsy about a country that our great-grandparents were forced out of in order to survive. Within my family I was alone in this: my sisters all wore Claddagh rings, went to St. Patrick's Day parades, and gave their children names with tricky clusters of *d*'s and *b*'s.

I was working at Berkeley, somewhat uncomfortably, as part of the cognitive sciences department. My marriage had just ground to a halt: my wife had been having an affair with a colleague for years, it had transpired. This revelation had pushed me into a minor dalliance, which had in turn prompted my wife to sue for divorce. I was living in the apartment of a friend who was in Japan on a sabbatical; the cuckolding colleague had moved into the house from which I had so recently been ejected. My soon-to-be-ex-wife had morphed into a vengeful harpy who had decided I should pay her astronomic amounts of alimony in return for minimal contact with my kids. Week after week, she refused to honor the custody arrangement our lawyers had thrashed out. I was pouring my entire salary into fighting this; I was having ill-advised affairs with two different women, and preventing their discovery of each other was causing me undue complications and evasions.

In the middle of this brew, my grandmother died and, according to the surprising instructions in her will, was cremated. The usual familial disagreements ensued as to what we should do with her ashes. My aunt favored an urn, in particular an antique Chinese ginger jar she'd seen on sale; my father wanted to go ahead with a burial. An uncle put out the suggestion of a family plot; another was keen to go the way of some kind of woodland, tree-planting deal. It was a cousin who said, shouldn't we put her with Grandpa?

We all looked at one another. It was the end of the wake: the priest had left; the guests were dwindling; the room was filled with crumpled napkins, crumbled cake, and wreaths of cigarette smoke. My dad and his siblings lowered their eyes.

The truth came out, as truths are meant to do at funerals: no one quite knew where Grandpa's remains were. The story was that, years ago, he and Grandma had taken what everyone agreed was their first vacation, to Ireland. Grandpa had retired from the business, and they had never seen the country of their grandparents, all their friends had been, they had a little bit put by, and so on and so forth. Fill in for yourselves the usual reasons why people go on vacation.

They flew to Dublin. They saw the Ring of Kerry, then looked around Cork, the Dingle Peninsula. They saw the famous dolphin. For some reason—no one knew why—they ended up in Donegal, the forehead of the dog, that slice of country squeezed in next to the British annex. Did one of their ancestors come from Donegal, I wanted to know, or perhaps the Protestant North? This latter suggestion was shouted down. They, and we, were 100 percent Catholic Irish, my uncle insisted. To suggest otherwise was a dire insult.

Whatever their ancestry, my grandparents were staying, for a reason that will never be known, at a B and B in Buncrana. My grandmother was filing her nails at what she would later always refer to as an "armoire"—my father was very clear on that point—when my grandfather turned from the window and said, "I have the strangest feeling in my legs."

She didn't look up. She would regret this. Daniel, she would say to me later, always look up, if someone says that to you, always. I can confidently report that no one ever has. In the event, she did not look up. She kept on with the nail filing and said, "So sit down."

He didn't sit down. He fell down, right across the carpet, knocking over the nightstand and an ornamental bowl that my grandmother had to pay for before checking out. A brain hemorrhage. Dead in an instant. Aged sixty-six.

I have the strangest feeling in my legs. How's that for your last words?

Long story short: my grandmother was of the generation that didn't make a fuss. Didn't create waves. They just swallowed whatever bitter pill life dealt them and got on with it. It would never have occurred to her to have her husband's body flown back to the States, to be honored by his numerous offspring. No, she didn't want to put anyone to any trouble, so she had him cremated the very next day, with the local priest in attendance. She did the deed, she checked out, and she came home. She had to pay an excess baggage fee to bring home his suitcase, a detail that always sent my father overboard with rage (he never did cope well with financial outlay of any sort). But what had happened to the ashes, nobody quite knew.

The plight of my long-deceased grandfather touched a raw nerve in me. I left the wake in a frenzy of disgust: it was somehow very typical of my family to go to the trouble of lugging home the clothes of a dead man but overlook his actual ashes. To have never asked my grandmother for the specific location of his final immolation. How could his remains have been forgotten, consigned to some lonely purgatory in a country where none of us had ever lived, alone, abandoned? No doubt I was imagining my own ashes being left to molder in some faraway place, my children never collecting them because they were permitted to see me only once a week, between the hours of 3:00 and 5:00 p.m., at a place of their mother's choosing. Because whenever this paltry, unjust amount of time came around, their mother left a message with their father's secretary to say the children were ill/on a school trip/had a test/couldn't make it that day. Because the legal system is irrevocably tilted toward the female parent, no matter how unfaithful or vindictive she is. Because, however hard the father tries—

I digress.

After I got back to San Francisco, I got hold of the names of all the funeral homes in that part of Ireland and, in between fielding calls from my lawyer, attending court appearances at which I might as well have thrown several thousand dollars into a trash can and dropped in a lit match, attending separate liaisons with my two lovers, trying to find an apartment where I could live when my friend returned from Japan (an eye-wateringly expensive three-bedroomed place because, the lawyer said, it was crucial to show I was "able to provide a home for the children"), I called them. I would sit at the kitchen table at 3:00 a.m., holding on to the end of a joint as if my life depended on it—and perhaps it did—and dial a number on my list. Then I would listen to the soft, cushiony vowels of the reply: "Hello." Said more like *hellouh*: the closing sound elongated, the tongue lowered, farther back than it would have been in the mouth of an American. There was no "how may I help you?" follow-up either, just a matter-of-fact *hellouh*.

It took me a while to get used to.

So, I would sit there in the dark, in my colleague's kitchen, surrounded by crayoned drawings by children who weren't related to me, insomnia raging through me, and I would ask: Can you help me, can you tell me, did you cremate a man called Daniel Sullivan thirty years ago, on a day in late May? Yes, to add to the surrealism of the situation, my grandfather and I have the same name. There were times, in the dead of the San Francisco night, when I felt as though I were trying to track down the ashes of my former self.

At my question, there was always a momentary pause and, after a scuffling, a few exchanges I was convinced were often in Irish, the thunk-swoosh of a filing cabinet being opened, the answer was always no. Said *nooooo*.

Until one day a woman (girl, perhaps—she sounded young, too young to be working at such a place) said: Yes, he's here.

I held the phone to my ear. I'd been in court that day, where I'd been told I had no further recourse: there was nothing I could do to ensure I could be part of my son and daughter's upbringing; there was no way to force my ex-wife to honor the contact agreement; I just had to hope "she would see sense"; and, in the words of my lawyer, we'd "come to the end of the road." At which I roared, in the domed vestibule of the courthouse, so that everyone in the vicinity turned toward me, then quickly away, all except my ex-wife, who walked steadily to the exit, without looking back, and even the swish of her ponytail was triumphant: "It's parenthood. There's not supposed to be an end of the road."

For something to come right, to have someone say, yes, here he is, seemed an impossibility, a tiny sweetener in all the oceans of bitterness in which I was currently drowning.

"You have him?" I said.

There was a slight pause, as if the girl was taken aback by my emotion.

"Yes," she said again.

"Well, where is he?" I'd heard that funeral homes dispose of ashes if they are not taken away by relatives. I wanted to know where he'd been scattered, so I could tell the family, and we could decide what to do with Grandma.

But instead of saying, We chucked him out the back door, into the sea breeze, into the nearest rosebush, over a convenient cliff, she uttered the unbelievable sentence: "He's in the basement."

For a mad moment, I had an image of Grandpa pottering about in a low-ceilinged but pleasant space, dressed, as he so often had been, in slacks, a mustard-yellow shirt, and a bow tie, spending the last thirty years rearranging storage jars or setting up a Ping-Pong table or sorting nails in toolboxes or whatever the hell it is people do in basements. We thought he was dead, I would shout. But he's just been in your basement all this time!

I cleared my throat and tightened my grip on the phone. "The basement?"

"Shelf four D."

"Four D," I repeated.

"When do you want to come and collect him?"

The question took me by surprise. It had never occurred to me that Grandpa would need to be fetched, like a child from a birthday party. I realized in that moment that I hadn't really expected to find him: the whole thing had been a distraction for me during the lowest point of my life thus far. To have found him was discombobulating, unexpected, unreal.

Ireland: I pictured damp hillsides of vivid green, stone bridges arching over silvering streams, women with an abundance of auburn hair running their fingers up the strings of harps.

"Next week," I almost shouted, "I'll come next week."

Which was how I ended up alone, in the middle of rural Ireland during spring break, ten years ago, alternately drinking myself into oblivion or eating takeout in a series of B and Bs with slippery bed-covers and single portions of milk.

I say "alone," when actually I was accompanied by my grandfather, who was sporting a small taped cardboard box and occupied the passenger seat of the rental car. He and I got along very well, which was not quite how I remembered it when he was alive.

"Remember that time you spanked me with a hurling stick for sassing you at table?" I would say as we bowled across the Irish countryside, which looked surprisingly close to how I'd imagined it, hump-backed bridges and all. Lots of sheep, though: more than I'd ever thought possible.

Or: "How about that time you told my sister that no decent man would have her because she ate a lamb chop with her fingers?"

Grandpa kept his counsel. He didn't even complain when I ground the gears on the stick shift or wavered to the wrong side of the road or ate only potato chips and Guinness for lunch or fired up a joint when it was way past my bedtime.

Then, one day near the end of my allotted fortnight, I was driving from the coast in the direction of the border. Grandpa and I were discussing whether or not we would head elsewhere to check out the scene—Galway, maybe; Sligo; or over the border to Ulster—whether or not we'd had enough of Ireland (I was pretty sure he had). I was rounding a bend when I caught sight of a child at the side of the road. Just crouching there, his chin in his palms.

There was something about him that didn't seem quite right. I hit the brakes and backed up slowly, lowering my window.

"Hey, kid," I said in my friendliest voice. "Everything OK?"

He stood up. He was barefoot, six or seven years old, and was dressed in a weird padded jacket thing that looked as though it had been made by free-spirited people under the influence of something fun.

He opened his mouth and the beginning of a sound came out. It might have been "I" or possibly "my." It was followed by silence. But not any kind of silence: a terse, freighted, agonizing silence. He stared intently at the ground in front of him, his jaw locked, his hands balled into fists. I could see his little chest struggling to draw in breath. He looked in my direction, then away. He was covering for himself pretty well, something I always find just heartbreaking: the bravery of it, the struggle, the small ways kids find to cope. The boy glanced skyward, in imitation of someone deep in thought or giving what he might say some consideration, but I wasn't fooled. I had, a long time ago, been a research assistant on a program for stuttering, and I was remembering all those kids we worked with, mainly boys, for whom speech was a minefield, an impossibility, a cruel requirement of human interaction.

So I took a deep breath. "I see you have a stutter," I said, "so please take as much time as you need."

He flicked his eyes toward me, and his expression was incredulous, stunned. I remembered that, too. They can't believe it when you're so open about it.

Sure enough, the kid said, in the rushed diction of a long-term stutterer: "How did you know?"

He didn't sound Irish, I wasn't surprised to hear. He looked like a blow-in, a settler—I'd heard there were English hippies in the area.

I leaned on my car window and shrugged. "It's my job. Sort of. Or it used to be."

"You're a sp-sp—" He stumbled, just as I'd known he would, over the term "speech therapist." Ironically, it's a phrase almost impossible for a stutterer to say. All those consonant clusters and tongue-flexing vowels. We waited, the kid and I, until he'd gotten out an approximation of the term.

"No," I said finally. "I'm a linguist. I study language and the way it changes. But I used to work with kids like you, who have trouble speaking."

"You're American," he said and, as he did so, I realized his pronunciation was more complex than I'd originally thought. There was English in there, mostly, but something else as well.

"Uh-huh."

"Are you from New York?"

I took out a cigarette from the glove compartment. "I'm impressed," I said. "You have an ear for accents."

He shrugged but looked pleased. "I lived there for a while when I was little, but mostly we were in LA."

I raised my eyebrows. "Is that right? So where are your mom and dad right now? Are they—"

He interrupted, but I didn't take it the wrong way: kids like him have to talk when they can, whether there's a gap in the conversation or not. "We had a house in Santa Monica," he blurted, not answering my question at all. "It was right on the beach and Maman and I went swimming every morning until one day the men showed up and Maman took the flare from the boat and she—she—she—"

He came to the end of this intriguing burst of articulacy and began to struggle in silence, cheeks red, the volatile confederacy of his tongue, palate, and breath dissolving into chaos and strife.

"Santa Monica is beautiful," I commented, after a while. "It sounds like you had fun there."

He nodded, his mouth shut tight, not trusting himself to speak.

"So you live over here now? In Ireland?"

He nodded again.

"With your mom? Your ... *maman*?"

Another nod.

"And where is she? Is she"—I wondered how to put this without sounding threatening—"nearby or ... ?"

He jerked his head behind him.

"She's back there?"

"Th-th-th-the ... t-t-t-tire ... bur-bur-burst."

"Ah," I said. "OK." I pulled up the hand brake and got out of the car. I smiled at him but didn't get too close. Kids can be jumpy, and rightly so. "You think she could use some help?"

Doglike, he dived into the bushes and reappeared on a track I hadn't noticed. He grinned and set off, zigzagging one way, then the next. We went around a bend, then another, the kid shinning up a tree and down again, turning every now and again to regard me with amusement, as if it was a great joke that he had procured my company like this. At the approach of another bend, he dived again into the undergrowth. There was the sound of a rustle, a giggle, and then a woman's voice: "Ari? Is that you?"

"I found a friend," Ari was saying as I came around the bend.

Up ahead on the track a van was raised on one side with a jack. A woman was crouched beside it, tools spread out around her. The sun was so strong that she was just a silhouette, and her hair was so long that it brushed the ground.

"A friend?" she said. "That's nice."

"Here he is," Ari said, turning toward me.

The woman jerked her head around and rose up from the ground. At this point, I could only register that she was tall, for a woman, and thin. Too thin, her collarbone standing out like a coat hanger from her chest, her wrists a circumference that suggested to me she might not possess the strength required to wield those tools. She had a mass of honey-colored hair, and her mouth was screwed up in a displeased pout. She was wearing a pair of overalls, rolled up over a pair of mud-encrusted Wellingtons. She was not at all my type. I remember consciously forming this thought. Too skeletal, too haughty, too symmetric. She had a face that seemed somehow exaggerated, as if viewed through a magnifying glass: the features excessive, the eyes overlarge, widely spaced, the top lip too full, the head disproportionately big for the body.

She tilted her head, she spoke, she gestured: she did something, I don't remember what. All I knew was that the next moment she looked perfect, startlingly so. This would be my first experience of her protean quality, the way she could appear to be a different person from second to second (a major reason, I've always thought, that cinematographers loved her). One minute, she seemed too thin and kind of bug eyed, if I'm honest; the next she was flawless. But too flawless, like the "after" illustration in a plastic surgeon's office: cheekbones like cathedral buttresses, a mouth with a deeply grooved philtrum, pearled skin with just the right number of freckles across the impeccably tilted nose.

I'd later find out that she'd never darkened the door of a plastic surgeon, that she was, as she liked to say, 100 percent biodegradable. I'd also find out that the filthy overalls concealed a pair of stupendously pneumatic breasts. But, at the time, I was thinking that I preferred women with a bit of curve on them, women whose bodies welcomed yours, women whose beauty was flawed, unusual, held secrets of its own: a touch of orthogonal strabismus, a nose as ridged and stark as that on a Roman coin, ears that protruded just a touch.

The bony Botticelli bent down, picked up some kind of wrench, and brandished it at me. "Hold it right there!" she shouted.

I stopped in my tracks. "Don't worry," I said, and almost followed this with, *I come in peace,* but stopped myself just in time; might I be just a little bit stoned still? It was possible. "I mean you no harm."

"Don't come any closer!" she yelled, waving the wrench. Jesus, the woman was jumpy.

"It's OK," I said soothingly, holding up my hands. "I'll stay right here."

"Who are you? What do you want?"

"I just met the kid out on the road. He said you had a flat tire and I came to see if I could help. That's all. I—"

She half turned, still keeping her eyes on me, and let off a long speech to the kid, in French. Ari replied and I noticed that he didn't seem to stammer in French. Interesting, I caught myself observing. *Non,* Ari kept saying, in a slightly exasperated tone. *Non, Maman, non.*

"How did you find me?" she shouted.

"Huh?"

"Who sent you?"

"What?" I was confused now. We seemed to be stuck in a bad spy novel. "No one."

"I don't believe you. Somebody's put you up to this. Who is it? Who knows I'm here?"

"Look," I said, fed up now, "I have no idea what you're ... I was just passing and I saw a kid all on his own at the side of the road and I stopped to see if he was OK. He mentioned the flat and I thought I'd come see if you needed any help. By the looks of things"—I gestured toward the van—"you've got it covered, so I'll head off." I raised my hand. "You have a good day." I turned to the kid. "Goodbye, Ari. It was nice meeting you."

"G—"" he tried. "G-g-g—"

I looked him in the eye. "You know what you can do if you get tripped up by the first letter of a word?"

Ari looked at me, with the trapped, ashamed gaze of a stutterer.

"Substitute something easier, something that launches you off on a different sound. I'll bet," I said, "that a smart boy like you can think of lots of other ways to say 'goodbye.'"

I turned and headed off down the track.

Behind me, Ari shouted, "See you!"

"Perfect," I threw back over my shoulder.

"*Hasta la vista!*" he shrieked, jumping up and down.

"You got it," I said.

"So long!"

I turned and waved. "Take care."

"*Au revoir!*"

"*Adios.*"

I got around the first bend before I heard feet behind me. "Hey!" she called. "Hey, you."

I stopped. "Are you coming after me with your monkey wrench? Should I be scared?"

"What's that you're carrying? Is it a camera? I know it's a camera. I want you to take it out and remove the film, here, in front of me, so that I can see you do it."

I stared at her. My main thought was for Ari: Should he really be living with someone so totally loco? No wonder the kid had challenges with verbal fluency, living with a mother suffering such extremes of paranoia, such delusions, such fears. A camera? Remove the film? Just for a moment, though, as we looked at each other, something flickered across her face that seemed familiar: the slight dipping of her eyebrows into a frown. I'd seen that expression before. Hadn't I? Did I know this woman? A disconcerting notion, when you're in the middle of nowhere, thousands of miles from home.

"Is it a camera?" she insisted, pointing at my hands.

I looked down and saw, to my surprise, that I was holding Grandpa's taped box. I must have reached for it as I got out of the car. He'd always liked a little air, had Grandpa.

"It's not a camera," I said.

She narrowed her eyes, for all the world like a police interrogator. "What is it, then?"

I gripped the now-familiar cube of cardboard, taped over its planes, slightly softened at the corners. "If you must know," I said, "it's my grandfather."

She pursed up her lips, raised her eyebrows: a minuscule arching inflection of her face. Really, it was too strange. Her face was so familiar, that expression so known: where had I seen her before?

"Your grandfather?" she repeated.

I shrugged. I was not, I felt, bound to provide her with any explanations. "He's been feeling a little under the weather lately."

"Seriously? You carry him around with you?"

"So it would seem."

She passed the monkey wrench from one hand to the other. "Ari tells me you help children with speech impediments."

I winced. "The term 'impediment' is generally considered to be a little pejorative. You might try 'challenged.'"

A diva-ish sigh. "Speech challenged, then."

"Well, I did. A long time ago."

Her extraordinary eyes—I'd never seen eyes like them; pale green, they were, with darker circles around their edges—flicked over me assessingly, desperately. Her exquisite porcelain face acquired an expression of vulnerability, and it was easy to tell that it was not an arrangement to which her facial muscles were accustomed. "You think he can be cured?"

I hesitated. I wanted to say I didn't like the term "cured" either. "I think he can be helped," I said carefully. "He can be helped a great deal. As a postgrad, I was involved in a research program to help kids like Ari, but it's not strictly my line of—"

"Come," she said, in the imperious manner of one used to being obeyed. I half expected her to click her fingers at me, like a dog owner. "You can hold the jack while I tighten the wheel and you can tell me about this program. Come."

I thought: No, I won't come. I thought: I won't be bossed around by some hoity-toity madam. I thought: She's used to getting what she wants because she happens to possess the face of a goddess. I thought: I will not come anywhere with you. But then I did. I steadied the jack while she replaced the wheel. I told her what I could remember about the dysfluency program while she turned the bolts. I looked away, with effort, when the hem of her shirt got separated from the waistband of her overalls. I did what a good man might do: I helped, then left.

Later that night, I was lying on the bed in the B and B, contemplating the remains of my dope stash, which wasn't, I was realizing, going to last me until my return. How could I have neglected to buy enough at that dodgy bar in Dublin? I didn't stand a chance in hell of getting any more around here. Would weed even grow in Ireland? I mused. Wasn't there just too much damn rain?

There was a knock at the door, and my landlady, a Mrs. Spillane, a woman with hair that stood out around her head, like dandelion down, and an apron surgically attached to her front, stood there. I had hastily stubbed out the joint and done that pathetic smoker's wave in front of me—why do we do that?—but her expression was that of a woman who knew she was being robbed but couldn't yet prove it.

"Mr. Sullivan," she said.

"Yes?" I said. I even pulled myself straighter, as if to withstand and refute accusations of getting high, alone, in the middle of nowhere, thousands of miles from home.

"This came for you." She was holding, I now noticed, a small parcel, wrapped in a calico bag.

"Thanks." I put out my hands to take it, but she pulled it away. She glanced up and down the corridor, as if checking for the presence of the FBI. "She wants to see you," she whispered.

"Who does?" I replied, noticing that I, too, was whispering. It appeared to be catching.

Mrs. Spillane examined me at our new proximity. I wondered for a fleeting moment what she saw: a large American man, starting to gray at the temples, the whites of his eyes scribbled with red calligraphy? Could she read, in its runes, my jet lag, my long-term insomnia, a dope habit, and unassailable paternal grief? Hard to tell.

"*She* does," my landlady said, leaning forward, attempting what seemed to be a wink.

Dope makes most people paranoid, but I couldn't blame on the drug my ever-present sense that the world was against me: I'd had it even before I'd started out on this bender. What was she saying to me? Was I missing something?

"I'm sorry," I began, "but I have no idea   "

She thrust the package into my hands. For a second, I had a mad notion that my ex-wife had somehow caught up with me and sent some noxious parcel: excrement, the semen of her lover, the severed head of the dog.

Then I looked down at the familiar blue tape bisecting some cardboard. It was Grandpa.

"Oh," I said. "How did—"

"You left it beside *her* car. When you were helping *her*."

I clutched Grandpa to me. I remembered placing him to one side in order to winch down the jack, but how could I have forgotten to pick him up?

"Sorry, Grandpa," I muttered.

"God rest his soul," Mrs. Spillane said sententiously, crossing herself.

"Yes," I said. "Thank you. Well"—I reached for the door—"I think I'll turn in and—"

Mrs. Spillane put her hand on the door to stop it from closing. "She wants to talk to you." She was whispering again.

"Who does?"

She sighed, exasperated. "*She* does."

"You mean the—the woman with"—I had, in my dope-addled state, to concentrate hard so as not to say *the great rack*—"the hair?"

Mrs. Spillane put her face close to mine. She was frowning, examining me, as if she had been considering buying me but was coming to the conclusion that I had too many defects.

"Do you know how to find her?" she whispered, with another glance over her shoulder.

"What?"

Mrs. Spillane hesitated. "You don't know?"

"Should I?" I said, wondering how long she and I could go on conversing in questions.

"She didn't tell you?"

I was floored for a moment but then came back with "Why would she?"

Mrs. Spillane said, "Hmm," thereby breaking the spell. She turned, abruptly, and said, "I need to make a telephone call."

I was left there, with Grandpa, standing in the doorway. I shut the door and leaned my head into its glossy wood. Something about seeing the water-flow grain of it at such close proximity made a decision rise in me like sap: I'd had enough. This cryptic nonsense was my breaking point. Enough with the rain, the dope, the evenings alone, the carting Grandpa around. Instead of igniting the rest of that joint, I was going to pack and drive to the airport. I'd get an earlier flight home: I'd gotten what I'd come for, and I couldn't take the surreal turn to the minds of the people here. I was a fish not so much out of water but way up the shore and over the beach road. I would leave Ireland and never come back. I would go home and try to repair what was left of my life.

I pushed myself upright. I crossed the room, flipped open my suitcase, and started tossing things into it. I was dithering about how Grandpa should travel—carry-on or checked—when there was another knock at the door.

Mrs. Spillane stood in the corridor, as before: the apron, the hair, the crossed hands. "She'll be expecting you tomorrow," she said, in a hushed, sepulchral tone. "The crossroads at ten."

"Huh?"

"I told her breakfast would be finished by eight-thirty, so you could come earlier, but Claudette said ten suited her best."

"Hang on a second—"

"I'm to give you directions to the crossroads. I'll have a map for you at breakfast."

She disappeared, stage right, and I was left staring at an open door.

Typical, I thought, slamming it. A woman like that would naturally have a pretentious name.

"She couldn't be called something like Jane or Sarah," I ranted to Grandpa as I hurled books into my case. "No, nothing like Amy or Laura or Clare. It would have to be something foreign and fancy, like Claud—"

Halfway through uttering her name for the first time, something gave way. It was as if the bricks and timber of an edifice were falling all around me. I suddenly saw, I suddenly remembered where I'd seen her before. She had been a dancer. Or was it a doctor? I'd seen her as an amputee, a murderess, a detective, a nanny. I'd watched her be French, Spanish, Italian, Persian. She'd escaped death and she'd died of cancer, car accidents, pneumonia, tiger attack. She'd killed and been killed. I'd seen her be fifteen; I'd seen her be sixty. She'd fought, punched, stolen, lied, cheated, saved lives, given birth, given head, shot, swum, danced, dressed, undressed, over and over again, for all of us.

To apply the word "famous" to her wouldn't be entirely accurate. Fame is what she'd had before she'd done what she did; what came afterward went beyond, into a kind of gilded, deified sphere of notoriety. These days, she was known less for her films than for having vanished right at the height of her career. Poof. Ta-da. Just like that. Thereby making herself into one of the most-speculated-about enigmas of our time.

I don't know if she'd thought ducking out like that would lessen her fame, but it had only the opposite effect. The press tends not to take such temerity lightly and the celluloid geeks—those oft-bearded types who will recite entire scripts at the drop of a hat, swap continuity errors, or spot background cameos by prefame actors—even less so. She was still, however many years on, the subject of much debate. They were always wondering how she had done it, why she had done it, where she had gone, if she was still alive, whom she might still be in touch with, and would she ever come back? They were forever trying to track her down, posting possible sightings of her on the internet, complete with smudged, grainy shots of someone who bore a passing resemblance to her. I'm not much of a moviegoer, but even I knew the contours of her story: her relationship with that director, their controversial collaborations, her tempestuous reputation, then her disappearance. Hadn't she attacked some journalist or photographer? Didn't she walk out in the middle of making some movie, causing some major studio to go into bankruptcy? Something like that. Whatever had happened, she had pulled off the thing that people of her ilk must dream about all the time: she'd left her life; she'd pulled the plug; she'd disappeared.

And I had found her.

There is a man at a desk. His head is bowed, forehead resting in his hands. The computer screen casts his hair, his clothes, in a cool, leucistic glow.

There is a man at a desk and the man is me.

I sit there, in my office, head propped on fists. I see: the edge of my desk, the nap of my trousers, the heels of my shoes, and, far below, a parallelogram of orange departmental carpet. I am still wearing my coat, still toting my bag. There is a vague smell off me, of offices, of crowded trains, of places I try to avoid. My bag jostles beside me in the chair, neither on nor off the ergonomically molded arm, as if fighting for its share of space.

From beyond the door comes the sound of students, rolling along the corridor, chatting, complaining, shoving one another. The click-clack of heels. An electronic plop as a phone receives a message. Someone saying, who would have believed me, anyway? in a cross voice.

The lecture is delivered. The words have been spoken, the sentence deconstructed. The students have been enlightened as to the difference between pidgins and creoles. They have the theory of creole grammar, hopefully, tucked into their heads. I stood in front of them for an hour. I moved through the lecture. I gave eye contact. I allowed time for questions. I did what I'd come here to do.

And now? I am meant to be leaving for the airport. I should be collecting my things, getting my desk in order, answering a few final e-mails.

Instead, I am unable to do anything besides sit at my desk. My mind zigzags, like a bluebottle, from Brooklyn to Nicola Janks, unable to settle on either one. My father, this goddamn party, and now this.

I raise my head. In the search box of my browser are two words. They have been there since I got back to my office half an hour ago.

"Nicola Janks," my screen tells me, minuscule pixelations arranged to form the letters of her name. I don't think I've ever typed it before, predating as it did the arrival of computers in my life. A strange thought, now, those years in which we existed quite happily without their constant presence.

The cursor, next to the *s* of "Janks," flashes on and off, awaiting instructions, my tap on the return key, a faithful hound, ready to do my bidding, to retrieve whatever I request.

I've been sitting here all this time, debating whether or not I want to know. Whether or not I should hit that key. What will happen if I do, what will happen if I don't? Will anything change, either way? The thought that swirls like flotsam on the surf in my mind is: please. Let it not be that year. Let it not have been then. Let her have died in the late eighties, the early nineties. Let her have made it into her thirties, comfortably so. Let her have had an accident, been hit by a car, knocked off her bike, fallen down a cliff. Let her have contracted some rare, incurable disease. Above all, let her have died quickly, painlessly, in the company of people who loved her. What more, after all, can any of us ask?

Just let it not have been in a forest, alone, in the velvet gray of dawn. *Please.*

When I was a kid, I used to love doing those puzzles where you get a page scattered with seemingly random dots. You have to connect them, number by number, with a pencil line, drawing form out of chaos, eliciting sense from mess. The part I liked best was about halfway through, when you could look at what you'd done, and what was to come, and try to guess what it was. A rocket? A tractor? A palm tree, a sailboat, a dinosaur, a beach? It could be anything. The best ones were those that misled you. You thought it was going to be a railway engine, but it resolved itself into a dragon with smoking nostrils. You thought you saw a cat, but all along you were drawing an iguana.

That same feeling of dislocation between what you thought you were doing and what you actually did envelops me as I sit there, as I press my elbows into the surface of my desk. All along I'd thought my life had been one thing, but it now seems it might have been something else entirely.

I unloop the bag from my neck and let it fall to the floor. I reach for my cigarettes, I loosen my tie, I twist my chair around, I shift some papers from one side of the desk to the other, and then, quickly, before I can stop myself, I turn my chair back around and hit the return button. I hit it hard. My finger joints throb from the impact.

The timer icon appears, tiny grains of electronic sand slipping through its waist. It flips itself, once, twice. Then a blue list appears. Library catalogues, mainly, from universities. Numbers and codes for academic papers by her, a link to a textbook she coedited, a mention of the radio program heard earlier, with an option to download the podcast. This, my eye sees, has a link for a biography, so I click on that and it unscrolls before me, the short life of Nicola Janks.

A novena of birth, nationality, schools, degrees, teaching posts, publications: how strange it is to be distilled in this way, as if we are in the final analysis just geography, coordinates, output. Is this what will be left of us all—computer-coded facts?

The four numbers at the biography's end slide into me, like a cold blade. That the year of her death is, indeed, 1986 seems at once devastating and inevitable. Of course, I think, of course it was then. I knew it already, I find. Perhaps I always did.

Five minutes later, I am moving across the gray concrete slabs that separate the university from the rest of the world. I need some air, a walk, a change of scene. I need to find a cab. Something like that. I cannot stay in that box of an office with my screen staring back at me. I have three cigarettes rolled inside my tin and I intend to smoke them, one after another, before I go to the airport.

I am moving along a bridge, the traffic grinding in contraflow along the pavement edge. There is roadwork ahead, a vat of boiling tar giving off a choking stench and great clouds of smoke. The river beneath is brown and swollen with rain, lapping oily waves at its banks.

When I reach the other side, there is a bench. I sit myself down on it. I start searching my pockets for a lighter. I have time, I tell myself, taking a snatched glance at my watch. Plenty of time. I am just going to take a short moment to steady myself, and then I am going to press on.

The bench is in one of those small parks—marooned green spaces that fill an empty lot on a street and you wonder, in this city, what might have happened there, what crisis could have occurred to clear the area of buildings. And it seems to me, as I sit there, among the ornamental hedges and genuflecting chrysanthemums, as I spark my lighter with a shaking hand and inhale the smoke, that my life has been a series of elisions, cover-ups, dropped stitches in knitting. To all appearances, I am a husband, a father, a teacher, a citizen, but when tilted toward the light I become a deserter, a sham, a killer, a thief. On the surface I am one thing, but underneath I am riddled with holes and caverns, like a limestone landscape.

A taxi, I am intoning to myself. I need to find one, then get a flight to Brooklyn, my sisters and my dad. I need to get on a plane and spend a few days there. I need to be at that party—and then? Then I come back here. Then I stay on track and get on with the life in hand. Then I do not start poking around, finding out whatever the hell happened to Nicola Janks, going off to uproot the truth. It is over and done. The woman is dead. Twenty years or more have passed. I am not going to drop myself down, like a speleologist, into those holes and caverns and start digging around. I have to focus, have to stop trembling, slow my galloping pulse. I have to put Nicola Janks on a shelf for a while, find a cab for the airport, and get my head around spending the next few days with my dad and—

There is a movement to my left. A man and his child, a girl, are sitting down on the bench. I glimpse a pair of scuffed trainers, the ones with flashing lights on the soles, trousers with the hems rolled up. The phrase "room for growth" floats unbidden through my mind as I turn to look at them. There is the girl; there is the father.

It is the child who draws my gaze. She is standing, one arm outstretched. I see that the arm is twisted and held out like that because she is scratching, in the desperate, driven, focused way that only an eczema sufferer can. She is tearing at her inner elbow, fingernails clawed and intent, seeking relief, seeking to feel something, anything, other than

33

the torment of her condition. I see the grim determination of the child's gaze, concentration under suffering.

Here, then, is another hole, another cavern in the life of Daniel Sullivan. Perhaps the largest, most devastating of all. I have to push off from the bench, to move, to force myself away, so great is the grief that has torn through me. I set one foot in front of the other, again and again, putting distance between me and the pair in the park. I have my gaze set on the road. I am treading carefully, as if the ground beneath me is not as firm and sure as it looks, as if it is riddled with underground rivers, as if at any moment a sinkhole may yawn open under my shoes. I am looking out for the lit sign of a cab. I have lost or dropped my cigarette somewhere along the way. The sensation that begins at my feet and trembles all the way through me is akin to the beginning of a seismic event.

Before I leave the park, I will permit myself one last glance at the child by the bench. I tell myself this as I move away. I see a cab, I signal, and it slows down. Just before it reaches me, at the curb, I turn. The girl is crying; the father is bent over his bag, searching for a cream, a lotion, anything. I crane my head to see, and the movement causes something to poke me in the ribs. I feel inside the pockets of my jacket, my palms sliding along the silky, slippery lining. My fingers encounter the reassuring rectangle of my passport. Folded into it will be my ticket. A flight to the States, my first in five years, a return to the house of my father. There it is, in my breast pocket, directly above my thudding, tripping, treacherous heart.

I Am Not an Actress

CLAUDETTE

London, 1989

It was almost the 1990s, the very start of the final decade of the millennium, and we had just arrived in London. We had not long ago left university. Just months previously, we had been holding the whole of critical theory in our heads, we had crammed all night to memorize the dates of European wars, the fluctuations in meaning of the imperfective aspect in Russian. We had entered exam halls, turned over the papers set down on the desks, taken up our pens, and known that these were the last exams we would ever sit.

The things we knew! The sequence of Shakespeare's plays, the defining characteristics of a villanelle, each and every muscle in the human hand, the myriad similarities and differences in the multiple translations of *The Iliad.* We were experts, in our way, with sharp spikes in our knowledge: we knew everything there was to know about one narrow field.

And now? Now we camped out on the floor of anyone who'd have us and we were looking for jobs.

Now we pored over the vacancy columns in the newspapers. Now we wondered what it was we were going to do, how to be, how to live. Now we realized that all the things we had learned were useless. That no one would ever ask us what degree we got. Or how to recognize a metonym or what were the dates of Chaucer or the dying words of Robespierre or the stages of Italian unification or the finer details of Disraeli's foreign policy. We saw that no one cared. All they wanted to know was: Can you type? Are you familiar with word processing, spreadsheets, phone systems? Can you fix a photocopier? Can you replace the carbon in a fax machine? Can you answer the phone while making coffee at the same time as opening the post and tidying the in-trays?

We wondered at times whether our degrees had been worth it.

It was very nearly the 1990s. We arrived in short skirts with thick tights, tiny T-shirts that showed our flat, childless stomachs, trainers in bright neon, colored cagoules bought from secondhand market stalls. We were hopeful. We wanted this to work. We looked at the clothes the people wore in the offices in which we temped. How did they do it? We wondered and studied. The trouser suits and spike heels, the shirts with crisp fronts and high collars, the handbags with tooled flaps and brass fastenings, coats of tweed that buttoned down the front. And the hair: straight and flat as paper, cut so that it swung cleanly around the cheeks. How to achieve these things when we had no iron, no fixed abode, no regular salary, nothing in our suitcases but creased clothes that weren't right for our new life?

We kept reading in newspapers and magazines that London was where it was at, the epicenter of cool, that the best bands were playing every night in pubs just round the corner. We never quite understood this. When we went to the pubs, they seemed dim and close, rows of people sitting with their backs turned, music from hidden speakers cutting through the smoke. London to us, then, was exhausting, a struggle to keep up the appearance of knowing what you were doing, of long journeys on the tube, of finding somewhere to write, rewrite, and print your CV when none of us had a computer. London was about interviews, about a desperate scramble to find a niche in this vast, threatening ecosystem, just a small one, a toehold, to pull off that magic pairing of job + flat, with any luck simultaneously, because one seemed impossible without the other. So we temped and stayed on the sofas of long-suffering friends or relatives or lovers until we could find the golden key to open the door, to persuade the city to admit us, to pass Go, to reach the point where we could say, yes, this is my address, and, yes, I would like to buy a monthly travel pass—no more messing about with day tickets for me.

We went out because the city was there and we were grown up and we were free, and because we couldn't impose all evening, every evening, on the people whose sofas we were sleeping on. We went to repertory cinemas in basements for all the films we'd heard of but never had the chance to see. We went to parties in warehouses in the east of the city where drum 'n' bass pulsed from speakers, and blokes in knit hats offered us cocaine and a famous artist was said to be about to arrive, any minute now. We arranged to see one another by phone, at work, snatched conversations, fixing on a café or bar that one of us knew about, one of us could identify. We would make it with time to spare, clutching our street maps and day tickets. Our sense of different locations began to mesh. One day we grasped that we didn't need to change tube lines to get from Leicester Square to Covent Garden: they were just five minutes' walk apart.

One of us landed a job, a proper job, at a newspaper. We were amazed. Some of us phoned others to discuss this occurrence. Some of us were jealous. Then another of us was appointed as an assistant at an art gallery. More phone calls.

The worst fear was not that the city might defeat you, not that you might not find that job, might not secure that flat, might fail to master the different tube lines, what color they were and where they intersected; the worst fear that kept us all awake at night was that you might have to go home. You might have to return to your parents and say, here I am. I couldn't do it. I didn't manage it. I couldn't pull it off.

More and more of us were finding work. One signed the lease on a flat right by the river, and there was a party, and you stood on the balcony and you breathed in the smoke and noise and splintered light of the city and you knew you didn't have much longer, that you had to do something quick.

You went into the temping agency again and you knew the woman didn't like you. You weren't sure why. You'd passed your typing test, you'd smiled nicely, you'd worn a clean blouse (borrowed without permission from the girl whose floor you were occupying that week, washed and replaced that night).

The temping agent glanced up when she saw you come in, then down. "Nothing this week," she said, and you were about to turn and go, when she added, "Unless . . ."

You stopped, at the top of the stairs.

"Are you interested in film?" she said as she lifted some papers on her desk, first one way, then the other.

"Yes," you said, "yes, I am." You were, as it happened, but you'd have said yes if she'd asked if you were interested in chicken farming.

"Something just came in from . . . the Film Society," she said, and it was as if you'd suddenly run up a hill—your pulse was galloping and your lungs were empty. This was it: this was your route in, your pass, your golden key, your way to effect the metamorphosis into adulthood. It took everything you had in you not to snatch the proffered piece of paper from her hand.

"It's only a few days' work and they're looking for someone with experience, but you could call. It might be worth a try. Fix a time to go in tomorrow."

"I'll go now," you said, groping in your bag for your map.

The Society occupied a building under a bridge at the edge of the Thames. When you stood at the entrance, gathering yourself before you went in, you had the river at your back and buses over your head, sliding in opposing directions, north and south.

The job required you to fold two thousand flyers and put them into two thousand envelopes. Two thousand address labels then had to be affixed and the envelopes fed, one by one, through a franking machine. You got the job: two days' work. You executed it in a damp-smelling room in the basement. You thought that might be it, but they said, Come back tomorrow. You came. You were sent to the printer's to collect a box. More flyers. More envelopes. The franking machine. You were sent the next day to the post office.

You watched everyone carefully. You saw what they did, how they spoke, what they drank. You made them their coffee without being asked. You took an old T-shirt and, after some deliberation, cut off its

arms and hems and wore it over a white shirt, just like the deputy pro-
grammer did.

At the end of two weeks, they said there was a permanent job as
an admin assistant in the office upstairs and would you like it as you
seemed to have a good work ethic, it wasn't very much money but it
was a start, and what did you think? You said, yes, yes, please, yes, I
would, yes, I have a good work ethic, I do, yes, I love to work, I love it.

You ran outside, filled with euphoria. You felt like a shaken bottle
of carbonated water. You wanted to shriek, you wanted to roar. You ran
up the steps and over Waterloo Bridge. You weren't looking where you
were going and you ran into a lamppost. A swelling the size of a door-
knob rose on your forehead. You didn't mind.

And you loved the job, you loved it so much. You answered phones,
you took messages, you made coffee, you inputted what you learned was
called data into databases (this turned out to mean typing addresses).
You were amazed that, at the end of the month, money appeared in
your empty bank account. The miracle of work! The next month, there
it was again. It seemed such a simple, alchemical transaction. You were
required to arrive at the office at 10:00 a.m., to stay there until the evening, doing whatever it was the people wanted you to do, and then they
gave you money.

You searched the narrow columns of the newspaper and found a
room in a shared flat: own bed, near tube, sixty pounds per week. The
room was marginally larger than the bed, overlooked a main road, and
had no curtains, but you didn't care. You sent your new address to your
mother, to your brother, to your friends, to all the people you knew. You
couldn't have been prouder.

The head of the Society was solicitous and said things like "someone of your caliber" to you. You didn't know what she meant by that,
but you smiled and tried harder not to reroute her phone calls accidentally. She let you sit in on meetings, go out on what she called
fact-finding missions, asked you to read documents for her. She wanted
you to "learn the ropes," she said, to "bring you forward."

She took you shopping and made you try on collared shirts in dark
colors, trousers that covered your feet, shoes with laces and stacked,
rubberized soles. You painted your room the white-gray of the London

sky. You had a drink with your friend on the newspaper and she told you the hours she worked, her salary, the difficulty of fixing a mortgage. Most nights, you went downstairs from the office and into the flickering dark of the Society's cinema and watched films until it was time for the last tube home. You ate popcorn for dinner. There was so much to know, so much to watch, so much you had missed out on. You didn't want to forget a thing, so you watched most of the films two or three times.

When directors or actors came to give a talk or a lecture, it fell to you to book their hotels, their flights, their restaurants. You made sure they had drink and food in the green room; you put them into a taxi at the end of the night. You were surprised, sometimes, by how nervous they could be. An acclaimed French director went away to throw up just moments before he went onstage. An actor who had appeared in huge blockbusters before producing a low-budget indie film said he couldn't go on without a double whiskey inside him.

You took care of it all, every whim, every request. You were good at this, you discovered.

You moved to a different flat; this one was closer to the tube. Your room was painted yellow and had a bed reached by a ladder. You would lie in it at night, when you got back late from work, and feel as though you were in the rocking cabin of a ship, being carried by night, that you might wake up in an entirely different place from the one in which you'd gone to sleep.

Opposite the bed was a small oval window. You wanted to take off the curtain, but you couldn't reach it. You liked to look out at the city at night. You told yourself you would paint the walls gray-white, but you never found the time.

You knew the city now. You were part of it. You no longer carried a map in your pocket. People asked you for directions and you could give them. You looked like a Londoner; you dressed like a Londoner; you walked like a Londoner, fast and without eye contact. You tried to phone your mother once a week, but you often forgot. Yes, you told her, I'm OK, everything is good, yes, I'm eating, yes, the job's fine. She didn't really understand what your job was. You suspected she was telling people you were a film director.

The Society held a series of events on the new wave of cinema coming out of Europe. You arranged flights for a group of young foreign-language directors and their entourages: some came from Berlin, Milan, or Barcelona, some from LA. There was great excitement about these events. Journalists rang, wanting interviews. Tickets sold out. The Society's head added more dates, and these sold out, too. You booked hotels; you liaised with assistants; you scheduled press days.

You darted in and out of the interviews. Phone calls came in all the time for the directors: producers calling from the States, journalists from other countries, wives, girlfriends, casting agents, managers. You fielded the calls; you wrote down the messages; you carried slips of paper around the building. There was a buzz, an almost-palpable frenzy. You gathered, from listening in on various interviews and phone calls, that these directors were all under the age of thirty. They were reinventing the parameters of film, expanding the potential of the medium.

There was a dinner. You booked the dinner. You didn't choose the restaurant—one in Soho, owned by an artist—but you called it; you confirmed the numbers; you discussed dietary requirements with all concerned. You sent out invitations to members of the press, carefully selected and vetted by the Society's head. You booked cabs when the time came; you went and told the various directors that the cabs had arrived; you rounded up the directors; you guided them to the doors, where the cabs were waiting; you gave directions to the drivers: over the river, to Soho.

As you shut the door of the last cab but one, something caught on your sleeve. You turned. A director had you by the wrist, his index finger hooked into your cuff. "Are you coming?"

You said, no. You said, not tonight. The truth was that you weren't invited, you were too lowly, too assistanty, but it didn't feel right to say so.

"That's too bad," the man said, in a mixture of American vocabulary and Scandinavian accent. He was Swedish, you knew, and had closely cropped blond hair. When he was with the others in the group, he seemed reserved and watchful; he didn't say much.

You shrugged and smiled. You gestured toward the final cab, where two other directors were waiting.

But he didn't move to get in. "Where are you going now?" he said instead.

Home, you said. I'm going to walk over the river, then get the tube.

The man lit a cigarette. "Is it OK if I walk with you?" He lifted one shoulder, then the other. "I've been indoors all day. A walk is just what I need."

What about the dinner? you said, and the man, Timou Lindstrom was his name, waved his hand, motioning the cab to leave.

"I'll go later," Timou Lindstrom said.

You walked. He walked. He told you stories about the other directors, some of them rude. He related an on-set anecdote from when he was a runner about an actress who asked him to help strap on her false breasts. You tried not to be anxious about the dinner: Would you be blamed if he didn't turn up? What would your boss say if there was an empty seat? Would he go to the dinner when you reached the other side of the Thames?

He showed no inclination to head to the restaurant. You reached Aldwych; you went past Holborn; you walked through Covent Garden. At Cambridge Circus you took the plunge and stopped. The restaurant is just up there, you said. You pointed. You smiled. You put out your hand for him to shake.

He looked at your hand and laughed. "You think I want to go to the dinner? You think that's why I'm walking with you? I hate those dinners. I hate those guys. They drive me mad with all their narcissistic jabbering. I'm walking with you because I want you to have a drink with me."

Oh, you said. Oh, I see.

You went for a drink. You were secretly proud that you knew of a place just round the corner, up some steps, and along a corridor. A row of grimy fairy lights framed each window. The table was unbalanced. Timou wedged it with a beer mat. You leaned your elbows on it to test: it no longer rocked back and forth. Magic, you said.

He asked you about your job, about London, about where you came from. You told him about your English father and your French mother, how they were wildly incompatible but had somehow made it work, about how your father had died when you were a teenager, about how you and your brother hated your suburban comprehensive school and lived only for the holidays, when your mother would whisk you back to Paris. She was, you said, the only mother who came to parents' evenings dressed in Chanel.

As you spoke, his eyes roamed over your face, as if he was collating information about you that he might use later, as if he was thinking up his next question, his next line of inquiry. Tell me more, he said while you were talking about the car ferry to France, about growing up bilingual; What kind of things did she wear, he said, when you were describing your mother walking into the school hall.

Timou told you about the script he was writing. It was about a group of friends who take a trip to a remote Swedish island. It unfolded in real time, he said, and he was just in the middle of describing the technical challenge of this, when he said, "Have you ever acted?"

You were so surprised that for a moment you said nothing. Then you shook your head, laughing a little, saying, no, never, maybe once or twice at school, but really not at all.

"Look . . . ," he began, then grinned. "I'm sorry, I don't even know your name. What is your name?"

Claudette, you said.

"Claudette," he repeated, took your hand and shook it; he was holding a drink with his right hand, so he shook with his left. It had a strangely unbalanced, one-sided feel. "I am pleased to meet you. Very pleased." He kept your hand in his for a moment longer than necessary. "I've never met anyone whose name suits them so perfectly."

You withdrew your hand. You took a swig of your drink. You weren't sure whether whatever was happening here—if anything was happening—was a good idea. Would it be embarrassing at work if you slept with this man? You hadn't been in the office long enough to judge. Did you even want to sleep with him? You'd never been with someone like him—your boyfriends, to date, had been students, as you had so recently been. You'd never slept with a grown-up. You felt you needed to decide where you stood in the next few minutes because things seemed to be moving quite fast. It wasn't right to lead people on, you knew that, so you needed either to cut and run or stay and see how things progressed. You dithered as you swished ice cubes round your glass.

43

Timou was still talking about his film, about how you should be in it. This irritated you at such a basic level that it was putting you off the whole idea of him. It was so shallow a chat-up line, so obvious, so well worn, that you felt insulted to think he might view it as effective. How dare he think that nonsense would work on you? Did he think you were a child?

You shoved your straw back in your glass as he told you he'd been watching you all week. You had, he said, a particularly mobile face, a way of frowning that he liked, a bone structure that took natural light well. That's it, you decided. You wouldn't sleep with him. You'd wrap things up, then head home.

"You'd be great in the role," he was saying, in a low voice. "Absolutely perfect."

You groped under the table for your bag. "But I'm not an actress," you said, lifting your bag onto your lap.

"That," he said, "is precisely why you are so perfect. I don't want actors in my film, people who have been trained, like circus animals, to display themselves to a camera in a certain way. It makes everything so formulaic, so conscious. I'm going to use people who have never been near a film set before. It will make things fresh and unpredictable. I want to rip up the rule book of filmmaking, and this is one way to take things a stage further. No professional actors. Real people only."

You stared at him. He stared back at you. It was like playing that game where you're waiting for one of you to blink first.

"I'm not making a pass at you," he said and, you couldn't help it, you blinked. "I swear. I don't mix work and romance. I have a girlfriend back in Gothenburg," he said, then added: "We went to art school together."

"But I have a job," you said. "And I don't want to be an actress."

He reached out for a strand of your hair. It was long but not as long as it will be later. He lifted it to the light, then tugged it, as if it were something he required and it was inexplicably stuck.

"Well," he said, "how about making an exception, just this once?"

Down at the Bottom of the Page

NIALL

San Francisco, 1999

Niall Sullivan waits, standing on the school steps—his father is, of course, late. He holds his arms slightly away from his body so that the early fall air may pass around him, between his limbs and his torso, between his fingers where webs might have been in another life. His skin, the outermost layer of him, prickles and seethes like lava. If he stands still enough, his clothes won't rasp against it. This is one of the ways Niall has developed to deal with his eczema. Coping strategies, the doctor calls them.

At the sound of his father's car coming around the corner, Niall steps sideways, twice, then back, a move that reminds him of the knight on a chessboard, and conceals himself behind a pillar.

He opens his schoolbag, pulls out his binoculars, loops their strap over his head, and leans around the pillar just enough for a clear, close-up view of his father, sitting behind the wheel of his car.

Daniel, he thinks to himself, *arrives nine minutes late. Facial expression tense, gloomy—worse than this morning.*

Niall was recently allowed to withdraw his first ever book from the adult section of the library. It had been about asteroids, and the layout of the page had been different from anything he had ever seen before. The text had been scattered with small numbers, and right down at the bottom of the page, in very small type you had to squint to read, there were extra facts. Footnotes, his father had told him they were called, when Niall had asked, and shown him how the numbers linked and guided you to the right information. Niall had been enthralled by this system, struck by its beauty, the way there could be one main narrative and, right there, at the bottom of each page, additional helpful information on all the things you couldn't understand. He decided there and then that his life needed footnotes and that he, Niall, should be the one to provide them.

Squinting through his binoculars at his father, Niall commits his observations to memory. *Nine minutes late. Distracted, gloomy.* He packages them up. He files them neatly at the foot of his page, where he will keep them until later, until he's called on to refer back to them. There.[1]

As he watches his father, he is conscious of the thought entering his mind that to rub the inflammation of his wrist with the side of that binocular strap might feel good, might give him some relief.[2] He squares up to this thought. He looks it in the eye. He puts it from him.

Niall eases back his cuff to consult his watch, which is strapped, as always, over the top of his white medical gloves. He squints into the sky. He lifts the binoculars again. He watches his father for another minute and a half, during which time Daniel sits with his head in his hands, fidgets back and forth in his seat, appears to be arguing with himself, grimaces, rubs at his chin.

Niall couldn't say how long he has been making observations, gathering information, about his father;[3] he also couldn't articulate exactly

---

1. Daniel arrives nine minutes late. Facial expression tense, gloomy—worse than this morning.

2. It would, but only for a few minutes, after which it would be worse.

3. Untrue. It's been nine months, ever since he was given a spy set for Christmas. Contents: binoculars, notebook, fingerprint-dusting kit, pen with invisible ink, flashlight, Morse-code booklet. Also, a disguise of glasses and a false mustache, but Niall gave this to Phoebe, who put it on her stuffed dalmatian, where it remains to this day. Christmas, it should also be footnoted, was when it became possible to hear his parents talking back and forth, downstairs, when Niall was in bed, often in the kind of raised voices that he and Phoebe were not allowed to use.

what he's looking for. He just knows it is something that must be done. He tries it on his mother, tries to compile footnotes on her actions and movements, but she is more difficult to pin down. She seems to sense what he's up to, succeeds in eluding him, in finding his hiding places. Daniel has an air of absorption, of oblivion, that makes him a prime subject. There is, Niall has realized, a lot that Daniel doesn't notice.

The thing about spying, Niall thinks as he steps out from behind his pillar and starts making his way across the parking lot, is that things which at the time seem irrelevant might later turn out to be crucial. You just never know. Like the time he overheard his mother, on the telephone, say, in her instructive voice, *you ought to try living with a passive-aggressive,* and Niall had repeated the phrase to himself and had later asked his father what it meant. His father had told him "passive-aggressive" was an example of something called an oxymoron and then, after a moment, had asked him who his mother had been talking to. *Was it her cousin?* his father had wanted to know, and Niall had had to say, No, it was Chris. *Who's Chris?* his father had asked, and Phoebe had chimed in to say that Chris worked with Mommy and that one day Chris had been with Mommy when she'd come to pick Phoebe up from kindergarten and had taken them both for ice cream, that he and Mommy had split a sundae, except that Mommy said she shouldn't eat that kind of thing, and Chris said, *Whyever not?* but ended up eating way more than Mommy, which Phoebe thought wasn't fair at all. Their father, Daniel, had listened to this very carefully. He had, Niall noted, turned off the radio to hear it better. And when Phoebe had finished, he'd had his new faraway look on his face, as if he was thinking about something else entirely. Then he had said, huh, and Niall had footnoted this.[4]

He pops the catch on the car door and climbs in. His father jumps, just as he always does, gives him a huge grin,[5] and says, "Oh, hey. I thought I was going to have to come in and spring you out of there."

"Spring you out," Niall knows, is a reference to jail, which is entirely

---

4. Daniel turned off radio and said: huh.
5. Good things about Daniel #1: he is always pleased to see you.

appropriate for school, an establishment Niall likes and loathes[6] at the same time.

Niall fastens his seat belt but doesn't say anything; his father doesn't expect him to chat,[7] which is a relief after the rest of the world's population.

"So," his father continues as he swings the car out of the school gates and into the road, "I got us an appointment for two o'clock, which we should just about make, but whether we'll be seen on time is quite another matter."

Niall inclines his head. He touches his binoculars, which are now zipped inside his Windbreaker, feels the twin rims of their lenses. His schoolbag rests on his knee, and its presence there feels reassuring, apt.

"How are you doing, anyway?" his father says, without taking his eyes off the road. "You holding up?"

Niall lifts his shoulders, lets them fall, and the weft of his shirt fabric catches and claws at the worst parts of his skin. Not long, he tells himself, inside his head, not long to go.

His father reaches out and turns over one of Niall's hands. Together, they look down at the medical glove, which is spotted with rust brown at the wrist, at the finger joints, across the palm.

"Hmm," his father mutters. "I told her[8] we should have gone yesterday."

Niall curls his hand back into itself. Then he looks at his father. "You OK?" he says.

"Me?" His father seems surprised. The car pulls up at a red light and he glances at Niall. They look at each other for a moment. "I'm great," his father says, in a slightly hoarse voice, breaking eye contact. "Why wouldn't I be?"

The funny thing about his father is that Niall can sense what he's thinking and feeling. He can tune in to his father's mind as if it were a

6. Likes: the board, the desk-affixed pencil sharpener, the science lab, the periodic table, school trips. Loathes: lunchtime, recess, sports.
7. Good things about Daniel #2.
8. The clinic nurse? Or Niall's mother? Uncertain.

radio station.[9] Right now, he can tell his father is upset but pretending not to be. He has the simmering, maddened, slightly dangerous look Niall once saw in the eyes of a horse kept back from its race. This fills him with a specific kind of dread: when his father is in this mood, anything may happen.

Niall shifts his feet, left over right, then right over left, then left over right again, trying to discern which arrangement feels appropriate for now.

"Onward," he says, and his father revs the engine by way of answer.

Niall has been coming to the Pediatric Acute Dermatology Daycare Unit[10] his whole life. It's a place for the city's most severe, most afflicted: you don't get to come here if you have a bit of an itch now and then, a slight rash on the backs of your knees. This is for kids who are inflamed with eczema, head to foot, kids for whom normal clothes and unbroken sleep are impossibilities.[11]

So, once a week, Daniel does what he calls rearranging his schedule and he brings Niall here, to the unit, where nurses in hats and much-washed tunics mix ingredients in little ceramic bowls and click their tongues in sympathy as they smear Niall with the cool, claylike substance,[12] until he looks like a child ghost, a mime artist,[13] then wrap him, toe to neck, in merciful paste bandages. The relief can last a whole day, if Niall is careful, if he can manage to keep the wrappings intact.

So Niall loves the unit. It means twenty-four hours off his mad-

---

9. This is not something Niall can do with other people, except maybe Phoebe, but she doesn't count because she's only six and tells everybody what she's thinking all the time.

10. PADDU for short.

11. Other impossibilities include: sit on upholstery or carpet, pet an animal, wear underwear from regular stores, sleep in beds other than your own, go on sleepovers or playdates, remove your gloves, use soap of any kind, lie or roll or fall on grass, take part in any grass-based sport, swim in a swimming pool, swim in seawater, eat food with your fingers, touch trees or flowers or leaves.

12. A mixture of antiseptic paste, antibacterial ointment, paraffin, and steroid: Niall asked them and they told him.

13. One who works against a black background; Niall saw one once at an arts festival.

dening, exhausting condition. It means an afternoon out of school. It means that he gets to sit next to Daniel in the waiting room while Daniel grades papers.[14] His father always brings something to occupy Niall[15] if he has work to do: a magazine or a book or a set of magnets or, once, a pedometer, so that Niall could fix it to his belt and walk up and down the corridor, recording how many steps it took to get from the drinks machine to the UV-lighting room.

Today, though, his father is not grading papers. He has the papers on his lap. Niall can see the half-marked one at the top of the pile, in slightly smudged black ink, but his father is not looking at it. He is glaring at the ceiling, as if it has offended him in some way, and he is tapping the end of a marker pen against his teeth.

The hardest part, Niall knows, is the waiting. It is now 2:27, almost half an hour after their appointment. The heat in the room is cranked right up[16] and sunlight fills the space, softening the plastic covers of the chairs, making the stacks of wilting magazines hot to the touch. Niall crouches by the table, setting in motion the gyroscope that Daniel has brought him today, the glinting structure spinning away from his white-gloved hands.

The nurse appears in the doorway, a blue column of surgical scrubs against the off-beige of the clinic walls, and runs a finger down the list of names on her clipboard.

It will be Niall walking across the floor, in just a moment. She's going to say his name, he is sure.[17] He can see her lips, her jaw getting ready to form the initial *n* sound; he watches her draw breath. It will be his turn, he knows it.

---

14. Written by his students at Berkeley. Daniel says that most of them haven't even grasped the basics of sentence construction but that there is always the occasional diamond in the rough. That, he has said to Niall, is what I'm there for. The diamond? Niall asked. The occasional diamond, Daniel had clarified.

15. Good things about Daniel #3.

16. Too much central heating is one of the things that makes eczema worse. Other triggers include: dust, detergent, laundry or cleaning products, animal dander, nut and nut derivatives, egg, dairy, soy, perfume, flour, grass, soil, sand, pollen, saliva, latex, wool, synthetic fibers, paint, glue, leaves, seeds, wood smoke, gasoline, felt, shellfish, the seams of clothing, the labels of clothing, fabric trim, chlorine, polyester thread, soft toys, rope, fire starters, plastic cutlery, elastic.

17. Niall has been reading about methods of mind control. He is putting it to the test here.

The nurse speaks his name.

It is not his.[18]

Niall curls his gloved fingers—nails kept short, always, filed down to the nub, but even so—and takes a deep breath, like a swimmer catching sight of an enormous wave, like a hiker learning that there are many more miles to go. He is aware of his skin, his surface, his outer layer, responding to this disappointment, a heated surge between his clothes and that part of him he thinks of as his "self."

The itch, the discomfort, the rash, the inflammation, the redness, the maddening, distracting ailment: this is not him. It is not who he is. There is him and there is his condition. They are two entities, forced to live in one body.

It is 2:36. Niall swallows, pressing his clipped nails into his palms where, even through the layers of protective cotton gloves, he can feel their power, their force. Another half hour, maybe more.

He breathes again, shakes the hair out of his eyes, tries to concentrate on the gyroscope, but there is a stinging, torched sensation along his inner arm, between his shoulder blades, around his neck, circling his ankles like a tourniquet.

The door to the treatment room clicks shut, admitting that other family (a mom, a dad, a little girl, younger than Phoebe, with a raw, bleeding, scaled complexion that is not as bad as his). And he and his father are alone in the waiting room.

Next to him, there is a sudden, lunging movement. His father is up, out of his seat. He seems to spring forward, scattering papers and coats and spectacles. All the strength, frustration, and fury that Niall knows his father keeps coiled deep within him are about to be unleashed, and Niall quails. He flinches. He says, "Dad? Dad?" without even being conscious of deciding to speak because he knows that his father has been building up to this ever since he got into the car—before that, even. Niall doesn't know what his father is about to do—he never knows in moments like these—but what he does know is that it won't be good.

"Dad!" Niall hisses, in the hope that he can recall his father to himself.

But Daniel vaults over the coffee table, over the soft-cornered maga-

18. He decides to give up all mind-control experiments.

zines, the leaflets about emollients and skin-safe detergents, the unloved toys in plastic boxes. He crosses the room in two strides, and when he reaches the opposite wall, he stops only to seize a pen from his jacket pocket and Niall sees what Daniel is about to do.

"Dad," Niall says, "don't—please don't. Don't. You mustn't. Please. Dad?"

His dad doesn't listen. Niall hadn't really expected he would. When his dad is like this, nothing gets through to him[19]—he is insensible to pleas, reason, requests, begging. He brandishes his marker aloft, like a dagger, and then he begins to deface the dermatology advertisements, one by one, muttering as he goes.

"I cannot," he is saying, through clenched teeth, "look at these things for a second longer. The day has come, my friends. It's time for a bit of truth."

Niall has no idea if his father is addressing the posters or the people in them. What difference would it make? His dad has always hated these advertisements; they make him livid. They are stuck to each available space of wall and feature smiling children sporting organic cotton underwear or clothing with flat seams or scratch mitts that fasten around the shoulders. What enrages his father is that the skins of the models are perfect: pale, smooth, untroubled, at peace. They bounce on beds in the closed-end pajamas, they pose with their gloved hands clasped cutely under their chins, they gambol about on lawns, apparently unaware that they have been buttoned into a pediatric straitjacket, from which they will be unable to free their hands without adult assistance.

"I mean," his father is saying as he gives the grinning girl patches of dermatitis around her mouth and down her neck, "how difficult would it be to find a model with actual eczema? To feature a kid who genuinely needs this stuff?" He moves on to the children on the lawn, adding hives and infected staphylococcus spots[20] all over their legs. "Instead

19. Niall's mother calls it "Daniel's impulse-control deafness." Niall has no idea what this means.

20. The more serious result of scratching. If the skin is broken, the naturally occurring bacteria on the body gets in, multiplies, and the eczema becomes infected. It's not fun to have or to treat, as Niall has discovered many times.

they insult us by implying the condition is unphotogenic, unpalatable. It's hypocrisy of the most heinous kind. Why should we, of all people, be forced to look at this crap?"

He is working fast, graffitiing each poster in turn. He does it methodically, working from left to right. The boy in the buttoned scratch sleeves is acquiring a nasty inflammation on his torso, reaching right down to the wrists; a baby next to him now has oozing lesions on its neck and ankles.

Niall sits on his chair, clutching his gyroscope, riveted, appalled. "Dad." He whispers this to his father's back, terrified that a nurse might hear him, stick her head out of the door, and see his father engaged in this activity. What will happen if he is caught? Will he go to jail? Does that happen if you graffiti hospital posters?

"Yeah?" his father booms, without turning, evidently unworried about alerting any passersby.

"Dad," Niall whispers again, the word barely formed in his mouth. "Don't."

"Relax," his dad says, pen lid gripped between his teeth. "There's no one around. These things have had it coming, they really have."

"Please don't."

At the sound of footsteps in the corridor, his dad steps away from the wall, hops over the table, and sits down. Niall is finding he can breathe again when a nurse opens the door. He sits upright, alert, ready to rise. Help, is all he can think. Help is here, at hand, on the way.

But the nurse walks through the room without glancing at them and disappears into the corridor.

Niall feels his eyes fill, feels the burn take hold. His hands spring upright of their own accord and begin to tear at his neck in a sawing motion, back and forth, across the skin of his throat. The feel of it is an exquisite, forbidden, torturing release. Yes, he tells himself, you are scratching, you are, even though you shouldn't, but how good it is, how amazing, but how dreadful it will be when he stops, if he stops, if he can ever end it.

Next to him, he can hear his father searching his pockets for something, lotion or spray, whatever he can reach first. Then he is putting his hands over Niall's, getting his fingers between Niall's nails and his neck, but Niall is not letting go, not permitting him entry, he cannot stop, he cannot, his neck is clasped by a ring of fire, a dementing ruby necklace, and he must tear it off or scratch down, until there is nothing left of his skin, until he reaches bone and sinew and maybe then, only then, will the itching stop.

His father has forgotten the posters. Niall feels this. His father is holding him tight. Niall can smell his aftershave, feel the soft blue of his shirt. It is half embrace, half armlock. His father is getting control of his arms, his hands, forcing his fingers down. Niall can feel this happening and he is strong, he knows, especially when the itch is upon him, but his father is stronger. Niall is fighting, kicking, struggling. He can hear a voice somewhere, crying, no, no, let me go, get off me. His father is saying, it's OK, it's OK, over and over, into his hair, and at the same time he is manhandling Niall across the room, kicking open the door to the treatment ward, and calling out: can somebody help us, please, my son needs to be seen, he can't take it, he can't take it a minute longer, please, can somebody help him?

The noiseless shoes of the nurses come running.

Niall walks with the stiff-legged gait[21] that must be adopted when all your joints are pasted, gauzed, padded. He moves along the treatment ward—the nurses all smile at him, say hello. When he was small, his mother used to bring him, just the two of them, and when Phoebe was born, she would come too, and Niall would push her up and down the corridors in her stroller until it was time to be seen. Now Phoebe is in grade school; she can't come anymore. This makes her stamp her foot: when Niall comes home in his wrappings she will take one look at him and wail, why didn't you take me to the clinic, I love the clinic, why can't I go? His mother doesn't come anymore either because she's gone back to work.[22]

Niall wanders through the ward, past the nurses' station, and into

21. Like that of an astronaut, Niall has often thought, or perhaps a cowboy just come down off his horse.
22. With Chris, who likes to eat sundaes and chat on the phone about passive-aggressive people.

the room with UV treatment units, where there aren't usually many people. If he can pass enough time before returning to the waiting room, his father might decide it's not worth going back to school for the rest of the day. He might take him to the space and science center, where they can walk the halls together, stand under the pinpricked dome of the planetarium, and Niall can tip back his head to look up, far up, into space, safe inside his wrappings.

Niall takes a couple of rides in the elevator. He loiters for a while in the corridor. He wanders past the UV machines again, watching people turn blue under the lights. He visits the drinks machine but remembers he doesn't have any money in his pockets so makes do with the water fountain. When he thinks it's about time to find his dad, he makes his way back to the waiting room and is just about to turn into the open door, when he hears a voice say, "I do like your artwork."

Niall pulls himself up short, stepping behind the door. He knows that voice, he's sure. It's a woman who comes, as they do, on Wednesday afternoon, with her teenage daughter. She wears pantsuits, her hair arranged over one shoulder, and shoes that clip on the clinic linoleum. She always engages Niall's dad in conversation and sometimes Niall wants to say, can't you see he's working, he's grading papers, leave him alone.

"For the sake of argument,"[23] his father's voice comes out as a slow rumble—he's probably concentrating on his reading, "who says it's mine?"

The woman again: "How would you know what I'm talking about, unless it was you?"

"Who says I know what you're talking about?"

"I saw you look at the wall when I said 'artwork'—"

"What wall?"

"—which proves it was you."

A short silence. Niall can picture his father giving the woman his piercing, amused stare. "It does?"

Niall gazes at a display of leaflets. Advice about sun protection for sensitive skins. Antibacterial lotions. How to cope with facial dressings.

---

23. One of Daniel's favorite phrases of all time.

"So," the woman beyond the door persists, "where's your son?"

"In there."

"He went in on his own?"

His father must have nodded because there is a gap. Then the woman says, "Listen, I'm not giving you a hard time about the posters. I just wish I'd thought of it. Who wants to see an ad for eczema products featuring children with flawless fucking skin and—"

"Not me."

"Not you. Or me. Or any of us. Bravo," she says, "that's what I say."

"Fucking." The word presses into Niall's mind, like a thumbtack. Kids at school say it. A teacher sent someone home last week for shouting it at recess. He has never heard adults say it to each other like this, casually, thrown out, as part of a normal sentence. The silence beyond the door swells like dough in an oven, until Niall can bear it no longer and steps into the doorway, into the room. His father says, "There you are." The woman's head snaps around so that she can look at him, and could it be said she had been leaning close to his father, a little bit too close?

"Hi!" says the woman, baring her teeth at Niall. "You're looking very comfy and cozy there."

Niall plants himself in front of his father. "Let's go," he says.

His father glances at him, glances at the woman, then starts to shuffle everything into his briefcase: papers, pens, journals. He hands Niall his jacket, helps him on with it because it can be hard to insert a bandaged arm into a sleeve, his father knows this. Niall picks up the gyroscope from the table; it doesn't fit in his pocket so he carries it carefully in his hand. Then he and his father are trailing themselves and their possessions across the floor, and they are about to leave, they are almost safe, when the woman leaps up, comes after them, takes his father's arm.

"Your glasses," she says, and she is holding them out to him, their frail legs crossed over each other.

Niall looks at her and feels the pressure of her touch on his own arm, as if he and his father are neurologically interchangeable. He watches as his father turns, thanks her, accepts the glasses, which he is always forgetting,[24] and Niall sees that there is a small piece of folded paper tucked into them. Lined, yellow paper,[25] a kind that his father never uses. He sees his father seeing it but pretending not to. The glasses are slid into the breast pocket of his jacket with a few more thanks, and then they leave.

Niall doesn't know it, but there is something about this moment that will imprint itself on his mind: the geometric shapes of sunlight in the unit waiting room, angling themselves over chair arms and table-tops; his father turning from him toward the woman, the woman's voice saying, your glasses; the piece of yellow paper that his father accepted, then hid; the hard edges of the gyroscope pressing into his finger pads through the meshing of his gloves. In a matter of months, the unbeliev-able will have happened and his father will have disappeared from his life and he won't see him again for many years, his mother will say terrible things about his father, and Niall and his sister Phoebe will listen to these things and believe them, yet not believe them, all at the same time. Either way, his father will be gone, the house will be as if he was never there, and sometimes Niall will lie awake and wonder if he'd imagined his father, dreamed him up. Had he ever been there at all? Then he will think about the day his father produced a gyroscope from his pocket and they set it going together, on the table in the Pediatric Acute Dermatology Daycare Unit, and it spun, a perfection of balance, of poise, sending points of light streaming over the walls.[26]

24. Daniel has had five pairs in the last year.
25. In later life, Niall will realize it was legal paper, which implies that the woman was employed in that capacity.
26. The end.

It's Really Very Simple

PHOEBE

Fremont, California, 2010

I'm under the bleachers with the rest of the crowd from eleventh grade and they have a glass tube filled with something and it's bubbling away, with a kind of animal roar, and some of them are taking it in turns to inhale it and the air is wreathed with its chemical stench and I'm pretty sure it's not weed, and I'm not sure what it is but don't want to ask, and I'm regretting wearing the skirt I bought with Casey on the weekend. It's kind of short, a slippery fabric, and I'm having trouble keeping it so my underwear doesn't show. I'm wishing I'd worn cutoffs, like Casey, instead of this skirt.

You can hear the yells and whistles from football practice out on the field and the grind of cars from the road. I like the way, under here, the people up on the bleachers look like shadows as they walk up and down the steps. Shadows without bodies attached to them. Kind of like Peter Pan but the other way around.

I want to point this out to Casey, but she would raise her thinned brows and roll her amber eyes and say something like, God, Phoebe Sullivan, you are so weird.

Stella would have totally gotten it. She would have flopped onto her back, looked up, and said something like, yeah, in that drawn-out way she has.

I'm tugging down on my hem and I'm aware that Mike Lepris has been edging his way over to me for a while now. He has the glass tube in one hand and the lighter in the other. I know he likes me—his friend Carlos told Diane who told Casey who told me—but his eyebrows are kind of shaggy and his right thumbnail is really long and pointed, like the claw of a carnivore. I told Casey this and she said, Phoebe, he plays guitar, like that was supposed to explain everything.

I look over at Casey and see that she is leaning forward and she has the hem of Phil's T-shirt in her fingers. She yanks on it, then lets go, giving a peal of laughter, and I hear Stella's voice in my head, all deadpan: If she had a dance card, she'd be hiding behind it, saying, Tush and fie.

I don't know why I'm thinking of Stella all of a sudden and why I'm feeling so strange. Like I've been cut down the middle and I'm in two places at once, or I'm getting radio interference from somewhere, or I'm just a shadow, like the people up there watching the game, and the real me has gone off somewhere on its own. Dissociation, my brother said, that time when I told him I get like this sometimes. "Dissociation" is the word.

Mike Lepris is next to me now and Phil has his index finger resting on the frayed ends of Casey's cutoffs, and her face is all innocent, like, Nothing's going on here, but I can see her looking around, can see the strain of it, of what might be about to happen, in the corners of her mouth, in the creases under her eyes. She looks kind of like our cat does when she's pretending she's not about to jump up and lick the butter dish but you know she totally is.

It was only when I started this grade that Casey Trent and friends started smiling at me in the corridors and saying hi. Me and Stella had been best friends since first grade and had always hung out together, and then suddenly I didn't see her anymore because I was sitting at a lunch table with Casey, and Casey always had so many people around her that I couldn't see where Stella was so I couldn't invite her to sit down with us. I sort of lost track of her. Mom said she came over to our house a couple of times, looking for me, but I was out with Casey, at the mall or under the bleachers, and then she stopped coming, stopped calling. I see her sometimes, the back of her, with that old red backpack of hers, in the corridors, but we don't speak anymore. She sits two rows in front of me in Spanish, but she doesn't turn around, doesn't meet my eye. I noticed the other day she no longer wears the friendship bracelet I made her.

I don't really know what changed or when it happened. I used to be skinny. I used to wear jeans and loose shirts; Stella and I bought the same ones, mine with blue stripes, hers with yellow. Tits are so overrated, Stella told me when we went to the pool. We stood in the cubicle together and she put her hands under her boobs and pushed them up so that she looked like she was in one of those costume dramas. They just get in the way, she said. Here comes Pancake Sullivan, Mike Lepris shouted at me in math once. Was that really only two years ago? And then, last summer, pretty much overnight, my boobs just grew. Two hillocks, heavy as water, appeared on the front of my rib cage.

Have you stuffed your bra? my mom said to me one morning, her eyes narrow, the way they are when she's caught me in a lie. When I said no, my face all red, she looked at me hard, looked at my chest. Well, Christ, she said eventually, find something to put those in, you can't have them hanging around like that.

It was Stella who took me to the store. A lady with a tape measure took me into a changing room and said not to be embarrassed. Stella talked Polish to her while I tried on bras. A week later, school started and that was when I lost sight of Stella.

I'm jolted out of my thoughts by Mike Lepris. He's putting the hard glass mouth of the tube against my lips, his arm encircling my shoulders, and holding the lighter to the bulb. The tube bubbles furiously, emitting smoke like a dragon, and I turn my head away. I want to say, I don't do this, I haven't done this, but somehow there isn't time and I'm sure that some of the smoke has found its way into me, through the cave of my mouth and down my throat, where it stings and burns. I push it away, coughing, and Mike, next to me, is laughing and his arm is still around my shoulders and then his mouth is on my neck and his lips feel wet and rubbery, he is printing spitty ellipses on my skin, and I know he expects me to turn my head toward his so he and I can get started, and I know I probably should because, let's face it, I'm nearly seventeen and that's really too old not to have done this before, but I think about his pointed thumbnail and his heavy eyebrows that look as though they've been scribbled on his face with marker and him saying Pancake Sullivan all that time ago, and Casey and Phil, with his fingers by her cutoffs' hem and her hair that she winds into curlers every night, and then suddenly I'm up, I'm upright, and my skirt swishes down, as if relieved to be reacquainted with gravity, and I'm swinging my bag onto my shoulder and I'm walking away, toward the exit of the bleachers, and then I'm out in the sunlight again, away from that striped half-light, and they're calling me, some of them are laughing, Mike Lepris is shouting something, not Pancake Sullivan, not that, and Casey is calling my name, but I keep on walking.

It seems as if the side of my head is missing. I can feel air whistling through my skull, like a draft. I have to put up my hand to check if it's still there. It is. I touch my cheekbone, my hair, the shell-whorl of my ear. It's the strangest feeling. I tip my head one way, then the other, then stop because I'm worried my brain might roll out and fall on the ground with a splat.

I pass a boy I vaguely recognize and he is standing outside the gym door, spinning a basketball on one skinny brown finger. He's just there, in a slant of sun, a ball poised and balanced in motion. He's doing it for no reason other than that he wants to and he's good at it. I stop and watch the ball rotate and it doesn't appear to be connected to his hand and it seems like the most amazing thing I've ever seen so I laugh and give him a clap. He turns and looks at me, surprised, and I know it's because I'm judged to be one of the popular girls now, one of the untouchables, and I shouldn't really be acknowledging him. By rights, I should just walk by him as if he isn't there. Hey, Phoebe Sullivan, he says, and raises his hand and lowers it, showing off now, but he doesn't drop the ball. I want to say, how do you know my name, but I smile at him and walk on.

In the parking lot, I see someone who looks like Stella. She's wearing one of the overall things that she and I always used to buy if we found them in vintage stores and I'd forgotten the thrill of seeing one on the racks. Some of them have a name badge on the lapel and it seemed like the funniest thing to us to wear overalls with a name that wasn't ours. I remember finding one that said RANDY and we nearly got thrown out of the changing rooms because we were laughing so hard.

It is Stella, without a doubt. She has the overall arms tied around her waist, a red blouse on the top, the way I used to wear them. She's dyed the tips of her hair a bright, jumping blue and I can see it from a long way off. She's standing at the bottom of the school steps, talking to some boy, and this seems like the best coincidence ever. I set my course toward her. I'm going to say, Stel, where have you been, how could I lose you, let's walk together, do you want to come back to my house?

Then I realize it's my brother she's talking to. Niall is standing in the parking lot, arms crossed in front of him, car keys hooked on a finger. His hair stands up from his head, just like it always does, as if he's recently been electrocuted. I want to spread my arms wide and run toward them. My two most favorite people in the world, ever, here, in front of me.

As I approach, I see Stella turn her head and clock my presence. She turns back to Niall and I know what she's saying: Gotta go.

It's what she says at the end of every phone call, every day, every conversation, every lesson. Gotta go. You can spend the whole day with Stella, wound up in a long, meandering chat, and then, with two short words, it's over and she's gone. I used to tease her about it. You're about to say "Gotta go," aren't you? I'd go to her. Yep, she'd say, gotta go. And then she'd be gone. Over and out.

So Stella looks up at my brother—she's still only five foot two, even in her thick-soled boots, my Eastern European babushka genes, she used to say—says it, gotta go, and she wheels away, without another glance in my direction.

Niall pushes his glasses up on his nose and pats the skin of his inner arm, which is what he does when he gets the urge to scratch.

"What are you doing here?" I call out to him.

"Came to find you," he says.

My brother talks like this, missing out words that other people would consider mandatory. I asked him once why he didn't like prepositions and he frowned and told me I actually meant *personal pronouns*.

That was the name for little words like "I," "you," "we," et cetera. And I've never forgotten it: personal pronouns.

When I get to him, I throw my arms around him, which he doesn't normally like but it's OK when I do it. Here is what my brother smells of: paper, computers, cotton, emollient, toast, soap substitute, herbal tea, windowless rooms. My brother smells of hard work. My brother smells of intelligence, of all-nighters, of education, of dedication and sometimes, I think, loneliness. He wouldn't agree with that, though. My brother graduated from high school a year early with the highest grades ever in the history of high grades. He is legendary among the staff of this school. There are teachers here who still haven't gotten over him leaving.

Niall pushes my hair out of his face. When we were little, we had exactly the same hair, coppery red and curly, the hair of our ancestors from Kerry, but his has darkened to a near brown and I have blond highlights, these days.

He pulls away and looks at me, hard, hands around my arms. Can he smell the dope or whatever it was? Would Niall know what drugs smell like?

"A drive?" he says.

As the car speeds away down Mission Boulevard, I crack the window, push the back of my head into the seat, let the breeze do whatever it wants with my hair. Which turns out to be:

—tugging the side of it out the window
—tossing the top part up and over my head
—making single strands lash into my face and stick to my lip gloss
—pushing the right side in a circular motion, round and round, as if an invisible person between me and Niall is twirling it around their finger

I reach out and push the CD into its slot. Yes, my brother is the only person I know under the age of thirty who still uses CDs. You are guaranteed, in Niall's car, to hear music you've never come across in your life.

Sure enough, the car is filled with a loud, strange sound that is halfway between yelping and singing. Hundreds of women, somewhere far away, were recorded yipping and whooping while other people behind them hit rocks with sticks and jangled bells.

"Niall," I go, "what the fuck?"

Niall doesn't take his eyes off the road. My brother is the cleverest person I know, but he is kind of a monotasker.

"Mongolian throat singing," he says.

"Throat singing? Is that, like, a real thing or did you just make it up?"

"Oh, it's real. Listen."

We listen. The women are reaching a crescendo—a climax, Niall calls it, without any irony whatsoever—and the guys in the background are bashing away at their rocks and I want this never to end, this car ride, with my brother and the wind and the throat singers from Mauritius or wherever.

My brother is the coolest person I know. And he does it without even trying. This is what makes him cool; it's the essence of his inimitable coolness. He isn't cool in the way that the numbskulls at school would define cool. He's beyond that. He wears science-fair T-shirts that are slightly too small, and his hair grows out in all directions, and he would have no idea what the new movies are or what sneakers you should and shouldn't be wearing. I go and stay with him on weekends whenever I can, and when I got back from my last trip, Casey announced to the lunch table that I had spent the weekend visiting my brother, who was a postgrad at Berkeley, and everyone piled in to ask me if I'd been to wild parties, had I seen inside a frat house, was there a beer keg, had I gotten totally wasted, did I hook up with any of my brother's hot friends?

I didn't say that when I got there my brother was really psyched because he'd heard there was geophysical activity expected. I didn't say that my brother and I spent the night at his lab, that he rolled out a sleeping bag for me under a desk, that I fell asleep watching the flickering arms of the seismographs, that my brother was too excited to sleep, that he woke me up at 3:00 a.m. because a tremor had been registering and he wanted me to see it: Look, he said, look at that. Isn't it beautiful?

This is what my brother finds beautiful: scribbling needles on a seismograph. This is what I do on my wild weekends in Berkeley: watch dials in a lab. This is the coolest person on the planet: my brother, the seismologist.

"So," Niall says as we pull up at a red light, "what's the deal with you?"

I clear the hair from my face. "What do you mean?" I retort. "There is no deal with me. Have you been talking to Mom? What has she been saying? Have you—"

Niall is watching the road, watching his rearview mirror. "Rarely talk to Mom, as you know. What's concerning me is"—and he counts off on his fingers as he speaks (he's always loved a list, my brother has)—"your clothing, you and Stella, and the fact that you reek of crystal meth right now."

I feel like crying. Don't, I want to say, please don't. "What's wrong with my clothes?" I shriek, my face hot, my hands reaching down to tug at my hem.

"Are you high right now?" he asks, in the same, neutral voice.

There is a pause in the car.

"Phoebe," he says, and I'm shocked into listening because he doesn't usually do names, "you don't want to get into crystal, you really don't, you—"

"How did you"—I start to cry now because I can't bear Niall to be disappointed in me: that would be the worst thing in the world. "How did you know? I mean—"

"I know, OK?" he says. "It stinks. You stink."

"I didn't know it was that," I wail. Tears and snot are streaming down my face and I can barely speak for sobbing. "I didn't know what it was. I didn't take it, not really. A guy shoved it in my face and I turned away but I think a little bit might have gotten inside me. I'll never do it again, I promise. I promise, Niall."

"Nice people you're hanging out with. You need to stay away from that stuff. And that guy, whoever he is. You haven't seen what goes into that shit. You might think it's fun to get high now, but you know where it ends?"

"Where?" I say, in a tiny voice.

"In a long-term psychiatric unit, with you dribbling into a strait-jacket and peeing into an adult-sized diaper."

I laugh. I can't help it. "An adult-sized diaper? You have some imagination, Mr. Sullivan."

Niall turns to me. "You refute the existence of adult-sized diapers?"

"I don't know what 'refute' means, but I bet they don't exist."

Niall turns back to the road. "Huh," he says. "Shows how little you know."

"Since when do you know so much about adult incontinence?"

Niall swings the car to the left and we pull up outside a coffee shop. He pulls on the handbrake and unclicks his seat belt. He passes a hand through his hair and leans on the steering wheel, all without looking at me.

"Listen," I go, putting my hand on his arm. "It's fine. You don't have to worry. I don't do crystal and . . . I'm not going to hang out with that crowd anymore. And me and Stella, well, the thing is—"

Niall interrupts me to say something, a series of words. They hang in the air between us, clouding it like a swarm of flies. I can hear myself breathing, in-out, in-out, as if I've been running. My pulse is tapping against the skin of my neck. I'm thinking, it sounded as if Niall said, "Dad called me." But he couldn't have said that. It can't be that. Because we never see Dad. He left when I was six and he didn't come back.

The air-conditioning went off with the engine so the air in the car is suddenly thick with late-spring heat. My nose and throat are itching and sore, with hay fever or with something else, and I'm trying to make the words fit together so that they add up to some kind of sense.

"What?" I go.

"Dad called."

"Dad?" I say, as if I've never heard the word—which is kind of true, I'll think later.

Niall nods, turning to look at me.

"You mean . . ." I search his face to try and understand. "You mean . . . What do you mean? 'Dad,' as in . . . one of our stepdads?"

"As in our father."

"Our father?" I echo and am seized by an uncontrollable giggle because it sounds like I'm about to start to pray, like our grandmother does before meals, and it always drives our mother crazy: she starts rolling her eyes and sighing, and Grandma just doesn't stop, she keeps pounding through the words while Mom taps her fingers and stares out the window. I let out a laugh, but it doesn't sound like a fun laugh: it sounds kind of harsh and crazy.

Niall sighs and pulls off his glasses. Without them, his face looks raw, unformed, childlike. He rubs at the skin under his eyes and I suddenly see that his fingers and wrists are patchy and red. His eczema is back with a vengeance, colonizing his skin like an enemy army, and, when I see it, what he has just said sinks into me, water into sand, and it sits there in my belly, cold and wet.

"He called you?" I say. "How? I mean, when?"

"Today. This morning. He was in the States, in New York, he said, for the first time in years, and he decided on the spur of the moment to get a flight down here."

I turn to look out of the windshield. A woman is crossing the road with a bicycle. The bicycle is white and its turning spokes glitter in the sun. How simple, how elegant, her life looks to me: to be wheeling a bike, in the sun, in a yellow dress. "Why?" I hear myself ask.

"To see us."

The woman with the white bicycle has reached the opposite side of the road. I see that she has a dog in a basket at the front. The dog looks out, tongue hanging loose, ears pricked. I am consumed with a sharp longing to be that woman. I want her life, her dress, her dog. I want to be thirty and have a bike with a basket—what is the word for that kind of basket, there is one, I know—and be pedaling home to an apartment with long white curtains and bowls of flowers and a husband who loves me. I want to be over all this, to be past it, to be safe and unreachable in adulthood.

"When?" I say, at the same time as the word "wicker" arrives in my head, like a train at a station. Wicker, I think, with relief. The word is "wicker."

Niall is polishing his glasses on his too-small T-shirt. He puts them on; he pushes them up his nose. He tilts his head toward the coffee shop outside the car and I begin to understand, to read the situation, so I almost don't need to hear it when he says, "Now."

It's really very simple: me and Niall are sitting at a table opposite a man.

We chose these seats by agreement, one we reached without saying anything. Neither of us wanted to slide into the bench beside him. That much we both knew.

So we sit side by side, on chairs, facing a man.

The man is our father.

He has ordered coffee, Italian-style, in a tiny cup. It looks like mud but smells dark and rich. Niall has herbal tea because that's the kind of person he is. It's a flower sort, not berry: he says berry teas are an "abomination," which is one of my favorite Niall words. He's taken out the tea bag, and the tea is so weak it's barely tea at all. Have I mentioned my brother is the coolest person in the world?

I have a soda, no ice.

The man, my father, is asking Niall about Berkeley, and Niall is using his clipped-off sentences to reply and you can see that the man, our father, is thinking it's his fault and I want to say to him: It's OK, he always does that, it's not just you.

"So do you use that tunnel building place? Is that where the lab is?" the man is saying, and he looks so like Niall that it's really quite distracting. It was the first thing I thought when I walked in here: that man over there is like an old Niall. Then I realized it was him, the person we were here to see. Dumb Phoebe. He has the same hair that grows in, like, twenty different ways, the brow that juts out over the eyes, which sometimes look fierce and other times just puzzled, even the same hands. Wide, flat nails with big lumpy knuckles. As I look at his hands I get the sensation that I'm looking down the wrong end of a telescope at something far away and almost indiscernible. I can see this hand in mine, except I'm much smaller and I have to reach up to hold it, and the hand is warm and large and covers mine completely, and my feet are in little blue Mary Janes that I just know are new and I am being told to line them up with the edge of the sidewalk and to wait, always wait, until my dad tells me it's safe to cross. Check and check again, he is saying, and then keep checking while you cross because you can never be too careful. The hand covering mine. And it's odd because I always tell Niall that I can't remember Dad, not really. I remember the shape of a man's back standing at the kitchen door, looking out. But that could have been anyone. I remember the sight of bristles in the bathroom sink after he'd shaved, a bathrobe hanging off the back of a door, a briefcase in the hallway, shoes large as boats kicked off by the sofa, the noise of a typewriter coming from the den. Nothing more.

"And is it actually on top of a fault line?" he is saying, and Niall is nodding, and I am suddenly aware of something flowing between this man and Niall, the wide current of a tide, back and forth. Niall was twelve when Dad left; he had him for twelve years and that's a long time. There's no tide for me.

"How come you know so much about Berkeley?" I blurt, and even though it comes out as kind of rude, he turns toward me and you can tell by the eager, quick twist of his body that he's pleased I've spoken.

"I worked there for years," he says. "All the time I was living with you guys."

"You worked at Berkeley?" I say.

"Uh-huh."

"Like Niall?"

"Yes." He gives me a smile and he looks so happy to see me, his eyes traveling all over my face, and a sudden wave of something crashes over me and I can't tell if it's happiness or sadness. It kind of feels like both.

"I never knew that," I mutter.

Niall doesn't say anything. He just stares at his hands, which are upturned on his knees so that his palms are staring right back at him.

"Are you a seismologist too, then?" I ask.

"No." Dad shifts in his seat, moves his newspaper from the table to the bench. "I'm a . . ." and he says a word I don't understand.

"A what?"

He says the word again.

"What is that?" I ask.

"I study language and the way people use it."

I still don't get it, but I don't want him to think I'm dumb, so I shut up and nod. Niall has started, throughout this exchange, to rub at the skin of his wrist, and when he claws his hand, switching from using his palm to using his fingernails, I am putting out my hand to stop him, because you have to do that with Niall, have to remind him not to scratch, when I see that Dad is doing the same.

Dad has his hand on Niall's inflamed arm. "Still bothered with that, huh?" he says.

Niall shrugs.

"What have they got you on, these days?"

"The usual."

"Which is?"

"Steroids and emollient."

"Hmm." Dad puts his head to one side. He's tapping on Niall's wrist, where the skin is torn and red, the way I've seen Niall do sometimes, and I'm wondering how Niall is doing with this because he doesn't like to be touched, doesn't like to talk about his skin. "Same old, same old," Dad says. "You still see Zuckerman?"

Niall sits, his back in a curve. "Nah. Self-prescribe, mostly."

"You still go to the . . . ?"

Niall lifts his head and looks Dad in the eye. "Daycare unit?"

Dad stops the tapping. He withdraws his hand. I feel again the tide pulling between them. "Yeah," he says, fiddling with his cup, putting the spoon in and out.

"No," Niall says. "I don't."

There is a pause and I'm wondering if people are looking at us and whether any of them could guess the situation and what they would say if they did.

"So, what grade are you in now, Phoebe?" Dad says. "Tenth?"

"Eleventh," I go.

"Of course," he says. "Eleventh. How are you liking it?"

"It's OK."

There is another pause. Niall picks up his wet tea bag from his saucer. It weeps a stream of drops onto the table. He puts it back.

"Any classes you particularly enjoy?" Dad says.

I shrug. I want to leave, I think, and I'm wondering if Niall feels the same.

"Do you have any notion yet of—"

"Where have you been all this time?" I shout, because suddenly I'm mad, I'm mad as hell. How can he just walk into a coffee shop and ask about Niall's job and my grades and expect us to answer and pretend everything's normal? Because that's what this scenario feels like: normal. It feels outrageously, weirdly normal to be sitting here with our dad, and it is normal, except that it totally isn't.

"Where did you go?" I'm yelling. "What happened? How could you leave like that? Why haven't you come before?"

Niall is saying, "Don't," in that way he has, like the way he talks to the dog if it's barking or Mom if she's losing it, and he's scared, I can tell, because he knows he's the one who's going to have to deal with me after this. Not Mom, because we probably aren't going to tell her; not Stella, because she hates me now; not anyone.

"Don't, Phoebe," Niall is whispering, holding on to my elbow like a cop. "Don't."

"It's OK, Niall." Dad is calm. He is leaning forward, holding out a wad of napkins. "You're perfectly entitled to ask those questions."

I take the wad. I press it to my face and it feels good.

"It's a natural reaction," Dad is saying. "You're completely within your rights to yell at me."

I take the napkins away from my face to look at him.

"I would yell at me," he continues. "In fact, I often do. The thing is, Phoebe, I've been living abroad. But I wrote you both every month and again on your birthdays. I don't suppose you ever . . . got those letters?"

I shake my head. Niall stares down at his hands; he starts on his wrist again with all five nails, but this time Dad and I don't stop him.

"I used to hope one might make it through," he says, almost to himself, "just one. I would apply for permission every year, sometimes more, to see you, but it was never granted."

I picture all those letters, thirteen times ten makes a hundred and thirty. Mine and Niall's together makes two hundred and sixty. I wonder what Mom did with them. Did she burn them, throw them in the trash?

The thought makes me cry even more, and Niall is scratching, and Dad says more. He says that for a long time he tried to see us every week, but Mom always managed to thwart him, in one way or another. He says he spent all his money on court cases to gain more time with us and to try to enforce the time he was supposed to have, but it didn't work. He was totally broke when he went away—"broke and brokenhearted"—and then he met this woman and married her. He says he flew in this morning with the express purpose of tracking us down. "I was at Newark airport—about to go visit my dad, actually—and I've been thinking for a while that Niall is over twenty-one now. Legally an adult. So I've been planning to come, to give seeing you another go. But there I was, in the States, so I just got on a plane for California and I decided I wasn't going to leave until I found you both. And here we are."

He sits back in the booth. He picks up a spoon and looks at it as if he's never seen one before. "I never gave up on the hope I might see you both again," he says, apparently to the spoon. "There wasn't a day, an hour, a minute, when I didn't think about you. I want you always to know that."

I have no idea what to do with this information, so I take a huge slurp of my soda and it's gone kind of flat but, even so, it floods the back of my throat and I gag and cough, and Niall has to smack me on the back and he smacks me way too hard because he's never been able to gauge the appropriate amount of pressure for things—he's forever breaking jars or faucets or window catches by accident. And while I'm coughing, I hear Niall say, "So whereabouts do you live?"

Dad says, or seems to say, "Island."

"What?" I get out. "An island? Like, a tropical island?"

"Not 'an'— 'the.'"

"The island?"

"The country," Niall says, "not the landform."

I almost start crying again because I can't understand what everyone is talking about and Niall just seems to get Dad, in the way only he has ever gotten me, and I feel left out, and I hate feeling left out when it's Niall because Niall is the only one I'm 100 percent sure will never leave me out of anything—no matter how young or dumb I am, I know he'll include me in everything—and suddenly it seems there's this whole other unit I never knew about, with this man I don't remember.

"Island, island, island," Niall is saying.

"Island, island," Dad is saying, "you've never heard of island?"

"Of course I've heard of islands!" I shriek. "I just don't get—"

Then I hear Dad say, "Where the Sullivans came from," and the penny drops.

"Ireland," I say, and everyone breathes again. "As in part of England."

Dad goes to speak, then changes his mind. "Yup," he says instead. "You got it."

"Strictly speaking," Niall says, "it's not part of England. It's been an independent state, politically and fiscally, since—"

"It's next to England," Dad says hastily, giving me a smile, and I want to smile back, seeing him do this normal-dad stuff, smoothing things over between me and Niall, and again I feel that rearing sensation of something far away yet close, and I wonder if he used to do this when we were kids. He must have.

"And you're married?" I say.

He nods.

"What's her name?"

Oddly, he seems to hesitate. "Claudette."

"French?" Niall asks.

"Half," Dad says, and it strikes me that he does the thing Niall does, missing out words that other people consider mandatory, and I wonder if Niall got it from him.

A thought strikes me and I sit up straight. "Do you have kids? I mean, other kids?"

Dad nods again. "I do."

"How many?"

"Two. A boy and a girl."

"Like us?"

Dad smiles. "A girl and a boy, I should have said. Like you but the other way around."

"What are their names?"

"The girl is Marithe and the baby is Calvin. You want to see a photo?"

"Yes," I say, even though I sort of don't.

Dad reaches into his pocket and pulls out his wallet. Niall and I lean over to look. Some people are trapped behind a sheet of celluloid. A small girl in a blue dress holds the hand of a woman with long hair. She has a baby on her hip. The baby is looking upward as if something in the sky has caught its attention. The little girl stares out and it occurs to me she must have been staring at Dad, at Mr. Daniel Sullivan, our father.

As if he senses my thoughts, Dad says, "She reminds me a lot of you."

"Who?" I go.

"Marithe."

I stare into the face of the girl. She looks like a girl, nothing more.

"Look," Dad says, and he flips the photo over and there, on the other side of the wallet, are me and Niall. Aged about six and twelve, in the back garden, holding hands. Or, rather, I'm holding on to Niall's hand and he's permitting me to do so. And Dad's right. I do look like Marithe: the same tilted-up nose, the same red-blond hair, although Marithe's is long and I was never allowed to grow mine. Too much like hard work, Mom always said.

But Niall, as usual, is thinking about something else entirely.

"That's your wife?" Niall says, pointing at the woman with the baby.

Dad waits a moment before replying, "Yes," in a voice that's weirdly uncertain, as if he's not sure this is the true and correct answer.

Niall looks at the photo. He looks at Dad. He says, "Claudette," in a reflective, questioning tone.

Again, there is the sense of something flowing between the two of them and this time it doesn't make me mad: it makes me kind of happy.

Dad inclines his head.

"As in . . . ," and Niall says a word that could have been "whales" or "wills" or "wells" and I'm not really listening. I'm not interested in his wife, though she is pretty, in a skinny, boho, European sort of a way. I've got my eye on that girl, the way she's standing on one foot, the other raised as if she's about to make a dash for it. Go, I want to say to her, my little doppelgänger across the Atlantic, go for it.

"Wow," Niall says, in a drawn-out way. "OK."

Auction Catalogue

CLAUDETTE WELLS MEMORABILIA

London, 19 June 2005

From the private collection of Mr. Derek Roberts,
former personal assistant to Ms. Wells.

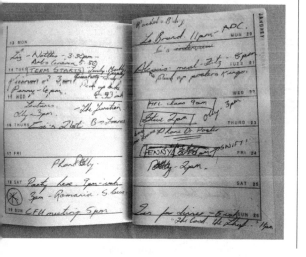

LOT 1

Date planner for the year 1989

Black-and-gold cover, some creasing to corners, notations on all pages in the hand of Ms. Wells.

Note to collectors: 1989 was the year Ms. Wells left university and moved to London. The diary records the dates of her final exams, the date of her arrival in London, the times of various job interviews, and, in late December, the evening on which she first met Timou Lindstrom.

LOT 2

Vintage scarf

Silk, dark red border with interlocking abstract design. Shows some wear; fading to one corner.

The scarf dates from the early 1950s and is believed to have once belonged to Ms. Wells's paternal grandmother. Included in the lot is a photograph of Ms. Wells with her hair tied up in the scarf, taken in late 1989 or early 1990 at a party on a rooftop in London.

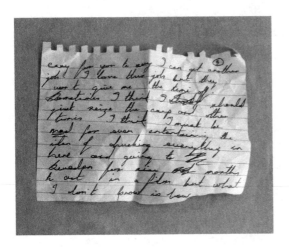

LOT 3
Book containing draft of a letter from Wells to Lindstrom
Some signs of wear and damage, as if it has been crumpled up, then flattened out. The text reads:

[STARTS]—easy for you to say I can get another job. I love this job but they won't give me the time off. Sometimes I think I should just seize the carp and other times I think I must be mad for even entertaining the idea of chucking everything in here and going to Sweden for six months to act in a film but what I don't know is—[ENDS]

The book is a copy of *The New Poetry,* selected and introduced by A. Alvarez (Penguin Books, London, 1962). Some discoloration to pages; notations in Ms. Wells's writing.

[BOOK NOT PICTURED]

LOT 4
Till receipts
Various, all dated 1990, some with notations by Ms. Wells. Includes drinks at a bar in Soho, dinner at a restaurant in Shoreditch, a pair of orange-and-blue trainers from a shop in Covent Garden, several London Underground tickets, several supermarket receipts, most timed in late evening, a bookshop receipt for *The Rough Guide to Sweden,* ed. 1990.

[NOT PICTURED]

LOT 5
Snow Globe of Westminster Bridge and Big Ben
Written on the surface in indelible black ink is:

In the event of homesickness, break glass. Timou L.

LOT 6
Copy of Mary Wollstonecraft's *A Short Residency in Sweden, Norway and Denmark* (Penguin Classics, London, 1987)
Some wear and tear to corners; written on flyleaf are the words "Claudette W." Marking page 156 is the stub of a boarding pass for a flight, London Heathrow to Gothenburg, on 02 March 1990, in the name of CLAUDETTE FRANCINE

WELLS. In the back is a note from Lindstrom, dated February 1990:

Dear Claudette,
What you said on the phone last night is true: it is a big step. But it's the RIGHT one, you know it is. Astrid and I were talking it over after I hung up. You love your job of course but think about this: is it better to facilitate films or to MAKE them?

You know the answer.

Astrid has found you a place to stay, with a friend of ours. We thought you would prefer a room in an apartment with a cool painter girl than a hotel room, yes?

See you then. We are going to have THE TIMES OF OUR LIVES. Everything is coming together for the film. Will tell you more when we see you.

Timou

[BOOK NOT PICTURED]

LOT 7
Marimekko shoulder bag
Jokeri pattern in lime green, 100% cotton, made in Finland. Some sun damage, small hole to stitching on one strap. Included in lot is a photograph of Wells, with the bag over her shoulder, on the island of Käringön, southwest Sweden. Also shown in photograph, from

left to right: Astrid Bengtsson, Timou Lindstrom, Pia Eklund, and unidentified man with border terrier dog.

LOT 8
Three strips of 8mm ciné film
Shot by Timou Lindstrom in a Gothenburg park, in 1990, showing Claudette Wells moving from left to right across the frame, wearing a light blue dress. Cut from a longer reel and kept by Wells; the finished and edited film is presumed lost. This is considered to be the first-ever footage by Lindstrom of Wells in existence.

LOT 9
Wells's Shooting script for *Out to the Island*
(original name: *Ut Till ön*) Numerous signs of wear, some damage to front and back pages. Front page bears the initials "CW" in graphite pencil. Notations, corrections, and doodles throughout in Wells's handwriting: fountain-pen ink, ballpoint, red pencil. On the back page is the following exchange, written at some point in the shooting, between Wells [CW] and Lindstrom [TL]:
[TL]—*Is she for real?*
[CW]—*It would appear so.*

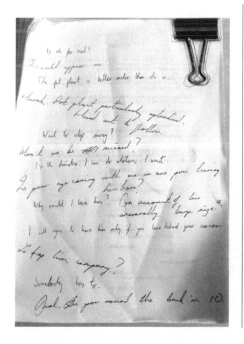

[TL]—*The potted plant is a better actor than she is.*

[CW]—*Harsh. Pot plant particularly splendid. Hard act to follow.*

[TL]—*Want to slip away?*

[CW]—*Won't we be missed?*

[TL]—*I'm the director. I can do whatever I want.*

[CW]—*Is your ego coming with us or are you leaving him here?*

[TL]—*Why would I leave him?*

[CW]—*On account of his unusually large size.*

[TL]—*I will agree to leave him only if you leave behind your sarcasm.*

[CW]—*To keep him company?*

[TL]—*Somebody has to.*

[CW]—*Deal. See you round the back in ten.*

LOT 10
Vintage dress
Navy crêpe with silk polka-dot detailing and red grosgrain trim. Worn by Wells to the London première of *Out to the Island*. Small tear in hem; topmost button is missing. Included in lot is photograph of Wells, at première, alongside her mother, Pascaline Lefevre, and her brother, Lucas Wells.

LOT 11
Three magazines
Featuring interviews with Ms. Wells, dating from 1991. Copies are signed by Ms. Wells across her photograph.

LOT 12
London Underground poster for *Out to the Island*
Shows some wear at corners and damage on left-hand side. Written on the back is the following:

Dearest C,
Look who it is!
   Astrid and I stole this last night: we got chased by a VERY angry man in an orange jacket. How does it feel to be looking down from the walls of Leicester Square station?? Tx.

Included in lot is original cardboard tube in which Lindstrom sent the poster to Wells, at her mother's address in Paris.

[NOT PICTURED]

LOT 13
Two postcards
From Lindstrom to Wells, sent from New York to Paris. Postcard one, dated November 1991, of a photograph of Gloria Swanson by Edward Steichen. Text reads:

C—OK, I admit it. The idea of you working with another director DOES bother me. I'm an idiot like that. But you must do this other film. Ignore my crazy possessive nonsense and say yes. Just make sure you're free in time to do my next film. Deal? Tx

Postcard two, dated March 1992, of *Lady in a Blue Dress* by Pablo Picasso. Text reads:

C—script currently looks and feels like this. Small, fragmented pieces that REFUSE to match up. Yet. Astrid says it's a good sign but I'm not so sure. All YOUR scenes are finished, however, and ready for you. Tx

LOT 14
Audiocassette mixtape
Made for Wells by Lindstrom, dated December 1991. Signs of wear to box; small crack on front. Tracklist in Lindstrom's handwriting in green ballpoint.

LOT 15
Paperwork
Pertaining to Wells's second film, *Lors de la Clôture de la Journée* (1992, dir: Robert Dinage), in which she played the girlfriend of an amnesiac. Included in lot is

contract, signed by Wells, shooting script, letters between Wells's London agent, Artemis Crane; her American agent, Paul Rackman; and the director. All pertain to contractual matters. Some coffee stains and wear to corners.

[NOT PICTURED]

LOT 16
Vintage leather document case
Belonging to Wells. Fraying to corners, surface scratches, some fading to rear. Contains half-used pad of blank paper and various tickets: a return journey from Paris Gare de Lyon to Chambéry-Challes-les-Eaux, dated 13.12.91, an entrance ticket to the Louvre, dated 10.12.91, an entrance ticket to Musées Nationaux, undated, a Paris Métro ticket for *section urbaine,* stamped 15.12.91.

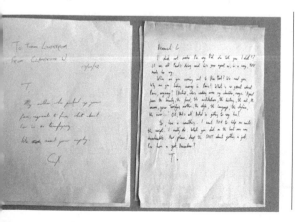

LOT 17
Correspondence by fax between Lindstrom and Wells
Numbering 16 sheets in all. Pages have been folded together, corners and outer pages show signs of wear and fading. Included in lot is a folder with a fleur-de-lis design. Small tear in back, some ink stains, fraying to ribbon.

Note to collectors: the lot pertains to correspondence collected and saved by Wells, so communications from Wells to Lindstrom are on cartridge paper; communications from Lindstrom to Wells are on fax paper. Some are typed, others handwritten.

[LINDSTROM TO WELLS] 17/02/92

Dearest C,
I did not make Pia cry. Did she tell you I did?? It was all Paul's doing and he's your agent so, in a way, YOU made her cry.
When are you coming out to New York? We need you. Why are you hiding away in Paris? What is so great about Paris, anyway? (Astrid, who's reading over my shoulder, says, "Apart from the beauty, the food, the architecture, the history, the art, the cinema, your terrifying mother, the style, the language, the skyline, the river ..." OK, that's all Astrid is getting to say here.)
So, here is something. I want YOU to help me write the script. I really do. What you did on the last one was invaluable. And, please, drop this SHIT about getting a job. You have a job. Remember?
Tx

[WELLS TO LINDSTROM] 17/02/92

T,

My mother, who picked up your fax, requests to know what exactly about her is so terrifying. We await your reply.

   Cx

[LINDSTROM TO WELLS] 18/02/92

C,

What's terrifying about your mother? EVERYTHING.

   Script collapsed in the middle. It reminds me of cakes my grandmother used to make. Don't know what to do. WHEN CAN YOU COME?

   Tx

[WELLS TO LINDSTROM] 19/02/92

T,

Cakes: if it hasn't risen, it's a sign you haven't stirred it enough.

   Do you think it's the same for scripts?

   Cx

[WELLS TO LINDSTROM] 21/02/92

T—sorry to send this by fax. I tried calling you but couldn't get through. I was just on the phone with Paul and he said he thought Astrid has left. Is everything all right? What happened? Are you OK?

   Cx

[LINDSTROM TO WELLS] 21/02/92

C—in a meeting (dull) so can't call (annoying).

   Yes, Astrid gone. Back to Gothenburg. What happened? YOU, of course.

   Txxxxxxxxxxx

[WELLS TO LINDSTROM] 21/02/92

T, I don't know what to say. I'm sorry. Cx

[LINDSTROM TO WELLS] 21/02/92

You're sorry? Why?

[WELLS TO LINDSTROM] 21/02/92

I'm sorry if I've unwittingly been the cause of problems between you and Astrid.

[LINDSTROM TO WELLS] 21/02/92

A and I were over the minute I met you. We all know that. Or do you mean you are sorry that A and I have split up?

[LINDSTROM TO WELLS] 21/02/92

Hello?

[LINDSTROM TO WELLS] 21/02/92

PLEASE don't go silent on me.

[LINDSTROM TO WELLS] 21/02/92

Claude? Don't do this.

[LINDSTROM TO WELLS] 22/02/92

*Can't sleep—worried about you.
Can you just give me one word?
So I know you haven't been tied
up by a crazy person or fallen into
the Seine or run away with the circus or got your hair tangled in a
rotating fan and are pinned to the
spot, in much pain? I am happy
to come to your rescue if any of
these things have occurred but I
may need coordinates.*
   Tx

[WELLS TO LINDSTROM] 22/02/92

*Not fallen into Seine, never been
tempted by circus life, hair fine
although out of control. Rather
like me, it would seem. Have
thrown caution to the winds and
booked flight to New York. Will be
with you tomorrow morning. We
can discuss coordinates then.*
   Cx

[LINDSTROM TO WELLS] 22/02/92

*xxxxxxxxxxxxxxxxxxxxxxxxxxxxxx
xxxxxxxxxxxxxxxxx*

LOT 18
Framed print of cloud formations

Entitled *Wolkenformen* and taken from a textbook. Shows illustrations of twelve different types of cloud. Oak frame, glass. Some signs of scratching on the front. Lower-left corner shows small split in wood. Writing on the back:

For C, my silver lining, with love, Txxx

NB: "Cloud" was Lindstrom's nickname for Wells. Lot includes photograph of Wells, with cigarette and dog, sitting in the Manhattan apartment she shared with Lindstrom, circa 1993; print can be seen on the wall behind her.

LOT 19
Two pieces of coral

Kept by Wells on her desk. Red organ-pipe coral (*Tubipora musica*) and blue coral (*Heliopora coerulea*), both native to the Indian Ocean. Provenance and significance to Wells unknown.

LOT 20
Five floppy disks

Used by Wells to save various drafts of the script for *When the Rain Didn't Fall*, the film she cowrote with Lindstrom in 1992. All covers show notations, labeling and corrections in Wells's handwriting.

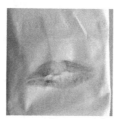

LOT 21
Tissue with lipstick blot
Made by Wells. From the set of *When the Rain Didn't Fall*, shot in late 1992.

LOT 22
Nine magazines
Most featuring Wells on the cover. Dated 1992–93. All are signed *To Derek,* by Wells.

LOT 23
Ashtray in the shape of a star
Aluminium, dates from 1940s. Included in lot is a photograph of Wells and Lindstrom on set, looking at a monitor together; Lindstrom has his arm around Wells; Wells is holding a cigarette and the ashtray in one hand.

LOT 24
Makeup bag belonging to Wells
Kimono design, gold leather loop, small ink stain to interior.

Contents are as follows: one large hairpin, seven small hairpins, two blue and white spotted hair clips, kilt pin, green Bakelite bracelet, small plastic dinosaur, enamel butterfly brooch, beetle cast in resin, two elastic hairbands, Chinese enamel bangle, double shell, one plastic doll's hand, one clear plastic button, one tortoise-shell button with four holes, one navy button with anchor design, one blue silk-covered button in paisley pattern.

LOT 25
Gray silk dress
Embellished with red and orange beading, worn by Wells at the 1993 Cannes Film Festival. Lot includes photographs of her arriving at the screening with Lindstrom. It was their first official appearance as a couple.

LOT 26
Pair of sneakers
In red lightning-flash print, size 39, worn by Wells in the early 1990s. Some signs of wear to sole and canvas upper. Included in lot is paparazzi shot of Wells, torn from the page of a magazine, which shows her wearing the shoes, running across a road in New York.

LOT 27
Greeting card
To Claudette Wells from her brother, Lucas Wells, dated 12

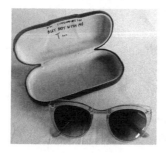

November 1993. Image shows a girl being towed by a younger boy on a bicycle past the Eiffel Tower in 1943: *Le Remorqueur du Champ de Mars* (The Tug Boat of the Champ de Mars), Robert Doisneau. Some signs of wear and damage—large central crease where it has been kept folded.

Text reads:
C, It is the most surreal experience watching your life explode from my position here across the Atlantic. I feel a bit like an astronomer traking [sic] the course of a comet and just hoping it doesn't crash. Please just know this: you can come here anytime. The house is ready (sort of) for visitors. Come, come, come. Wear a gorilla suit or similar so no one harasses you on the plane. Can you travel under an assumed name? Lx

LOT 28
Pair of sunglasses
Given to Wells by Lindstrom. Rose-colored frames, dark brown lenses. Good condition, scratch measuring 2mm on right arm. Case has leather outer and felt inner. Dented and shows signs of use and sun damage.

Written inside the lining is:
Be incognito but not with me. Txxx

LOT 29
Hospital ID band
Red plastic, severed for removal, inscribed in black ballpoint:

WELLS, CLAUDETTE F. 2/8/93

A medical number is also inscribed in blue ballpoint. NB: Various newspapers at the time reported a rumor that in the summer of 1993 Wells suffered a collapse during filming and was admitted to a New York hospital with "stress-related exhaustion."

LOT 30
Letter to a private security company
From Lindstrom, dated 4 December 1993, indicating that he wished to appoint a private security guard for Wells. The letter is on headed paper from Lagom Films, Wells and Lindstrom's production company, and is signed in Lindstrom's absence by personal assistant Lenny Schneider. Written on an attached sticky note, in Lindstrom's handwriting, is:

Lenny, process this but don't tell C.

Underneath, in Wells's handwriting, in black ballpoint, is:

Don't tell me what??

How a Locksmith Must Feel

A PHONE CALL, TO CALIFORNIA

Donegal, 2010

"Claudette?"

She has picked up so quickly that he thinks she must have been waiting by the phone.

"Daniel." It is half sighed, half murmured. "About bloody time."

Despite his surprise at this greeting, despite everything, he finds himself wincing, hoping the children aren't in earshot. Marithe has a far more colorful vocabulary than any six-year-old ought to have; Claudette's inability to refrain from swearing in front of their children is his one and only complaint about her as a mother. And one, he tells himself, over and over, isn't so bad.

"Hello to you too," he says, nonplussed. "Are you OK?"

He hears the sound of the television surge forward, then die away, and he can picture her, knows exactly where she is in their house, what she is doing: she is walking away from the sitting room, where the woodstove will be fired up, where the dog will be lying, stretched out like a hairy hearth rug, where Marithe and Calvin will be sitting, leaning up against each other, on the sofa, Marithe with her thumb in, slackly, watching cartoons. Claudette will be heading, on bare feet, over the splintery boards of the corridor into the front room, where she can swear at him with impunity.

The urge to be there with her is so strong he has to lean his head into a convenient lamppost, grit his teeth, set his jaw.

"Am I OK?" she says. "Well, frankly, I've been better. The question is, are you OK?"

"I'm fine," he says. "Why wouldn't I be? I was just calling to let you know that I'm not at my dad's yet. I kind of—"

"I know you're not at your dad's," she interrupts.

"You do?"

"Yes. Your sister called me and—"

"Ah." There is a rising sensation in his chest, a small tide of dismay. He should, he now sees, have called her before. He should have tried to explain something to her, about the holes in his life, the underground rivers, about the sudden towering urge to fix as many as possible.

"—told me you'd just taken off. There they were, waiting for you in Brooklyn, making lunch for you, when you sent some incoherent text message saying you were at Newark airport but that you weren't going to be able to make it that day."

"Now," he says, swallowing, "about that. The thing is, I meant to go. Obviously. I really did. I mean, I was there, wasn't I? But then—"

"Where are you?" she says. Her voice is low, forlorn, and the sound of it fills him with nothing so much as the desire to put his arms around her, to hold her head to his shoulder.

"Fremont," he mutters.

"Where?"

"California."

A sharp intake of breath. He listens to the ensuing silence. There is my home, he thinks, there is the noise of my house, the lives of my wife and children. He wants to bottle this sound, to stopper it, so that he can take it out and give himself a dose of it when needed.

"I caught a plane straight out of Newark for San Francisco."

"But . . . what happened to New York?"

"I did go. I was there. And I'm going back there now. Right now.

I'm heading to the airport to catch a flight back tonight. The party's not until tomorrow. I've got loads of time."

"Daniel, what are you doing in California?"

"I . . ." He presses his fingertips into his eye sockets. "I had to . . . I wanted to see . . . my kids. My other kids. I had this sudden . . . I wanted to straighten things out with them."

"Oh," she says, taken aback. This is clearly not the answer she was expecting. There is a moment of silence. "And did you manage to see them?"

"I did. I saw them just now."

"That's great, Daniel. That's wonderful. I've always said you should just turn up. How did it go?"

"It was . . ." He tries to articulate what he felt when he saw them, after a gap of so many years, how they appeared in the doorway of the coffee shop and walked toward him across the floor. It wasn't so much a case of recognition, more a sensation of rightness, the idea of something being where it should be, something finding its place. He knows now how a locksmith must feel when he creates the key that finally releases an old rust-shut lock, or a composer when he finds the note to complete a chord. They had changed, Niall and Phoebe, yet were exactly the same, and he, Daniel, had been filled with a crazed kind of delight and delirium at seeing them, their hair, their hands, their feet in their shoes, the way their clothes sat on their bodies so precisely and so uniquely. Your *faces*, he had wanted to exclaim, your *fingernails*. Just look at you both.

In several years' time, in the middle of the night, Daniel will receive the news that Phoebe has been killed in an accident and he will find that during her funeral he will be picturing her as she was on that day in the coffee shop, sitting before him after so long, her hair hooked behind one of her perfect pale ears, a charm bracelet encircling her wrist, her knee almost touching her brother's.

As yet, of course, he doesn't know this. Nobody knows this. He doesn't know that he will receive e-mails from her once a week for the rest of her life, that he will, for that short time, see her regularly, her flying to Ireland, him flying to the States; he will take her out to dinner, she will order for both of them, they will discover a mutual taste for spicy Thai soup; he will buy her the books she needs for college, a warm winter coat, a pair of leather gloves. For now, Daniel is walking along a Fremont street and he is raising himself up on his toes to answer his wife, banging his hand into the wall of a Laundromat. "I saw them," he is saying, with unadulterated, unalloyed joy. "They came, Claude. And they were amazing, as amazing as they ever were."

"I'm really pleased for you. Really, really pleased."

"Thank you." He sighs, touched by her support, her understanding, her calm. Everything, he sees, is going to be all right.

Then she says, "Could you not have told me first?"

"Well, the thing is—"

"Could you not have called to tell me why you didn't turn up in Brooklyn? Could you not have been a little bit more forthcoming in the single text message you deigned to leave on your sister's phone? Could you not have let us all know before?" And here it comes, he thinks, the emotive articulacy that moviegoers paid to see. "It's your father's birthday, Daniel. He's a frail old man and he was expecting to see you yesterday. I know there's a lot of history between the two of you, but he didn't deserve that. Not at all."

Silence roils between Fremont and Donegal.

"I'm sorry," he says. "You're right. I should have called you. I don't know what I was thinking. It's hard to explain, but I'm kind of as surprised as you are to find myself—"

"Is this about someone else?"

"What?"

"Are you seeing someone?"

"Claudette. That's ridiculous."

"Is it?"

"Yes."

"Because you'd never do a thing like that, would you?"

He sighs. "I admit that my track record in that respect is not perfect but, come on, you know I wouldn't do that to you. Who else would I ever want?"

She lets out a puff of air. "I don't know."

"Come on, I'm not that man." He wants to say, aren't you mixing me up with your ex, but he can see that this isn't the time, so instead he opts for more reassurance: "Sweetheart, I swear to you it's not that."

"Swear on your life."

"I swear."

"On the children's lives."

Unseen by her, he smiles. He loves her for her sense of melodrama, her extremity. "I swear on the children's lives."

"OK," she says slowly and clearly. "Know this, Daniel Sullivan: if I find out that you are lying to me—"

"I'm not."

"—I will cut off your balls."

"OK."

"First one, then the other."

"Got it." He hears himself emit a slightly nervous laugh. "Thank you, wife of mine, for that very graphic and precise picture." He dodges a man holding the leashes of no fewer than five dogs and sidesteps a leaking gutter. "So," he says, in an attempt to get the conversation back to the realm of normality, "what have you guys been doing today? Anything special?"

"Well," Claudette says, "remember I told you I wanted to try to build that winch? I realized—"

"That what?" He isn't sure he heard her right.

"Winch. I realized—"

"Did you say 'winch'?"

"Yes, the winch. We talked about it last week."

"We did?"

"When we were out by the well that evening. With a bottle of wine. Remember?"

"Er . . ." Daniel casts his mind back to a recent evening by the well and can remember her talking, pointing to the barn and saying something about ironmongery but can recall only his attempts to grope her in the dark. She'd been wearing a diaphanous dress thing and not a lot else. "Sort of."

"Well, I managed to get hold of the right kind of rope, strong enough to hold both kids, I mean, but—"

"Hang on a second. You mean this—this winch is for ... what? Stringing up the kids?" He tries to think of a way to begin to object to this plan, coming up only with "Claudette."

"What?"

"Are you sure? I mean ... have you thought about ... ?" Daniel flounders for the right approach. He knows that her somewhat-overblown and baroque parenting is just an expression of her sublimated creative urges. It's the way she works off all the energy she once used for making groundbreaking films. She has to do something with all that fire and spark, he reasons. But he draws the line at rendering his children airborne in a homemade fucking winch. "I'm not sure this sounds entirely safe."

"I knew you'd say that," she says. "Which is why we're doing it while you're away. They want to put on a play, you see, for when you get back. Marithe has been making Calvin a unicorn costume and—"

"Well, is there any chance it could be a terrestrial-based play? And we can discuss the winch when I get back."

"And when will that be?"

"When will what be?"

She exhales. "When are you coming back?"

"Next week, as planned. But, now you mention it, I was wondering ..." He comes to a standstill outside a grocery store. Banked up in bright pyramids are oranges, peaches, nectarines. All he would have to do is extract one single fruit from the wrong place, and the whole perfectly balanced display would come crashing down. He pictures orbs of fruit bouncing like rubber balls all over the sidewalk, around his feet, into the gutter.

"You were wondering what?" Claudette prompts.

"How would it be if I"—he has to turn away from the grocery display, so strong is the urge to unleash chaos—"extended the trip by a day or two? I may not, I don't know. It's just a possibility. Would it be all right with you? I know it means you'd be on your own a bit longer with the kids, but you'd have time to rehearse the unicorn extravaganza and it shouldn't be—"

"Are you thinking of staying on with your family?"

"Um," he says, slowly, "not exactly."

"I don't understand," Claudette says. "Where would you be in these two days?"

"The thing is," he says, aware that he hasn't consciously made this decision, aware that this is the moment in which the decision appears to be making itself, imposing itself upon him, and hasn't he always lived his life like this, or used to? "The thing is," he says again, "there's something I was thinking of following up. Just a very small something. When I get back, I mean. I'm going to see my dad now, but it's just occurred to me that I could change my flight to come back via London. I might take a day or so because there's not much on at work and there's something I have to see to. Maybe. I wanted to run it past you. Just two days. Maybe three. I'm not sure."

There is a pause.

"You're not sure?" she repeats.

"No."

"Can I ask why?"

"It's very . . ." Daniel gropes for the right word, the exact term. How to communicate to Claudette the towering fear he has at letting even a molecule of what happened twenty-odd years ago leak into the life they have carved out for themselves? Because this is how he sees it, as a gaseous poison, bottled, stoppered, sealed, never to be opened. "It's a bit complicated, Claude. Too complicated for me to tell you over the phone. There is someone I might need to go and find."

"Who?"

"No one you know. Someone I was at college with."

"For fuck's sake, Daniel," she shouts. "This is about a woman, isn't it? You just swore to me on your children's lives that—"

"It's a guy!" Daniel yells, startling a couple drinking coffee at a table a few feet away. "He's a guy called Todd, OK? I knew him when I did that year in England and I thought I might go ask him something."

"What? What do you have to ask him?"

Daniel scans his mind, takes stock of the situation. Can he tell her over the phone? Can he give a brief-enough description of things? Can he go into the minutiae of what happened, all those years ago, what might have happened? He can't even remember if he's ever mentioned Nicola to Claudette.

"I told you," he says, "it's very hard to explain."

"Well, try me," Claudette says, "and I will attempt to rally my meager cerebral resources."

"Claude," he murmurs, "come on. Don't do this. Please just trust me, OK? You know you can trust me. It's just two or three days to go to Sussex and then I'll be right back and—"

"Sussex? Why Sussex?"

"That's where Todd lives. Did I not say?"

"No, Daniel, you omitted to mention that. I can't believe you're—"

"Look," he interjects, "I don't even know if I'm going to do it yet. I may not, I may just come straight home, but I wanted to talk it over with you first and then I'll decide whether or not—" He hears Marithe's querying voice in the background, in French, and even though he doesn't speak the language, he knows she's asking is that Papa and can she talk to him, and Claudette is saying, *Non, ce n'est pas Papa,* and he thinks his heart will break, right there, right then. He doesn't know how to survive this.

"Go on, then," she cries. "Bugger off to Sussex, go and see this *friend* I've never heard of, see if I care, see if—"

"You need to calm down, OK?" he says, in as reasonable a voice as he can manage. "The kids can hear everything you're saying and—"

There is a clatter on the line, then the flat monotone of a cut connection. Claudette has hung up.

Enough Blue to Make

CLAUDETTE

New York, 1993

Claudette balances in her bare feet on the edge of the bathtub. One hand grips the sill, the other pincers a near-expired cigarette. She squints up at the New York sky—a hazy china-blue bolt of cloth, cross-stitched with white vapor trails—and a plume of smoke drifts from her mouth out of the window.

She has been looking out at the apartment windows across the air vent. Most are obscured by blinds or drapes, but there is one, directly opposite her, where some people are sitting around a dinner table: two couples, various children, a narcoleptic cat stretched out along the dresser behind them. Claudette watches their mouths opening and closing, their arms moving, the hands lifting cutlery, putting it down. It's like watching the rushes of a film without headphones. One of the women goes to the stove, comes back, goes again. The other darts at one of the children with a cloth. One of the men has a child on his lap; he holds an arm about the boy's rib cage. Something white flies about the boy's face and, for a while, Claudette wonders what it is—birds, scarves, some kind of toy? By straining her eyes and leaning farther out of the window, she discerns that the child is wearing gloves. A small pair of white gloves, rather like the anarchic cat in that story about the brother and sister forced to stay inside all day.

Claudette is wondering why a child might choose to wear white gloves when something her father used to say about the sky tugs at the edge of her memory. She frowns, her hand poised in midair. What was it? She almost has it. Enough blue to make—something. A pair of trousers? A sailor's trousers? It was said in the tone of buoyancy and optimism. It could be lashing with rain, but he would point through the windshield of the car and say it: look, enough blue to make—whatever it was. But what was it?

Claudette allows the ash to fall from her cigarette into the waiting toilet bowl below. She will ask Lucas next time she speaks to him. He will remember, she is sure. He's the kind of person who—

The bathroom door opens and, just as it always does, crashes against the tiled wall, dislodging the towel rail hooked over it, making a startling, metallic clang.

Timou, in practiced fashion, leaps sideways, catches the falling towels and rail in one hand, and, with the other, pushes the door shut behind him.

"Nicely done," Claudette says from her position on the edge of their bath.

Timou regards her, half amused, one eyebrow raised. "So," he says, "you are hiding in the bathroom? Like a truant?"

"No," she says.

"And you're smoking?"

She takes a drag of her cigarette. "Certainly not."

"It looks," he says, replacing the towel rail, "very much like smoking to me."

Claudette exhales. "I don't smoke. I never smoke. You must be imagining it."

Timou comes toward her. He wraps his arms around her legs and buries his face in her midriff. "Those things will kill you," he mutters, his voice muffled.

"Really?" Claudette stubs out the cigarette and hurls it from the window. "I never heard that before."

"I don't want you to die of cancer."

She runs her fingertips over his shorn hair, sleek as the flank of a cat. "What do you want me to die of?"

"Nothing," he says, into her abdomen. "You are never to die. It is simply not allowed. Never ever. At least, not until I do."

"How come you get to die first?"

"Because I said so. I—how do you say it?—booked it first."

"Bagged," she murmurs. "Bagged it first. But I'm not sure you can bag the order in which we die. Surely it's the kind of thing we need to discuss and agree on. We might have to draw up a contract. You can't just—"

"Cloud," he interrupts gently, "you know there's a journalist in our living room, right?"

She doesn't answer.

"He's there, waiting for us."

She stretches her hand into the air beyond the window. It is heavy, balmy, stirring, filled with noises. Air-conditioning units hum, car horns, a siren, music from a stereo or perhaps the bar on the next block, the clatter of an engine somewhere. The soundscape of a city going about its Wednesday-afternoon business.

"Do you ever wish," she says, almost to herself, "that we could just make films? Just make them and send them out into the world to fend for themselves, without talking about them, without explaining, without anyone ever seeing us, without—"

"I've given him coffee," Timou says, ignoring this speech, "but there's a limit to how long we can expect him to wait."

Claudette rakes her outstretched fingers back and forth through the air. The diners opposite are all on their feet, lifting dishes, milling about the kitchen, their backs to the window.

"Cloudy?"

"Mmm."

"What does 'mmm' mean? 'Yes, Timou, I'm coming right now'? Or 'I'm going to pretend this isn't happening and maybe walk out halfway through, like last time'?"

"Mmm," she says again.

"You know, they gave you a nickname in that article."

"Which article?"

"The one you walked out on."

"What was it?"

"I don't remember . . . It was to do with running but it sounded like rivets or metalwork. Bolting? Something like that."

She thinks for a moment. "The Bolter?"

"Yes, that was it."

She laughs and pulls in her hand, surprised. "Like Nancy Mitford?"

"Eh?" Timou tilts his face back to look at her. "You've given yourself a reputation for bolting. You know that?"

She puts her arms around his shoulders and lowers herself down off the bath until she is face-to-face with him, his features blurringly close, his stubble sharp against her cheek. They are pretty much the same height, which often surprises her. He is so much stronger than her, so much more of a physical presence: that he should reach the same point as her on a height chart seems ridiculous.

His arms lock, just as they always do, around her rib cage so that she can barely draw breath. "Just don't bolt from me," he whispers, "OK?"

"I won't."

"Promise."

She smiles into his face. "I promise."

He kisses her and she closes her eyes. His mouth is hot, his body pressed against hers. He is like an anatomy figure, each of his muscle groups standing out beneath his skin. She has never known anyone else with Timou's focus, his drive. Whatever he sets his sights on, he will work toward with a singular determination, letting nothing and no one distract him, an oil tanker on course.

When she feels him pulling at the waistband of her skirt, she opens her eyes. "Timou," she says, "the journalist."

He is unzipping his trousers and pushing them down with the same intense urgency he does everything. "Oh," he says, "so now you're worried about the journalist?"

"Listen"—she starts to laugh—"this is ridiculous, we can't, we have to—"

"Come on," he says, divesting her of her knickers with a deft downward movement, "you have to strike while the eye is hot."

"The eye?"

"It's not correct?" Timou's breath scalds her ear.

"No, it's . . ." She's half smiling while trying to think straight, which is hard when Timou is lifting up her shirt, unhooking her bra. There is a slight buzzing in Claudette's head, distant, disconcerting. She feels as though she has heard this colloquial misstep before somewhere; it feels important that she remember it, remember this. "Iron," she gets out. "While the iron is hot."

"OK." He is lifting her, pressing her up against the cool tiles of the wall. "Whatever."

Claudette tries to clear her mind, to navigate her way to the source of this unease. The eye is hot. But then it slips away, bobbing out of reach. She forgets all about it, her legs stretching out so that her feet may once more find the rim of the bath.

The air-conditioning in the living room must be faulty. It appears to be churning away, the long white curtains lifting in the movement of air, but the atmosphere feels weighty and moist, like that of a greenhouse.

Claudette shifts in her seat, tucking her still-bare feet beneath her. Her hand separates a length of hair and she smooths it, twirls it, loops it, twists it between two fingers, feeling its roots tug gently at the side of her scalp.

She tunes in briefly to the conversation going on around her.

"So, *When the Rain Didn't Fall* is your third film, Timou. Are you pleased with it? Is it what you wanted it to be?"

"The finished film is never what you envisioned at the start," Timou says, leaning forward, elbows on knees, and she thinks, not for the first time, How good he is at this part of things. The chat, the sell, the promotion. He turns into someone she doesn't know, someone edgeless, amenable, open. "The process is a dialogue between self and vision. As a filmmaker you are constantly battling against your own personality, your own set of values, your own aspirations. You have to trust the film. You have to let it find its shape. I spent three months in the editing suite with this one—"

I? thinks Claudette.

"—and it felt more like excavation than creation. More a sense of digging for what is already there ... "

Claudette allows her attention to recede, to take wing. She looks around the apartment, their apartment, where they have lived now for almost a year, and she wonders what the journalist sees, what he will take from it. The coffee cups stacked on the shelves, the marble-topped table, the postcards tacked to a corkboard above the phone. Two of Paris, one of Stockholm, one of Sydney, one of a Cumbrian lake, several from the modernist exhibition she and Timou went to the other week. The sea-green alcove and desk where, until recently, their assistant, a film student from Québec, sat. The abstract-design bag Claudette bought in Sweden suspended from a hook, Timou's collection of scarab beetles trapped in resin, the paperweight with a dandelion clock inside.

What would people think of them, looking at all these things, these possessions? What do they tell of—

Timou is touching her arm. Claudette starts. They are both looking at her, Timou and the journalist, whose name, she now realizes, she hadn't quite caught. Justin or Gavin or Josh—something like that. "I'm sorry," she says. "What did you say?"

The journalist puts his head to one side, spectacles flashing. She has forgotten, too, whom he writes for. Is it a film magazine, a niche publication that preaches passionately to a small readership of the converted? Or is it a broadsheet that will detail what she is wearing, what wallpaper she has, what kind of nail polish she favors?

"I was wondering how you found your first stab at directing?"

"Me?" Claudette says.

"Yes. The on-set gossip"—he puts the pen to his mouth, bites it with his small, pointed teeth, and sits forward in his chair—"was that you spent as much time behind the camera as in front of it. I heard this from a reliable source. I was just wondering how you found it. Did you enjoy it? Is it something you'd want to do again, maybe on your own next time?"

"Um ..." She casts a look at Timou, whose expression is unreadable, opaque. He is looking sideways but not quite at her; he appears to be transfixed by the edge of the table. His right ankle is making a small repeated motion—up, down, up, down, up.

They are, she sees, waiting for her to speak; the journalist is looking from her to Timou and back again, eyebrows raised, pen poised above pad.

"Well," she says, "I've always enjoyed every . . . every aspect of film-making from . . . from . . . The thing is, Timou and I, we . . . we talk everything through and . . . and being with Timou has . . . well, I've learned a lot from him and—"

"This is a joint project," Timou says over her. He takes her hand in his, moves it so that it is caught between his palm and his thigh. "Clau-dette and me. The film will have a joint credit, both for direction and writing."

Claudette blinks. She keeps her hand very still. The air-conditioning unit lets out a slight wheeze, a sigh. The journalist sits up in his chair and starts to write furiously on his pad, nodding as he goes.

"What fascinates me," Timou continues, "about collaborating with Claudette is that it is impossible to tell where her vision ends and mine begins. It is a truly symbiotic, sympathetic partnership. Why should, we thought, the roles of actor, director, writer be so defined? Why not loosen things up and see what happens? Blur the boundaries, turn received hierarchies and structures on their heads. The only way to forge something new is to—"

Into Claudette's mind comes a sudden incursion: the sight of the back of the Québécoise film student's head and shoulders as she sat at her desk in the alcove. Claudette had painted it for her, in sea-green emulsion, so that she, the assistant, would have her own space, would feel that she had some territory, however small, in the apartment, which belonged to them. It had seemed important to Claudette, as she roll-ered on the paint, as she fixed the shelves to the wall, as she laid out a holder for pens, a wrist rest for typing, a headset, so the girl wouldn't have to cradle the phone between shoulder and ear, thereby giving her-self neck strain. The girl had been their first assistant—she and Timou hadn't needed one before—and Claudette had wanted to make her feel welcome, taken care of, valued. But something—what could it have been?—must have been missing, something off-key, because after only two months, she had left, without giving notice, without saying why. There was just a note left stuck to the computer screen one morning: *I won't be coming back.* No signature, no explanation, nothing. Claudette had peeled it off and stared at it for some minutes, baffled, surprised, because she thought she had been good to the girl, thought she had been kind, generous, a good employer. She had given her money for cabs, if the girl had worked late; she had never minded when the girl took a long lunch. If she, Claudette, was out of the apartment all day, scouting locations, at fittings or shoots or casting meetings, she had always made sure the fridge was stocked, that the heat was on. What could it have been?

Claudette feels the urge unfurl within her to stand, to move, to walk about, perhaps to leave. It rises from her heels, up her legs, and snakes its tendrils around her middle, reaching up her back to her neck, her head. Timou seems to sense this change. Maybe her hand, beneath his, has twitched or trembled, because he grips it with a firm, steady pressure. Without looking at her and unseen by the journalist, he is giving her a message: hold tight, stay put, I know you hate this but it will soon be over. She finds the impulse to move hard to resist, always has done. *Claudette cannot sit still,* her school reports used to say. *Assieds-toi!* her mother would admonish at the dinner table. She is thinking how good it would be to walk down Eighty-Sixth Street, to stroll through the light spring air, to watch the people passing her, to feel the city roll beneath her soles, to glide past shopwindows, diner tables, scaffolding, ice-cream parlors, deli counters, to let her bones be shaken by the rumble of subway trains, far beneath her feet, to let this conversation, this interview, this encounter, spool out of her so that a small space can open inside her head and she can start to think.

Because to think is what she cannot manage, not here, not now, not with this man who is sucking words out of Timou, out of her, and feeding them into his notebook. This man, who is sitting in her apartment, in the chair her mother bought for her, in a flea market downtown, a beautiful thing it is, with planed-oak arms and woven strapping. Does this man see its beauty, its craftsmanship? Claudette doesn't think so.

She cannot think—she cannot think at all. She wants to dwell on the final frames of the film they have edited because something is not quite right, something is unbalanced, and she cannot see what it might be. Is it the dialogue in the corridor, between her character and the man playing her husband? Does it go on a beat or so too long? Should they cut out the last exchange? Or is it that it needs more sense of time passing? An intervening frame or two of the street outside, devoid of people?

Claudette cannot decide. There is no deciding to be had when this man is talking, when Timou is talking, when there is no space, no rest, here in her own home, the very place she ought to be able to think best. How can she make this most important of decisions—the closing minutes of the film!—when her mind is filled with the back of the Québecoise assistant's head?

Smooth, glossy hair, she had, the color of charred wood; she wore it up, mostly. Claudette can picture it now, how vulnerable the nape of her neck seemed, how the ponytail flicked between her shoulder blades as she turned her head to answer the phone, to type something on her keyboard, to call through to Timou, if he was working in the bedroom. How sometimes, when Claudette returned to the apartment, the girl's hair would be wet, as if newly washed, pulled through its band, the ends drying in the central heating, which Claudette had been so careful to turn on because it was such a cold winter they were having, so very cold. Strange, Claudette found herself thinking, to wash your hair in such cold, in the middle of the day.

Claudette cannot bear it anymore. She has to move, has to activate her frame. She takes out her hand from under Timou's and pushes herself from the sofa, causing Timou to shoot her an alarmed look, but she's not going far. She steps across the carpet, across the floorboards, and it feels good to be in motion, to have uncurled herself from that sofa, which can have the unpleasant habit of swallowing you whole, an upholstered Venus flytrap. She passes the window, reaching out to graze the white muslin curtain there, and she comes to a stop at the alcove.

The desk is neat, ordered. Which, Claudette reflects, it should be, since no one has sat there since the girl left, so abruptly, just under a month ago. Only this week Timou has been interviewing people to replace her. A keen but slightly frightening woman from Boston. A man, Lenny, who lives a few blocks east of here.

There are still a few notes in the girl's handwriting sticking to the paint of the alcove wall. *Paul called for CW,* reads one. *TL to confirm dates,* reads another.

Claudette pulls this last one from the wall and holds it close to her face. *TL,* she sees. *TL to confirm.* The girl had narrow, closed-off handwriting. She favored rollerball pens in bright primary colors and made her descenders markedly longer than the ascenders. Claudette runs a hand along the top of the computer, across the number pad of the phone.

In a way that doesn't feel like realizing something, learning something, but instead like uncovering a fact you had known a long time ago, she knows why what Timou had said to her in the bathroom sounded familiar.

Strike while the eye is hot.

When the girl said it to her, Claudette had been standing right here, just behind where the girl was sitting—her hair caught up in a damp ponytail, the nape chalk pale, a few stray strands reaching the collar of her maroon sweater—and they had been looking at details of nightclubs because, Timou said, they needed to shoot a scene in a basement restaurant: a nightclub could easily be mocked up to look like a restaurant, and nightclubs were always empty during the day. The girl had been holding photocopied pictures of two basement nightclubs, one in each hand, and saying that she had heard back from one manager, who said it would be OK, and the other hadn't returned her call.

"What do you think we should do?" Claudette had said, leaning over her shoulder to see the two images.

The girl had shrugged inside her maroon sweater and then she had said it: "We should strike while the eye is hot."

Claudette, glancing from the images to the girl and back, had had to suppress a smile. The eye is hot: she rather liked it. Hot eyes. Flaming vision. She would never, in a million years, have corrected her. She wasn't that kind of person and certainly didn't want to be that kind of boss.

"You're probably right," she had said instead. "Why don't you call them back now?"

She rests her hands on the edge of the desk. The room, the rug, the scarab beetles, the street outside, the journalist and Timou, especially

Timou, seem to fade, as if someone somewhere has turned down a dial on the world. The sounds, the light, the colors all become dim. It is just Claudette, her breathing, and the desk now. Nothing else. Just her and her mouth, which keeps itself open, drawing in air and pushing it out, over and over, because it doesn't know what else to do.

Where Am I and
What Am I Doing Here?

DANIEL

New York, 2010

Somebody is saying my name.

"Danny?"

The word reaches its arm down whatever hole I am hiding in and gives me a sharp shake. My head jerks on its neck and the mumbling monologue that seems to have been going on in the background of my mind comes to an abrupt stop.

"Danny?"

I find myself leaning—or is it lying?—on some forgiving, yielding surface, in a strangely uncomfortable position: legs twisted to the side, arms flung out. The position of someone who has fallen from a great height.

Have I been asleep? Was I sleeping? Where am I and what am I doing here?

"Danny," the voice says again.

My head appears to be filled with smog, my vision wavering and pricked with vibrating points of light. I have come to in a place unfamiliar to me. I seem not to be in full command of my faculties. But, hey, I tell myself, screwing up my eyes against the glare, you've coped with worse. And: doesn't this remind you of the bad old drug-taking days of your youth?

What materializes around me is a room. There is a high window to my right, a ceiling with meandering cracks above my head. Lace curtains make a hesitant advance into the air, then, held back by their pole, retreat. Advance, retreat, advance, retreat.

I know this room. I see where I am.

I am lying, unbelievably, on my parents' bed in Brooklyn. The side that was my mother's, next to the window, beside the painted nightstand, under her reading lamp. The very spot, ladies and gentlemen, where she died.

This takes me a moment to get my head around.

I am just straightening out my legs, pushing my hair back off my forehead, when I hear the person say my name again.

"Danny?"

For a moment, and just for a moment, the notion enters my head that my mother is calling to me from the afterlife, from the wide blue yonder. Have I summoned her simply by lying here?

"Yeah?" I get out.

"Jeet?" the person says, or seems to say.

"Huh?" I lift my head from the pillow. Across the room, in a chair beside the door, sits a woman. It is, I hardly need tell you, not my mother or, indeed, any other supernatural incarnation. This woman is possibly in her seventies. She is wearing a loose caftan thing and her hair is pinned up in a kind of topknot; there are many colored beads slung around her neck, and her fingers glitter with rings. Do I, I am asking myself, recognize her? I must. She seems to know me: she's using, after all, my childhood diminutive. But is she an aunt, a cousin—what?

"Danny," she says again, leaning forward in the chair, "jeet?"

We stare at each other for a moment, she and I, each of us struck by the unaccountability, the incomprehensibility, of our situation.

"Jeet?" I repeat warily, and as I say it I know what it means. She is asking me, in pure Brooklyn, Did you eat?

I almost clap my hands together. Jeet. How could I have forgotten that? I am going to write it down, as soon as I can find a pen.

The woman pushes herself out of the chair and comes toward the bed. "You look like you could do with a little sustenance. You want me to make you up a plate?"

I stare at her from my prone position. The rings, the multiple necklaces, the long white hair. It comes back to me that I am at my father's birthday party: the sounds of chatting and cutlery reach us from the door. I came in here to the bedroom with the idea of calling Claudette, of speaking to the kids, of taking ten minutes out for myself to consider what to do, where to go—home to my family or off to Sussex in search of Todd?—but instead I must have fallen asleep. Jet lag can do strange things to one's body clock. There in my hand, in fact, is my cell phone: evidence of my better intentions.

So I have located myself in time and space, but I still have no idea who this woman is. I search her face for traces of the Sullivan brow, the Hanrahan jaw, any clue at all, but there's nothing. I cannot recall ever meeting her before. Could she be a friend of the family, one of my sisters' mothers-in-law?

"Er," I say, struggling to raise myself on my elbows, "no, thanks. I'm good."

She puts her head to one side, looking down at me with an encouraging smile. "Tired?"

"A little."

She reaches out and straightens a book, a box of tissues on the nightstand. I see that it bothers her that I'm lying here like this, and an old, rebellious flame kindles itself somewhere inside me. Why, I want to say to her, shouldn't I lie on my mother's bed if I want to? What's it to you anyway?

I cross my feet, put my hands behind my head. Not going anywhere, lady, not any time soon.

"You want me to help you up?" she says, this tiny old lady who stands so proprietorially in my mother's room.

I laugh. "That's kind of you but a little ambitious, don't you think?" I gesture down at myself. "I'm at least double your weight."

She nods. "You're probably right."

She adjusts the box of tissues again and, as she does so, it comes to me who she is, what she's doing in here, addressing me by my family name, why she might not like me lying like this with my shoes on the comforter. She is my father's wife, the woman he met a few years ago at some social for elderly people—a church thing, was it, or a dominoes game? Something like that. I didn't fly out for the wedding, so have never met her, apart from a brief introduction when I came through the door.

I swing my legs off the bed and sit upright, my head swimming only slightly. Myrna—is that her name? I'm almost sure it is.

"I guess I should get up," I say. "How's the party?"

Myrna adjusts one of her necklaces, disentangling it from the others. "It's going great," she says. "Your father sent me to look for you. Everyone was wondering where you'd gone."

"Oh, sorry about that. I just came in here to . . . um . . . make a phone call and . . . well . . . the thing is . . . I needed to I need to decide whether or not I should . . ." I look up at her, this woman who agreed to marry my father, the woman who sleeps in this bed every night now. What could have persuaded her? I wonder. How would anybody think that hitching herself to a man like my father was the right choice to make in life?

I once put this very question to my mother, when I was about fifteen, and it didn't go down too well. The memory sits uneasily within me, like a surgical pin in a broken bone. I came into this room (I say "came" when, in fact, I must have crashed through the door, filled with ire at my father's latest infringement on my liberty—as I saw it) to find her sitting on the side of the bed. She must, I see now, have come in here for a break from the Sturm und Drang going on in the apartment. Funny how you realize that only after you become a parent yourself. Here she was, a book open on her lap. And it was the book that seemed to me, in that moment, the essence of my frustration, its absolute cathexis.

You see, my mother's idea of a good time was to spend the evening rereading *The Divine Comedy,* whereas my father liked to have several beers and watch the game. That they were woefully mismatched seemed a given, a background presence in our lives; like others of their generation, they just got on with it, circling around each other, making the best of it. But my mother, I remember, often wore an expression of abstraction, of distance, as if her thoughts were elsewhere, exiled to a place none of us could reach.

What I wanted to know, in that moment, as I stood there in the bedroom in front of her, was how it had come about. What had led her to this terrible mistake, what had tripped her up, what had deceived her into thinking this marriage was a good decision for her?

"Why the hell," I remember yelling at her, in the cruelty and myopia of youth, "did you marry that guy? What possessed you?"

She started to admonish me for cursing but couldn't manage it. Instead she looked at me, right in the eye, and she said my name: "Danny." And she began a sentence she never finished. I would, to this day, give almost anything to have heard it in its entirety, but, then, life is full of unanswered questions, as we all know. "Danny," she said, "the truth is that all this time I have . . ."

She didn't get any further. You know why? Because she started to cry, with such overwhelming immediacy that she couldn't speak. I had never seen my mother cry before. She was not an emoter, not a crier: she conducted herself always with an enigmatic calm. To see her racked with sobs, tears pouring down her face, was a shock of the most visceral, horrifying kind. I think I said, sorry; I think I said, Mom; I think I said, don't. But perhaps I said nothing at all.

Either way, I never made the mistake of asking her again.

And now I am the one on the bed, looking up at my father's second wife. In order, I think, to stop myself from putting the same question to her as I put to my mother that day, and also to attempt to plaster over that awful memory, I blurt out the following: "I'm facing a dilemma, Myrna, and I don't know what to do."

"Oh?"

I don't really know where I am going with this, but it seems preferable to be talking about dilemmas, rather than my father's attractions as a husband. "Maybe you can help," I say wildly.

Myrna's penciled-on eyebrows shoot up but, to her credit, she attempts a smile. "I can try."

"I . . . Well, it's kind of a long story but I—I just found out something about someone I knew a long time ago. And it has come as something of a surprise to me. Now, do I go and find an old friend who will be able to explain a lot more about what happened, who will be able to give me some answers? Or do I go home to my wife and forget the whole damn business?"

Myrna regards me, her fingers pressed to her lips. Maybe I have misjudged this situation. Maybe Myrna is not a person to whom you can put this kind of question. Maybe I should just shut the hell up, go back to the party, get a plate of food, talk to my relatives, and wish my dad a happy birthday, then get myself out of here and go home.

"This thing you found out," she says, after a moment, "is it to do with another woman?"

I point my finger at her. "Myrna," I say, "you are an astute thinker. How did you guess?"

She shrugs. "I've been married four times, Danny. There's not much you can teach me about the way men are."

"I see that," I say. "Then I have to say that I'm intrigued as to what you make of my dad, the ins and outs of his mind, because no one has ever been able to—"

"Your dad misses you a lot."

"Er, I really—"

"He's very proud of you."

"Myrna, come on, I—"

"I would never presume to comment on your relationship with him—it's not my place to interfere—but I know it's a source of great sadness to him that he has so little contact with you and your family."

"With all due respect, I'm not sure you fully—"

"When," she interrupts, "are you going to bring that wife of yours to meet us?"

The idea of me ever bringing Claudette here strikes me as improbable, hilarious. I laugh. She laughs in response. We laugh together. "I really can't say!" I exclaim, and we laugh some more.

I stand. I gather up my cell phone. I straighten out the bed.

"Your wife," Myrna says behind me, "is she a good woman? Does she make you happy?"

"Oh, yes," I say, sliding my phone into my pocket. "I managed to pick a good one this time."

Myrna reaches up and straightens my collar and tie, a gesture that seems oddly intimate for someone I've just met. "You know," she says, brushing at the lapels of my jacket, "your father always says you got all of the brains and none of the sense."

"He does?" This interests me a great deal. "Well, he may have a point there."

Myrna smiles at me as we stand in the room where my mother died. "I would go home, Danny, if I were you," she says, and she puts her arm through mine, as if we're about to take part in a country dance, and propels me toward the door. "Leave whatever this is alone. What can be gained from turning over old coals? Go home to your wife. But first come and eat. OK?"

The Kind of Place You'd Have Trouble Getting Out Of

LENNY

Los Angeles, 1994

"I ... hate ... LA," his boss gasps, between breaths. "I don't know ... how much longer ... I can take it."

Lenny feels his head nod, like one of those toy dogs people have in the backs of their cars.

"The air," his boss continues as he runs beside him, limbs moving seamlessly, mechanically, "the traffic, the people who can't get their asses out of their cars, the rivalry, the naked ambition of everyone, everywhere. I hate all of it."

Lenny, wobbling slightly on the bicycle, nods again. He isn't required to do much else and he's heard this speech—or versions of it—several times.

"Have you ever been in a more self-obsessed culture, a more venal city, than this?"

Lenny swings his head back and forth, then has to straighten the handlebars of the bike, and steer around a rollerblader, oblivious and sleek, as she slaloms past them. Timou lets out a *tchau* of annoyance at her, as if he—in his biodegradable, organic-cotton T-shirt, sourced from Scandinavian forests and dyed with the feathers of chickens fed on locally sourced grain or whatever the fuck it is he's wearing today—and only he has the right to run in Venice Beach at nine in the morning, accompanied by his reluctant PA, who is meant to be taking notes, meant to be recording his every passing thought, but is currently concentrating only on not falling off the bicycle and wondering when they might be able to stop for breakfast.

Bicycles are not within Lenny's comfort zone; boardwalks are not places he has ever enjoyed; exercise is not something with which he is at ease, especially in public, and in particular when that public consists of nerve-frayingly attractive women in Lycra and running shoes or surfer dudes with rippling abs and low-slung shorts. Neither is he entirely happy with the idea of holding a Dictaphone while riding a bicycle, while dodging street sellers and buskers and dozing down-and-outs, while trying to filter what is important from what is irrelevant in what Timou is saying.

All in all, Lenny wishes he were back in New York. He would give anything right now to be waking up on the Upper West Side, three blocks away from where he grew up, six blocks away from where he went to kindergarten, with the noise of sirens threading up to his window, able to step out and buy a lox bagel from the corner deli before walking to Timou's office, where he has a desk next to a window: there, he can take calls, put his feet up on the trash can, hide those black-and-white cookies in a drawer to keep him going during the long hours of Timou's conference calls.

Instead Timou has decided to relocate to LA for a while. He told Lenny this last month as he passed through, wearing—it pains Lenny to recall—a wet suit, unzipped to the waist. As if it was no big deal for Lenny to uproot his life in New York, to sublet his apartment, to sift through his clothes to find something suited to the climate of California, to attempt (unsuccessfully, Lenny fears) to put on ice the girl he's been tentatively dating, to trade in his subway tokens for this: a bicycle, bafflingly referred to by Timou as "the hybrid."

When Lenny had asked why they needed to go to LA, Timou had

snapped a pair of goggles down over his eyes. "Economic and creative practicality, my friend," he said. "Claudette is shooting that ghost movie there and the next script isn't going to write itself. So, right now, where she goes, I go. And where I go, you go. Unless you want to start finding your replacement." He had grinned and yanked up the zipper on his wet suit. "I'm going to swim the East River. I will be back in one hour."

Timou has, over the last while, developed a thing for Ironman triathlons. Lenny had explained this to his almost-girlfriend that night over dinner. The obsession started after Claudette won an Oscar and began to get roles in big-budget studio projects. It seemed, Lenny had said to the girl, to be Timou's way of coping with this unexpected development in their lives. Claudette only took those roles, he hastened to add, if they fit between her projects with Timou. That was, of course, where her heart really lay.

And so while Claudette was off filming elsewhere, Timou did a triathlon. Lenny knew the stats but didn't reel them off for her: 2.4 miles of swimming, 112 miles of cycling, 26.2 miles of running. It was how Timou switched off between projects, Lenny told the girl. He and Claudette had just finished an indie about a woman and her elderly father and he was preparing for their next film—about a group of friends at a funeral—by training for the Ironman triathlon in Arizona. Timou was not a man, Lenny told the girl, who knew the meaning of "downtime."

"Of course," Lenny had said, making an expansive, circling gesture with his wineglass, "the endorphins clear his head, pave the way for creativity."

"Uh-huh," said the girl, in a way that suggested she might require some convincing on this subject.

"And Timou's in the middle of securing some American cofinancing for the next film, which is an exciting new step," Lenny had said, increasingly desperate, "so it's important we show our faces in LA."

He had actually said that word: "we." He'd leaned on his elbow—debonairly, he'd hoped—his chin on his hand.

The girl had toyed with her food, glancing at him from under her brow, as if she knew that Lenny was not, as he'd hoped, on his way to being promoted to assistant director but being kept firmly as assistant. Oh, that elusive compound noun: so easy to say yet so difficult to attain.

"Also," Lenny had continued, "Claudette is working in LA for the next few months and . . . "

The girl had perked up at the mention of Claudette. People usually did, since the Oscar, since all the heat about her in the press, about how difficult she was, how she walked out of interviews, argued with directors, stormed off set, refused to answer questions in press conferences. Claudette had, inadvertently perhaps, made her life more difficult than it had ever needed to be. Not that Lenny would ever say that to anyone, this girl least of all. But some part of him would have liked to call up Claudette, to speak with her over the phone, to explain how things worked from his perspective. It's easy, he imagined himself saying during these telephonic chats, you just need to toe the line. Or even give the appearance of toeing the line. You need to smile for the cameras, you need to avoid leaving the house in eccentric getups, you need to stop fighting the paparazzi and use them instead to your advantage. Work them. Play nice. Be nice. Then they will stop hounding you. Nice doesn't make the gossip pages; nice doesn't sell.

In the restaurant, the girl had actually put down her fork and sat up straighter as soon as Claudette entered the conversation.

"Do you have much to do with her?" the girl asked, in a low, urgent voice, leaning forward over the table. "What's she like? Is she as much of a nightmare as everyone says?"

Lenny had paused, considering his options. To say that he had never met Claudette would make him seem at best ineffectual, at worst unimportant. Since he had started working for Timou, Claudette had been away almost all of the time, off around the world, either filming or promoting. She never seemed to come to the office; she'd been there, once or twice, but Lenny had always had the misfortune to miss her, left only with the tantalizing trail of perfume laden with lime or musk or rose. He'd picked up a scarf she'd left behind—cashmere, by the feel of it, navy with white squares, again that distracting scent—and given it to Timou, who had tossed it onto a filing cabinet, where it had stayed for several months. He'd taken her calls, of course: the modulated British accent, the inhale on the cigarette, the careless "Is Timou there? No? Could you ask him to call me, please? Thanks, Lenny." Always addressed him by name, always remembered. Which is more than can be said for her spouse.

"She's"—Lenny had circled his wineglass again—"much as you'd expect."

The girl's face fell.

"Very down to earth," Lenny hazarded. "And yet . . . amazing . . . like no one else you've ever met."

"And is it true that she scooped up her dog's shit and threw it at that photographer? Did she really do that?"

Lenny swallowed hard, a long ribbon of pasta snaking whole down his throat. "I think reports of that were greatly exaggerated. That's not . . . who she is. And you have to remember the pressure she's under, constantly, all the time. They provoke her, because they know they'll get a reaction, get a good photograph of . . . of . . . "

"Of her losing it," the girl said, tossing down her napkin, "and looking like a total crazy psycho."

Lenny does not, as he pushes down on each pedal, one after the other after the other, think the girl will take his calls when he gets back to New York, whenever that might be.

"So I said to him," Timou is saying as he jogs beside the bicycle, "'What do you think?' I don't know if I can use him. I mean, he's had so much work done. His face doesn't have the range of expressions it once did, yes?"

"Mmm," Lenny says, to cover all bases. "I really—"

Timou holds up a hand. "Here is where I sprint." He takes off, an arrow from a bow, shoes flashing on the path, legs moving like pistons, arms slicing through the air, shoulders powering. Just to watch makes Lenny feel exhausted. He wipes his brow, presses down on the pedals, and the bike slowly responds. He passes under palm trees, under awnings advertising surfing meet-ups, past a gray-haired man mumbling a throaty song about trucking, past alternating clouds of incense–marijuana–incense, past open-fronted stores filled with clinking crystals and drifting tie-dye, the sea dragging a blue line through one side of his vision.

Timou is in what he calls warm-down mode when Lenny catches up with him: finger to the pulse in his neck, one eye on his watch, running on the spot.

"So, today," he says, without preamble, "we need to call that location guy in Rome and we need to fix a meeting with Rex at Paramount. Can you find me a pair of those swimming shorts? You know the ones I like. But first could you call Claudette, see if she will have a chance to get to the script today, ask her when—"

"You want me to call Claudette?"

"Yes." Timou fixes him with a frank gaze. "Is that a problem?"

"No." Lenny gets down off the bicycle and sees, with relief, with joy, that they are outside a café. A disappointingly granola-and-smoothie-type place but a café all the same. "But you want me to ask her if she's . . ." Lenny flounders. He isn't sure if it's low blood sugar or something else.

"To remind her to start her rewrites."

Lenny is having trouble processing this one. "Isn't she shooting today?"

"Yes." Timou drops to the ground and starts doing push-ups.

"So she probably won't have time to get to your script."

"Of course she will. There's always lots of time on a set like that in between shoots. She can get some work done then."

Lenny thinks he understands, but he cannot help having one more go at this conundrum. "You want me to ask Claudette if she can do her rewrites between takes of this other film? The ghost story?"

Timou stops with the push-ups and springs upright. "Yes," he says. "Why not? It's not as if this film takes up much mental space, whereas our film is—"

There is a sudden noise, persistent and grating as a circular saw. Lenny jumps. "Oh," he says, in rather effeminate surprise, pulling Timou's cell phone from where he has stowed it in his pocket. "That's her now," he says. He holds the phone out to Timou.

"Answer it, would you?" Timou says, curling into an ab crunch.

"Hello?" Lenny says, feeling his heart start to gallop in his chest. He can't help it. He still finds it a thrill to speak to her.

"Timou?" she says.

"No, it's Lenny."

"Oh. Hi, Lenny, how are you?"

"Fine," Lenny says, then regrets it. But what else is there to say? "How are you?" he tries.

"Not too bad. Is he there?"

"Er . . ." Lenny waggles his eyebrows at Timou, indicating the phone.

"Is he exercising?" She sounds very near, as if she's standing just at his shoulder.

"Yes."

"Well, I need to talk to him. Just hand over the phone, would you? I'll talk to him while he jumps up and down or whatever it is he's doing."

Mutely, Lenny holds out the phone to Timou. Timou lies back on the concrete, raising one leg, then the other.

"Hey," he says. ". . . No, not yet . . . I'll check with Lenny . . . Really? Oh, no, Cloudy . . . I'm so sorry . . . You're not going in at all? How come? . . . Did you tell Matt already? Was he mad? . . . It will put back shooting . . . I don't know, a week maybe . . . OK . . . OK . . . Sure . . . I will. Or maybe Lenny will. An hour or so. Maybe less. OK, see you."

Timou snaps the phone shut, leaping upright in one coiled movement. He sighs. "She wants a tofu steak," he says, in the manner of someone delivering bad news.

The very words make Lenny feel nauseated.

"Right now," Timou says.

They stand, Timou and Lenny, on the sidewalk, for a brief moment united as men baffled in the face of female caprice. The sea turns and turns behind them.

"I don't know why they call it morning sickness," Timou murmurs. "It seems to happen at any time of the day or night. She says she's not going in today."

"Oh," Lenny says. "*Oh.* Claudette is . . . ? I didn't know. Congratulations, Timou. That's . . . well, that's great."

"You think?" Timou looks at him, properly looks, not just seeing the face of another employee.

Lenny swallows. When are they going to get some food, some water? How much longer does he have to wait? "Of course," he says. "It's wonderful. We should celebrate."

"Don't tell anyone," Timou points his finger at him. "We can't let it out—the press will be all over her."

"Of course."

"She'll be mad I've told you." Timou scratches his head.

"I won't tell anyone. I promise."

"OK." Timou starts to stride toward the café. "Can you take a tofu steak up to the house?"

Later in life, Lenny won't recall much from his brief years working in the film industry, but he will remember meeting Claudette Wells.

Several months after he stands in Venice Beach, he resigns his post as Timou's personal assistant. He spends some months drifting, living in his parents' spare room, staring out of the window and wondering what to do and where to do it. Then he finds a job in the administrative office of a theater. He lives once again in New York; he rides the subway, he carries papers and books and pencils in a canvas knapsack, he eats a lox bagel every morning for breakfast.

He reads about Claudette's disappearance while waiting on line in a deli. The man in front of him is holding a newspaper and Lenny happens to glance over his shoulder and there is her photograph on the front page, and his heart behaves as if assailed by a strong wind, swooping up, then down, when he sees the headline. The article contains the words "erratic behavior" and "devastated boyfriend" and "financial disaster for a major studio." For the next month, all he sees, when he picks up a newspaper or a magazine or turns on the TV, is her face looking out at him, as if to say: now you see me, now you don't.

Throughout the furor of her disappearance, he doesn't tell anyone that he once worked for Timou Lindstrom—not the people in his office, not the actors rehearsing in the theater, not the girl he is dating. He doesn't tell anyone that he met Claudette Wells, that he stood in her living room, that he touched her hand, lightly and for a moment. He never tells anyone about it: not once. He keeps it to himself, not because he is afraid his new friends wouldn't believe him, but because to speak of it would be betraying her in some inexplicable way. He met Claudette Wells and, a short time later, she was gone. Dead, some people suggested, drowned in the Baltic Sea; run away, said others. Either way, she vanished, slipped out of reach, never to be seen again.

As the weeks slide past and she still isn't found, he finds himself thinking more and more about Claudette Wells, about the set of her shoulders, about her unwavering gaze, about how perfect she was, too perfect, surely, for the Swedish sea to claim her. She would have escaped, he tells himself as he sits at his desk, folders, invoices, and rehearsal schedules spread out in front of him; she would have found some exit, some rabbit hole, and wriggled through.

The oddest thing, he thinks as he gazes out over the air-conditioning units of the block opposite, as he watches the others around him answering phones and typing into their computers, was that he hadn't wanted to go, had almost asked to be excused the errand, almost hadn't gone at all. He'd been fed up when Timou had handed him the tofu steak and the keys to the car. He hadn't wanted to steer that tank-sized vehicle through the molasses-slow LA traffic, down the twelve-lane highways, gripping the steering wheel, letting the automated voice of the car's electronic Ariadne issue him instructions, which he took, blindly, gratefully, as if his life depended on it. Which, in a way, it did. The tofu steak perspiring inside its brown-paper wrapping, the cell phone chirruping and shuddering on the dash—but he couldn't answer it now, not now, as he counted off exits, scanned green signs, moved his foot on and off the accelerator, straining to hear the soothing tones of the car's automated warnings.

The house was up a long, winding road, high in the parched hills. The properties there were ringed by eight-foot walls, sealed up with electric gates. Security cameras turned their convex eyes toward him as he passed, driving so slowly that several times the engine nearly cut out.

He could never have missed it. He hadn't seen a pedestrian for miles, but suddenly the road was filled with people. Black cars, people on stepladders, machinery, figures standing in groups. For a moment, Lenny thought he'd arrived in the middle of some crisis, some accident. But, disconcertingly, at the sight of his car, they all rushed toward him, en masse, a wall of black clothing. Lenny hit the brake, put his arms up to shield his face. He was convinced, for a moment, that he was about to get carjacked, assassinated, robbed.

Then he realized they were photographers, ten or twelve of them, gathered outside her gates and now swarming around his car.

Lenny was surrounded, lenses aimed right at him, their eyes blacked out, like those of insects. They thought he was Timou. He was driving Timou's car; they thought she might be in the car.

His pulse was erratic, tachycardic, as if he was on the verge of a panic attack, but he managed to lower his window to speak into the intercom. The photographers instantly recognized him for the nobody he was and the lenses disappeared.

The intercom emitted a male Mexican-accented voice, instructing him to drive in, right up to the house, and the gates swung open. Lenny revved the car, once, twice, before seeing it wasn't in drive. His palm slipped on the stick, sweat gliding between skin and leather, and he had to slow his breathing, look down, focus on the task.

The driveway was curving, steep, oppressively sylvan. On both sides, sprinklers emitted a noise like air escaping a tire. The house appeared, through the trees, as retina-searing flashes of reflected light. There was a mower, droning back and forth on a flat, artificially green lawn, a pair of maids in white uniforms, bearing piles of what looked like laundry, traversing the drive; there was a stuttering buzz from the trees at the left of the car, and Lenny saw a figure with a chainsaw and visor, lopping off low-growing branches. It turned to watch his car pull up on the gravel.

The house was glass, with an exposed structure of steel, the windows opaque with mirrored sky, surrounded on all sides by trees. A maid opened the door onto a hallway of polished blond wood where the doors were concealed, masquerading as walls. It was the kind of place, Lenny thought, you'd have trouble getting out of once you were in. He was shown into a room the size of a basketball court, windows on three sides, thick, ankle-swallowing rugs on the floor, angular chairs set to face the view over the city haze, books lining the whole of one wall, floor to ceiling. The door was slid back, just enough to permit entry or exit, and beyond it, a pool waited, its surface impassive, mercury-still. A man with a necktie worn over a T-shirt, shades pushed back on his head, was speaking in staccato bursts into a cell phone: "She won't do it . . . Why would she? . . . I'm telling you now . . . No way, no way . . . Forget it . . ."

By the window a crop-haired woman, in platform shoes and the merest hint of a dress, was typing very fast on a laptop, frowning at the screen. She acknowledged his presence—sweaty, baggy shorts, hair falling in eyes—with a minor flex of an eyebrow.

Lenny looked at the humming, implacable pool; he looked at the necktie man; he looked at the tofu steak, limp now and sticky. A person, some kind of gardener, Lenny guessed, slipped in through the door, pulling off visor, gloves, a scarf, and he was thinking it was the same person he had seen sawing branches off the trees and also: they let the staff use that door?

Then he realized it was her. Claudette Wells. Tossing dusty gloves onto the pale blue sofa, hair pinned up in two woven braids, like an Alpine maiden, a pair of filthy jeans on her, coming toward him with a smile on her face.

He was instantly amazed and terrified. The emotions surged up in him, vying for supremacy. Was he amazed? Was he terrified? He had no idea. He was neither; he was both. There she was, in front of him, and he had no idea what to say, no idea how to hold himself, how to be, to stand, to breathe. She forced everything out of his head until it was filled with nothing but white light.

"Lenny," she said, her head to one side, a slight question in her voice.

He raised the tofu steak in his hand, as if it was some kind of entry ticket. "Uh-huh," he managed.

"It's so nice to finally meet you."

"Mmm."

"I've talked to you so often on the phone it's as if I know you." She was looking at him searchingly, holding his hand in hers. "It's good to put a face to the voice."

"Yes," he said. "Likewise." He shook his head. "I mean, I already . . . well . . . "

She smiled properly, cutting him off, revealing those teeth that he knew casting directors had asked her to fix—the gap in the front—but she had always refused.

"Where's Timou?" she asked, still with her eyes on his, still standing very close, disconcertingly close in the enormous room.

"Uh," Lenny had to think, "swimming."

"Swimming," she repeated. Eyes on his, hand still holding his.

"Or . . . cycling?"

"Cycling."

"One of the two."

She released his hand. Lenny went to rub it, as if he'd trapped it in a door, then stopped himself.

"Well," she said, smoothing the placket of her shirt—a ratty denim thing with a missing button at the neck, possibly Timou's, Lenny thought—passing a hand over her brow, "we wouldn't want to interrupt the training, would we?"

The man in the necktie had appeared at her side. "Claudette," he murmured, and Lenny recognized the faux respectful yet possessive friendliness of a certain type of factotum. This was Claudette's assistant, his equivalent, and the man did not like the idea of another assistant being in the room, a rival to her attentions.

She turned. "Yes, Derek?"

"I've got . . ." He leaned forward and whispered something into her ear, his lips brushing the whorls of her braids.

She shook her head. "Tell him we'll call back." She glanced around her, as if trying to work out where she was. "Drink," she said to Lenny and, in her clipped British accent, it sounded like a command. Lenny actually looked about him for a glass or even a bowl, ready to do her bidding.

"Are you thirsty?" she asked, a hint of amusement in the question.

"What? Oh, yes. I am. I mean, please. If that's OK."

Instead of instructing one of the staff to fetch a bottle of water from some chilled cabinet concealed somewhere within the wood paneling, she crooked her finger, beckoning, indicating he should follow her.

He did.

In the kitchen, she hauled open the door of a cavernous refrigerator, extracted two bottles of water and a lime. Lenny watched, mesmerized, as she sliced the lime into quarters, then put a glass on the counter in front of him. Her water she swigged straight from the bottle, pushing the lime into its neck only when she'd downed half.

"So," she said, standing on one bare foot with such poise that Lenny wondered if she did ballet, "where are you from, Lenny?"

He put down his water, determined not to glance at the plate of pastries on the counter to his left. "New York."

"And how are you finding LA?"

"It's been"—the trouble was that the stool he was sitting on had barely enough surface area for one buttock, let alone two, so he was obliged to perform a sort of lopsided crouch—"you know, interesting."

"Good." She swapped feet so that she was standing on the other leg. "You found somewhere decent to live, I hope?"

An image of his rented room, glaringly bright without so much as a blind, the woven wall hangings hammered into the plaster, the row of cacti, with dust held in their spikes, flashed through his mind. "Yeah, it's fine."

She smiled, as if to acknowledge—and forgive—the lie. She reached out and prodded the pastries toward him.

"Go on," she said. "Help yourself." And she took one, a *pain au choco lat,* Lenny would always remember, and ate it in five decisive bites. Lenny tried not to watch: did women like her really eat that stuff? He found himself glancing at her stomach: impossible to tell, under that loose shirt, which was in itself a kind of clue, he supposed.

"And tell me this," she spoke through the pastry, in the same conversational tone, "is Timou sleeping with that art-director woman?"

Lenny put down his glass with a clash. All he could think was that he had, his entire life, been a terrible liar. As a child, he used to get into trouble for things he hadn't even done, so badly did he handle interrogation. He could never think on his feet, come up quickly with an excuse, had no aptitude for dissembling. It was a quality that intrigued him in others: how to convince people of something entirely untrue. He looked at her; he looked away, his face and neck hot, steeped as he was in the knowledge of his utter ineptitude with situations like this.

"I . . . ," he said, gripping the edge of the counter, unable to meet her eye ". . . I really . . . Not at all . . . I don't think . . . I just—"

"I'm sorry," she said. "It was very wrong of me to ask."

"I don't know who you mean and—"

"It wasn't fair of me to put you on the spot like that and"—she drew in a slow breath, pulling herself up to her full height—"I shouldn't have done it. I apologize."

The horror of the moment stretched out before Lenny, like the water of a lake. He hadn't been able to lie. He had given the game away. He would, in all likelihood, lose his job. Timou, terrifying Ironman, would tear each limb from his body. His career, his livelihood, his ambition—killed, with one simple question.

Lenny gripped his water with a profound unhappiness. Claudette balanced on one foot, gazing out at her trees.

Without warning, a power tool of some sort started up outside the house, a thin mosquito drone. Claudette tilted her head, as if its sound held some kind of meaning for her, then ran a finger through the chain about her neck. Lenny picked at the label on his bottle, his mind still scanning for things he should have said: What art-director woman, what are you talking about, what a ridiculous idea, of course not, whatever gave you that impression? Any of these, he told himself miserably, would have done. What kind of an idiot can't drum up a single platitude in this scenario?

"It's OK," she said, in a casual voice that wasn't fooling anyone, consummate actress though she was. "I knew anyway."

"If you think Timou would ever," he tried, "do anything like that, then—"

She turned upon him a look so piercing, so wounded, that he immediately fell silent.

Lenny stood abruptly, the stool he'd been perched on crashing backward to the floor. "I should go," he announced, groping to reinstate the stool. "I need to . . . I should let you . . . "

She said nothing, but nodded, putting down her drink.

In the hallway, as she walked ahead of him toward the door, he watched the soles of her bare feet, revealing and concealing themselves to and from him, in turn, over and over. He caught hold, briefly, of what it would be like to live in this house, with her as your girlfriend, your wife. Just for a moment, he could feel it, that life, as closely as something you might wear: these rooms, those yellow oblongs of light thrown along the floor, that pool there waiting for you in the morning, the murmur and chatter of the sprinklers outside, the restless stirring of the trees, the drone of the mower, and her, turning toward you, one of her braids escaping its pins, holding out her hand to you at the open door.

Show Me Where It Hurts

MARITHE

Donegal, 2010

Tables are useful, Marithe thinks, for a number of reasons. She draws her feet toward her so that she is entirely tented inside her nightdress and counts off these reasons on her fingers.

You can eat off them. You can draw and cut and glue on them. You can stand on them, although that isn't allowed unless you're a grown-up and you're putting up Christmas decorations—great swatches of green-smelling fir branches to be pinned to the beam. You can also hide under them.

People, Marithe knows, tend to forget you're there.

She lifts her eyes to the underside of the table above her head. On it, she knows, are the scattered remains of breakfast: coffee cups, plates, bowls, spoons, knives, breadcrumbs, Calvin's bib encrusted with porridge, the saltcellar, her uncle's elbows.

Marithe knows this last one only because her grandmother, who must always be called Pascaline—not Granny or Nana or even *Grandmère* or any of those other names—keeps stopping her flow of conversation to say, "*Lucas, tes coudes!*"

Pascaline is Marithe's mother's mother. She never wears trousers or shoes with laces. She doesn't put her arms through the sleeves of her cardigan but wears it draped on her shoulders like a cape; she has a special chain with clips at either end to keep it from slipping. And she always talks French when she tells people off.

They have been talking in low voices, her uncle and her grandmother, since her mother left the room. Her mother, Marithe knows, has gone outside and, from the sounds of hammering and bashing, has started mending the outhouse roof.

They appeared yesterday, these visitors, and it seems to have been a surprise: usually when people are coming, Marithe's mother will draw her a calendar so that she may cross off the days until they arrive. But this time, no calendar. Just a hurried dash into the car to collect them from the airport, through the gates, her mother toiling out into the rain, on her own, driving the car through, then getting out again to shut them, on her own, while Marithe and Calvin waited in the car.

"This much is clear," Marithe hears her grandmother say, from across the room. "It is not good."

"Come on," Lucas says, through a mouthful of food, probably bread, "we've got no reason to think that yet."

"I am not so sure," Pascaline says. "It is bound to be another woman. Why else would he suddenly take off like that? To England, he says, but can we believe that? He could be anywhere. Old habits die hard, especially in a man like Daniel. When you think—"

"Wait a minute," Lucas interrupts, "when you say, 'a man like Daniel,' do you mean American? Because I'm not really in the mood for sweeping bigoted statements and—"

"No, of course I don't mean American. I mean . . ." Marithe's grandmother hesitates, turns her head to gaze out of the window, and sighs. "I mean someone who is so . . . different on the inside from how they are on the outside. Is there a word for that?"

Lucas turns a page of the newspaper he is reading. "Don't know," he says, with a yawn. "Anyway, what makes you say that about Daniel? I don't think he's like that at all. I've always thought that, with him, what you see is what you get."

Pascaline is silent for a moment. Then she says, in a voice so quiet

that Marithe has to strain to hear it, "On the surface, Daniel is so charm-
ing, yes, so charismatic, but underneath it is a whole other matter. *Lucas,
tes coudes.* I have always felt that Daniel has a—how do you say it?—a
strong streak of destroying himself. A—"

"A self-destructive streak," Lucas corrects, mumbling through
another mouthful.

"Yes, that. I can see why Claudette fell for him, of course I can, but
he is the archetypal self-destructive charmer. He cannot help himself.
He feels on some level he doesn't deserve her, doesn't deserve all this. I
have seen the type before."

Several things happen at once. Her uncle shifts irritably in his seat,
uncrossing and recrossing his legs, the edge of his socked foot coming into contact with Marithe's arm. He says something to Pascaline,
very fast, in French, and Marithe catches the words *l'enfant* and *ici* and
Marithe knows she has been found.

But Pascaline doesn't stop. She merely switches into French. "*Évide-
ment cela veut dire qu'il y a une autre femme. Qui vit dans le Sussex
peut-être. L'homme ne—*"

"Oh, *arrête*," Lucas grumbles, "*arrête.*"

" *peut pas résister. Nous devons nous demander comment protéger
Claudette. Et si il a dit à l'autre femme qui elle est et où elle habite. Tu
as pensé à ça?*"

Marithe sees that Pascaline doesn't know or has forgotten that Claudette and Ari speak French together all the time. Marithe has grown up
hearing the language, imbibing it from birth; it has spooled through
her head for as long as she can remember. It is the secret language of
her mother and her brother, that older, darker, almost-adult, who has
suddenly gone from their house when he used to be here all the time, in
the room opposite Marithe's, and the pain of that disappearance, which
she hadn't known was coming, is so severe that she cannot always keep
it in. She is sometimes compelled to stamp into the garden and fling
clods of mud at the garden wall, hurl rocks at the old well, which her
father hammered shut with planks of wood, but you can still hear its
depth, its existence, in the echo, if you hit it in the right place, with the
right stone.

Marithe shoots out from under the table, a blur of nightdress, socks, unraveling plaits, and, ignoring the cries and admonishments of her uncle and grandmother, runs across the room, weaving through furniture, past playpen and stove, past the dog, who has caught something of her motion and thinks that an adventure is in the offing, past the stacked dishes of the kitchen and out of the back door.

She leaps from the worn stone of the step, stamping on some Wellington boots, and stands for a moment, poised at the edge of the lawn. The air is moist, heavy with unfallen rain. The tops of the mountains are swathed in scarves of soft gray.

What to do, which way to go? Climb the aspens, splash through the stream, feed the hens, visit the tree house, head for the tire swing, build a fire, go to the fairy den that Ari made for her last summer, search for smooth pebbles in the water butt, find one of those reeds that Lucas knows how to pierce in the right place to make a music pipe. The world seems to Marithe to be suddenly crammed, overloaded, a spectrum of possibilities. How can she choose just one, how can she ever decide which way to turn, when the place is so full, so teeming with choice? There is a fire raging somewhere within her, it seems, and none of these things can put it out.

She moves sideways along the path, one foot crossing over the other, "sidling," it's called, her father told her—"Good word, huh?" he had said, with a wink—and she takes care that the dew-drenched flowers don't catch and clutch at her hem. Nothing slows you down like a wet nightdress. At the corner of the house, she pauses to do up every last button of her cardigan, right to the top. It doesn't seem so long since it was summer, since she was out here in the garden in nothing at all, since her mother sat feeding Calvin on a rug on the lawn, but now the air is sharp, her breath leaving her in white explosions.

Just coming into view now is the well. Marithe eyes it, as you might a sleeping enemy. Her father took some planks from the barn—her mother had been annoyed when she saw, said she had been saving them for something—and hammered them down over the wet, mossy mouth. Marithe thinks she can remember what the well looked like before, when it used to open, when the cover used to lift off. Someone—was it Ari, her father, her mother?—had lifted her so she could see down,

down, down, a tunnel into the earth, and there, at the bottom, was a distant, watery girl, gazing back up at her.

It must have been Ari who lifted her. Marithe has a memory of her father sprinting out of the house toward them, shouting something, snatching off his reading glasses, and chopping them down through the air. No, he was saying, no, get away from there, put her down, and Ari saying, s-s-s-sorry, s-s-sorrysorry.

Marithe bends at the knees, selects a stone from the path, and hurls it toward the covered well. Its arc, she sees, as soon as it leaves her hand, is all wrong. Too high, too short. It falls between her and the well. Marithe sighs.

The words *une autre femme* slide unbidden through her head. She turns her head, first one way, then the other, almost as if she expects someone near her to have spoken them aloud. But she is alone. She mouths the words silently, making them into one continuous sound, then separating them into three. *Une autre femme.*

She bends and tries another stone, then another, but both of them veer off to the side, and she hurls a handful, wildly, up into the air, without even bothering to see where they land.

She runs. Around the house, past the aspens, past the fairy den, past the barn, where she catches a glimpse of her mother's feet in work boots, high up on the tiles, the leather tool belt that Marithe covets and is sometimes allowed to touch.

She arrives at the door of the henhouse, breathless and hot. The hens are crowding and groaning at the wire, turning upon her their beaded, glistening eyes. They have a hen each, she and Ari and Calvin. Marithe's is tawny, with a red comb and yellow feet, Calvin's black, and Ari's white.

She unlatches the door and scatters the feed on the ground. Calvin's is first out, clawed feet held fastidiously high, a throaty tutting coming from the glossy throat, then hers. At the sight of Ari's white hen hesitating, scratching, then plucking at the feed, the fire that has been burning away inside Marithe seems to flare and crackle.

"No," she says to the white hen. "No, you don't."

She picks up the hen, her fingers closing about the breast feathers, and the ugliness of what she is about to do seems only to fuel the fire. The frail heartbeat flutters under her hands.

She flings the hen back into the henhouse and slams the door. The hen stumbles on contact with the ground, the soft curve of its breast pitching into the dust, but it rights itself and struts in a circle, letting out a mournful croon.

Marithe watches the remaining two hens eating the feed. She cannot look at Ari's hen. She cannot. The sight of it falling like that into the dirt, its little legs folding: her fault, all her fault. And Ari had asked her to look after the hen while he was away. Her, not their mother, not their father.

The wail seems to come from somewhere else. It isn't her making that noise, no. It must be some creature somewhere, in pain, in grief. All Marithe knows is that she is stumbling in her mismatched Wellingtons away from the henhouse, toward the trees, and the gray scarves have unraveled from the mountains and the aspens are letting fall a shower of yellowing leaves and her mother is there. Her mother is there. She is catching Marithe in her arms and Marithe is being lifted off the ground and pressed into her mother's neck, her mother's heavy rope of hair. What happened, her mother is asking, are you hurt, did you fall, show me, show me where it hurts.

"I was . . . I was horrible," Marithe sobs into her mother's sweater.

"You were horrible?"

"To"—she can barely say the name: oh, how awful, the way the bird stumbled like that—"to—to Iceberg."

"To who?"

"Iceberg."

Her mother sits down on the wall, with Marithe on her knee, her arms clasped about her in a circle. Marithe presses her face into the interlocked wool of her mother's sleeve.

"What did you do?" her mother asks.

"I—I—" Even to say it is too dreadful. "I didn't let her eat. I shut her back in the henhouse."

Her mother takes her face in both hands and tilts it up. She regards Marithe for a long moment, and when she does this, Marithe knows she is looking down, right to the bottom of her, that her mother can see all of her and thinks it will be OK.

"When is he coming back?" Marithe asks.

Her mother continues to look into her eyes. "When is who coming back?"

Marithe glances away, at the gravel of the path, at the tools slotted into her mother's tool belt. She picks at a loose thread in her mother's cuff. "Ari," she says.

"Half-term," her mother says. "Three weeks from now. Twenty-one sleeps. So, not too long to wait." She stands and puts Marithe back on her feet.

"Would you like to go and let Iceberg out?"

Marithe nods. She takes several steps toward the henhouse, then turns.

Her mother is still there, watching her, hands resting on her tools. She smiles at her and nods, once, in encouragement, in acceptance.

"What is a self-destructive streak and why is another woman a bad thing?" Marithe asks.

Her mother's face becomes puzzled. "What was that?"

"Another woman. Why is another woman a bad thing?" Marithe sees that her mother still looks confused so she says it in French as well. "Une autre femme."

"What makes you ask that?"

"Pascaline was saying it. To Lucas."

Without a word, her mother turns and sets off toward the house. "Maman?" she yells. "Maman! Qu'est-ce que tu racontes?" And now the secret language is shouted and fast, and Marithe cannot grasp it: it's too slippery, too eel-like, it spools past at a terrific rate. Lucas is coming out of the back door after his mother and the three of them stand in the middle of the lawn, Pascaline and Claudette facing each other, Lucas trying to get in between.

Marithe turns away from them and goes slowly toward the henhouse where Iceberg is waiting, her head cocked to one side, her moist black eye full only of trust, of faith, of certainty.

Severed Heads and Chemically Preserved Grouse

TODD

The Scottish Borders, 1986

A wedding.

The bride and groom are young, newly graduated, and have the kind of open good looks that will last them a few more decades. They will be successful; they will have good-looking children; their house will have white floors, cabinets of glassware, and bright toys in baskets. Their walls will display scenes from this day: their former selves, posing beside a lake, in an artful line with their families, in the center of their group of friends. The bride will wish, in years to come, that she hadn't listened to her sister in the matter of eye-shadow color. Did her sister deliberately derail her appearance on this, the most important day of her life, by suggesting the moss green, which drained all hue from her complexion? Or was it an accident? The groom will rarely look at the photographs and, when he does, will be struck most by how many of the guests—considered, at the time, to be crucial presences in his life—he no longer sees.

What neither of them can know, looking at these photos of people dressed in their best, holding themselves together, presenting their faces and smiles to the camera, is how much their wedding, coming so soon after graduation, so early in their twenties, set off ripples of paranoia and fear among their peers.

Is this how it will be now? the lines of younger guests in the photograph are thinking as they smile and pose, as they hold up their champagne glasses to the camera. Are people starting to get married? Have they really reached that age? Are they to attend weddings on weekends? Is this the start of it all? A strange parade of ceremonies, rehearsal dinners, receiving lines, after-parties, their friends unrecognizable in stiff, elaborate dresses and immovable hairdos. The unfathomable lists of required items. What are fish forks and butter knives and occasional vases, and why do their friends need them, and why must they buy them in exchange for attending this peculiar event?

The bride's father does something important in a bank (no one is entirely clear on this point), and the wedding is taking place in the Borders of Scotland, a locale the majority of the guests have never visited. There is, here, a turreted, moated country house, surrounded by woods so dense and green they have a vaguely menacing, fairy-tale air, crowding in where the manicured lawns of the house stop. One would do well not to wander into them, not to stray from the paths, not to follow music you might hear from somewhere among the trees.

Peacocks pick their way over the graveled drive and scream at their reflections in the parked cars. It is quite a lot colder than most of the non-Scottish guests—that is to say, the younger crowd, the couple's friends—would have expected for June. The women, no more than girls, shiver in the mist that seems to roll all day long off the loch, in through the forests, their flesh goosebumped under their thin, short dresses, their ankles mauve above their strapped heels. The ones who thought to bring shawls or jackets clutch the fabric around themselves. The men cup their cigarettes in their hands, as if for warmth, shoulders raised inside the inadequate cloth of their rented suits.

They traveled up, in groups, the previous night, from London and the south; some, the more organized ones, by train; the others in an assortment of cars, borrowed mostly from friends or siblings. They stopped, noisily, at various places on the way: York, then an unsuspecting village in Northumberland, at Holy Island, where they disembarked from their vehicles and waded off the causeway into the encroaching tide. They paused at service stations to buy crisps and chocolate, magazines and deodorant, cigarettes and contraceptives. They behaved, every one of them, in all of these places, in a manner so raucous it verged on shrill, so uninhibited it suggested hysteria. Someone got hold of a can of shaving foam and covered another's car in white froth. The men picked up the women and they had a piggyback race to the toilets. A felt-tip was acquired from somewhere and anyone sleeping was decorated with a black mustache.

They are, all of them, unused to the ceremony they are facing. They are all keen to display—to one another, to themselves, to the world in general—their disregard, their reluctance, the lack of store they set by such a public commitment. They all want to say: we are too young for this, we will never come to this, not us, not ever. And yet, and yet, of course, most of them will.

Todd Denham, who has spent most of the night awake, on driving duty, at the wheel of a borrowed and antediluvian Nissan, wriggles his feet farther into the bearskin rug and takes a gulp of his drink. The infernal circus of photographs is over for the guests, and they have been allowed back inside, where they are being plied with drink and snacks, to cover for the absence of the bride and groom, who have been whisked away by said photographer to pose beside a stone lion or the small loch or in some other equally demented situation.

Inside, the place is all corniced ceilings, cloakrooms with deep basins, polished-wood bars that reek of peaty whiskey, stone corridors, trays of tiny foodstuffs arranged as daring acts of balance: dill on top of salmon on top of crème fraîche on top of velouté on top of caviar on top of an oatcake. It is staffed by people dressed in tartan: the men in kilts, the women in sashes, which, to Todd, who has worked in a fair number of hotels himself, look restrictive and impractical for catering. He starts to count the number of times he sees a female member of the staff hoick her tartan sash back to its rightful place on her shoulder. Just take the damn thing off, he wants to whisper to the one nearest him—

a lovely thing of around fifteen with a low hairline and an oval face, a schoolgirl, no doubt, doing a weekend job for extra money. No one here will give a monkey's.

As if sensing his stare, the girl blushes, a tide of red rising from the neckline of her blouse, past her jaw, and into the roots of her widow's peak. She is conscientiously not looking at him, he sees. The tray she is holding starts to wobble. He wonders, for a moment, what she does with the money she earns. Goes up to Glasgow after school on a Friday to buy—what? Nail varnish, cheap perfume, clothing of which her nice country mother wouldn't approve, magazines that the teachers at her probably private school would deplore, rakish shoes, colored nylon underwear. What do teenage girls do with their money?

Todd takes a canapé from her tray without registering what it is and drops it into his mouth, still musing about the girl. He wants her to look at him, just once, just to prove he exists. He has no sexual interest in her—he's twenty-four, for God's sake, and even when he was fifteen he didn't want to sleep with fifteen-year-olds—but there's something about her stolid poise, her determined refusal of him, that makes him feel dangerously insubstantial, inconsequential. No one has spoken to him for a while, here in this room, which is teeming with conversation: people chatting, exclaiming, communicating. Look at me, he wills, as he explores the canapé with his tongue—it is damp tasting, a hint of cheese, a dash of fish. Something herby. Revolting. He has to swallow hard to stop himself gagging.

She doesn't look but whisks away her tray and walks off toward a group of middle-aged women, who are engaged in a mass exclaim over the bride's shoes.

Todd swallows the remains of the canapé, rinses his mouth with wine, then looks about the room to see what he can do next. He sees the bride stick her head around a door and gesture frantically to one of her bridesmaids, who assumes an expression of bewildered fear. He sees the photographer, with increasing sweaty desperation, trying to get a small boy in some hideous sailor getup to stand next to the bride's mother. He sees, through the window, three or four postgraduate students, like himself, cavorting on a small patch of lawn, removing their shoes and throwing them at one another. He sees his flatmate, Suki, standing in the doorway, blowing smoke over her shoulder. He sees that no one is looking at him: not a single person.

Todd feels the familiar idea grip him. The dare, the risk, the chutz-pah of it. His heart trips into a faster rhythm and his hand finds its way into an inner pocket of his jacket and begins to stray through the contents. A small bottle with a safety cap, its sides invitingly cool but no good in this one-handed instance. A foil blister pack, half gone, of—something? He doesn't recall. Two, no, three torpedo-shaped free floaters, one with an elastic give to its surface, the others powdery. A single round pill, possibly Valium, and three paper tabs.

Todd takes drugs at times like this not so much because of the tidal push and pull of the chemical craving, although there is that, but because he likes to test if he can. If he can pull it off. He gets almost as much of a kick from seeing if he can get away with it as he does from the drug itself. Can he stand in a room of an appallingly expensive, stupendously ridiculous charade of a party, full of self-satisfied people his parents' age—doctors, lawyers, military men, auctioneers—and pop some pharmaceutical products without one of them having the faintest inkling what he is up to?

He opts for the single round pill. Maybe Valium, maybe something else. An upper, a downer, Todd doesn't know. His hand moves in a swift swoop to his mouth; the hard casing fits beautifully into the arch of his palate. Then he swallows and it's gone.

Undetected! Once again! Todd bares his teeth in triumph, exhaling loudly. A woman in a turquoise suit and matching hat turns and looks at him with concern and veiled fear, then away.

Todd doesn't like to think of what he does as "dealing." He has a particular dislike of that word. His cousin "deals," operating out of a flat in Leeds, with a client list, a team of runners, an exclusive phone line, the works. What Todd does is small fry by comparison. He hooks up friends. He sources particular demands, mainly from his cousin, who is always happy to help. He distributes—gently, he likes to think, carefully, selectively—throughout the university. He is known to certain people; he gets calls from friends of friends, needing something for a party or a rave or a weekend away. He supplements his paltry grant with the resulting cash: he pays his rent, he buys winter shoes, he staves off his library fines, he feeds the electricity meter, he goes to the cash-and-carry for large bags of rice, tins of beans, packets of noodles. Survival stuff, really. No flash cars and clothes for him.

Unlike his cousin, he doesn't look like a dealer. And he has the perfect cover: he is an academic, a postgrad, a supervisor, an expert in fictive nonfiction. He looks like what he is: a person on the verge of genteel poverty, a person who spends too much time indoors, bent over books, a person much wedded to libraries. He does not, by any stretch of the imagination, look like a drug dealer.

He also operates under the strictest of rules. No drugs during the week: Saturday nights and special occasions only. He's not an idiot. He knows his brain is his only asset, his only means of long-term employment, and he intends to keep it in good working order. Everyone needs a place to think, as Daniel is always saying.

He feels a jab at his back, and a voice close to his ear says, "I saw that."

Suki? Todd looks over to where she had been a minute ago and the place by the door is vacant.

"Saw what?" he says, without looking around.

"Give me one," she says, jabbing him again with something sharper than one ought to be carrying at a wedding.

"One what?"

"Whatever it is you're having."

He turns. Suki is behind him and the sharp object turns out to be the corner of her clutch bag. He shrugs at her and grins. "Don't have anymore."

"Liar."

"I don't. Honest."

"Liar!" she hisses, stamping her foot.

"But if you'd like to make a different withdrawal from the Todd Denham pharmacopoeia, you're more than welcome to step into my office."

Suki sighs, losing interest. "Maybe later," she mutters. "So," she sifts through her bag, searching for a lighter, "how many of the guests here today do we think have slept with the bride?"

Todd surveys the room, speculatively. "Male or female?" he asks.

Suki rolls her eyes. "Male. Obviously. She's hardly the type."

"Really?"

She pulls her how-stupid-you-are face. "Of course not. Save your tawdry lesbian fantasies for another time. Now, what do we think?" She points at a heavyset, shaved-headed bloke, who looks vaguely familiar to Todd. "Him, for sure."

Todd points at a blond man from his eighteenth-century-travelogues seminar. "And him."

Suki nods sagely, then swivels her eyes around the crowd. "Possibly him."

"What about what's his face from anthropology?"

"And not forgetting Daniel."

Todd turns to look at Suki. "Daniel hasn't slept with her."

Suki raises an eyebrow.

"He hasn't. I'm sure he hasn't."

"I heard otherwise." Suki tilts her head. "And what's more I heard it was last week."

"Last week?" Todd looks at the bride, who is patting the back of her elaborate hairdo with anxious fingers, and then at the groom, who is in his shirtsleeves, laughing at something someone is saying to him. "No way," he says. "He didn't. He wouldn't. Not now. He hasn't been doing that lately, not since . . . Anyway, she's not his type."

"Does he have a type?" says Suki, opening her eyes wide. "I had no idea. He's always been so *egalitarian* in his choices. Or, at least, he used to be, before the whole Nicola debacle." She stands on tiptoe and swivels her head from left to right. "Where is he, anyway?"

Todd has to stop himself answering immediately. He always knows where Daniel is. It's a thing with Todd that he can track him, like a sniffer dog. "Downstairs, I think," he says casually. He prefers to keep this ability, this talent, private. Then adds, "Want to go and find him?"

They descend one of the three staircases—the medium-sized, twisting one that gives onto a low-ceilinged hallway with fringed lamps and peeved-looking grouse in glass cabinets. They pass an alcove where a woman in a flesh-colored frock is locked in a frenzied grapple with a man in a white shirt. Suki glides by, but Todd leans in and gives a theatrical cough, startling them out of their embrace, forcing them to look up at him with dazed mascara-smeared faces.

At the bottom of the staircase a gaggle of children in party clothes is being ineffectually herded by a harassed mother in a sweat-darkened dress. She turns to Todd and Suki and, seemingly without seeing them, shrieks, "I warned them about serving ice cream! But did they listen?"

In answer, Suki puts a cigarette into her mouth and lights it, all in one hand movement. The mother stares, first at Todd, then at Suki, as if she can't believe her eyes. Todd starts to laugh, gently at first, then finds he can't stop. He has to lean on Suki and, when she removes herself outside his reach, he has to resort to a handy bookcase. Is this the first effect of the Valium? Hard to say. Something is silting up his veins, that's for sure, rolling through his brain. It feels like a missed night's sleep but with softer edges. His limbs have a pleasing weight to them and the lights around the hallway have acquired refracting penumbras.

"Penumbra," he says, possibly aloud, to the books in the bookcase. "Pen. Um. Bra."

Suki removes her cigarette. "Shut up, Todd," she says briskly.

The gaggle of children turns suddenly, like startled cattle, and stampedes through a doorway, the mother running after them. Todd is repeating her words over and over, inside his head, trying to get the exact pitch and register of her Scottish accent. I *warrrn*ed them about *serrrv*ing *ice* cream. But did they listen? Said more like *lus-un*.

In front of them is a display of stags' heads. Daniel is nowhere to be seen. He has momentarily fallen off Todd's radar, wandered out of range. Todd takes a thistle from a floral arrangement and places it in the mouth of the largest stag. Suki strikes up a conversation with an earnest-faced bearded boy.

Where is Daniel? Todd feels an unspecified, nibbling anxiety. He headed this way a quarter of an hour ago—maybe more. He said he needed some air. Or was it a drink? Something like that.

Todd is just about to reach out and touch Suki's arm, to tell her he doesn't know where Daniel is and should they go and find him, when he becomes conscious that he is twisting his head to look at the door. Someone is entering. Later, he will recall that he heard her before he saw her: that clack-clack of her boots, the jangling metalware of her bag.

Nicola Janks is moving through the hallway. Or someone who closely resembles her. This person has her glossy, clipped hair, her heavy fringe, the crimson startle of her lipstick, but it is as if she herself is a candle that has been left burning too long. The flesh has melted off her in—what?—a matter of weeks. Her clever fox face is hollowed out at the cheeks, under the eyes: skin stretched over skull. Her hands, clutching that bag of hers with multiple zippers, are reduced to wizened claws, marbled with blue. Her sternum sticks up as a ridged spur from the neckline of her dress.

She passes them with a tilt of her head and a grimace, as if simultaneously to acknowledge and dismiss their shock.

"Hello, sidekicks," she says, from the corner of her poppy-red mouth.

She doesn't alter her stride. Todd and Suki swivel their heads to watch her go.

"Did you see?" Suki is hissing as Nicola Janks ascends the stairs, at precisely the same moment as Todd is whispering, "What's happened to her?"

Todd stands up. He sits down. He stands up again. He says, "We have to find Daniel. We have to warn him."

Suki says, "Fuck." Then she says, "Did you know she was invited? How come she was invited?" She screws up her face and moves it close to Todd's. "You stay here," she says, pushing him down on a convenient tweed stool. "Keep a lookout for Daniel. If you see him, make sure you keep him with you."

She disappears up the stairs, two at a time.

Todd watches the comings and the goings of the hallway. The earnest-faced boy goes into a room, then comes out again surprisingly quickly. More children in party dresses or possibly the same ones. The bride's mother, walking fast in her aubergine court shoes, her mouth set in a grim line. A couple, not the ones from the alcove, the man's hand inside the woman's dress. The mother of the ice-cream comment: she wanders through the hall, glances at Todd, then away, her face tense and alarmed. Suki, in her dragon jacket, gives him a sidelong look as she passes.

Suddenly someone is patting his cheek with an open palm and saying, "Hey, Denham, what's going on?"

Daniel is there, in front of him, his shirt untucked, his jacket gone. "Denham," he is saying, "wake up, man."

"I'm awake," Todd says. "I wasn't sleeping." He stands up to prove it. "Where have you been?"

"Everywhere." Daniel grins at him. "Nowhere."

Todd looks at his friend. Daniel is swaying slightly. His pupils are enormous, blasted into the blue of his irises, his skin pale and moist. He smells of stale wine, of woodsmoke, of mud, of outdoors and something else. Todd frowns. Daniel is due to fly back to the States in less than eight hours. Family emergency, as it's termed on all the necessary forms. Todd had to go to the head of Daniel's department yesterday and explain to him that Daniel's mother is dying—sent home from hospital, he'd said, unfortunately, yes, a matter of weeks—that Daniel needs to go back to New York for a while, a month or two at the very least. Todd had arranged a flight for him, starting in Glasgow, early tomorrow morning.

The thought makes Todd feel unbalanced, as if he's missing some vital limb. He has no idea what Daniel will face when he gets home. Todd pictures darkened rooms, lowered blinds, bedside tables full of pills, a body under blankets. Lots of weeping relatives. The works.

He doesn't let himself think about what it will be like in the flat without Daniel, with no one in the room above him. How he will write his thesis conclusion alone, with only Suki and her cursed hamster for company. How he will get through the last few weeks of term, the rapid acceleration in teaching, the panic of the final-year students and their last-minute seminars. How he is going to face all this without Daniel, Todd doesn't know.

He wants to formulate some way to say this to Daniel. To say: don't go. No, not that. He has to go, his mother is dying, for God's sake. To say: don't go for long. Make sure you come back. To say: life without you is unthinkable. But to say any of these things seems impossible here, in this hallway full of severed heads and chemically preserved grouse and abandoned wineglasses, with Daniel in front of him, his face mushroom pale, his pupils shot.

"What have you taken?" Todd asks instead.

Daniel swings his head around to look at him. His face is distant, dangerous. "Huh?"

"Daniel," Todd whispers, taking his elbow, "what did you take?"

"Nothing," Daniel slurs. "I don't know. It wasn't much."

"Much what?"

"Nothing," Daniel says again.

"How many times have I told you—"

"'How many times have I told you,'" Daniel mimics, in the voice of a chiding mother, pulling his elbow away. The movement seems to unbalance what equilibrium he has, and he staggers sideways, into a table, then a stool, then the floor, a vase recoiling from his shoulder, an antler giving way to his flailing arm. Thistles, water, and snapped antlers litter the tartan carpet in a confused arc.

"Right," says Todd. "Let's go." He takes Daniel's hand. "It's OK," he says to the people gathered around them, staring at Daniel in horror. "I've got him." He levers Daniel up off the floor, brushes broken glass and thistle particles off his clothes, then manhandles him out of the door.

The air outside is sharply cool, the sky fading to indigo ink. Small flies circle the lamps. Daniel leans against him, breathing unevenly.

"Listen," Todd says, as they stagger together over the gravel in a strange, forward-momentum waltz. "I need to tell you something, but first I have to say that you mustn't take stuff that doesn't come from me, OK? I've told you this before. You've got no idea what's in it. What comes from my cousin is pure. You know that. But everything else is—"

"What a place," Daniel exclaims, still leaning on him. "What a fucking place. Look at it." He flings out an arm, then seems to peer at something. "Are those mountains?" he asks, pointing at a line of peaks beyond the trees.

"Yes," Todd says. "The thing is—"

"Are you sure?"

"Am I sure about what?"

"That they're mountains. They look so . . . so far away."

"Hmm. Daniel, the thing is—"

"Aha!" Daniel yells, ecstatic, yanking his hand out of Todd's inner pocket and up into the air. "What have we here?"

All the time they were walking together, yakking about mountains, Daniel had been searching Todd's stash. Pickpocketing him, in effect.

"No," Todd says, feeling his grasp on Daniel's frame loosening and slipping. "Really don't, Daniel. Give it back."

Daniel pushes him away and Todd has to stop himself snatching at him, grabbing him by the chest.

"Don't be such a whaddayacallit," Daniel says.

"A what?"

"Party pooper."

"Come on," Todd says, holding out his hand. "You really don't need any more."

"Au contraire, Pierre," Daniel says, with a smile, brandishing the tab.

Todd makes a leap for it, but Daniel, at six foot whatever, snatches it effortlessly out of his grasp.

"Let's see," Daniel says. "One for me, one for you, and one for—"

Todd makes another futile leap. "Daniel, listen. We saw Nicola."

This seems to make an impression. Daniel stalls, the plastic wallet high above his head, like a child answering a question. "Nicola? My Nicola?"

"She's here."

"Here?"

"At the wedding."

"This wedding?"

"Yeah. And—"

"Oh." Daniel slides a palm down his face. "That's kind of . . . I mean, why now, why here, why on earth—"

"She seems . . ." Todd swallows. "She looks . . . different," he finishes weakly.

Daniel cocks his head, as if having trouble hearing the conversation. "Different how?"

"Um . . ." Todd tries to order his thoughts. "She looks . . . thin."

"Thin?" Daniel says again, his hand falling to his side. He smiles, a crooked half smile, and shakes his head. He shakes it so hard and for so long that Todd worries he will fall over. "No, no," he says, his voice blurred by the movement. "You're forgetting. She's always thin."

"No." Todd spreads his hands, helplessly. "This is different thin, unhealthy thin—"

Daniel is still shaking his head. "You've got it all wrong. She doesn't do that anymore, she got over that, she—"

"Daniel, she looks really ill. Suki thought so too. How long is it since you saw her?"

Todd isn't really expecting a coherent answer so is surprised when Daniel says solemnly, "Five weeks and three days."

Todd leans forward and closes his hand around the plastic wallet of tabs. "Suki and I wanted to find you to—"

Daniel snatches the tabs away.

"You have to get on a plane in a few hours," Todd says, holding out his hand. "Daniel, come on. You can't fly home like this. You're going to need to talk to Nicola. And what about your mum? What about—"

Daniel's expression shuts like a book. He slaps a tab onto his tongue, closes his mouth. He places one in Todd's hand, then turns, without a word, and takes off toward the lake.

When Todd and Suki heard that an American exchange student was being billeted in the vacant room in the eaves of their graduate flat, they were not pleased. They pictured a toothy type with trainers and V-necks and white socks. They pictured someone who might, of all things, attend church. Americans were religious, weren't they? He would have hot-dog–scented breath, a penchant for soft rock, and a backpack full of college sweatshirts. He would want to join fraternities.

"Typical," Suki muttered darkly, shaking the fuel up the U-bend of her lighter. "Why couldn't they put him downstairs?"

Todd, sitting opposite her in their kitchen, nodded. Downstairs was a flat full of foreign graduate students, mostly scientists, who worked hard, wore ties, and looked permanently cold and shocked after about October.

"Or in college," Suki continued, painting her nails with the fluorescent yellow tip of a highlighter. "That's what the Yanks want, after all. Gargoyles and quadrangles and all that shit." She recapped the pen and tossed it among the debris of the table: mugs with desiccated tea bags dried onto their rims, plates smeared with baked-bean juice, a crust of bread, possibly whole wheat, a library book about poststructuralism for which neither Todd nor Suki was willing to take responsibility, two ashtrays, a folder, an alarm clock with a blank digital display.

Todd and Suki had lived together for the two years since graduation. Their success as flatmates was predicated on two things, in Todd's opinion: first, they had never been close friends before they had shared a flat so had arrived with no expectations or preconceived ideas of how cozy and wonderful it was all going to be and, second, they had never slept together.

Suki was not his type any more, he was sure, than he was hers. He had once compared her to the chocolate bittermints his mother sent him at Christmas—small, dark, sour, an acquired taste—and she had reached over and snapped his pencil in two. She had eaten the rest of the mints: it was her right, she said. They kept their bike keys in the empty box, which lived beside the kettle.

Two years of harmony, or as much harmony as you can get between the precious, late, and only child of two Highgate psychoanalysts, and a stressed, overstretched, cash-strapped graduate, who was the first person in his family to get to tertiary education. And now a third party was about to be catapulted into their midst.

"I hope he's not going to be *friendly*," Suki snarled, slapping shut her book on post-Newtonian cultures.

As it turned out, they needn't have worried on that score. It was a while before they caught their first glimpse of their new flatmate. The only signs that he'd actually moved in were the appearance of a packet of pungent Italian coffee in the kitchen, a red toothbrush in the bathroom, and, one morning, the pale, elongated balloon of a condom floating in the toilet bowl, transparent and alien as a sea creature.

"I take it that thing's not yours?" Suki said, without looking up from her lecture notes, as Todd entered the kitchen.

"Er, no." Todd shook the cereal box and found it empty. Then he turned, suddenly offended. "But it might have been."

Suki snorted, turned a page, then another.

Todd sighed. He flicked down the switch on the kettle. The state of his romantic life had begun, of late, to bother him. He didn't know how one obtained sex here. It was the least erotic place in the universe, he'd decided. Undergraduates were off-limits—the faculty frowned on that sort of thing—and the graduate girls were all intent on their books. How, then, had this American made a conquest so fast?

A few days later, a woman entered their kitchen. It was midafternoon. She had streaked hair spilling over one shoulder and she was wearing a T-shirt emblazoned with the name of a band from Manchester. It reached almost to her knees but, despite this, it was possible to tell that she was naked underneath. Neither Todd nor Suki had ever seen her before.

She opened the fridge. She got out a loaf of bread, a slab of butter, then found a plate. She proceeded to make two sandwiches.

"*Hello*," said Suki, in what might appear, to people who didn't know her, as a friendly manner.

The girl turned. "Oh," she said, shaking her hair out of her eyes. "Sorry. Dreadful manners. Hi. I'm Cassandra."

"Hi, Cassandra," Suki said, then jabbed him with her pen. "Todd, say hello to Cassandra."

"Hello, Cassandra."

Cassandra cut her sandwiches into quarters, arranged them on a plate, then left. They heard her climbing the stairs to the attic. Only minutes later, it seemed, came the muffled crack-crack of the headboard hitting the wall.

"Well," Todd said, reaching over to switch on the radio, "I guess he likes sandwiches."

One night, fueled by a heat-and-eat macaroni and cheese from the corner shop, and some excellent dope from Marrakech, Suki and Todd decided to break into the American's room. They tiptoed, shushing and nudging each other, up the stairs to the attic. Suki had brought one of her credit cards to slide into the lock, but there was no need. The door was ajar. At the sight of a desk chair, draped with an empty leather jacket, Todd lost the impulse for snooping.

"Maybe we shouldn't . . . ," he began, stepping back to the edge of the small landing, but Suki had pushed the door and walked in.

There was a long pause. Todd strained his ears for an exclamation, a comment, anything, but Suki, uncharacteristically, was silent.

"What?" Todd said. "What's in there?"

His mind flashed through options—strange sex toys, disturbing pictures, a dead body. His? The American's? Had he hanged himself or overdosed and been lying there for days?

"Shit," Suki murmured, and Todd could bear it no longer. He pushed through the door, stepping on Suki's foot and banging into the desk.

The room was much as Todd had last seen it—low, slanting ceilings, bare window out onto blackened branches. A desk in the corner, a bed squeezed in next to it. But the walls were filled with words. Hundreds of them. Written in slanting black capitals on index cards and tacked to the faded floral wallpaper.

Villain, was the first one Todd saw, and next to it, *animosity.* He turned his head. *Silly* and *hierarchy* jumped out at him. Next to the door: *dizzy, annoy, pagan, profane, doom, fatal.*

Suki padded forward and gave one of the cards a tap with her thumbnail. She let out a long, swooping whistle. "Mad," she whispered.

"What?" Todd whispered back.

"Mad as a hatter."

"Do you think?"

"Yep. Totally lost it."

"Not necessarily," Todd whispered. "Maybe there's some . . . I don't know . . . scheme behind it all. I mean—"

"Scheme?" Suki hissed, pulling her cardigan sleeves down over her hands. "Do you see any evidence of schematic thinking in this?" She gestured around her so violently that the word *discreet* fluttered to the carpet.

Todd bent to pick it up, then changed his mind. "Perhaps we should—"

At that moment, they heard the front door slam shut. They leaped toward the landing and hurled themselves down the stairs and into their own rooms, then shut the doors.

The very next day, coming back from a lusterless seminar with some first years, none of whom had completed the assignment he had set them the previous week, Todd entered the gate and nearly tripped over a figure hunched over an upturned bicycle.

"Oh," Todd said, righting himself by clinging to the low wall. "Sorry, didn't see you there."

The person stood. He was wearing an enormous black overcoat, thick-soled workman's boots, and the Mancunian band T-shirt. He had black hair that was shaved at the sides but obscured most of his face; his eyes were an incongruous, startling gas-flame blue.

Todd experienced a spasm of doubt, of fear. Was this person about to hurt him? Was there any way he could dart around him and reach the door first? Was there any conceivable scenario in which he, Todd, could outrun, outwit, outsmart this person?

Then the person smiled, whacking Todd on the upper arm in what seemed to be an amiable way, and began to talk: "Hey," he said, "you must be Todd. You're Todd? The elusive Todd. I've seen your name on the doorbell and letters and things. Yours and Suki's. Now, you can tell me this, is it Suki or Sucky? How do you say it? Suki? OK. Got it. So, listen, what can you tell me about bicycle chains? I've been grappling with this thing for half an hour and I hate to admit defeat. I thought we were going to be able to work together for a while there but then the fucker went and reneged on me. Are they always like this? I haven't had a bicycle since sixth grade, but they tell me it's compulsory around here. Kind of like an admission requirement. Hey, are you hungry? I made a whole load of chili. I've got a girl coming over later but I made so much—"

"Cassandra?" Todd managed to get in.

"Oh," Daniel Sullivan pulled a wry face under his heavy black fringe, "no. Cassandra turned out to be very ... Well, never mind. This girl I met in the library yesterday. She's kind of the opposite of Cassandra, in a lot of ways. Sort of big-boned and generous, you know? Anyway. So I made the chili and ... Are you going in? Me too. We'll go in together."

They went into the flat, Todd and Daniel. They ate chili. Todd explained his thesis to Daniel. Daniel played some of Todd's vinyl. Todd asked him about the words on the walls and Daniel said he was trying to mine potential patterns in semantic amelioration and pejoration. Todd had no idea what Daniel was talking about and tried to understand as Daniel riffed on attitudes to language change: decay or evolution?

When the girl turned up, she was dismayed to see that the loquacious American exchange student, who had so charmed her in the library the day before, had a friend with him. A pale, nervous sort of friend who fiddled with the record player, turning up the volume and, when she was speaking, had the unnerving habit of muttering inaudible asides to Daniel, making Daniel smile and occasionally laugh. The whole effect was very off-putting, not to mention the way they both insisted on reading out the words stuck to the walls in medieval English pronunciations. All in all, it was a very disappointing evening, she told her friends later. She would never again accept dinner invitations from strangers in libraries.

Some weeks into their second term of living with Daniel, Suki marched straight into Todd's room without knocking and shook him through the blankets.

"You'll never guess who the penthouse guest was last night," she said into Todd's ear.

"Don't care," Todd said blearily, his lids shut tight.

Suki waited for a moment, then said, "Nicola Janks."

Todd opened his eyes.

Nicola Janks was, scandalously, several years older than them. Todd and Suki knew her only by sight—and reputation. She had her own house, her own car, a lectureship, that elusive triumvirate of letters after her name, and a burgeoning sideline career as a media pundit. She stuck out, somewhat, among her rather more conservative colleagues, in whose breasts she elicited paranoia and envy in equal measure. She had written books on gender and society, which were published by mainstream publishers and sold in actual bookshops, not just academic ones. She wrote features for broadsheets. She appeared on the radio and, occasionally, on television, where she said things like "the toxicity of accepted phraseology" and "the impossibility of neutrality in the camera's gaze" and "eating disorders are a cry for autonomy, for gender-role recalibration." She stalked about the corridors and quadrangles in a swooping black cloak thing, leaving behind her a trail of fascinated and awed undergraduates. Todd had always thought she looked like a crow, albeit a rather glamorous one.

That she had descended from the heights of proper grown-ups with mortgages and insurance, tenure and television appearances, to their dingy flat—and Daniel—was astonishing. What was more astonishing was that she stayed put. She and Daniel cooked dinner together. They went out to films. They drove about town in her little red car. She renamed him Dan: she would call the flat and ask, "Is Dan around?" The flow of other women through Daniel's room ceased altogether. Daniel assumed the preoccupation and equanimity of a man in a permanent adult relationship. He was sober, mostly calm; he worked hard. He was also absent, several nights a week, because he was staying over at Nicola's.

On these evenings, Todd would stand in the doorway to Daniel's abandoned room, pushing the door away from him and letting it swing back, over and over again. This was not a development he had ever expected.

And then Todd and Suki returned from the cinema one evening to find Daniel at the kitchen table, already one-third into a bottle of whiskey. "Ever seen the inside of an abortion clinic?" were the words with which he greeted them. He squinted, as if he was having trouble seeing them, proffering the whiskey. "Let me tell you," he said, taking a swig, "it is not a happy place."

This was considered by all concerned to be a hiatus, an interval, if you like, in the drama that was Daniel and Nicola. But it turned out that there was one final scene to be played out.

The next day, apparently still inebriated, Daniel was observed to resume certain old activities. He was seen, haggard and pale of face, making effortful phone calls from the hallway. Todd and Suki assumed he was on the phone to Nicola, who had stayed up in London for a few days to recover, with a friend. He apprehended Suki in the kitchen sometime during the afternoon and asked her whether she had ever considered that pro-lifers might have a point. Suki said, no, of course I bloody haven't. And: go to bed, Daniel, sleep it off. Around dinnertime, Daniel suddenly disappeared out of the door before Todd could stop him. Todd ran out into the road to call after him, to say, where are you going, come back, but it was too late. Daniel was off, unsteadily, weaving from one side of the road to the other, on the bike that always looked too small for him.

It was Todd who, later that evening, met him on the stairs. Todd was going down to see a showing at the repertory cinema, and Daniel was coming up, with a wavy-haired woman from the teacher-training course. They were both drunk, and the woman was wearing Daniel's coat.

Todd wanted to say, Daniel, stop, what are you doing, think about this. But whoever does, in these situations? There was nothing for him to do but stand to one side, letting his friend and the woman lurch past.

The following morning played out with all the precision, ill timing, and miscommunication of a farce—or, perhaps, a tragedy. Nicola Janks drove up to the house in her little red car, a day or two earlier than expected. Suki, who happened to be watching from an upstairs window, later said she climbed out of the driver's seat with a caution and slowness that suggested the act caused her pain. She was coming up the garden path before Suki thought to warn Daniel, by which time he was coming down from his room. As was the trainee teacher.

Suki was darting out of her bedroom, thinking she could forestall the disaster, get to Daniel in time to warn him, to enable him to put Nicola off until he'd got the wavy-haired woman—whose name no one, afterward, would ever remember—out of the way. But what was forgotten in the melee was that Daniel had given Nicola a key.

All parties met on the landing: Nicola coming up from the passageway, Todd and Suki arriving from their rooms, Daniel and the woman descending from his.

It will be disagreed upon, later, as to what Nicola was carrying. The heavy black-leather bag will be a given, but Suki will say it was also a spray of lilies. Todd will insist it was a bag of breakfast groceries—croissants, a baguette, a pot of jam. The kinds of things grown-ups buy. Either way, what she is holding, be it flowers, groceries, or both, slides to the floor.

Nicola stares, her arms empty. Her gaze moves from Daniel to the woman and back again. She is deathly white, bloodless. She leans against the wall. Daniel begins to talk and talk, his arms thrashing through the air, his hands raking through his hair. Todd and Suki withdraw to their rooms. The wavy-haired woman bursts into tears. Then she leaves.

Nobody tries to stop her. Daniel fetches a chair. Nicola sits down. Then she gets up. She tries to go. Daniel bars her way. He is shouting by this point. Nicola still says nothing, which, everyone later agrees, is not like her. Daniel tries to stop her from going down the stairs. It's only when he puts his hands on her, on her arm, that it happens. She hits him. Right across the face and only once. A crack of a blow, just below his left eye. It is an act done quickly, efficiently. And then Nicola Janks leaves.

There is a clearing in the trees. Todd has decided some time ago—it is unclear exactly when—that the right thing to do is to walk around its perimeter, around and around. The thick carpet of pine needles has begun to be trodden down in a circular rut, in a way that is pleasing to him.

Someone has lit a fire. Probably Daniel. He's good at that sort of thing. He'd been some kind of scout or whatever it was they had in America and could tie knots and build shelters and create emergency stretchers out of coats and branches.

It was Daniel who started the splinter party in the woods. He had come in here after his conversation with Nicola by the lake and, because he was Daniel, people began to follow him. Where's Daniel? they said. Where's he gone? Because they always did. Daniel was one of those people whom others follow. It's because, Todd has often thought, he doesn't appear to want or expect it. It just happens.

People are gathered around the fire: flittering figures and a lull of voices, pierced by the occasional shriek, burst of song, or exclamation. Suki had been here—she's gone now—and Todd has a definite recollection of her saying it was getting much too fucking feral for her liking, and stalking off back to the house, the dragon on her jacket disappearing into the crisscrossing branches of the trees. There are a few people from uni, various hangers-on, boyfriends and girlfriends acquired since graduation. There is a bottle of whiskey, which tastes hot, and vodka, which tastes cold. Todd has experimented by taking alternate swallows and shared his insight with Suki, before she left, but she pulled a face and said, take it easy. When he told Daniel, he had leaned in to listen, then nodded, very slowly and for a long time.

There is a ghetto blaster, which appeared from somewhere, hanging by its handle from a tree, and the firelight seems to leap and flare in time to the heavy beat. The rhythm finds its way into Todd's very body and he has to stop walking to check that, yes, his pulse is keeping time.

This seems to him an amazing, revelatory thing.

Daniel is crashing about in the undergrowth, yanking bits off trees and hurling them onto the fire: branches, leaves, logs. His face is shuttered, intent, wheaten in color, his suit torn in several places, his hands muddied and cut. The fire is getting larger and larger, the fierce flames reaching up toward the trees above.

When Todd came upon him and Nicola beside the lake, or loch or whatever it is they call it up here, Daniel had been saying, "Jesus, look at you, you're breaking my heart."

Nicola had laughed that throaty laugh of hers. "How ironic," she'd said, in her brittle, atonal voice. She took a quick, nervous drag of her cigarette. "Anyway, it's nothing." She shrugged as she exhaled. "Just an old demon reasserting itself. I'll be right as rain."

Daniel put out a hand to touch her, but she stepped away.

"And," she said, flicking her ash to the ground, "you don't exactly look the picture of health yourself. Been burning the candle at both ends, have you?"

Daniel scratched his head. "Something like that."

"I can well imagine."

"No," Daniel said quietly, "I don't think you can. I've been"—he dragged his hands through his hair—"I don't really know what I've been doing. I'm just ... My life seems to have been diverted onto this whole other track. I can't sleep, I can't work, I can't do anything even close to—"

"Poor you," Nicola interrupted. "Is that what you want me to say? That it must all have been so terribly difficult for you? That—"

"No," Daniel cut in. "Stop it, Nic. You know I don't mean that. It's just that when I look back to that day when ... that day in London, when ... that day of the ... you know ..." He took a deep breath, as if trying to order his thoughts. "When I look back to that day, I—"

"You know what I feel when I look back to that day?" Nicola spoke over him, in a tone so low that Todd had to strain to hear.

Daniel looked at her. "What?"

"That I don't recognize myself. I remember wondering if I was making a huge mistake." She throws her cigarette to the ground, turning to address him. "If I was doing the wrong thing. I felt so certain, at one point, that I should be keeping it, that I should be binding my life to yours. And now—" she brought up her hands to her face—"now I have to question my judgment, question everything, because I obviously had no inkling of the kind of person you really are. I don't know how I could have misread you so badly, how I could have failed so spectacularly to see you for what you are. I can't believe I ever even considered having a child with someone like you. I look back to that day," she said, "and ask myself how I could have been so wrong about you."

"You weren't," Daniel muttered.

"I wasn't what?"

"Wrong about me. Not then, not that day."

She let out a small scoffing noise and turned away. Daniel lowered himself to a rock and, just as Todd knew he would, got out his tin and papers and began rolling himself a cigarette. His movements were deliberate, careful, but his hands, distributing the tufts of tobacco, were shaking.

It was only when he put the cigarette into his mouth that he spoke: "I'm flying back to New York tomorrow."

"I heard," Nicola said, smoothing back her hair. She bent at the knees and selected a pebble from the ground. "I'm really sorry about your mother." She weighed it in her hands, then tossed it toward the loch.

There was a moment's silence, then a splash, out on the water. It made Daniel turn his head.

"Are you coming back?" she asked, searching for another pebble.

"Of course," Daniel said quickly. "In a month or so. Maybe two."

She must have picked up a handful of stones because Todd could hear her sifting them in her palm. "Well," she said, "perhaps I'll see you then."

"You certainly will." Daniel stood. He came over to her, put one arm around her, then the other, and this time she didn't pull away. "And while I'm gone," he said, "I want you to get well. OK? No more of this demon." He seized her face between his hands, forcing her to look up at him, and Todd thought that perhaps he should go now, that perhaps he'd seen enough. "OK?" Daniel said again. "You have to start feeding yourself, Nic. It's as simple as that."

Nicola nodded, whispering something, and the two of them were pressing their foreheads together and Todd was backing away, crouching low so they wouldn't see him, so they wouldn't be disturbed, but a branch or reed or something must have caught his ankle because one moment he was upright and the next he was on his side, winded, lungs empty, and Nicola's voice was its usual sarcastic rasp, saying, "Spying again, are we, Mr. Denham?"

There are people here in the forest Todd doesn't know. Two blokes who said they worked with the groom, a girl with pale hair, who spoke in an accent like Daniel's. Todd had mentioned this to Daniel and he had rolled his eyes. She's Canadian, he'd said, as if it ought to have been obvious. There were a few wanderers-in from the wedding party, which was still going on back near the house, in a large tent with blue fairy lights and a band playing hits from twenty years ago. Todd and Daniel had been back several times to get supplies and the bride was dancing in her stockinged feet on a near-empty dance floor, arms in the air, eyes shut, hair fallen to her shoulders.

There had been a moment when Todd thought the Canadian girl with the slight lisp might like him. She had sat on a log with him and they had passed a joint between them and she had told him that her ancestors had emigrated from a valley like this, somewhere in Scotland, six generations ago.

So it had seemed possible that she was interested in him. But then Daniel had come crashing through the trees with more firewood in his arms and thrown it in one go onto the fire, making sparks and glowing smuts float up to mix with the leaves. Then he had reached over and changed the track on the ghetto blaster and the girl with the ancestors had got up to dance in the kilnlike glow and then, after a while, Daniel had said he was going to look for more wood and the girl had stopped dancing. She'd said could she go with him but Nicola had been there and she had stood up quickly, followed Daniel into the trees, and the Canadian girl had sat down again on the log.

Todd and Daniel had a room in a B and B that Suki had booked for them: Todd knew this. But somehow it seemed foolish to leave the fire. It made no sense, especially as the sky above the tangle of branches was beginning to drain of its dark and drop a moist, grayish film into the forest. It made no sense at all. What made sense was this: to lie down on the spread of pine needles, next to the fire, as close as you could. There were so many pine needles. Thousands, millions, of the things, all exactly the same. Laid across and underneath and on top of one another, forming the most comfortable surface ever. It seemed miraculous to Todd, their similarity, their uniformity. He said this to Daniel, who was lying on the other side of the scarlet embers: Isn't it amazing?

Yeah, Daniel replied, with a yawn. Oh, yeah.

There arrived an interlude. Todd could see the pine needles near his head and then it seemed he was back in his childhood bedroom, only it wasn't the same. One of the walls was made up of thick bushes that pressed in on his bed, on his eiderdown. Somehow he knew his brother was on the other side of the bushes but he couldn't get to him, couldn't reach him, because the bushes were so sharp, so spiked.

Someone was swearing. This became clear to Todd. Someone was stumbling about near his head with heavy feet, picking things up and swearing.

"What?" Todd mumbled, keeping his eyes closed. It seemed only minutes since they'd gone to sleep, seconds perhaps, but he could tell that the fire was out, that it was early morning. Somewhere above them, birds were screeching in horrible unison, an orchestra of mis-tuned violins.

"My flight," Daniel was saying hoarsely, off to the left, "my fucking flight."

Todd sat up. He was instantly awake. His head felt ringingly empty: it was clear to him what he had to do. He had to get Daniel to the air-port. He had to get Daniel to his flight.

Daniel was leaning with one hand against a tree, yanking on his shoe. He was dressed—that was something. Mud-stained trousers, a torn jacket, hair hanging in his eyes.

"It's OK." Todd got to his feet, the axis of the ground tipping only for a minute. "It's OK." He looked at his watch. He tapped it. He held it to his ear. There was an answering, reassuring click-click of mechanical motion. "We've got time."

"We have?"

"Yeah."

Todd grabbed his jacket off the ground, where he had apparently been lying on it. "We need to get to the B and B, get the car, and drive to the airport."

"OK."

"It'll take us . . . I don't know . . . an hour. At most."

"Right." Daniel seized him by both arms, pulled him close. "Slap me."

"What?"

"I said, slap me."

Todd looked into his face. "Really?"

"Yeah." Daniel rubbed at his bloodshot eyes, eased open his jaw, once, twice. "Go for it."

Todd slapped him with one hand, then the other.

"Thanks," Daniel said, shaking his head.

"So," Todd began, "we really could—"

"Oh, man," Daniel said. He was looking past him at something.

"What?" Todd turned.

Nicola Janks was lying on the ground, near to where the fire had been.

Todd and Daniel regarded her. She was on her side, legs tucked up, feet bare. Her lips—pale without their customary red stain—were slightly parted, her eyes shut tight.

"Is she sleeping?" Daniel whispered.

Todd put his head to one side. He considered her one way, he considered her the other. "Looks like it."

"Should we wake her?"

Todd looked at his watch. He went over to her. He tapped her ankle with his toe. Nothing. He tapped her again. He looked at his watch. He looked up at his friend. Daniel looked back at him, his face blank. He seemed to be waiting for Todd to speak. A long moment passed.

"Is she OK?" Daniel said.

Todd bent over her. He touched her arm. Her skin was cool as marble.

"Did you give her anything?" Todd asked as he leaned over her face.

"No," Daniel said, quickly. "I don't think so. Unless . . ."

Todd could see, in the morning light, that the roots of her hair were brown. A nondescript dun color. So the raven sheen was all a construct, he thought. He could also see that Nicola Janks was so thin you could see each bone of her frame: the ulna and the radius of the arm—the terms reached him from a distant biology lesson—meeting the humerus with aligned precision.

"Unless what?"

"I might . . . She might have had some of that . . . "

"Coke?"

"Yeah."

"You gave her coke?" Todd hissed, gesturing at her emaciated form. "In this state?"

Daniel looked stricken. "I . . . don't know. I might have. I . . . I don't really remember."

"Jesus, Daniel. Where did you get it, anyway?"

"This . . . guy. At the bar."

Todd sat back on his heels. He thought about Daniel's plane. He imagined it waiting on the tarmac at the airport. Perhaps it was being cleaned right now, a team of women in overalls entering its aisles and rows, armed with sprays and cloths and wipes. He thought about Daniel's mother, about the oxygen tanks and lowered blinds.

He picked up Nicola's wrist in his fingers and waited.

The forest inhaled, a breeze sifting through the trees, a shower of needles falling some way off, behind them.

"She's fine," Todd said, dropping her arm. "I can feel her pulse. She's just sleeping. Look, why don't you go to the B and B, wake Suki, and get her to drive you to the airport?"

Daniel thought about this, shifting from foot to foot. "I don't know." He scratched the back of his head.

"Go," Todd said. "I mean it. I'll take care of this. Of her. I'll explain the whole thing. But just go. You'll miss your flight. Off you go."

Daniel looked away from him, through the trees, toward the light.

"Go," Todd said again. "Run. I'll see you when you get back."

Something Only He Can See

LUCAS

Cumbria, 1995

Lucas moves by instinct through his dark garden. If he thinks about it, he will stumble, but if he lets his muscle memory guide him, he will be fine. He rounds the patio, makes his way past the rockery, and comes upon the black mass of the big evergreen tree sooner than he'd expected. He slides in behind it, to a space between its fronded branches and the wall. He places the walkie-talkie telephone receiver, brought with him so Maeve doesn't have to get up from the sofa to answer it, in his coat pocket.

Only then does he light his cigarette.

He doesn't want Maeve to spot the orange glow through the dark. Nicotine is known to inhibit sperm motility or give it two heads or make it go round in circles or something like that. He doesn't remember, even though she's told him countless times. It's just one cigarette, he tells her inside his head. It can't possibly zap all his spermatozoa. Can it?

He shivers inside his all-weather down coat and draws on the spunk-mutating cigarette, eyeing the neighbors' house, a slate-covered villa, like theirs. It's a second home, of course, as most in the village are, lit up only on weekends. This lot are from London, where the dad works as a banker, and has four children. A shocking, unjust number, really, when you think about it. The mother just seems to pop them out, one after another, her stomach permanently inflated, her breasts constantly being heaved out of her garments in the back garden for some infant or other to nourish itself. Lucas can't look anymore; Maeve avoids the garden on weekends.

He and Maeve have lived here for five years, since giving up their jobs as social workers in Manchester and downshifting to this Cumbrian village, starting a business taking schoolkids on Outward Bound–type adventures. From their back windows, you can see green fields and hills bisected by rivers and a white waterfall. Maeve takes the little children on nature walks, sketching or dam building; he leads the older ones up Helvellyn or instructs them on how to build a shelter in the wild.

Real children fill their days, he thinks, as he takes another drag, and would-be, wished-for, imagined children fill their evenings, their weekends, their nights.

He is just leaning sideways to get a better view of the neighbors' pantry, where the eldest child—a pale, almost-wordless boy of around ten—is standing on a ladder, hand deep in a canister of what is possibly raisins or chocolate drops, when the phone rings. His sister—it has to be. He knew she would call tonight.

"Is that you?" he says, putting it to his ear.

"It is indeed," Claudette's voice replies. "I see your phone manner hasn't improved."

"No," he says. "It hasn't. What in God's name do you want?"

She laughs, as he knew she would. "I want to know about today. How did it go?"

Lucas inhales deeply on the cigarette and considers how to answer this. Should he say that he and Maeve waited for a whole agonizing hour in the embryo-transfer room, which had no windows and very little light, save for a cone cast by a lamp on the doctor's table? Maeve on the bed, covered with an insufficient blanket—Lucas could see her shivering with the cold or the anticipation or perhaps both—and the doctor holding up an X-ray to the light. Lucas exhales his smoke into the chill Cumbrian night air. How to distill the magnitude of what happened today into the smallness of a reply?

"Well," he flicks away his ash, "it went. We had two embryos put back."

"Oh." She lets out a sigh. "Good."

"We saw them."

"You saw what?"

"The embryos."

"Really?"

"They showed them to us on this screen up near the ceiling."

Backlit in green, the embryos had hovered above them, like notions, like deities: vast, beautiful, terrifying. Geometric in structure, they were like a proliferation of soap bubbles or the huge, heavy blooms of flowers. Lucas had wanted to shout Oh, and Hello, and There you are. He thought they were the most exquisite things he had ever seen. Maeve's hand held his in a fierce, cold grip. He had wanted to shut his eyes in a final, desperate wish but dared not tear his gaze from that screen, from those illuminated sea creatures floating in their aquatic dish. Please, he said to them, please, please.

"One of them," he says to Claudette, "we were assured, was of top, sure-to-be-a-winner quality."

"Thank God. That's great. I've got all my fingers crossed for you."

"That doesn't sound entirely comfortable."

"I don't care. This has to be your time, it just has to be."

He presses his back into the wall of the shed. "Let's hope."

She shifts position or someone near her says something.

"Where are you?" he asks.

"I've just got up."

A typical reply from his sister: most people would not be able to decode this kind of Claudette crypticism but, to Lucas, it's second nature. It tells him that she's probably not at home, in either LA or New York, that she's taken off somewhere but isn't ready yet to say exactly where, that she and Timou have either had a row and she's done a runner or they are in a good phase and holed up together in some dazzling tropical retreat.

Then there is that noise again. A snuffling. A sense of her moving, her attention being divided. And then he realizes.

"How's my nephew?" he says. "How's the"—forcing himself to form the word they never say, the collection of letters they never use—"baby?"

"Fine." She snips the word, as if with a very sharp pair of scissors. "How are you?"

He wants to say to her, please don't. Don't not talk about him. Don't pretend Ari doesn't exist for my sake.

"No," he says, pushing himself to joviality. The cheery uncle: fond but distant, involved but relaxed. He's almost convinced himself. "Tell me properly. How is he?"

"He's . . ." He senses her thinking. What to say? What not to say? How to navigate this? "He's sitting up on his own now. He's reaching for food. He's got your eyes."

"Oh," Lucas says.

"And his hair's starting to curl. He's basically a mini you."

And that's enough, he wants to say. Any more and I won't be enjoying this, I'll just be coping. Any more after that and I'll be unhappy. Next comes despondency, then despair.

But Claudette senses this. God knows how, but she does. He loves her for that, his sister, loves her for the fact that she moves things along, tells him about a letter she had from their mother, about a script her agent is telling her to do.

"So," she says, "how long is it until . . . "

"We find out if it's worked or not?"

"Yes."

"Fourteen days."

"That seems like a long time."

"I know. The two-week wait."

"How are you going to fill the days? Have you got any plans?"

"For the next two weeks?" Lucas thinks about this. "Not ask Maeve every five minutes whether she has any symptoms. Not follow her to the loo to see if everything is OK. Not call the doctor. Just keep our heads down, I guess, our hopes low, our fingers crossed. There's not much happening at work at the moment, it being winter, so we were thinking we might—"

"You don't fancy a trip, do you?" Claudette interrupts.

"A trip?"

"A quick change of scene. For both of you. With me."

"You mean to LA?"

"No, not LA. Somewhere else."

Lucas smiles, takes a drag on his cigarette. "OK," he says, "spit it out. Where are you?"

They are waiting, Lucas and Maeve, on a strip of gravel outside the thing like a cattle shed that serves as an airport in this part of the world. He has a rucksack at his feet, a hat with earflaps pulled down low on his head; Maeve is huddled inside her waterproof. The wind comes at them horizontally, whipping through a line of ragged trees to tug at the fastenings of his jacket and toss his hat strings in a manner that feels distinctly derisive.

Lucas is experiencing a falling sensation in his midriff, a premonition that this trip is a mistake, one of Claudette's less inspired impulses, and a suspicion that he has exercised a gross lack of judgment in agreeing to come. It is a feeling all too familiar from his childhood, from the many times his sister persuaded him to do something with her, lured him into acting as her accomplice, to tackle something or attempt something, and halfway through the execution, Lucas would be overtaken with dismay, with regret: how had she convinced him that this was a good idea? How badly were they going to be punished? Making a zip wire from a bedroom window to the ground. Rigging up a makeshift bridge across a flood-swollen river. Rescuing an injured bird from a high branch. Hauling off their mother's mattress to act as a crash mat for somersaulting off the windowsill.

And, now, almost thirty years later, here he is again, agreeing on the spur of the moment to drop everything and meet his erratic and hopelessly unreliable sibling in the middle of nowhere. What's more, dragging his possibly (maybe, hopefully, goddamn-better-be) pregnant wife along with him. Maeve had done nothing to deserve that kind of treatment. What was he thinking, leaving their business, their house, their bonsai-tree collection, and embarking on a trip of mysterious and possibly spurious purpose? It's only a couple of days, he'd told Maeve, when she'd fixed him with her stare.

He knew she'd been thinking about the last time they'd answered one of Claudette's late-night suggestions of a trip. They had met up in Rome. Claudette and Timou got into a flaming row on the Ponte Sisto (it was to do with what an Italian location scout had said to them earlier in the day, about artistic ownership or the challenges of collaboration or something along those lines). The two of them were going at it, Claudette furious and tearful, Timou gesticulating and yelling, when a gang of photographers had turned up and started taking pictures. Claudette had turned on them and hurled a handful of stones (they were small stones, she insisted to the carabinieri afterward, tiny, just gravel really, not rocks, not boulders, not at all), and when one of the photographers, struck in the face and bleeding, called Claudette a word that implied her profession was something other than acting, Timou had yanked him off his scooter and punched him. They had all been kept at the police station until the middle of the night. Maeve had murmured to Lucas, as they sat with their backs against the interview-room wall, never again.

Outside the airport, a bicycle creaks past, powered into the head-wind by an octogenarian with a pipe. Maeve clears her throat, raises a hand to her mouth; Lucas manages to stop the words Are you OK, and Do you feel sick, from making it out into the air. He is forced to do this, on average, every three minutes, has to stop himself from saying, How do you feel, do you feel anything, are you nauseous, just a little bit, a lot, is your sense of smell enhanced, do you feel tired, more tired than normal, less, do you feel anything out of the ordinary, anything at all, has it worked, do you think, oh, please, for God's sake, let it work.

"Um," Maeve says. "Is she definitely coming?"

"Yes."

"You're sure we're in the right place?"

"Yup," he says, with a confidence he doesn't feel.

Maeve swings her head from side to side, shivering again in the blasting wind. "She arrived yesterday?"

"Two days ago. Maybe three."

"And she knows we were on this flight?"

Lucas shrugs. "She booked it."

Maeve snorts. "I very much doubt that."

"Well." He sighs. "She would have asked one of her minders, or whatever they are, to book it, I suppose, but I don't—"

"Is she traveling with her minders? Do you think this might be one of them now?"

She points at a blue car circling the rockery roundabout. The car pulls up at the curb and a person of indeterminate gender steps out wearing a moth-eaten, ankle-length garment, mirrored sunglasses, and an alarming balaclava.

"I hardly think so," Lucas murmurs, and Maeve gives a laugh.

The doors to the cattle-shed airport flap open and shut, the bicycle creaks on.

"Oh, God," Maeve breathes, "he's coming over."

"Quick," Lucas whispers. "Look busy."

They turn, in unison, to examine a peeling bus timetable behind them. When Lucas casts a look over his shoulder, the person from the car is sidling up to them. He decides not to risk eye contact but to look steadfastly away, as if fascinated by the line of wind-battered trees. Maeve affects deep interest in the timetable.

"Got a light?" the balaclava person says, in a thick Irish brogue.

"No," Lucas says to the trees.

"Go on, give us a light."

"I don't have one. I don't smoke."

"Liar."

Lucas spins his head just as the sunglasses are lifted and the balaclava pulled down. His sister is grinning at them.

"Jesus." Lucas cuffs her on the shoulder, then hugs her, then cuffs her again. "Don't do that."

"I never knew my Irish accent was so convincing. I'm going to remember that." She hugs Maeve, jiggles the car keys in her palm. "Well, are you going to stand there all day or are you coming?"

"We're coming," he grumbles. "What else would we bloody well be here for?"

Before they get into the rental car, Lucas and Claudette must stand in the freezing gale to argue about who should sit where. He thinks she should drive; she is sure it should be him. He counters that she can't map read but she can drive; she says, Try me. Maeve opens the back door, muttering that she often wishes she had siblings but at other times she's glad she doesn't. Claudette says he can't map read because he doesn't know where they are going.

"True," he says, and clicks open the driver's door, "so why don't you tell me?"

She slides into the passenger seat, slams the door, and the relief at being in a confined, windless space is enormous. She unfolds a map, talking about a slightly longer route that goes past a beautiful mountain. Her hair spills out of the constraints of the balaclava. The last time he had seen her, six months ago, or was it seven, it had been dyed brown, but it's back to its original color. As a child, her hair had been pale gold, almost colorless, hanging down her back in plaits that flicked from side to side like whips; their mother had braided them each morning before school.

She looks at him, map in hand, the balaclava still obscuring the lower half of her face.

"What are we doing here?" he says, with a patience he doesn't feel. "Can I ask that now?"

"I . . . ," she begins, her voice muffled by the balaclava, then stops.

He frowns, looks at her more closely, leaning toward her, as if to avoid missing any clue she might drop. A film location, a meeting with an obscure Irish writer, some bizarre photo shoot: he and Maeve had speculated on all of these. But, looking at her in this rental car, on this bleak, wind-battered road, quite alone, quite unchaperoned, he realizes it's something completely different.

"What?" he says, seized with a sudden foreboding. "What is it? Are you OK? Is it Timou? What's happened? What's he done now?"

"Nothing," she says. "Nothing's happened. I just . . . I was thinking . . ." She glances away from him, out of the window. "I need your help with something."

"With what?" Lucas asks.

Claudette turns to face him and her eyes are bright, almost defiant. "It's hard to explain. Better that I just show you."

He turns to Maeve, to roll his eyes at her—Claudette and her bizarre whims are common ground between them—but the jokey utterance forming dies on his lips because, in the backseat, he sees two things simultaneously. His wife with a face that is stretched and still and also pleading. And a baby seat, one of those that fits into a car backward. Over its black plastic side, it is possible to see the soft curve of a tiny head, covered with dark down.

"Oh," he says. "The baby's here."

Claudette looks at him; she looks at Maeve. "Well, I could hardly leave him behind," she says, "now could I?"

Rain hurls itself against the windshield in staccato gusts; the wipers flail back and forth, Sisyphean in their ineffectuality. Lucas has to lean forward to see the road before them. Through the rain, through the steamed-up windows, it is just possible to make out the louring bulk of mountains at the sides of the road, huddles of trees, the pocked surface of rivers.

Claudette and Maeve are talking, as they always do, as they have done since they were all teenagers at school. About the kids they took up Helm Crag the other day, about Claudette's search for a nanny, about the script she is currently reading, about Pascaline's unfathomable penchant for broken furniture.

"Left here," his sister throws in, interrupting a monologue about the many chairs of their mother's in which it is forbidden to sit. Lucas knows both these women, probably better than anyone else in the world, and he knows that, underneath their surface conversation, Claudette is not mentioning the embryos and how they might be faring, how they have eleven more days until they find out whether they have stayed, whether they have hung on, or whether they have fallen, drifted, feathers on a breeze, to somewhere beyond reach, beyond recall. She isn't mentioning the cost of the treatment, or that he and Maeve have no more embryos in storage, that this is their last chance. He also knows that although Maeve is asking about Timou and the next film, what she is really thinking, what she is really saying to Claudette, is: if only. And: please. And: I'm terrified, I don't know how we'll cope if it doesn't work, I don't know what we'll do.

A rough track unribbons before them, the car climbing and climbing the side of a hill of gorse and moss and bare gray rock. Claudette gets out, again and again, to open and close five-bar gates.

"Is this right?" Lucas asks as she gets back into the car, bringing with her the scent of bracken, of weather.

Claudette nods, brushing rain from her brow.

"Are you sure?"

She nods again.

The wheels skid and flail against grit, but they turn a corner and suddenly, before them, is a small clearing, cut through with a stream, silver birches gathered at its banks. Lucas edges the car forward, and out of the mist appear shapes, angles, and planes, faint at first but then more distinct. He peers ahead, straining his eyes, wondering if he had seen anything at all, whether whatever it is might just vanish, as mysteriously as it had arrived. But, as he looks, it resolves, assuming corporeal form. He can make out a window, a wall, a roof.

By the stream, in the lee of a meander, stands a stone house. It has casement windows in peeling white paint, a tiled roof, a front door, which stands half open, like a door in a fairy tale, as if they are to be lured from their lives into a parallel adventure.

"There!" Claudette says, with an odd flourish of her hand, as if she has pulled off some magic trick, as if she summoned this vision from the earth itself. "Want to see inside?"

At that moment, there is a noise from the back, like the wingbeat of a small bird. Both he and Maeve turn, in unison, toward the baby's seat. Claudette doesn't take her eyes off the front façade of the house. "Oh, he's woken up," she murmurs, pushing open the door. "Perfect timing."

Lucas passes through the doorways of the house. Green shoots are pushing up through gaps in the floorboards, curling their fingers through slits in the window frames, insinuating themselves into the plasterwork. Strips of wallpaper in what was once the dining room have given up their adhesion and slumped, defeated and ignored, to the floor. The place has a damp, vegetal scent. No one has lived here for a long time.

In the kitchen there is an old, blackened stove, still bearing a kettle, as if thirsty visitors might arrive at any moment. There are cobwebbed plates in the rack above the algae-stained sink, a tin of baking soda, sealed shut with rust, on the shelf, a curled shoe sole by the range. The lead of a long-departed dog hangs on a nail by the back door, its leather cracked and peeling, waiting for its canine familiar.

Lucas paces. He looks at the ceilings, at the walls, at the cartography of damp climbing the wainscot. He walks to the front of the house; he walks to the rear. He forces open the back door and stands there for a moment, the step worn alluvial smooth beneath his feet; he considers the side of the mountain, the copse of aspens at the ramshackle fence. The rain has stopped, blown over, and the land is sodden, lush and green, illuminated with fallen water.

He climbs the stairs, keeping to the wall side. Safer that way, although there is no woodworm, no rot that he can see. On the landing, he turns his head one way, a big room with a bay window, overlooking the stream, and the other, a claw-footed bath overhung by a mildewed heater. He moves forward through a doorway into a space with low, slanted ceilings, two tall windows, vague shapes of things at the walls. He is treading across the floor, intending to look out at the view from here, when it comes to him what the shapes around him are: beds, small beds, lots of them, pushed back to the walls, tarnished brass knobs on their tops, one with symmetrical curlicues on its side, one with a canopy, rotted now, of course, and curved wooden runners at its base. To rock a child, he supposes, to lull it, to soothe.

What is the word for that kind of bed? he wonders, looking at it as if he's never seen such a thing before, so ornate it is, like a miniature marquee. The walls, he sees now, are decorated with depictions of toys. He can make out, through the dust and decay, a striped drum, a toy soldier, a teddy bear with a ribbon around its neck. So, a nursery. For a family with—how many?—six children. He counts the beds, turning in the middle of the room. Six. The number rolls around his head. Seven, if you count the baby.

As his mind admits the word "baby," it supplies him with another: "cradle." He looks again at the canopied bed with the rockers. Cradle. You would place the baby in there, under the canopy, which would once have been draped with fabric and lace—he's seen such things in museums, in costume dramas—and then it goes to sleep, just like that.

Astonishing, he thinks, how small babies are. He looks from one end of the cradle to the other. How can an entire person fit in there? He'd caught a glimpse of Claudette's baby, Ari, his nephew, before Claudette had strapped him into a kind of papoose thing on her front. Dark curls, a frown, pursed lips, and, yes, eyes that reminded him strangely of his own. He and Maeve had looked, they'd made themselves look, they'd stood behind her as she lifted him from his car seat, they'd exclaimed things to the air about how beautiful he was, how sweet, how lovely. He could feel the steel in Maeve as they did so, the effort it took her. Claudette slotted Ari into the sling without turning around. Lucas saw a socked foot, a curled fist, a cheek creased by sleep. He wanted to take Maeve's hand but didn't dare. Then Claudette had turned and given them both a level look that told them they weren't fooling anyone, one hand curved over the baby's head. Right, she'd said, let's go.

Maeve, he thinks. She mustn't come into this room. It must not happen. He turns toward the door, as if to bar the way.

He can hear them downstairs, in the drawing room—a place with a high ceiling, a huge marble fireplace, the skeletal remains of a sofa, the floor strewn with disgorged horsehair. His sister's voice is telling his wife that it was an old hunting lodge, built as a weekend retreat by the landowners of a big house near the village. The big house is gone, she is saying, lost in a fire years ago, during the Troubles. This is all that's left, she says.

He can hear the murmur of his wife, their footfalls, and the high yips of another voice—Ari's. He can hear Claudette speaking to the baby in quiet, soothing murmurs.

Lucas looks again about the room. A hunting lodge where seven children once slept, under pictures of drums and teddy bears.

"Hi," a voice behind him says.

Lucas whirls around, as if caught doing something wrong. Claudette is standing in the doorway. The balaclava disguise is gone; her hair surrounds her, like a cloak. She is herself again, unmistakably so.

"Maeve"—he panics, gesturing around him—"she mustn't—"

"It's OK," Claudette says. "She's gone outside. She wanted to see what was growing in the back garden."

Claudette comes into the room. She touches her finger to one of the beds, to the wall. The baby is a marsupial mound on her front. "If I buy this place," she says carefully, not looking at him, "is it OK to put the paperwork in your name?"

They stand together in the nursery, Claudette and Lucas and Ari.

"Legally," she continues, "it would belong to you. Or appear to belong to you. I'd need your signature, nothing more."

Lucas considers these words: the paperwork, his name, his signature. He realizes that he has known all along what this trip was about, what it means, this house, this valley, this clearing.

He can hear Maeve in the garden below; she is digging or scraping at something. He can hear water running around the house, off the tiles, down the gutters, through the drains.

He clears his throat. He isn't sure what to ask but knows there must be something. "But," he begins, "what about . . . "

She gives a tilt of the head, a minuscule movement, as if to recall something she has forgotten.

"It's in the middle of bloody nowhere, Claude," he whispers. "You couldn't get anywhere more remote than this. You wouldn't ever . . . I mean . . . you're not actually going to . . . use this place. Are you?"

She lifts her head. Their eyes meet.

He tries to read her expression. "Claude? What's going on? What about Timou? Does he—"

"It's just a house," she says, and breaks away from his gaze, walking toward the window. "In case I ever needed to . . . get away. It would be somewhere to come, somewhere to be. Just for a while."

"How long is a while?"

She shrugs, still with her back to him. "It's just a house," she says again.

Lucas comes to stand next to her and together they look at the mountain, which is obscured by a girdle of cloud.

"You have to promise me one thing." Each of his words appears as a swell of steam on the windowpane.

"What?"

"That you won't do anything without telling me. You won't disappear and leave me to wonder or—"

"Of course I won't. I couldn't. I'd need your help. Just don't . . ." She hesitates. "Don't worry if . . . if you're told that I . . ." She shakes her head, marshaling thoughts. "Don't necessarily believe what you're told. Hold steady and wait until I get in touch. Because I will. You know I will."

"Oh, God." Lucas puts both hands up to his face. He covers his eyes, as he used to do when she forced him to play her version of hide-and-seek, with her always the hider and he the permanent seeker. "I don't even want to fully understand what you're saying to me right now. The whole thing sounds like a ragingly terrible idea. I can't begin to imagine what Mum will have to say about this when she—"

"She's not going to say anything because you're not going to tell her," Claudette says, in a severe tone. "You know she'd go off the deep end." She lays her hand on his arm. "I need an answer, Lucas. Preferably today. I need to know whether or not I can put it in your name."

He sighs. He twists his head from side to side, as if to free himself from some invisible shackle. He sighs again, then says, "OK. Fine. Put it in my name."

"You agree?"

"Yes. Against my better judgment, I agree."

"That's lucky," she says, with a grin, "because I already transferred the money to your account. You've got a meeting at a solicitor's this afternoon. I'll drive you, but I'm not going to come in. They have to believe that it's yours."

At that moment, Ari lifts his head from her breastbone and twists around in the sling. He raises his hand and seems to point at something beyond them, beyond the window, at something only he can see.

"Ah dang-nang-nah, ah bleuf, ah blee," he says.

It is a long and complicated utterance. His fist opens and closes. Lucas looks at him, properly; his nephew looks back at him, fixing him with an intent, questioning gaze. What a child, he is about to say, but doesn't because at that moment he feels, for the first time ever, not quite the presence but the possibility of another child, to the back and slightly to the side of him, a form, a being, standing at his leg. It isn't so much a visitation or a haunting, just the idea of someone who might yet appear, might still exist.

Lucas puts his hand to the worn wood of the sill; he concentrates on this sensation, careful not to turn around, to scare it away. On the greenish glass in front of his face, his exhalations appear, then fade, appear, then fade, the unseen showing itself, over and over, the invisible making itself known.

The Tired Mind Is a Stovetop

DANIEL

Sussex, 2010

It is just after 3:00 p.m., Greenwich mean time, and I am standing in the parking lot of a secondary school in an unprepossessing town in the English commuter belt.

This is not a sentence I've ever constructed before; I have never put that collection of words in that particular order.

I am lurking, in my crumpled clothes, in the shade of some trees, partially hidden by a car the exact shade of bile, my bag at my feet. My heart has taken it upon itself to perform a series of trips or tricks inside my rib cage: a type of cardiac pratfall. It has decided to miss or stumble over every tenth or eleventh beat. The effect is one of unremitting anxiety, interspersed with spikes of panic. I have to press my hand to my chest, as if to reassure my heart, to tell it to behave. Sweat prickles along my hairline, inside my collar. I'm fine, I tell myself, tell my heart, We're fine. But what if I somehow miss Todd? What if I don't find him? What if I drop dead of a heart attack right here? Would the police be able to track down Claudette, to reunite her with my lifeless body? Is there enough ID on me for them to locate her?

The clutter of brick buildings in front of me is silent. The doors are shut. The windows are still. But it's almost the end of the school day and, any minute now, the place is going to erupt into activity and I will, I think, come face-to-face with my erstwhile friend Todd Denham for the first time in twenty-four years.

A short internet search at Newark airport revealed that the vinyl-loving, cardigan-wearing, Derrida-reading Todd of the late 1980s is now a high-school teacher in Sussex. It cannot be him, I told myself as I sat in a slightly too small airport chair, staring into my laptop screen. It must be another man with the same name.

But click on a PERSONNEL tab for the school, and there is his biography: born in Leeds, England, attended such and such a university, now teaching media studies. It had to be him.

Outside the school, I take a deep breath, I take two, I ignore another bungled heartbeat. I pick up my bag. I put it down again. I knock my temple, lightly at first, against the peeling bark of a eucalyptus tree. I have to stay on top of this situation, whatever this situation turns out to be. I have to keep my wits about me.

The automatic doors of the school sweep open and I stand straighter. A janitor-type person in overalls steps out into the searing sunshine, carrying a toolbox. He comes down the steps and disappears around the side of the building.

I watch as the automatic doors suck themselves shut.

Here I am, I think, loitering outside a school, lying in wait for someone in order to ask him whether or not I left a woman dead in a forest. Just an average day, then. Nothing to see here.

The doors trundle open, trundle back.

And something pushes its way into my thoughts. A rare appearance, this one, and I think it's because there is something about the school entrance that reminds me of the linguistics department in that university in England. It's not the ranks of cacti embedded in gravel or the woman behind a reception desk, who is wearing a thick layer of beige makeup (reminding me, unpleasantly and fleetingly, of my first wife), or the aquarium where neon-hued fish circle in their filtered environment, coshed by boredom. No, it's those double electric doors, curved in shape, which open and shut with a hesitant glide, creating momentary parentheses around those who pass through. There is something about the noise of them, the whoosh-clunk as they open and shut, open and shut.

I have done an assiduous job, all these years, of keeping Nicola from my thoughts. I have staved off recollections, reassessments, memories of her. But here I am, waiting and waiting, and I'm thinking about Nicola, my first love, and also, in the simultaneous way you can, especially when jet-lagged, as if the tired mind is a stovetop that can keep several burners chugging away, keep more than one pan boiling, I'm thinking how glad I am that Claudette, my current love, my hopefully permanent love, doesn't go in for much makeup. She's not a devotee of the caked slap that some women coat and obscure themselves with.

I'm also thinking—and this has just occurred to me—whether it is possible that I married my first wife as a reaction to Nicola. (I dislike the word "rebound": we *Homo sapiens* are not rubber balls; we are surely more complex, sentient beings than that, our choices are surely more finely nuanced.) I'd always thought that that marriage was in some ways a response to the death of my mother, me seeking stability, permanence, distraction, but now I wonder if it didn't have something to do with my severance from Nicola.

The thing is, I called Nicola from the States. I called and called but never got an answer. And so I wrote to Nicola. I can recall this with perfect clarity. A couple of months or so after my mother died, while I was still in the States, having been delayed by a small and unfortunate brush with the New York Police Department, it was becoming clear that I wasn't going to make it back to England. So I went to Manhattan, to a stationery shop, where I bought a pad of heavy-grain creamy notepaper, and with it I wrote Nicola a letter. I worked and reworked it until it was perfect. I told her I was beyond sorry, that I was a shit and an idiot, that I still wanted her, if she still wanted me. I told her I'd been offered a research-assistant job at Berkeley and that she should come out there and join me.

No reply, of course, which rankled and stung, heaped pain upon pain. It was one thing to refuse someone, but not even deign to reply? I was dumbfounded by that, her lack of response. I remember hurling stones into the river one night, denouncing her to the impassive gulls that swung above me: I spared them no detail of her heartlessness, her narcissism, her cold, careerist outlook on life, her callous disregard of love, of men, of unborn children.

In most species, the injured male will withdraw, go to ground, nurse his wounds in private, only reemerging into the light when he appears whole again. And so I took myself to Berkeley, to the Sunshine State, where no one knew me, where I had no commitments, no history, no reputation, nothing. I began all over again, thrusting Nicola from my thoughts, seeking ways to smother my love for her so that it would no longer smolder within me. And so, ergo, my first wife. She was, it strikes me now, the opposite, the anti-Nicola.

Again, the school doors ease open and shut.

So here's what I remember about Nicola and sliding doors. That I had seen her around the university—she was, after all, pretty hard to miss. She was part of the social sciences department, which shared an atrium with literature and linguistics, complete with a set of curved automatic doors. I'd done a little homework on her, found out who she was, established that she was single. I'd turned up at her lectures; we'd talked afterward; we'd been in a group that had gone for coffee. There was no feeling, though, that I was getting very far, in any real sense. She gave off this aura of indifference, aloofness—which only, of course, served to sharpen my desire.

One evening, I sat through a lecture on the sociological and political ramifications of female psychiatric disorders. I even, I recall, took some notes. At the end, I went up to her and suggested dinner sometime.

She didn't answer, so I think I emitted some vapid theorizing about the position of male disorders within the parameters of feminism, et cetera, et cetera. She carried on sliding her notes into her bag, throughout my rambling speech, and then she turned around. "What do you want, Daniel?" she asked me, her chin raised.

"I wanted to ask you ... about your ... your position on the male perspective ... whether you—"

She cut me off with a toss of her gleaming hair. "What do you really want?"

I held her gaze. I shoved my hands into my pockets. I took them out. "To take you to dinner," I said. "And then to take you to bed."

Her eyebrows shot up, disappearing under her bangs. She looked me up and down. "I see," she said. "Well, I appreciate the candor. Shall we go?"

We went. I was battling astonishment and still getting my bearings in the situation—doing some quick accounts in my head as to where I could take her to eat and whether I could afford to pay—when, ahead of her on the escalator on the way out, I felt her lean forward, felt her breath on my neck, her hand on my shoulder. She bit me on the ear. This brilliant, beautiful, bold woman nipped the cartilage of my upper ear between her gleaming incisors.

What else was there to do but to take her firmly by the wrist, pull her off the escalator, past the notice boards, and into a conveniently accessible restroom? It was quick; it was wordless; it was anything but gentle. I kicked open the door with its picture of a wheelchair; she reached to snap on the light as I pushed her up onto the handbasin. Her pantyhose got ripped; my glasses got broken; she dragged her nails across my butt, which stung to some considerable degree, later, in the shower.

Afterward we stood panting into each other's hair. I was wondering what to say, how to break the silence, what does anyone say in that situation, when one of those automated air-freshener things suddenly went off, somewhere near the ceiling, making her sneeze. She always was a little atopic around cleaning products. She sneezed again. We made the necessary adjustments to our clothes. I righted a lock of her hair that had fallen the wrong side of her part.

She picked up her bag, straightened her jacket, and looked at me, not quite smiling. I saw she was about to speak and I braced myself, unsure of what was coming.

"So," she said, "where are we going for dinner?"

I am roused from my soporific reverie by a sound like water rushing over stones: a susurration, a sense of motion.

A thousand teenagers are pouring out of the school. Once through the bottleneck of the doors, they break, regroup, and bond as groups of three or four. They call to one another in their particular argot: pure Home Counties cut with Teen American. A lot of yips, heys, elongated vowels. They swing bags through the air. Hair is flicked, stroked, tossed.

Trousers are worn tight but low; shoes unlaced. The females link arms with their chosen peers; the males perform mock violence upon those they recognize as their tribe. Most, if not all, display what I think of as "the screen hunch": head bent, eyes down, one hand engaged in fondling, stroking, manipulating a phone.

I scan them all as a whole, a large, seething organism. I look for one that reminds me of Ari, of Niall: I find a boy with Ari's height but none of his rangy elasticity. I see someone with a jacket like Niall's, but his face is too wide, too tan. I seek out one with the same coloring as Phoebe and Marithe but there isn't a single child who matches the coppery fire-tone manes of my daughters.

And then a man comes out through the glass doors. He has no beard, no cardigan, and hardly any hair. But there is something in the set of his shoulders, the way he grips his briefcase.

My first thought is: no, it can't be him, this is some nondescript middle-aged man with a shirt and tie and male-pattern baldness. My second thought is: yes, it is him, it has to be him. My third, and most uncomfortable, realization is that when he lays eyes on me he will undoubtedly go through the same mental process

Todd Denham, the new Todd Denham, with midbrown slacks pulled up just a little too high and a buttoned-up checkered shirt, comes down the steps. He navigates his way through the groups of kids. He doesn't meet anyone's eye. His face is cast down to the ground. He tugs, then smooths his bangs and I remember it, that gesture, a compulsive thing he did as he was walking, when he was thinking.

I'm expecting him to approach one of these parked cars, get out his keys, sling his briefcase into one of the passenger seats, at which point—I have it all planned—I will appear and say . . . what? Remember me? Remember a forest? It has been circling my mind, the question of what her death might have meant for Todd. He was the one on the ground, there, with her. The one left behind. The one who took the rap, who pulled the wool over my eyes to save me. The one who would have had to pick up the pieces, face the music, deal with the situation. I cannot imagine what might have come next for him as I flew away home. Police, ambulances, questioning, suspicion? Even just that moment of being left in a forest with a dead girl: how do you go on from that?

It is regrettable, I know, to spring this on him, to have to do this here and now, in front of his pupils, but what choice do I have?

I am just about to break cover when I see that Todd is walking past all the cars. He is picking up his pace and heading out of the school grounds, on foot.

I follow him for a block or two. He walks quickly—I remember that too—head down, as if searching for something dropped or lost. We make our way past a row of houses in that beamed, fake Tudor-style that this part of England apparently went crazy for a while back and then onto a shopping street that could be picked up and placed down anywhere in the Western world and nobody would think anything was amiss. Dry cleaners, bakeries, supermarkets, a pet shop, a café, with unenticing and tired-looking scones arranged on doilies in the window.

Todd pauses outside a newsstand, looking perhaps at the day's papers, but then moves on. He seems to hesitate at the door of a grocery store, briefcase dangling at the end of his arm, but again thinks better of it.

I am just about to increase my pace, to catch up with him, to tap him on the shoulder, enough already with the private-detective act, when he disappears. Just like that. Vanishes off the street.

I almost break into a sprint. To have come this far and lose him. How typical would that be? I am hurrying, sweating, swearing, panicked as I reach the place he dematerialized, and find myself looking into the window of a Chinese restaurant.

ALL YOU CAN EAT, the sign reads. BUFFETT. The misspelling barely registers, which is a testament to my extreme mental agitation. There, behind it, partially obscured by reflection, is Todd Denham, holding an empty plate, lifting up the lids of some big, aluminium platters, one by one.

I go in, I accept a plate and a napkin from the girl at the door, I walk past drumlins of *chow fan*, mountains of prawn crackers, swamps of wonton soup, and I catch up with Todd by the spring rolls.

"Hello," I say, putting my hand on his arm.

He starts and pulls away, in reflexive surprise. He always was a jumpy sort. He glances at me, his face startled but blank and, seeing no one familiar, he glances away again.

It's taking him a moment but it's coming, I know it is, I can see it, here it comes, and—there it is!—the realization dawns.

He looks at me again. "Oh," he says, his face twisted with incredulity, with shock. "*Oh.* Jesus."

I am just saying, facetiously, with a smirk, "No, just Daniel," when Todd's plate tilts. A cascade of *chow fan* and spring rolls falls to the floor, and how pretty it looks there, in a way, on the red carpet, but how annoying too, as it's all over my shoes and trousers.

There follows an interlude of wiping and sweeping: the girl at the door gets involved, and someone else in the same uniform, with a dustpan and brush and damp cloths. Todd and I grapple and apologize and bump into each other as we help and hinder.

Then order is restored and we are seated together at a table and the girl is there with a pencil and pad so Todd and I have to go through the motions of ordering jasmine tea and draft beer, listening to the price options, for all the world as if he and I do this kind of thing every week: getting together over Chinese.

Eventually, the girl leaves and we are alone, facing each other.

"What are you doing here?" is Todd's opening gambit. His face is unsmiling, his manner bordering on unfriendly. His hands, I notice, are gripping the sides of the table.

"Working," I say slowly, registering this hostility. "I'm in Sussex for . . . a conference. Thought I'd look you up."

Todd, to his credit, clearly doesn't believe this for a second. He dabs at his forehead with a paper napkin. "Why now?" he says.

"Excuse me?"

"I said, why now?" He screws the napkin into a tight sphere in his fist. "I mean, it's been, what—thirty years?"

I am, I admit, a little taken aback by his manner, and also horribly dismayed. This coldness of his can only confirm my worst fears, surely. Am I looking across the table at a man looking back at a murderer? Is this the expression a person assumes when reacquainted with an unwelcome specter from their past? I had, I now see, been counting on a little more bonhomie, a tad more recollection of the warmth that once existed between us, but that now seems like the expectation of a madman. Why, if the circumstances under which we parted all those years ago were what I think they were, would he be even remotely pleased to see me?

"Twenty-four," I say, in a nervous, strangled voice. "Around that."

"So, nothing at all from you for twenty-four years and then, all of a sudden, I'm treated to an appearance in a Chinese restaurant." Todd moves his teacup from one side of his plate to the other. "How come? How did you find me?"

"Well, I guess it was the internet."

"You didn't think of calling ahead?"

I shake my head. "No. I . . . It never occurred to me that you—"

The girl appears at our table, with a tray of drinks. Todd and I fall silent, lean back in our chairs. She seems to take an inordinately long time to set down the beers, then adjust the angle of the teapot spout to her liking.

"Look," I say, when she's finally gone, "I realize we haven't seen each other in a while. I'm sorry to barge in unannounced, but I need to know . . . I wanted to ask you . . . What I don't get is the . . . the . . ." I grope for the right word, coming up with: "attitude, I mean." I wince internally. It's the kind of thing we'd say to Ari, when he's refusing to do the dishes or tidy his room, so I amend it to: "The hostility. I thought . . . I thought we were—"

"Friends?" Todd puts in, his neck jutting out of his shirt collar. "Were you going to say you thought we were friends?"

"Well," I say, "we were, weren't we?"

"I'm not sure you know the meaning of the word," Todd murmurs, then stands, taking his plate with him. He does that thing men do when they're wrong-footed or ill at ease, fingering the silky length of his tie, altering its position. He moves toward the buffet, or buffett, with his plate and starts loading food onto it.

I sit for a moment, staring into my glass of beer. The necklace of foam at its edges, its glistening amber eye. The idea of drinking it makes my belly lurch. I take a scalding swig of tea instead, then go up to Todd, who is raking through a vat of noodles with an insubstantial serving spoon.

"I don't know why you would say that," I say, careful to make my tone neither conciliatory nor accusing but somewhere in between. "I always consider you to have been . . . I think of our friendship as—"

I stop because Todd is snuffling with derision.

"As what?" he says. "Such a good and valued friendship that you would go to the States, apparently for a month or two, and not only never return but never write, never call, never even bother to let me know that you're not coming back?"

I think this over. "Is that what happened?" I say. "Really? I did that?"

Todd ignores me, opens the lid of a serving dish, examines the contents, lets it fall shut. He roots in a heap of rice, taking one spoonful, then two. I stare at him as he does this, at his hands, at the food. All this antagonism, I realize, isn't to do with Nicola. It's because I ran out on him. It's because he's hurt, he's angry with me—still—for not coming back. This I had not expected, but perhaps I should have.

"I guess I did," I say. "I had no idea that you would see it like that, when really I—"

"It's still the same shtick with you, then, is it?" Todd brandishes a pair of tongs at me.

"What do you mean?"

"Oh," he mimics, in an appalling American accent, "I had no idea, it's not my fault, I'm just a big dolt, I'm so sorry, I didn't know, I didn't think, I had no intention of riding roughshod over you and all your feelings, you're my best friend, Todd, but I'm just going to fuck off back home and never contact you again—"

"Come on," I let out, "you can't still be holding on to stuff that happened a lifetime ago. I was a mess at the time, and while that's no excuse—"

"You're right," he says, piling his plate with slippery, slithering noodles. "It's no excuse. You could still have picked up the phone."

With that, he turns tail. He sits himself down at the table, takes a sip of his beer, and begins to eat. He eats with a regular motion, seemingly without enjoyment: it is the automatic slaking of a human need, nothing more.

I stand a few feet from him, my hands dangling uselessly by my sides. I consider leaving, just picking up my bag and walking away. No one need ever know this happened. I could package up this unpleasantness, this humiliation, somewhere small and airtight, and need never think of it again.

This man, though, has what I want. He holds the key to what happened. He is the only one I can ask: this is my only chance of finding out. If I blow this, that's it. I will never know.

As I stand there, hesitating, wondering what to do, I recall something my mother told me, as a child. Apologize, she would say, apologize, and people's defenses come down and everything will be better.

I sit down. I take a mouthful of tea. I regard the man opposite me: he seems smaller, somehow, than I remember, shrunken, sitting there in his checkered shirt, chewing his way through his dinner, avoiding my eye. No wedding ring, I see, and somehow this doesn't come as a surprise. There is something very unmarried, uncoupled, about him. I wonder how he ended up here, teaching in high school. I want to ask him what happened, what about your academic career, what about your record collection, your in-depth knowledge of eighteenth-century travelogues, your devotion to the blurred lines between fiction and nonfiction?

But I don't. Instead I put down my teacup. I sit up straight. I say: "I'm sorry, Todd. I really am. You're absolutely right. It was very wrong, very remiss of me, not to call you. To fall off the grid like that. There is no excuse for it. I apologize unreservedly."

He looks up. He meets my eye for, it seems, the first time.

"I'm sorry," I say again. "It was a shitty way to treat you. You didn't deserve it."

He looks at me for a moment longer, chewing, then swallowing the last of his mouthful. Then he inclines his head and he's almost smiling and there seems, in the atmosphere between us, a kind of flowering, an unfurling, a glimmer of what used to be. And there it is, right there, the legacy of my mother, Teresa Sullivan, in action.

"There's something I wanted to ask you, actually," I say.

Todd examines my face for a moment, then says, "Go on."

"It's about Nicola."

His expression is unmoving, his cutlery held in mid-air, in a position Claudette would not condone in the kids.

"You remember Nicola?" I say. "Nicola Janks?"

A hesitation. He digs with his fork through his plate for something. "Of course," he says.

"It only recently came to my attention," I hear myself say and I am wondering why I sound so formal, as if I'm addressing my students, "that she died, shortly after—"

"You didn't know that?" he asks quickly, laying down his fork. "Before, I mean?"

"No, of course not. I only found out a few days ago. I was listening to the—"

"You had no idea?"

I shake my head. "No. As I said—"

"I thought"—he frowns, prods some noodles to the side of the plate—"someone would have called you."

"Well, no one did." I take a deep breath. "But really my question is how you could have . . . I don't even know how to put this . . . I'm sure you know what I mean without me saying it. Don't you? It isn't, really, the kind of thing you could ever forget." I try to gather my thoughts, to focus on what I need to say. "That time in the forest. How could you have . . . kept it to yourself like you did? How could you have done that? To me—and to her. You knew that she was . . . you knew . . . but you didn't say anything. You know what I'm talking about, right? We understand each other, here, don't we? What I'm struggling with right now is how you let me just—"

"Is that what this is about?" Todd pushes his plate away, places his elbows on the table, holds his head in his hands. "That's why you've come?"

For a moment, neither of us speaks.

Then he says shakily: "Look." He inhales once, twice, his face trembling. "It's not something I'm proud of."

I almost say, I'm not surprised. But I want him to go on, so I opt for a neutral "Hmm" instead.

"I . . . It was a long time ago . . . I was . . . I don't know . . . I guess I was upset, hurt, angry. All of the above. It was a mistake. I'm willing to admit that. I've felt terrible about it, obviously, ever since."

He raises his head and there is a chill spreading through my abdomen, like a stain. The worst has been confirmed. I did run off and leave the dead body of my girlfriend in a forest. I did that. I, Daniel Sullivan, was happy to turn my back, to walk away. I didn't know at the time, but perhaps I kind of did. I'm finding it hard to meet Todd's eye, to hold his gaze. What the *fuck*? I want to scream. What were you thinking? You were the one on the ground, with your fingers on her nonexistent pulse, you were the one who said, she's fine, go. Run, Daniel, run.

I want to slam my hands on the table, I want to reach out and do some damage to the craven, sweating face in front of me, but I don't. I don't know what to do; I don't know what to say. The chill is reaching my shoulders, my neck, and I feel as though I may never speak again. Is this, I find myself wondering, how Ari feels when he's about to stammer? That uncertainty, that doubt, the risk that words will never come again, that it's just silence from here on in?

"I don't know what to say," I manage.

"I don't get . . ." Todd passes a hand over his face. "How did you find out? It was so long ago. Was it Suki?"

"Huh?"

"Did Suki tell you? Has she—"

"I told you," I murmur, distractedly, over him. "I heard it on the radio."

"—been in touch with you? How did she know? Did she find it? Did she read it? She must have done. It was hidden in my room. She was always going through my room."

"What?" I say.

"I didn't know she knew," Todd is muttering, almost to himself. "She never said. She always was a devious little . . . Look, it was a stupid thing to do, I know that. I had no idea there was even a possibility that Nicola wouldn't make it. Never. If I'd known she was in that state, I would never have taken it, of course I wouldn't. You were the one I was angry with, not her. I only took it to get back at you. Everything always seemed to come so bloody easily to you. All you ever had to do was crook your fingers and everyone came running. But I shouldn't have taken it. If you only knew how much it's weighed on my conscience ever since, I—"

"Wait," I say, "wait. What are you talking about?"

Todd looks at me or past me, his face distorted, stricken, guilty. "The letter."

"What letter?"

"Your letter."

"My letter?"

"The letter you sent to—" He stops. He scans my face. The silence seesaws between us. His expression folds, shuts up tight. "Um," he says. "Are we at cross-purposes here? What are you talking about?"

"The wedding," I say, confused, the jet lag slowing me down. "The party. Up in Scotland. Remember?"

"Mm-hmm." He nods vigorously. "I remember."

"We slept in the woods. Nicola was there, and then I left the next morning."

"Yes." He nods again and again.

"And Nicola was on the ground. You said I should go, that she was fine."

He's still nodding and saying, "Mmm, mmm."

"But she wasn't fine, was she?" I prompt. "She was dead."

Todd frowns, as if presented with a mathematical equation he can't solve. The nodding turns slowly into a shake of the head.

"She was dead," I repeat, "and you told me to go. You wanted me to catch my plane."

Todd still shakes his head.

"You covered for me," I insist. "You knew I gave her the drugs and you covered for me. You told me to go so I could get out of the country."

Still shaking. He has a small, peculiar smile on his face: a little twisted one. "No," he says, "you've got it all wrong. I can't believe you don't know this, that you . . . that all this time . . . It's so odd that you never . . ." With effort, he readjusts his face, to one of gravity, of seriousness. "She didn't die that night, Daniel. Not then. She was very ill. I had to take her to hospital just after you'd gone. I called an ambulance. We had to dodge some tricky questions, but I managed to plead ignorance. They pumped her full of vitamins and stuff, treated her for the cold. But she made it through. She was OK. I drove her back south, in her car. Remember her car?"

"Yes."

"The red one? I drove it." He sounds mystifyingly proud of this, even now. "I got her home. I stayed with her for a while and—"

"You stayed in her house?"

"Yes. The hospital said I should. Said she shouldn't be left alone. She was getting better." He meets my eye. "She really was. She was making an effort, you know, to—to get well. And I was looking after her. For you. I took care of her. I knew that was what you'd want."

"So what happened?"

"She"—again, that look of opacity, almost craftiness—"got worse again. By December, she was hospitalized."

"With . . . the eating thing?"

"Yes."

"And she died?"

He nods. "They called me. Her heart gave out. A weakened valve. I think she had less of a chance because of those other episodes when she was younger. Anyway, I got a call, like I said, from the hospital, asking me for her next of kin." He gives a shrug and I have to turn away.

I find myself swallowing and swallowing, as if to keep something down, as if there is something in me fighting to get out. I have to consciously push images from my mind: Nicola as frail as a bird, a hospital bed, her house, which was beautiful, painted dove gray with woven rugs on the wooden floors, bookcases lining the stairs. Who would have come to dismantle it, to cart away all those books and rugs? Who would have been the first over that threshold? Did they come with boxes and garbage bags?

Todd is standing, lifting his bag, pulling out his wallet, and tossing money onto the table. My mind is thrumming, bruised, overworked, but somewhere a veil of fog lifts.

"Hey," I say to him as he starts to leave. "What were you talking about before?"

"Nothing," he says, without turning around. "I don't know."

He says goodbye to the girl at the door and steps out onto the pavement.

"Wait," I say.

He walks away, in the opposite direction from the way we came.

"Todd! Wait!" I catch up with him. "What was all that before? The thing you're not proud of?"

Todd shrugs. He increases his pace.

"The thing that was so long ago," I say. "You thought Suki had found something in your room." It comes back to me. "The letter."

"I'm not sure," he murmurs. "We were ... at cross-purposes. I thought ... I thought you meant ... something else."

His evasion fills me with the kind of rage I haven't felt for a long time. I grab his arm. He pulls away, his face disgusted, fearful, but I don't release him. We grapple in an undignified, middle-aged sort of way on the pavement of a commuter town, and I seize him by the lapel of his jacket. I press him against a lamppost.

"You said," I breathe into his face, "it was a letter I wrote. A letter I sent."

"No," he tries again, "I was ... mistaken. Let go."

"What letter was it?" I say, and the answer slides into my head, like an envelope under a door. "It was that letter I wrote to Nicola, wasn't it? The one I sent from New York. The one where I asked her to come join me in Berkeley."

Todd doesn't answer. He is panting, perspiring under my grip.

"Wasn't it?" I spit. "You took it, didn't you? You hid it from her."

I let go of him suddenly. I don't want to touch him, feel his flesh under my hands, have the fabric of his clothes bunched in my palms. He staggers sideways, almost falls, but rights himself. We are both breathing heavily. The sun sears our skin, scalds our heads.

I lean against the wall of a closed sofa shop.

"That's why she died, isn't it?" I say. "Because she never got the letter. She knew I'd write to her. She knew it wasn't the end. But she never got it. Because you took it. You read it, didn't you? You read it and found out I wasn't coming back."

I come toward Todd, who is straightening his jacket, brushing himself off, with affronted fastidiousness.

"You shitty, selfish, lying bastard!" I yell, jabbing my finger into his chest. "You realize, don't you, that you killed her? You did that to her. It was you."

Todd laughs. He actually laughs, a dry, sarcastic chuckle. "No, Daniel," he says. "I think you'll find it was you."

He slides sideways, away from me, then sets off down the pavement. He moves quickly, so quickly that his trouser hems flap and catch around his legs. He breaks into a run, and his gait is the same as it always was: bandy-legged, his arms stiff by his sides. He reaches a bus stop just as a bus is about to pull away. He boards, and the door closes behind him. I get one more glimpse of him, moving down the aisle, searching for a seat, a place to put himself, before the bus pulls out into traffic and he is gone.

Oxidized Copper Exactly

CLAUDETTE

Goa, India, 1996

She is being held in an upright position by a chair. She can feel it pressing into the bones of her pelvis, the small of her back. Her feet are together on the metal rest, hands folded in her lap.

She avoids the eye of the woman in the mirror: she resembles her yet is not her. It is indeed a puzzling conundrum.

Air, artificially cool, passes back and forth between her teeth. Where the chair touches her bare skin—her elbows, the backs of her thighs—it draws out a sticky sweat. She is wearing clothes that don't belong to her. Over them someone has put a beige robe, the kind that swathes the body and fastens behind the neck: an outsize bib. It must be polyester because she can feel her skin heating inside it, like a chicken in foil. She has told them she prefers natural fibers for this climate, but they must have forgotten and it doesn't seem worth making a fuss.

Two people stand over her. One of them is picking up sections of her hair and wrapping them around heated pincers, and it seems to her a lengthy and pointless act because it is doing nothing but make her hair look exactly as it did before. The other has the kind of belt sported by workmen but, instead of hammers and wrenches, this one is filled with pots and colors and powders. This person is dabbing at her face with tiny brushes and damp sponges.

Neither of these people addresses a word to her or even looks her in the eye. One smears her cheeks with a claylike substance while the other suddenly seizes a brush and begins to back-comb her hair, spritzing clouds of foul-smelling spray in her direction. Murder by chemical attack.

Her head is tugged backward and she has to steel herself not to cry out every time the brush makes a lunge for her face: What are you doing to me? Please let me be, please stop.

And all the while they continue a conversation above her head:

—*He was like, whoa, and I was like, yeah.*

—*Totally, totally out of it. And I mean. Out. Of. It.*

—*Because she gave me this look and I was just, you know, hey.*

Her script is on her lap, beneath the robe. She knows it's there because she can feel the edges, paper sharp, against her wrist. She knows it, she's almost sure. When she gets there, the words will come, as they always have. But what if they don't? What if today is the first day when the words clog and jam, like cogs in a faulty machine, refusing to emerge? What if Timou has made changes to the words she wrote for herself to deliver? What if he's done that again, without telling her? She will have to challenge him, question these alterations, in front of the whole crew, and she knows they will all stand there, motionless, listening, as she and Timou bat objections back and forth.

Already she feels that this is a bad day. She has the kind of headache where it hurts to turn her eyes, to move her jaw. She cannot tell yet whether it is an ordinary pain or if it will bloom into the kind that takes her over, replaces her with itself, consumes that part of her that is still her. It will insinuate itself into her body, like a dybbuk, and she will be forced to stand outside herself, watching. She has become prone—this is the term, she believes, it is what the doctors have said—to three-day-long attacks during which the world becomes filled with spikes and shards of light, so bright, so dazzling, that she is unable to believe that no one else can see them. Quite usual objects will flare and glitter: the coffee machine, the bonnet-shaped head of a lamp, the latch of a window, a pair of sandals, the baby monitor. Everything becomes intolerable: the outlines of flowers on the mantelpiece, the circumference of a plate. People approach her and they carry with them unbearable flaring coronas, like prophets or devils.

Claudette suddenly becomes aware of her foot. It is jiggling at the end of her leg, spasmodically: up, down, up, down, like the freeze-frame on a VHS. She looks at it there, as if it is disconnected from her. How can it do that? How can it focus so beautifully on something so—

"Look up, please," the makeup girl says.

Claudette looks up to the ceiling, where a fan circles its blades above their heads. The soupy air around the three of them yields the scent of deodorant, insect repellent, hair spray, the acrid taint of wet mascara, a chemical fabric conditioner, a whiff of marijuana—local, Claudette guesses.

With a gunfire of static, the robe is un-Velcroed from her. The two attendants take a step back in unison, their heads to one side. One darts forward with a comb to tease a strand of hair into place; the other screws up her face in what seems to be a dissatisfied grimace.

"I'm not sure about the . . . "

"Mmm," the other agrees.

They stare at her. Seconds jerk by on the clock up near the ceiling. Then they shrug.

The taller one looks, if not quite at then near her.

"You're done, Ms. Wells," she says, with a smile that reveals pink, healthy gums.

Thank you, Claudette says, thank you.

She steps out of the door and it is as if she has entered an oven. The heat swarms in at her face, her neck; it finds its way, immediate, insistent, under her clothes. India, she tells herself, they are in India. She had forgotten this. Hard to remember when you are escorted—like a child, like a criminal—from hotel to set and back again, when each of your meals is delivered to you on a tray, before you even realize you are hungry, when the person at the end of the room-service telephone speaks impeccable English and already knows your likes and dislikes, your requirements, your date of birth, your taste in decor, sleepwear, thread count, toiletries, beverages, reading matter, music.

Waiting for her at the trailer door is a person with a clipboard and headset. He doesn't greet her but speaks about her into his microphone. "Ms. Wells is leaving makeup," he narrates, stepping in beside her. "We're heading toward the set right now, ETA two minutes. Oh, she's stopped to pick up something. No, we're on our way again. Yes, hair and makeup finished. Yes."

She walks through groups of people. They part as she approaches, like iron filings repelled by a magnet. They look at her, then away quickly, too quickly, as if she might be enraged by their gaze, as if looking upon her might turn them to stone. She puts up a hand and touches her hair. Stiff with lacquer, texture like cotton candy. It can't be her hair, no, not at all.

Without warning, someone appears, stepping into her path, and lassos her around the neck with something. A spotted scarf. Claudette stops, examines this person at close quarters. It is a woman in her twenties. She has black lines drawn in a beautiful arch on her eyelids, wispy bangs, lips stained blackberry purple, a brooch of a bird in flight pinned to her collar. She is tugging the scarf to the side, tying it, frowning, retying it.

"I like your bird," Claudette says.

The girl starts, as if a statue has spoken. Her hand flies to the brooch.

"Oh!" she says, flushing deep crimson. "Well, thank you."

"It is the green of oxidized copper."

The girl glances up at her, and her expression is one of fear. Why, Claudette wants to say, why are you afraid of me?

"Stopped for wardrobe," the man with the clipboard mutters into his mouthpiece. "Shouldn't take too long."

The girl plucks at the scarf with trembling fingers, eyes lowered. Oxidized copper exactly, Claudette thinks, or absinthe or arsenic. Wasn't arsenic once used as wall paint? She imagines Victorian children running their fingertips along it, their clothes brushing up against it, lethal atoms adhering to the cloth, making their way to the skin, to the blood, where they spore and spin through the veins like—

"That's it," the girl whispers, and steps away, out of Claudette's path. Claudette isn't sure what else to do, so she walks forward.

"OK," the man with the clipboard says, "on the move again. Just about to pass catering. Yeah, Ms. Wells is all good for wardrobe."

Claudette stops.

"We've stopped," the man says.

She turns her head one way: catering vans, the staff staring at her. She turns it the other way: a large truck containing scaffolding, rigging.

"I don't know, she's just looking around."

She suddenly recognizes the source of her trouble. She can pin-point what she needs, why she has this bolus of unease in her abdomen. Of course.

She turns on her heel; she walks back the other way.

"Er . . . we're on the move but we're going the wrong way . . . I don't know . . ." The man has to break into a trot to keep up with her. "I've no idea. Ms. Wells? Er, Ms. Wells? We need to go this way. They're wait-ing for you. Ms. Wells?"

It's easy to step things up. Claudette spends thirty minutes every day on a running machine. Her limbs glide into a sprint. The back-combed hair bounces back and forth on top of her skull, the scarf unravels and streams behind her.

By the time she arrives at the trailer door, the man with the headset is far behind. She climbs the steps and yanks open the door.

"Ari?" Claudette says. "Where are you?"

She is listening for the rhythmic pad of his feet, the mellifluous rise in his voice, saying, Maman, Maman. She has to hold that small body in her arms, has to press her cheek to the silk of his hair, has to look into those grave hazel eyes, she has to. Just for a moment.

But the nanny is coming toward her: she has Ari's sweatshirt in her hands; she is holding her finger to her lips and shaking her head. "He's just this minute gone to sleep," she is saying.

The disappointment is physical: a plummet in the stomach, a clenching surge in her headache, a tensing in her forearms.

"You just missed him."

She has to gulp at the air in the trailer so as not to cry.

"OK," she says. "It's OK." She moves toward the door of the little bedroom. "I'll just sit with him for a minute."

Ari is lying on his side on top of the quilt, arms stretching out, as if seeking something. She can see that the nanny has given him the wrong blanket, not the one he likes, with the folded-over edges and the loose thread in the corner. And his velvet-faced fox is still on the shelf. She gets down the fox. She places it next to him on the bed. She dares to stretch out a hand and touch the tips of his hair but no more. She sits herself on the edge of the bed. She absorbs the breathing of her son. The room is clouded with his particular scent—citrus mixed with biscuit mixed with milk. She takes in the movement of eyes under lids, the shell-curl of his toes, the creases at his wrists. When she hears the trailer door slam open and a voice asking, Where is she, she stands and tiptoes out of the room, shutting the door behind her.

There is a man standing by the door. He wears headphones slipped down around his neck. He is tanned, his hair clipped short; the muscles of his chest and arms stand up under the white cotton of his shirt.

"What's going on?" he says.

This man is Timou. The idea seems stranger and stranger by the day. This is the man who once walked with her over the Thames and to a bar in Soho. A lifetime ago he met her at JFK Airport, holding a sign with a picture of a cloud. They used to live together in Greenwich Village. He was the one who came into her hospital room after Ari was born and cried, his hand seeking hers, saying could she forgive him, could she ever forgive him, that she was his life, that he would do anything, anything at all, that he would never be so stupid again. She had been stunned, split, speechless, a tiny baby on her shoulder, her chest fizzing: it hurt to sit, it hurt to lie, it hurt to breathe. Even then, she had trouble convincing herself that he was this man and not a very close look-alike.

And now here he is again, the person purporting to be her partner, her man, her other half, her coparent, in her trailer. Behind him, outside the door, she knows, four or five people will be waiting. They follow him around all day. She doesn't know how he stands it.

"Claudette?" he is saying.

He is, she sees, expecting her to speak. So she does.

"I had to see Ari," she says, and the words come out with relative ease and they sound, to her, reasonably normal. "Sorry."

A tendon flexes in Timou's jaw. There is, just for a moment, a flash of light just above his shoulder, like a camera going off or a small firework. Did anyone else see that? she wants to ask.

"Right." He passes the papers he is holding from one hand to the other. "Well, can you come to set now?"

Claudette considers this. She doesn't think so. She doesn't think she can. She feels her head shaking, no.

"My darling," he says, coming forward and placing his arm around her shoulders, "there are one hundred and fifty people out there"—he points with a pen that Claudette thinks he must have stolen from her desk, as it's the kind she likes—"all waiting for you to show up. You know that? One hundred and fifty people. And we can't do a thing until you decide to grace us with your presence. We're totally stuck without you." He attempts a smile. He is trying, Claudette can see this, he is being kind, but she can feel the tension radiating from him, feel the jitter of it in the bones and sinews of his arm about her neck.

"Half an hour," is what she comes out with. "Give me half an hour."

Timou sighs. He does his effortful grin again. The kind you might give to a recalcitrant child or a mentally deficient person. He steps back and presses the pen—she is convinced it's one of hers—to his forehead. The outline of it crackles like lithium on water.

"All right. Half an hour. You can have half an hour, if you need it, of course you can." He points at her with the pen. "But no more, OK?"

"OK," she says.

He moves his black shape out of the trailer door, into the heat and daylight, and then he is gone. Claudette blinks as the door slams. She turns to the nanny and to her PA, Derek, who has appeared from the kitchen area, phone in hand.

"Could you please give me a moment?" she says, as pleasantly as she can.

Sure, they say, of course, we'll go get a coffee, we'll see you later, take as long as you need.

Then they are gone and Claudette is alone. She feels the silence fasten itself around her like a cloak.

She stands for a moment, in the middle of the trailer. Ari is asleep in the bedroom; the door is in front of her. How she longs to take off these clothes, to loosen her hair from its clasp. What a relief it would be to slip them off until they pool around her ankles so she could step out of them, kicking them away from her. She would go into the bedroom and, without waking Ari, she would pull on that dress in faded indigo cotton, those sneakers with the lightning-bolt pattern.

As if to quash this line of thought, she steps up to the door and peers out of the tinted glass. Nothing. No one. A few small figures over by the catering van. She assesses the distance between the door and the black SUV parked beside the trailer.

What unfolds next in her mind takes the form of a film she might one day make, and one she alone will write and direct. She envisages a self that is not quite her but looks like her. This person is going into the bedroom, changing into her indigo dress, lifting Ari, who stays magically asleep, into her arms.

No, Claudette thinks, she would first have to find their passports because she couldn't look for them if she was already holding Ari. So, she looks for the passports before lifting him. Or would she perhaps have everything ready? A bag, prepared and hidden, filled with all the necessary documents, their French passports, details of secret bank accounts, into which she would have been siphoning money? Yes, that would work better, would save time, would cut to the chase.

So, a bag. Pulled down from a shelf somewhere. She is already in the dress, the sneakers, no need to show the change. Next, this Claudette, the one who isn't quite her, would shake out her hair and stuff it under a wide-brimmed hat. The nanny's. She would pick up the nanny's sunglasses, the nanny's security lanyard. She would put them on.

How simple and yet so effective, Claudette thinks as she stares out of the trailer window at the line of people waiting at the catering van. How simple it would be to lift Ari into her arms. To pick up the velvet fox and the favorite blanket. Simple to strap him into his car seat, to stow the bag in the back. It would take this Claudette, the escaping Claudette, a moment, when she sits in the driver's seat, because it has been so long since she's driven herself anywhere, but it will come back to her the minute she puts her hands on the wheel. Simple, too, to drive to the gates, to wave the nanny's pass at the security guard. How lucky that the nanny has the same build, the same hair color, as her, so very lucky that is; the thought, of course, had never crossed her mind when she hired her, not at all.

And then? Claudette runs a fingertip back and forth along the seal of the window, planning the next scene. They will be zooming, unstopped, undetected, outside the set, away from them all. The problem would be, Claudette thinks, as she sees Timou and his minders appear in the distance, over the brow of an incline, where to end the scene. What would come next?

If she had things her way, with this film, the on-screen Claudette would pull up at a river, swollen and brown with fallen rain. Ari would be completely happy to get out of the car, to stand there, beside the river, beside the SUV, while she opens the car doors and releases the hand brake and rolls the vehicle into the water, just enough so that a small part of it still shows. She envisages what this will look like: the SUV roof sinking beneath the oily current, the swirling eddies swallowing it, digesting it. She envisages the tire tracks stretching from the road all the way to the riverbank. An accident, they will think. Police will be called, trucks, pulleys, divers. It will be a while before they realize that the car is empty, was always empty, and by that time she and Ari will be gone.

Tricky to film, of course, expensive, but so effective, so devastating, so final.

She leaves the door, leaves the scene of Timou and his people getting nearer and nearer. She goes into the bedroom and looks down at her son. Ari has his fox tucked under his arm, his thumb in, his face tilted up toward her, absorbed in perfect, untrammeled, trusting sleep.

Claudette has to press her face to the bed next to him to rally herself, to support her own weight, so searing is her sense of entrapment, the futility of such fantasies. She has sketched for herself the cage door left momentarily ajar, she has caught a flash of a life outside this one, something beyond, something other.

After a minute or so, she hears the screech of the trailer door handle and hastily blots her tears on her sleeve. Staying, she tells herself as she stands up, means you get to do this work. You get to make this film. You get to finish it, then edit it, then send it out there. Then you get to make another. What, she asks herself as she walks toward Timou, as she makes herself smile and nod at him—yes, she's fine, she's ready now, and the relief in his face is enormous, expansive, and it makes her think for a moment that, yes, he loves her and, yes, she loves him—what would she do without this work? How would she live, how would she feed and occupy her mind? Isn't this what she wants? Where else could she find a valve, a vent, for the restlessness that has simmered inside her mind since she was a child? What else would she do with it, if not this?

She reaches Timou. He puts an arm around her shoulders, as if taking possession of her, holds the nape of her neck in his hand. They go down the trailer steps, and as they walk together, he is murmuring in her ear about what they are about to film.

She has no idea, as she walks with him, as she listens to him, as she interjects to say, let's try it the other way first, that all is not lost. That it won't be long. That a plan will unfold, a chance will arrive, the script will write itself.

She must, for the moment, keep her expression neutral, guileless, as she walks toward the set, Timou next to her, as people around them adjust their headsets, stand a little straighter.

She has no idea that, a couple of years from now, after this film and halfway into the next, she and Timou and Ari will be sailing the Stockholm archipelago with Timou's parents in their yacht. A week's break from filming in the city, a sequel to the movie about infidelity, featuring the same couple five years later. She has been suffering from more headaches, more vision disturbances, flares and flashes, sparks and stray lights, and a doctor has diagnosed acute stress, has told Timou that Claudette needs complete rest for a week. So here they will be, sailing the archipelago.

The Lindstroms haul up the anchor, unfurl the sails, uncoil the ropes, shouting to each other about this way or that way or this wind direction or that compass point. They run up and down the deck in their natty rubber shoes, calling to each other in urgent voices. She sees, as soon as they pull out of the harbor on the first day, that she has made a terrible mistake in agreeing to this trip. She hates the keeling motion of the hull, the water reeling by, the menacing flap of sail, the wild veer of the boom, the way she must fold herself and her child into a corner so that everyone else may run about unimpeded. The ever-present terror that

Ari will be swept overboard, into the unforgiving water. She hates the cabins, the low ceilings, the cramped, airless beds. But, as Timou says, where else can they go? Where else will they be unbothered, unrecognized, unless they are at sea, in constant motion, never touching land?

In India, the people on set are making their way toward her, they are speaking, they are holding out their hands, as you might to an animal that may or may not make a run for it.

Not too far away in time, there will be a morning in a boat in Sweden when Ari will wake early, too early, before 5:00 a.m., and Claudette will raise herself from the cabin bed, careful not to wake Timou. She will pick up Ari, she will soothe his nightmare, and, to chase it away entirely, she will take him up on deck.

Outside, the world is another place. She and Ari emerge from the hatch into a blue-lit dawn so still that she wonders for a moment if something has happened to her hearing in the night. The boat is moored in a channel between three islands, low-lying, wooded, their striated granite sides like the hides of sleeping leviathans.

She looks around her. She had come up here with the idea of showing Ari what the dawn is like, with the idea of letting the rest of them sleep, but as she stands there on deck another notion spreads its wings. She can feel the flex and strain of its feathers, the febrile power of its muscles.

"Wait here," she says to Ari. "Don't move."

She ducks down again into the humid stillness of the boat, listening. The cabin door to where Timou is sleeping is shut tight. His father snores beyond a second door. From a space under Ari's bed, she slides a backpack: she has it with her always, never lets it far from her reach. With deft movements, she shuts the door, climbs the ladder, lowers the hatch after her, and smiles at her son.

"Shall we go for a row?" she says.

So easy to step into the little rowboat, to hold out her arms for Ari, to untether themselves, to push off. The plash-suck of the oars through the brackish waters. She keeps an eye on the contours of the yacht. If Timou or his parents were to appear—no harm done. What could be more natural than a woman taking an early morning row with her son?

But no one appears. No voice calls her back no shouts are raised.

The yacht is motionless, anchor down, curtains shut tight, sails tied. A heron standing on coat-hanger legs in the reeds turns its face toward them, then away, as if to say, I never saw you.

She reflects, then, and only for a moment, on the film she is rowing away from. Half-made it is, half-realized, as yet in that state where it has the potential for perfection, for something outside their reach. Those small inhibitions and compromises have not yet crept in. It will be good—would have been good. She has that feeling. The script has an inner balance, a momentum, an endoskeleton all of its own. Shouldn't she wait, shouldn't she finish it? Can she really be considering throwing it up, abandoning it in its unformed state?

She keeps rowing. She rows until the muscles in her arms are aflame, until they have rounded the headland to a different gully, a different set of islands. The little boat comes to rest on a sandy shore where the pebbles are sharp underfoot and each rock is furred with waving green. She lifts Ari out of the boat, then pushes it back into the choppy waters, oars trailing loosely.

"Let's walk to the jetty," she says to Ari, and he takes her hand, without question, and she turns her head to see the double set of footprints obscured and smoothed by the waves.

By 7:00 a.m., she and Ari have boarded a ferry to Stockholm, she in a hoodie and large glasses. By the time Timou wakes, showers, makes coffee, discusses the plan for the day with his parents, wonders where Claudette and Ari might have got to and when they are coming back, they are in a taxi for the airport. By the time Timou sees that the rowboat is gone, they are boarding a plane. At around lunchtime, it seems to the Lindstroms that they have been away a long time, even for someone as flighty and capricious as Claudette, but by now it is too late. They have gone; they have escaped; they have found their loophole and have slipped through it. The next day, Timou will receive a single line on his pager: *I'm sorry. Cx*

In India, however, Claudette is walking across the set, toward the men in headphones. She raises her hand, in a gesture of supplication, of defeat, of admission. Yes, she says to them, I'm ready, I'm coming, here I am.

The Girl in Question

TERESA

Brooklyn, 1944

Teresa had been engaged for a week, her fiancé back in occupied Europe, when a young boy ahead of her on the subway steps slipped and made a grab for the grille under the handrail. She was close enough to see a loose wire slice into his hand, almost heard the clean butcher-swish of metal through flesh.

He cried out, in the voice of a much-younger child, crumpling to the ground. People, stepping off the late train, flowed around him, and she was crouching beside him, already pulling a scarf out of her pocketbook, when she noticed a man sprinting back up the steps, saying, "Jackie, Jackie, what happened?"

Blood was coursing in three neat lines from his finger and into the lap of his raincoat. His face was white, his lips pale under his cap.

"It's cut to the bone," she said to the man—the boy's father, she assumed—without taking her eyes off the child, "I'm going to tourniquet it."

"Are you a nurse?" the man said.

"No, a librarian," she said, adding, "but we do a first-aid course as part of our training."

She tied the scarf, once, twice, around the boy's palm and put her hand on his shoulder. The man was hunkered down next to her; she was aware of laced shoes in a dark-caramel leather, a coat that smelled of rain-damp wool, but nothing more. Her attention was entirely on the boy.

"You'll be all right," she said as she pulled tight the final knot. "Does it hurt much?"

Jackie lifted his eyes to her and nodded. Lips still pale, she noted, in her first-aid manner. His irises were the blackest she had ever seen, entirely swallowing their seeing centers, and brimming with sup-pressed tears.

"He'll need stitches," she said, closing the flap on her pocketbook, dusting down her coat.

"You think?"

She and the father raised the boy to a standing position between them.

"You'll need to get him to a doctor," she said, still looking at the boy.

The man passed a hand through his hair. "My sister's going to kill me."

"Your sister?"

"Jackie's mother."

So, Teresa thought, not father: uncle. She finished rearranging her coat and turned to look at the man for the first time. Her initial thought was that he was familiar. I know you, she almost said, don't I? We've met, surely.

She could tell he was having the same thought: his expression was one of confusion, hesitation, tempered by a strange, cautious joy.

She doesn't know it at the time, but she will think about this moment again and again, the two of them standing on the steps of the subway station, a boy between them, a pool of blood at their feet, trains arriving and departing above their heads. She will play it over and over in her head, almost every day, for the rest of her life. When she lies in the bedroom of her apartment with only hours to live, her daughters bickering in the kitchen, her husband in the front room, weeping or raging, her son asleep in the chair next to her, she will think of it again and will know it is perhaps for the last time. After this, she thinks, it will live only in the head of one person, and when he dies, it will be gone. She finds herself hoping that the man will, in a few days' time, happen to read the death notices in the paper so that he will come to her funeral; she knows he would come, without doubt, that he would sit near the back, that he would bring well-chosen flowers, nothing too gaudy, that he would speak to no one. She knows that people will look at him and wonder who he is, what his connection is with her, and perhaps conclude that he knew her via the library. No one, she knows, would guess his true link with her, not even Daniel, her son, who naps next to her, looking washed up and burned out and too thin and already grieving, who guesses and divines too much about people, always: it is his blessing and his curse.

On the subway steps, Teresa and the boy's uncle looked at each other, in something close to shock or fear. She was filled with an urge to apologize, she wasn't sure for what: I didn't know, she wanted to say, I didn't realize.

She broke the lock of their gaze first. She fit her gloves onto her hands, feeling her skin slide against the wrong side of the leather. "Have you money for a cab?" she said, as if to her hands.

"A cab?" the man repeated, dazed.

"To get the boy to a doctor."

She wasn't going to look at him again, no, she wasn't. For the first time, an image of Paul floated through her mind and, in an effort to recall herself to herself, to her life, she clenched the fingers of her left fist to feel the pressure of her engagement ring on the neighboring digits.

Then she did look and the same sensations hit again, like a row of dominoes toppling into one another: the towering sense of recognition, the disbelief that she doesn't somehow know him, the ridiculousness that they do not know each other, the impossibility of their not seeing each other again.

"Yes," the man said, delving in his pocket. "I have money for a cab."

"Good," she said, and she thought again of Paul, of his mother, of her parents, her sisters, as if they were all there, on the subway platform perhaps, looking down on her as she stood with this man. She was seized with a terrible dread and it propelled her away from the man and the boy, down the stairs, made her pretend not to hear him yell after her to wait, to hang on a minute. "Good luck," she threw over her shoulder, and was gone.

She didn't see him again for a week, for seven days and seven nights. She went to and from work; she cooked supper; she ironed her clothes. Her mother tried to get her to write to Paul, to ask if they could set a date for the wedding during his next leave. Her sisters fought over who would get to be maid of honor. She went to the movies, twice, with her friend Maureen. She received a bundle of letters from Paul, some dated two months previously and held up in some mysterious wartime net; she read some of them; the others she put in the tin box under her bed. She locked herself into the bathroom for hours on end, until her brother hammered on the door to let him in, for pity's sake, a man has to go. And at the library she conducted a search about love at first sight.

Teresa was not a romantic. She was not what she thought of as an airy-fairy type of girl. She had never dated anyone other than Paul, and when news of their engagement had been made public, she discovered, in people's expressions of surprise, that it had been expected she would never marry. She'd had the misfortune to be born tall in a time when women were meant to be petite, neat, fit nicely under the arm of an accompanying man. As a newborn, her mother was fond of telling anyone who would listen, she wouldn't fit into the crib; her feet had stuck out of the bottom, "like ninepins."

Who could have predicted, then, that one of the most eligible boys in the neighborhood, Paul Sullivan, whose parents ran a general store on Vinegar Hill, would start to pay court to the bookish, lanky eldest daughter of the Hanrahans when he was home on leave from fighting in Europe? She didn't, at first, understand what he wanted: she assumed he was asking her to the movies, to walk back from mass, because he wanted to date one of her sisters. But, no, it seemed it was she he wanted, and when he sank to his knees in the middle of the Brooklyn Bridge on a drizzly evening, how could she have done anything other than nod, turn herself slowly, like a speeding ship, toward that alternative destination of wife-and-mother to escape her predicted role of librarian and maiden aunt?

On her lunch hour, she sat in the park and thumbed through *Romeo and Juliet* but found nothing in there to alleviate her turmoil: all that palm-to-palm stuff and the holy kiss seemed strained and constructed. It hadn't felt like that at all. It was as if someone had reached into her with an electrical wire and given her such a jolt that her heart had been obeying a new rhythm ever since. She tried Anna and Vronsky's meeting but became distracted by how silly and unworthy of Anna's love she always found the count. Over the following days, she took with her to her park bench Donne, Browning, Byron, the Brontës, and Christina Rossetti. But nothing came close to what she had felt on the subway steps.

A week since the meeting and she found, in an anthology of love letters, something by Hazlitt: "I do not think that what is called *Love at first sight* is so great an absurdity as it is sometimes imagined to be. We generally make up our minds beforehand to the sort of person we should like . . . and when we meet with a complete example of the qualities we admire, the bargain is soon struck."

She raised her head, tilted it one way, then the next, as if the words were the ball bearings of a puzzle, seeking a resting place in her skull. Not so great an absurdity, she murmured to herself, and something touched her shoulder, and there was Mr. Wilks, the head librarian, saying that someone was here to see her. Teresa stood and smoothed her hair and tried to breathe above the cantering of her heart because she knew who it would be—she'd known he would come, somehow and soon.

And there he was, by the inquiry desk, without a hat this time but still in his wool coat, a package gripped in his hands. Again, they looked at each other in confusion, and Teresa wondered how this had come about, what had happened there on the steps as Jackie sliced open his finger.

"For you," he said, breaking the spell, holding out the package to her: brown paper, knotted twine.

"What is it?" she said as she took it.

He grinned. "A scarf. A new one. Yours was—"

"Oh, really, you needn't have. I—"

"—all stained and ruined, and my sister said it was the least we could do."

They both took a pause, looking away, then back at each other. One of the elderly librarians, behind them, cleared her throat, snapped shut a drawer.

"How is your nephew?" Teresa asked, rather formally.

"Jackie?" He grinned again. "Fighting fit. Got six stitches and couldn't be more proud of them."

The colleague behind her coughed again, and Teresa, not knowing what to say next, where to take things, said, "Shall I walk you out?"

Outside the library, as the revolving door released her into the winter air, he was there; he took her hand, he guided her to one side so that they stood out of the way of people going about their business, out from under the lit portico, so that a light rain fell on them, flecking his face and lashes.

"I don't even know your name," he said urgently, at their new proximity.

"Teresa," she said. "Teresa Hanrahan. Yours?"

"Johnny Demarco." He squeezed her fingers in his. "It is," he said, with a smile on his lips, "very nice to meet you."

"Thank you for the scarf."

"I hope you like it. I chose it. It's a little brighter than your other one, but I thought, hey, she needs something to bring out those blue eyes of hers. You wouldn't believe the trouble I've been to to deliver it. I've been to every library in Brooklyn today, looking for the girl in question, just to—"

"I'm engaged," Teresa said.

He gave her a long look. "Huh," he said. He stepped sideways and slumped against the library wall. "Huh," he said again. He took out a lighter, put a cigarette in his mouth, and stared up into the darkening sky. "Well," he said, inhaling, "it figures, I guess."

"I didn't . . . ," Teresa began, "I don't . . . "

He let out a short, mirthless laugh. "Me too, actually." He took a drag of his cigarette. "I mean, sort of. Almost."

"Oh," she said, trying to master the surge of grief, of jealousy, rising in her chest.

Johnny Demarco flung his cigarette to the ground and turned toward her. "So, what do you want to do?"

It was four years before she saw him again. Brooklyn was a big place and the Italians and the Irish, although celebrating the same festivals, the same masses, had different parks, different streets, different shops.

Paul said they should open the store on Easter Monday; his mother disagreed, as evidenced by the thin line of her mouth, the heft with which she slammed down the skillet onto the stove. Teresa had no opinion on the shop's opening times—she couldn't have cared less: she wanted only to go into the next room, to place her head on the cool pillow, pull up the covers, and sink into the novel she had borrowed last week and of which she had managed only fifteen pages, the children and the store keeping her so busy.

But open they did, afternoon only, to appease Mrs. Sullivan. So by lunchtime on Easter Monday, Teresa had been to mass, cooked the lunch, installed the toddler in her playpen in the back room and the older girl with a game of counting out dried beans, under the sometimes-watchful eye of her grandmother, and was standing behind the wooden counter, the shop overalls straining over the mound of her third pregnancy—another daughter, as it would turn out.

She was shifting from foot to foot, serving a half-blind neighbor from the next block, when she heard him before she saw him: "... but just for a minute, OK?" he was saying.

The woman with him was beautiful, she saw, the discovery causing her equal parts pain and pleasure. She was small, with a gloved hand hooked around his sleeve, her hair curled and set in the latest fashion. When they turned toward her counter, she saw that the woman's belly was the shape of her own.

"Something cold, Johnny, a soda or a Popsicle," the wife was saying. "What do you think?"

It happened: he saw her. She saw the recognition, the shock, ignite in his face. Their eyes locked, just as they had done four years previously, and the room, the voices, the shop, the customers, the shelves and shelves of jars and cans and flour, all fell away. It's you, he seemed to be saying to her, and she answered, yes, it is.

The neighbor fussed between two types of canned beans and the wife talked about which soda she liked best and would it be cold, what did Johnny think, and how hot it was today for April, and Teresa held on to the counter, as if caught in a gale.

When the neighbor finally shuffled away, Teresa raised her chin a notch and took a deep breath. The wife was selecting a soda from the refrigerator and Johnny said, "Hello again."

"Hello," Teresa replied, her eyes flicking toward Paul, who was up a ladder on the other side of the shop.

The wife put down her soda on the counter with a look of inquiry.

"This is Teresa Hanrahan," Johnny said. "She . . ." He seemed to lose track, his conversation falling off a precipice into nothing, causing his wife to glance sharply at him.

"Sullivan," Teresa heard herself correcting. "I helped out your nephew one time when he'd gotten himself in trouble."

The wife rolled her eyes. "You mean Jackie? Always in trouble. I'm Lucia," she said, "seeing as my husband has forgotten to introduce me."

Teresa nodded at her.

Lucia's eyes flicked down Teresa's overalls. "You too?" she said.

"Yes."

"Your first?"

"Third."

Lucia's eyebrows went up. "Third? I tell you, I will never get to three. This one's been so much bother already. I told Johnny the other day, I'm stopping at one, honey, that's it for me."

Teresa reached for the bottle of soda, eased off the cap, and handed it back to her. "Well," she said, "you might change your mind."

"Never," Lucia said as she headed for the door.

Johnny stood where he was for just a shade too long. No one else would have noticed, Teresa told herself afterward: of this, she was almost sure. He laid his hand on the broad, worn wood of the counter, exactly opposite Teresa's. He mimicked the arrangement of her fingers: first two curled under, thumb and final fingers pointing outward, as if in salute, as if in welcome or perhaps farewell. Then he was gone.

She counted the years: one and then two and then three and then four and then more. Paul's parents moved out to live with one of his sisters. After a decent interval, Teresa asked Paul if they might make the room into a bedroom for the girls, and he had nodded. He got a friend who was a carpenter to come and build bunk beds for three.

They invested, at her suggestion, in a large refrigerated counter so that they could make fresh sandwiches for the lunchtime customers. Seven years, eight years, nine years. The girls started helping in the shop after school, doing their homework at the shop counter. Teresa, having thought there would be no more children, was surprised to find herself pregnant once again. She gave birth to the baby who would turn out to be her last, a boy, Daniel. She walked the floor with him in the night—he was always a sleepless, restless baby—and she discovered that if you stood on tiptoe in the front room you could see a section of the flat dun-colored East River.

Even as a baby, Daniel loved the river. Teresa would push him down to the shore and he would sit forward, as if straining to hear its noise of wind, boats, lapping tide. When he was walking, the two of them would go down there together, in the mornings, when the girls were at school and the shop quiet, Daniel buttoned into a knitted jacket and Teresa in a head scarf to keep her hair in check. He would reach out his palm toward Manhattan, his infant sense of distance and scale persuading him that those tall towers of steel across the water could be his, if only he could just stretch far enough.

It was a treat for Daniel, the ferry trip that day. Aged almost four, it wasn't necessary for him to attend preschool every day, was it? Paul shook his head, but said nothing when Teresa, on a whim, kept the boy at home with her for the odd morning. Why shouldn't she? she demanded during an interior debate on the subject. He was her last, her late baby, why shouldn't she enjoy him for a little bit longer?

So she had promised him that, the first fine day of spring, they would take the ferry to Manhattan. Daniel hop-jumped all the way to the ticket office, and when they were allowed onboard, he ran from one end of the boat to the other, shouting something indecipherable to the gulls.

How was she to know that he would be on the boat? That he would see the back of her head through the window, come out, and sit down next to her, laying his newspaper on the bench.

They didn't speak but looked out at the approaching Manhattan skyline. She felt the outermost finger of his hand brush hers. She didn't move away. Behind her sunglasses, she shut her eyes.

"I think about you," he said, "every day."

Teresa nodded.

"And nobody knows."

She nodded again. She felt the juddering power of the boat's engines, carrying them inexorably forward; she felt the thick, tarlike surface of the bench beneath her skirt, painted and overpainted in repeating layers; she felt the featherweight of mascara on her eyelashes, the straps of her slip as they rested on her shoulders, the grip of her sunglasses on the backs of her ears. She heard him sigh, heard the slide of fabric as he crossed his legs.

"Has it ever occurred to you," he murmured, "that we could go away together?"

"Too late for that," she said. "Where would we go?"

"I wish," he began, "I wish . . . "

She turned to look at him. She saw that the hair at his temples had started to turn silver; the skin around his eyes was scored with lines. His shoes were still immaculate, laced, polished leather; his hair was longer, still combed to the left.

"What do you wish?" she said to him, years after they had first met.

"I wish, that day at the library, that I'd gotten hold of you and told you how it was going to be," he said, in a rush. "I wish I'd grabbed you then and never let you go, before it was too late." He took up his newspaper, as if he would crush it between his palms. "I don't know what we were thinking."

Teresa took off her sunglasses, folded them into themselves so she could look Johnny Demarco in the face when she said, "I don't know either. But we made our choices and we have to live with them."

"Then I will promise you one thing," he said. "That wherever I am, wherever I go, I will find some way to let you know. And you must promise me the same. So we can find each other if . . . if things change."

She nodded. "Johnny, I promise, of course I promise, but—"

At that moment, something barreled into her leg. She gasped with the pain of it. It was her son, panting, flushed, his jersey askew. Teresa was shocked at momentarily forgetting about him and at the rush of love she felt for him as he stood there, lolling against her leg, elbows pressing into her thigh. It was a pure, animal avalanche of feeling, this. Look at him, she wanted to say, just look at this child. Was there ever a more perfect boy? She seized him, his hot body, the birdcage of his ribs, and pressed kisses into his hair, as if the scent and sense of him might save her from all that was uncertain and dangerous in the world.

"Your son?"

"Yes," she said, without taking her face out of his hair. "This is Danny."

Johnny leaned forward. "Hi, Danny, how are you?"

Daniel looked at the man. The man looked at him. In later years, he will recollect only dimly the trip he and his mother took on the ferry. He will recall it as a series of sensations: a sock that kept slipping and wrinkling under his heel, the startling white undersides of gulls as they wheeled above him, a girl throwing pizza crust up into the air for them, the amber beads of rust on the rails. And this: the unaccountable sight of his mother sitting with a man who was not his father, her skirt with the sailboat print arranged around her, the man turning toward her and whispering words that Daniel knew were unsettling words, persuasive words, frightening words, her head bowed, as if in prayer.

The Dark Oubliettes of the House

DANIEL

Donegal, 2010

No cabdriver around here is stupid enough to attempt the climb to the house: the track is too steep, and wet weather turns it into a pebbled, rivered slipway. So my baggage and I are unceremoniously dropped at the side of the road.

The sight of the track, winding up through the trees, produces in me such a surge of joy, of relief, that I start up it with haste, my unsuitable city shoes sliding and slipping on the grit. I have been across the Atlantic and back; I have seen my estranged children; I have sat across a table from a man I haven't seen for half my life; I have heard tales I would rather not hear; I have absorbed information I don't yet know what to do with; I am broken- and lame-hearted, but I am home, I am here. I have made it back, and this feels like an achievement against all odds, as if I am treading the fields and vineyards of Ithaca.

The first three gates I vault. I actually hurl my bag over, then enact a full leap, so great is my homecoming joy. The third time produces a twinge in my lower back, so I resolve to unlatch the rest.

I climb quickly, enjoying the increase in heart rate, the rapidity of my breathing, the motion of my limbs. I have been too much sessile these last few days, my muscles atrophied by airplane seats, my vertebrae stiff and compressed. I will, in a matter of minutes, be seeing my family again, my loves. I will have them in my arms and I will be breathing the air of my house, my home.

The thought makes me want to break into a sprint, but I am not the athlete I fleetingly was.

I am not worried that Claudette failed to pick me up at the airport. No, not at all. I tell myself this as I pass beneath the sodden branches of trees, as I move through the gates, as the distance between me and the house shrinks. Not at all. Maybe I wasn't entirely clear about flight times in my voice mail. Maybe she's taken the kids out somewhere. I said in the message that I had managed to see the person I needed to find, but I didn't say any more. The thing is, I find myself asserting to myself—

Without warning, a pheasant explodes from the undergrowth to my left, a scolding, pyrotechnic whir of iridescent green and umber. I jump back in surprise, letting out a yelled expletive. The bird plunges, swoops, then soars above the trees and is gone. The path and its woods seem unsettled, noiseless, after this interruption.

The thing is—I return to my defense, addressed, it would seem, to the leaves, to the tree trunks, to the pebbles pushing up beneath my thin shoe soles—if I am to account for myself to Claudette, I have to do it face-to-face. I have thought about this many times, over the past week or so, and have pictured it after the kids are in bed. I will draw her toward the big sofa next to the stove. The dog will be curled in its basket. We might have an open bottle of wine on the table. She will turn to me and I will tell her—what? I had a girlfriend who died. I had a girlfriend who had an abortion. I had a girlfriend who had been ill, on and off, for years with an eating disorder. I had a girlfriend who was one of the most intelligent people I'd ever met and somehow I accidentally got her pregnant. I had a girlfriend who, against my wishes, had a termination and then—and then—

I haven't figured out the "and then" part yet. Claudette, as I might have mentioned, takes a rather dim view of infidelity, in its myriad forms. She is, you could say, somewhat black-and-white on the subject. This is all Lindstrom's fault, of course, not mine, but because of him I need to be careful about how much I tell Claudette. Do I come clean about having slept around on Nicola or not? Is it something I should confess or relegate to the file of Things Claudette Doesn't Need to Know? Does the story hang together if I elide that detail?

I click the final gate into place, walk around the corner, and there is the house before me. The sight of its gabled windows and single turret ought to be accompanied by a resounding orchestral chord, so happy am I to be home. I hasten through the front garden and down the path. No lights gleam from the windows: I am pretending not to notice this. There is no car parked out front.

I call their names into the moist, soft air. It is close to the end of the day: they ought to be inside, perhaps having their tea, but they might still be out, romping on the back lawn, feeding the hens.

"Marithe! Claudette!" I yell. "Calvin! I'm home!"

The trees, the clouds, the mountainside, accept the noise, fold it into themselves. Nothing comes back.

I fit my key into the lock, push the door. There is no frantic clatter of dog claws on the hall floorboards, no shriek of children. The house breathes a cold sigh into my face as the door swings shut; the place has a sepulchral silence. Again, I call their names. I am ever the optimist.

I move through the hallway, past the staircase, which holds a dim, fading light in its curves, toward the back room. And when I open the door, I know for certain that there is no one here, that I am alone, that the house is empty.

The stove is out, the plates are stacked up on the shelves, the dog's bed is empty, the kids' toys and colored pencils are not strewn over the floor but stashed in their baskets. It could be a room in which there has been no human habitation for a long time. The paper stars studding the ceiling show themselves with a tarnished, lusterless gleam. This house has an odd habit of returning to the atmosphere of its former destitute and deserted state: I never forget, it seems to say, if we've been away for longer than a day or so, my stones and mortar are steeped in decades of human neglect.

I sit down in one of the dining chairs. I sink forward until my forehead comes into contact with the grain of the tabletop and there I let it rest.

I have always, I realize, half expected her to do something like this, history having a history of repeating itself. How could I have been so stupid? How could I have gone off-piste like that when I should have known it would push her to this? How could I have abandoned my post, knowing my wife as I do?

Claudette has gone. She has taken the kids. She has pulled off her speciality, her pièce de résistance: the mysterious, comprehensive, and complete disappearance. And I am left alone, discarded, steeped in the knowledge that it is entirely my fault. I am, in short, Timou Lindstrom the Second.

I have often, from the victorious ramparts of my hitherto successful marriage, wondered what it had been like for Timou when Claudette disappeared on him. How I have pitied him, with a certain amount of vainglorious superiority, as I imagined him waking up that morning on the yacht. Pictured him getting breakfast, perhaps going for a swim, as yet unaware of what nefarious webs were being spun around him. I have plotted those hours of the morning, the midday, the afternoon ticking by, as irritation must have given way to concern, concern to anxiety, anxiety to panic. How would it feel for your woman and child to evaporate, to vanish off the face of the earth? To be left like that, so definitively, so humiliatingly, not to mention publicly. What must it have been like to face the world's media, with their questions, their demands, their allegations, with a heart well and truly pulverized?

I have always hoped that he knew Claudette well enough to half expect it, as I have, and to recognize that it wasn't so much him she was escaping as her whole existence, a life she had unwittingly signed up for at an early age, a milieu she was whirled into without much forethought. I have wished that for him at the very least. I have, as you can probably tell, a certain sympathy for the man. It was two months before Claudette permitted Lucas to get in discreet touch with Timou to say that he knew where they were and, if Timou wanted, it could be arranged for him to see Ari.

Two months of not knowing where they were or if they were coming back or if he'd ever see them again. Two months of facing dogged media scrutiny, suspicion, and accusation.

I have also wondered what might have transpired if Timou hadn't flipped them the bird, hadn't written them both off. According to Lucas, there was a pause, a sigh, then Timou's exact words were *Send them my undying love.* Then he'd hung up. End of. But what if he had said, Yes, Lucas, take me to them? If he had said, I want to see my child, I am desperate to see my son. Part of me wonders if Claudette might have been waiting for that, for Timou to step up, to man up, to order his priorities so that Ari (and, by default, she) came out on top. Did she retreat to this house as a strategic move in a long psychological game of chess? Had she been waiting for Lindstrom to come to his senses?

I once hinted at this theory as we were getting ready for bed and she paused in the act of braiding her hair in front of the mirror. She turned and gave me a long, disbelieving look. The hair slowly unraveled and spread itself about her shoulders. Then she pointed her hairbrush at me, bristles first, and said, you can't possibly mean that. She crossed the room; she took the book I was reading out of my hands; she gripped the fabric of my T-shirt. The answer, she said, her face close to mine, is no. Absolutely not. "I have never," she said to me, "and would never wait for that man. The best decision I ever made was to walk away from him."

I made her wait a second or two before I took hold of her, before I flipped her backward onto the bed. "That was your best decision?" I said, pulling at the sash of her robe. "That?" At the time, she was laughing, pretending to fight me off; she finally agreed to demote it officially to second best and rate marrying me her finest moment of decision-making.

Which is, of course, I theorize as I sit with my head resting on the table of my deserted kitchen, exactly the answer she'd known I'd want. Did she say those things just to please me? Was she just humoring me? Has she been pretending all along? Had she just been waiting for my first slipup before she pulled a vanishing act on me? Has my whole marriage been a sham?

I raise my head, weary of myself, of my life, of my mind and its endless, circling tracks. Get a grip, I tell myself as I rise to my feet, think about this rationally. You and your wife have had an argument. You changed your plans without telling her; you extended a trip. While it's not impossible that she has another bucolic hideaway up her sleeve, just waiting on the off chance that she decides to exit her life again, it's highly unlikely. So, all may be resolved if you talk it through with her. All you have to do now is find her. Simple.

I get down the coffeemaker, fill it, put it on the stove, and fire up the gas underneath. The wheezing draw of its workings, its acrid vapor, go some way to calming me, to helping me think—always have.

Where would Claudette go?

I look around the room, taking in the sofas, the stove, the armchairs set facing each other, the table with the candelabra, the collection of antique mirrors, the photos of the children at various ages, the long curtains of fraying chinoiserie silk, with an endlessly repeating scene of a bridge with pagodas, where a hundred identical women with a hundred identical parasols wait for a hundred identical men in triangular hats who are inexplicably hiding themselves in some bamboo. Calvin is making short work of the embroidery in the curtains' lower reaches: most of the women have been divested of their parasols, and the men's cover has been pretty much blown, leaving them out in the open.

When I first saw the room, it looked nothing like this. The curtains were still waiting for Pascaline to discover them in some Parisian vintage store; the stars hadn't yet formed themselves into ceiling constellations; the walls weren't blue but a stained and faded distemper, showing signs of the mildew that had only recently been scrubbed away. Claudette and Ari had been living here for eighteen months, just the two of them. Workmen had been here, in the time between her buying it and her moving in, but only intermittently and erratically. The roof had been fixed so the house wasn't open to the elements, but the whole top floor was still uninhabitable and there were still big sections of floorboards missing, the dark oubliettes of the house exposed for all to see.

She and Ari, then, were mostly inhabiting this room. When I first came, there was the stove, a table, a makeshift kitchen, and two iron beds dragged close to the fire. Their whole life, their whole shriveled world, was there for me to see, and I was, frankly, dumbfounded. I had not expected her to be living in that way, in a decaying, rotten, forgotten building site. I'd only known her a short while, it was true, but when I came to the house and saw their beds, the stained walls, the state of the place, I saw not an intrepid and intriguing woman who had evaded notoriety and set herself up in a new life. I saw a woman half-crazed with loneliness and paranoia, and a kid so traumatized by events in his past that he could barely speak.

It took her a week or two to permit me to come up the track and over the threshold. Against all better judgments, I turned up that day at the crossroads, driving with one hand on the wheel and the other clutching the directions that Mrs. Spillane had drawn for me in leaky ballpoint. I didn't really know why I was going. Curiosity, I suppose. I have often based decisions on what the more interesting outcome would be, and that morning as I ate Mrs. Spillane's rubbery breakfast eggs, I had been weighing my options: flying back to the States or keeping a rendezvous with a reclusive ex–movie star.

No contest, obviously.

It was like a crossroads from a folktale illustration. Dry-stone walls hemmed it in on all sides, green fields stretched away from it, there was a slightly wonky signpost, and—best of all—it had a cross. Did you ever hear of anything more literal to adorn a crossroads? A great blackened wood thing it was, looming beside the road. There was one of those little shrines that you see all over Ireland, recessed into the wall and painted white, with a rain-blurred image of the Virgin, a long-extinguished candle encased in glass, and numerous offerings left there by the hopeful, the devout, the desperate.

She was there. The car was pulled in at the side of the road, half of its wheels parked on the shoulder. And she and Ari were, strangely, sitting on its roof. I peered out of my misted-over windshield to be sure of this. Yes, there they were, on the car roof, shrouded in hooded coats, each with a pair of binoculars tilted at the sky, apparently oblivious to the veils of gray rain coming at them horizontally.

"So," I hailed them as I got out of my car, "this must be the place."

"Shh" was her first word to me.

(Does it, in fact, even qualify as a word? I'm not sure it does. "Phonic" might be more accurate. Her first phonic to me.)

"What are you looking at?" I asked, in a more modulated tone.

"Two hawks and a buzzard," she answered, without looking my way.

I peered into the sky. I could see nothing but the iron-hued under-side of a cumulonimbus, the rain needling my eyes. Far up in the distance I could make out a black shape or two, holding their stillness in a place of turmoil and current.

"The buzzard," Ari burst out excitedly, removing his binoculars to look at me, "the buzzard—the buzzard—the b-, the b-, the b—"

She had lowered her binoculars by this time and was regarding her son, and her face showed nothing but the desire to help him.

"The buzzard," she put in for him, "caught a mouse, didn't he, Ari? At least, we thought it was a mouse. It might have been a small rabbit."

She raised her binoculars again. I looked at Ari; he looked back at me.

Is it weird to say that I've always felt Ari in some way chose me? That he decided or divined in that moment what should ensue from that meeting? I don't mean that Claudette wasn't given a choice—clearly she was, and so was I. Either way, the next thing that happened was that Ari launched himself off the car. He stood, on that slippery, rain-covered roof, and leaped, all in one movement. Straight into my arms.

I caught him, of course. My parental reflexes weren't that rusty. You see a kid flying through the air, and you reach out, you make sure you're there to cushion the landing. He felt different from Niall, from Phoebe. I remember thinking this, with no small pang of pain. He had lighter bones, somehow, a springier, longer feel to his limbs. He lacked the solidity, the familiarity, of my own children. And his hair, as it lay against my cheek, was finer and curlier.

So there we were, he and I, locked in an embrace, on a lonely, wind-battered stretch of Irish road: the fatherless son and the sonless father.

I threw him up in the air, of course, because that's what you do when a kid leaps into your arms. There's no written rule on this, but everyone knows it's next on the agenda. I didn't even have to warn him before I tossed him up. He knew it was coming and so did I.

The first time wasn't so high that it would frighten him. He laughed, so I did it again, higher this time, high enough so I could clap once before catching him.

His fine hair flew into a halo and his face was stretched in delight and fear. Again, he was yelling, again, his fingers gripping at my sleeves, again. Up he went, down he came, up, down, with me catching him each time under his arms.

When we finished, we were both breathless. I put him down on the road, holding on to him until I knew he'd found his balance, but he gripped me around the legs, pleading for more, because that, too, is the way these things are done.

"So, tell me," I said, my palm on top of his damp curls, looking up and down the road, "where can you get a decent cup of coffee round here?"

The answer was in her car, from a flask, but it wasn't coffee; it was hot chocolate.

"Jesus," I said, as I took my first swallow. I'd been expecting some watery beverage made from powder, but this stuff was hot, thick, dark, and impossibly good. It was like whipped, creamy soup, like molten magic, like nothing I'd ever tasted before. "What in the world—"

"Maman makes it," Ari interrupted in a rush, his head pushed between the two front seats, where his mother and I were sitting, "with special chocolate beans."

"She grows chocolate beans?" I said, looking at her, but her face was turned away, obscured by hair. "Now that is an impressive skill."

Ari gave a peal of delighted laughter and whacked me on the shoulder, the lightest feather of a punch I'd ever received. "No. You don't grow chocolate beans."

"Oh, yeah? Where do they come from, then?"

"You buy them."

"I bet she grew them."

"She didn't!"

"She strikes me as the type who might have a secret chocolate tree in her backyard."

"They don't grow on a tree!" He turned to his mother. "He thinks they grow on a tree!"

She turned her face toward him, making her large eyes even larger. "Maybe they do," she whispered.

"They don't," he said, with only a hint of doubt. "I know they don't.

Grandmère sent them from Paris. You told me." He gave her seat a nudge, and the movement caused hot chocolate to slop over the side of his cup.

"Oh," she said, in dismay, as hot rivers of chocolate trickled down her coat sleeve, pooling in the folds and pleats.

"S-sorry, Maman," the kid was saying. "S-s-sorry, s-s—"

"It's OK," she was saying, "don't worry," and I was saying the same and mopping at her sleeve and her hair with my handkerchief. Ari was still apologizing, or trying to, and she was telling him that accidents happen, and I was still wiping away.

"Ari," she said, putting her hand on his, "it doesn't matter. OK? Now, why don't you go outside and play?"

We watched through the misted windshield as Ari made his way over the wall and into the field. I shifted in my seat. The peculiarity of the situation washed over me: here I was, squeezed into a car with a former movie star who most people assumed was dead. What was I doing here? What could she possibly want from me? I was also, I remember, giving myself a firm talking-to. I knew what I was like around women, especially attractive ones, and there was no way I could allow myself to go on hormonal autopilot with this particular specimen. This was Claudette Wells, for Chrissake. I really needed to keep myself in check. She probably had armed security guards just out of sight who could be summoned at the merest lift of one of her slender fingers.

"You know," I said, because I had to say something, had to break this silence, and I held aloft my chocolate-stained handkerchief, "I'm seriously considering putting this in my mouth and chewing on it so as not to waste a single drop."

She let out a laugh. "Don't let me stop you. But please bear in mind that there is plenty more." She proffered the flask and I allowed her to pour an inch or so into my cup.

"You have an amazing kid," I said, keeping my gaze on the curvature of her wrists, her sweater cuffs, her fingernails, almond shaped, they were. I think I had decided that minimal eye contact was the way forward if I was to avoid inappropriate auto-flirting. "He's really quite something. So responsive and smart."

She looked across at me. I permitted myself a micro-second of contact with those startling feline eyes, but no more.

"Thank you," she said. "I always think so, too, but I have to admit a certain amount of bias. Do you have children?"

I cleared my throat. "I do." It was on the tip of my tongue to tell her about my legal wrangles, my parental anguish, but something stopped me. The thought crossed my mind that it wasn't the kind of thing one told women—single women, mothers, beautiful ones—in case they thought you were a deviant or a criminal. "I do," I said again. "Two. A boy and a girl. Older than Ari." Then I saw in a rush of panic that this might represent me to her as a married man. "They live with their mom. My ex. Ex-wife. We're not together. We separated. Split up. Got divorced." Why, I was asking myself, was I so keen to dispel the idea that I was attached? What was I thinking, that this was some kind of date? What was going on in my head? Was I insane? "I'm divorced," I heard myself say, one last time, just for good measure, just in case she hadn't quite gotten my drift.

"Oh, I'm sorry," she said. "About the divorce, I mean."

"Don't be," I said. "I'm not." I rolled my eyes in her direction but found she was looking at me, so turned wildly to the landscape, the clouds, the rain-polished gleam of the road before us. "So," I addressed the dry-stone walls, "what about Ari's dad?"

She was still looking at me; I could feel it. I drummed my fingers on the dashboard.

"What about him?"

"Are you and he still together or . . . ?"

"Separated," she said, giving each syllable a staccato emphasis. "We never actually married."

"Ah. OK. Maybe that makes things simpler."

"Not really," she said, with a wry smile.

"Ha. You're right. I don't know what I'm saying. 'Simple' is probably the most inaccurate word ever for these situations, isn't it? We'd need its exact opposite, its complete antonym. 'Complex,' maybe, or 'labyrinthine.' 'Tortuous,' 'convoluted,' 'tricky,' 'byzantine.' Any of those might be more apt." I managed, with great effort, to shut my mouth, and my gabbling mercifully ceased.

"Well," she said, after a moment's silence, "we've all been there."

"Mmm," I said, but what I wanted to say was: Really? You've been there? You? You have made mistakes and gotten yourself into unresolvable situations with unsuitable people, just like us ordinary mortals?

Then she said, "You're probably wondering why I asked you here today."

"No," I said, thinking, Hell, yes. "Not at all, I just—"

"How long do you plan to stay in Donegal?" she asked and, caught off guard, I looked at her. Her face was impossible to read and seemed suddenly and uncomfortably close to mine in the steamed-up little car. A minuscule crease appeared between her perfectly arched eyebrows. "If you don't mind my asking," she said.

"Not at all. The thing is . . ." I faltered, mesmerized by the separate strands of her eyelashes, which seemed so intriguingly dark in comparison to the golden sheen of her hair, by the constellation of freckles that plotted itself across the bridge of her nose.

I attempted to hijack and drag my renegade attention back to the conversation. It was a question, I was almost sure. But what had been the question? That was the question. "Sorry," I said, "what did you say?"

The crease had deepened to a frown. "I just wondered how long you were planning to stay around here, but you don't have to say, if you'd rather not. Obviously, it's none of my business and—"

"I really don't know," I said. "Could be a while." My leg moved convulsively against my bag, inside which, I knew, and my leg knew, was an airline ticket with tomorrow's date on it. "I'm just, you know, traveling around a bit. Rented a car. Thought I'd see a bit of the old country." The old country? *The old country?* Had I actually said that? "I don't have to be back in the States until the beginning of next semester. So. It could be a while."

"Oh." Her expression cleared and she smiled at me, an astonishing, wide, beatific smile. "That's great. You see, I was wondering, and I know it's a big favor and you must please say no if you'd rather not . . . "

She was off, explaining something about whether or not it would be possible for me to do some sessions with Ari while I was there. I watched her hands, moving through the close air of the car, as she said that of course she would pay me for my time and reimburse me for any expenses incurred. I watched the tresses—because it was the kind of hair which warranted that noun, usually confined to usage only within fairy tales—move on the surface of her coat. I watched the timpani beat of her pulse in a vein that traversed the hollow in the lee of her collarbone. It was taking everything in me not to say, *smile at me like that again and I'll do anything you want.* My twenty-something self seemed to be riding in the ascendant today, for some reason, and I had to tamp him down, tie him up, gag him, at all costs. There was no way I was letting him out, giving him free rein in this car. I experienced briefly, disquietingly, a flitting image of a pay phone in the dim hallway of my English-exchange-year house, and I banished it quickly, without permitting myself to ask why.

"You know," I said, holding up my hand to stop her, "I would love to help you—"

"Thank you," she burst out, "thank you so much."

"—but I'm not sure I'm the man for the job. I'm not qualified to help someone like Ari. I'm not a speech therapist or even a specialist in developmental dysfluency."

"But those things you said to him, about starting off with another sound or finding a different word, they were—"

"All things I got from doing a research-assistant job, a lifetime ago," I interjected gently. "I'm a linguist. I specialize in language change, in the genetics, if you like, of what we say. I really don't know very much at all about the challenges that Ari is facing. I wouldn't feel confident in . . . "

She placed the flask between the seats and the droop of her head, the tremble of her hands, were heartbreaking to witness. I caught wind suddenly, and for the first time, of her keen isolation, the bravery it must take for her to be there, alone with the boy.

"There must be practitioners within reach," I said. "You're not that far from Belfast, are you? A couple of hours' drive? Even Dublin, if you had to. You could quite feasibly find—"

"It would be tricky," she cut across me, looking away, out of the window, at where her son was running through the wet field, dragging a fallen branch after him.

I took a breath. "Look," I said, "I get it."

"You get what?"

"I get why it would be tricky. I know who you are. I didn't know yesterday, when we changed the tire, but it came to me last night, when Mrs. Spillane let your name slip. I don't know why the penny didn't drop right away. I suppose the last thing I was expecting to find here was, well, you."

She bit her lip. "I have to ask if you—"

"It's OK," I said. "I'm not going to tell anyone. I can keep a secret."

"Can you?"

I nodded. "Sure."

She brushed some strands of hair off her face and lifted her chin. It was a gesture that would become infinitely familiar to me, but I didn't know that at the time.

"Thank you," she said, and the words had an air of finality to them. I could see that the conversation was over: she had extracted as much as she could from me and now she would return to whatever it was she had here. I could see that I would step out of the car, say my goodbyes, drive back to the B and B, then travel on to America, home and work, the task of finding an apartment, and the struggle to see my kids. This encounter in the middle of nowhere with a woman of ineffable mystery would, in a few weeks, have taken on the quality of something dreamed, something made up. Had I really sat in the car of Claudette Wells and looked out with her into the rain, at the mountain and the flat, steely waters of Lough Swilly beyond?

I was swigging the dregs of my cup, looking around for a place to put it, about to take my leave, when the car door opened and Ari clambered in, hair plastered seallike to his scalp, jacket wet and glistening.

"Will you come to the beach with us?" he said, with perfect clarity, a huge grin on his face looking from me to her and back again. "We're going there n-n-now and we're going to have f-fish-and-chips and then we're going to—"

"Ari," his mother murmured, "Mr. Sullivan probably has other things to do. He is on holiday and we mustn't—"

"It's Daniel," I said. "Call me Daniel. And I don't have anything else to do. I'd love to come to the beach." I gave Ari a smile, then allowed myself to look his mother full in the face for the first time that day. "As long as that's OK with you."

I stand now in our kitchen as my coffee brews. I look at the phone, resting in its cradle. I look at Marithe's colored pencils, standing upright in their pot, tips sharpened to arrowheads. I examine a stack of laundry, a skyscraper of folded underwear, leggings, sweaters. I am a detective at the scene of a crime. Nothing escapes my gaze. I look again at the faded chinoiserie curtains, at the women endlessly crossing and crossing their bridges, and it all falls into place. I know exactly where Claudette will have gone.

The Logical Loophole

MAEVE

Chengdu, China, 2003

Maeve wakes with a jolt. She is lying on her side, and it is stiflingly, oppressively humid: she is damp with sweat and tangled in the sheets. The room is filled with a strange, shrill noise, like that of a malfunctioning machine or burglar alarm. It seems to drill into her ear canals and vibrate there at a persistent, painful frequency. She sits up and leaps from the bed, almost in one movement.

There is a silhouette across the room. Maeve can see its cutout shape against the never-quite-dark hotel windows. It is a child, standing in a cot, hands gripping the bars. Maeve fumbles for the bedside lamp and clicks it on.

The situation becomes illuminated.

She is all the way across the world, without Lucas. It is the middle of the night. Hard to tell what time exactly: the road outside seems to grind at all hours, with lights and trucks and horns.

She is alone in a hotel room, with a child.

The child is making a noise.

It isn't so much crying, Maeve thinks as she stands there, because that would involve different notes, pauses for intakes of breath, tears even. This is more high pitched. It is one note. There is no letup in its timbre, no pause. It is a call of distress, of grief, of abandonment.

Maeve puts out her hands for the child and lifts it into her arms. This is what you're supposed to do at such times; she knows this. She tries to emulate this lift and hug, but the baby has other ideas. It arches its back, leaning away from her, as if to get a better look at her, as if to assess whether it wants to be held by her. Its eyes are black, wide, terrified, the skin around them drawn and wet.

"It's OK," Maeve tries. She pats the baby's back. "Shhhh, it's OK."

The baby's arms are held out stiffly from its body and it turns its head from one side, then the other, as if to look for someone in a position of higher authority, someone it recognizes.

"Don't cry," Maeve croaks, although crying herself now. "It's me, Maeve." Then she corrects herself: "Mummy, I'm Mummy, remember?"

The child lurches back in her arms, heels pressing into Maeve's abdomen. Everything about its body is saying: I don't want to be hugged by you. I don't like you. I don't know you. Amazing, one part of Maeve's mind is telling her, how a child of only a year and a half—or two perhaps, impossible to know exactly—can express this without a single word.

Maeve inhales. She must remain calm. She must keep it together. Everything is going to be all right.

Maybe the baby is hungry.

Maeve seizes on the idea. Hungry! Of course! Why didn't she think of that? Just hungry, that's all: she doesn't hate Maeve, she doesn't want Maeve to put her down, she just needs a bottle.

Maeve puts the baby back into the hotel cot and goes into the bathroom, where she prepared the formula earlier. She takes one of the bottles, all brought from home two days ago and sterilized this morning (can it only have been this morning, the same day as this one? It feels like weeks, months, lifetimes ago), and counts in the right number of scoops.

She's doing this, she really is, she's coping, she's being a parent. A mother. She wishes, not for the first time today, that Lucas was here, that Lucas was with her, not waiting uselessly at home.

She comes back into the bedroom, walking with new confidence and purpose, shaking the bottle.

"Look what I've got for you!" She hears herself trying a new, sprightly voice. "Milk!"

The baby is still in the cot, still standing, still making the endless noise, which is beginning to sound a little hoarse, a little desperate and mad, but Maeve wills herself not to be discouraged.

"Here!" Maeve says and goes to pick her up again, then gets halfway before seeing it isn't going to work because she's holding the bottle and so has to clumsily lower her back down, turn, place the bottle on the bedside table, and pick her up.

Again, she feels horror and reluctance reel through the child. Maeve grits her teeth, sits down on the bed, trying to maneuver her into a sort of sitting position in the crook of her elbow. That's how you feed an infant, isn't it? They are supposed to bend in the middle somehow and use your body as a kind of chair, but this one doesn't seem to bend. She is rigid, livid, stricken. Maeve has got herself a nonbending baby.

"There, there," Maeve hears herself say. She hooks one arm around her shoulders and makes a lunge for the bottle, which she has positioned just out of reach, a movement that elicits a scream from the child, a proper noise of fear, so by the time Maeve has got the bottle in front of her face, she is too upset, too rigid with panic, to drink it.

Maeve tries putting the nipple into the child's mouth, but her lips are stretched out in a scream and won't join together to suck. She tries wetting her open mouth with a few drops of milk, so the baby gets the idea, but it just drips out again and down her chin.

They stare at each other, Maeve and this baby, alone in a hotel room, far from home. Maeve sees: black eyes, creased into crescents, but still seeing, still knowing. She sees hands, heartbreakingly small and soft, with fingers clenched and thumbs outstretched, each nail just a shade too long and ingrained with some kind of blackish substance. Should she have bathed her after all? She had balked at this, after they had made it back to the room, the baby and her, after they had staggered through the odyssey of their day: the long wait at the Social Welfare Center, the endless checking and rechecking of forms, the handing over of the envelope of cash (clean, unmarked, new American dollar bills, so many of them, more than Maeve had ever seen), and then the door opening and a facilitator coming toward her holding what looked to Maeve like a mannequin with black hair held up in a single elastic band and a face with an expression that was devastatingly grumpy, wary, skeptical.

What, though, had she been expecting? That the child would toddle toward her, beaming, arms outstretched, ready to be swept into a hug, ready for all the affection and desperation and fierce craving that builds up, as behind a dam, from—count them—fourteen years of childlessness, five rounds of fertility treatment, three near-but-not-quite adoptions?

Maeve has thought about the moment when she would meet her child for the first time, over and over again, mostly when she is alone. She has taken the idea out, like a gift, and viewed it from all angles, invented and embellished and pursued every possibility. Ever since she and Lucas, exhausted and worn down by UK procedures for adoption, had decided on adopting from China, she had pictured herself and him waiting in a clean but functional orphanage entrance hall. It would be gray concrete, communism-sparse, with kindly young staff in uniforms, rows and rows of iron cribs, plastic toys lying on the floor, yellow curtains, the smell of rice cooking. There they would be, and there would be babies. Hundreds of them, lined up, each with shining hair and a tiny face, and one would be for them. It would be theirs. They would pick it up and take it home and then they would all live happily ever after. Simple.

What she had not imagined was being bused, with other parents-in-waiting, to a place like the Social Welfare Center, which looked like a department store or shopping mall, with an enormous, towering apricot façade and a fountain outside with statues of featureless concrete children endlessly pouring urns into scummy water. She had not imagined waiting in a room that seemed more suited to low-budget civic weddings than adoption handovers, with swags of metallic-bright fabric, fake rubber plants in brass pots, long trestle tables with white cloths, a dais in the corner with an empty microphone stand. She had not imagined that the children would be brought in, one by one, held up like raffle prizes, the names of the intended parents shouted out loud so that you had to concentrate, you had to listen, so as not to miss your cue. What a thought: to have come this far and then be scuppered, left babyless again, after a moment of inattention or a failure to understand a Chinese-accented pronunciation of your surname. She had not imagined doing this without Lucas, but the last two times—two!—they had come to Chengdu, having been told that there was a child, a baby, for them there; they had found that by dint of actually being in China they had missed a crucial telephone call on their home phone in Cumbria, which, remaining unanswered, meant that their baby had been allocated to someone else.

The logical loophole of this had floored Maeve but not Lucas. You go, he had said, when they'd opened their mail to find a picture of a small Chinese girl with blunt fringe and a yellow romper. You go and I'll stay by the phone. I shan't leave it for a minute. I won't even go to the loo. Maeve had giggled at this and said, what will you do instead? and Lucas, without missing a beat, said, I'll get a bedpan, one of those big Victorian porcelain ones, and you'll have to empty it when you get back.

Maeve has to grip the bottle hard, so hard she's worried she might crack it, with her need of him. What would he say to her, what would he think, seeing her handling this so badly?

Maybe, she thinks, as she looks down at the hysterical and miserable child in her arms, she just isn't meant to be a mother. Maybe she should take her back tomorrow —she should catch that bus again to the place with the apricot façade and find the people who gave her the child and say, I couldn't do it. I was no good, she doesn't like me, I can't do it.

A minute later, Maeve has laid the child on the bed and picked up the phone, dialed a number, waited for the purr-click-purr of an international connection trying, trying, trying its best to make it, to succeed, to get where it wants to be, and then suddenly, miraculously, Lucas is speaking into her ear and she is replying.

"The child hates me," Maeve says. There is no good way to break it to him, she has reasoned, there is no way to soft-pedal the fact that they have come to the end of this road, the end of all roads, and are going to have to return the baby. "She's miserable. She hates me. I can see it in her eyes. We have to give her back."

Lucas says: "Where are you?"

Maeve says: "The hotel."

Lucas says: "Go and see Claudette."

Maeve does as she is told. She pretty much always has: first by her parents, then teachers, then lecturers, then bosses, then doctors and a whole host of other, less medically qualified experts in the business of conjuring babies, either from your own body or alternative sources. And see, Maeve thinks, where it's got her. Here. Nowhere. Worse than nowhere.

She picks up the baby, however, keening now with a hoarse, rending cry, goes out of her room, along the corridor, and knocks on another door.

Her sister-in-law opens it. Her face is creased with sleep and she is wearing a nightdress, a loose white thing.

"Oh," she says, pushing her hair out of her eyes. "OK."

She ushers Maeve through the door, past the sleeping form of Ari, who is stretched out under a sheet on Claudette's bed, thumb in, fox by his side, and into the bathroom.

Claudette shuts the door.

"Now," she says, turning around, "what's up with you two?" Maeve answers by bursting into tears, the first tears she has allowed herself all day, possibly because of the lovely, inclusive sounding "you two," possibly because Maeve cannot take this sound anymore, not a minute more—she has come to the end of her tether, the end of her rope, the end of the road. There is no more—of anything.

"Shall I take her?" Claudette asks tentatively, not wanting to grab the child, Maeve sees, against all instincts. Maeve nods, then watches as Claudette lifts the child, the baby, into her arms, watches as Claudette balances on the edge of the bath and sits the child on her knee, expertly, Maeve thinks, competently. And all the while Maeve tries to explain, tries to make Claudette see the magnitude of this disaster: She won't stop crying, not at all, she doesn't like me, doesn't want to be with me, she'll have to be given back, all a terrible mistake.

"Might she be hungry?"

"I tried feeding her," Maeve wails, brandishing the bottle, which she finds she is still holding. "She didn't want it!"

Claudette presses her palm to the child's cheeks, her brow, runs a finger around her collar. How calm she is, how good at this she is. How the child there, on her lap, presses against the white nightdress and makes the curve of her pregnancy evident.

When Lucas had called Claudette to ask her to go to China with Maeve to collect the baby, for moral support, he said, to help on the flight—wasn't it easier for her to travel, these days, now that she had a married name she could hide behind?—Claudette had said yes, her voice hesitant, careful. Maeve was listening from the other side of the room and she already knew what was about to happen. There is one thing, she'd heard Claudette say, and Lucas had looked at Maeve across the room and he loudly cleared his throat over the ensuing utterance. Maeve had waited a moment, checking herself, checking herself all over, as a person might after a fall down a flight of stairs, but she had at the time been filled with a joyous optimism about the photograph of the toddler in a yellow romper, so had shrugged and nodded at the same time. It didn't matter, she'd said to Lucas as he held the phone to his ear, frowning. It's OK.

He had asked her again later, as they booked the flights, as they scoured the guidebook to find a hotel different from the one they had stayed in before, which had been infested with cockroaches. Was she really OK to go with Claudette, who was now pregnant? Maeve looked at him. Claudette had pulled off something astonishing, breathtaking, escaping her old life and resurfacing, like a diver, into something new: a new house, a new country, and, most surprising, a new husband. Of course she's pregnant, Maeve said to Lucas. You didn't see that coming?

Now she doesn't feel so blasé, so generous, sitting there in a stifling, boxy bathroom, with a child who loathes the sight of her, and her beautiful expectant sister-in-law, who already has one child and will be able to go on having them, as many as she likes, whenever she likes.

"You know what," Claudette is saying, starting to unhook the fabric loops on the child's jacket. "I think she might be hot. What's she got on under here?"

Claudette peels off the jacket and drops it to the floor. She lifts a jersey over the child's head. Off come padded pants, leggings, tights. A second jersey, a shirt, a T-shirt, a pair of socks. Maeve sees the child, her child, emerge from layer after layer of orphanage clothing.

When Claudette finishes and the baby is sitting on her knee, wearing just a diaper and an undershirt, Maeve has her hand over her face.

"Oh, God," she says, "I can't believe I didn't think of that. What's wrong with me? How could I have put her to sleep like that, in all those clothes?"

"It's not your fault," Claudette says, dabbing at the baby's perspiring brow with a damp washcloth. "How could anyone dress a child in that many layers in this climate?"

"I can't believe I didn't check!" Maeve cries. "I changed her diaper, but I must have been on autopilot because everything I took off I just put back on! This just shows, doesn't it, that I'm not cut out for this, that—"

"It's OK," Claudette says, laying a hand on her arm. "She's OK."

And she is. The child, Zhilan, she is called, which means "iris orchid"—Maeve looked it up—sits on Claudette's knee, looking first at Claudette and then at Maeve, her gaze one of startled astonishment, her mouth parted in a tiny, round O. What am I doing, she seems to be saying, in a bathroom with you, and why was I wearing all those clothes?

Maeve looks at her. She looks and looks. If she was a liquid, she would drink her; if she was a gas, she would breathe her in; if she was a pill, she would down her; a dress, she would wear her; a plate, she would lick her clean. Her hands gripping the hem of her undershirt, her toes flexed in midair, the place at her temples where the black hair crowds in. Her eyelids are the shape of a bird's wings, her rib cage delicate branches. Her realness, her corporeality, the way her lungs go in and out, the way she turns her head to look around, take Maeve's breath away. She cannot believe she is here, cannot believe she is hers.

"She might," Claudette says, "be ready for that bottle now. What do you think?"

Maeve sits down. She makes herself ready, and when Claudette stands, Maeve opens her arms to take the child.

A Jagged, Dangerous Mass of Ice

ARI

Suffolk, 2010

"Just a moment," the counselor cried, and hurried to cram the remains of his lunchtime sandwich into his mouth, sweep his desk for telltale crumbs, crumple the greaseproof wrapper in his fist, and drop it into the bin. "I won't be a minute." He grabbed the file from his in-tray, swallowing an unchewed hunk of hummus-clogged bread, and flipped open the cover.

Ari Lefevre Lindstrom Wells Sullivan, he saw. He had to read it twice. *Aged 16.* He let his eye travel down the page as he took a swig from his water bottle. Lives in Ireland, mother, stepfather, attended this school for a year, subjects taken, blah, blah. But the counselor's eye was caught by one particular detail: *Previous schools attended—none.* He sighed and his head gave a single shake. He took a dim view of homeschooling. He turned his swivel chair and stood up.

A child—he opined, to an audience comprising his bookshelf, a watercolor of a Scandinavian lake, a Newton's cradle, his effigy of a Yoruba deity, picked up a long time ago on a gap-year placement—is a social being. He or she requires, needs, nay, craves the company and instruction of his or her peer group.

The counselor crossed the room, pausing only to light a candle on the mantelpiece. He had a handle on the session to come now. He felt inspiration, confidence, assurance, surge through him. He loved this job, he loved it. He could help this Ari Whatever Hatchback Peugeot Whatever he was called, he knew he could. He could picture the child who would be waiting beyond the door, in all probability nervously, fearfully, although perhaps covering these emotions with the rough façade of teenage bravura. Ireland, the file had said, so the counselor imagined the offspring of some Celtic hippie types. Auburn dreadlocks, a whispery Irish inflection, dressed in felt and hemp, that particular brand of drivelly, directionless, formless homeschooling written all over him. Couldn't read until he was eleven, could barely count, even now. He, the counselor, would bring him out of himself, give him that direction, inspire him to exert himself in more mainstream educational channels, show him that there are other ways to live, besides weaving one's own clothes, straining one's own cheese, splitting one's own logs.

The counselor flung open the door to welcome this waif, this refugee, this victim of overparenting.

He beheld a figure in dark clothes seated in the armchair outside his office. One foot balanced on the opposite knee, a newspaper folded on his lap, where a crossword was being filled in with a gold fountain pen. Polished leather ankle boots, navy sweater, narrow trousers, and the kind of angular-framed tortoiseshell glasses usually worn by architects or web designers, black curly hair worn neither short nor long. The counselor thought: This cannot be him. He thought: This must be someone else. A parent? No, too young. An older sibling of one of the pupils?

"Oh," the counselor said. "I was waiting for Ari . . . ," he floundered. "Ari . . . Le-something . . . um . . ."

The person nodded. Really, it was a quite extraordinary outfit—it made him look as though he'd stepped straight out of the pages of a French novel; he ought to have been wearing a beret and smoking a Gauloises and expounding the theory of existentialism in a café on the

Left Bank. Extraordinary, especially because most of the pupils at the school preferred to dress like off-duty rap stars, in ridiculously capacious jeans, sleeveless T-shirts, and baseball caps worn backward. The person stood, recapped his fountain pen, laid a jacket over his arm, and extended his hand. He was tall, this boy, with the kind of rangy, muscular thinness found in greyhounds.

The counselor took the outstretched hand, bemused, trying to remember if a teenager had ever offered to shake hands with him before. Then he recalled himself to his script. "Ari," he said. "Welcome."

"It's *Ari*."

"Excuse me?"

"You said *Ari*, with the emphasis on the second syllable. It's *Ari*." The boy smiled. "Inflection on the first."

The counselor let go of his hand and motioned him inside. "I see," he said. "Well, thank you for clearing that up."

He felt better when seated behind his desk, when he had the file open before him, when he had the boy situated on the couch, which was sagging and enveloping, designed to make his subjects relax.

But Ari wasn't in it for long. He was up again, almost immediately, his legs unfolding beneath him, to examine the Yoruba figure, the Scandinavian lake, to run his eyes over the bookshelves.

"So, tell me," the counselor began, "how are you finding the school? You've been here—how long? A year?"

"An academic year," Ari replied, without breaking off from his examination of a Moroccan bowl. "Just under."

The fountain pen was gripped in his left hand, the counselor noticed, where the boy clicked the lid on and off, on and off. *Compulsive tics?* he wrote on his notepad.

"And before that you were homeschooled?"

"I was."

"By your parents?"

"My mother."

"And your mother is . . . "

The boy turned an expressionless stare toward him.

"A teacher?" the counselor hazarded.

Ari shook his head and seemed to be suppressing a smile.

"So, help me paint a picture of your homelife. It's you, your mother, and"—here, he checked the file—"three siblings?"

"Two."

"And they are—how old?"

"Six and one."

"Do they attend school?"

"No."

"Whose decision was it for you to come to school here?"

Ari picked up and put down the Yoruba deity. He shrugged. "Mine. And Daniel's."

"And Daniel would be . . ." The counselor flipped through the file.

"My stepfather," Ari supplied.

The counselor put down his pen and placed his hands on the desk. "Ari," he said, in a lower voice, "why don't you come and sit? Take a seat. Now, tell me, what kind of a relationship do you have with your real father?"

Ari rolled his eyes. He sat, crossed one leg over the other, laid the newspaper on the floor beside him. "Are these standard questions? Do you ask everybody this? 'Help me paint a picture of your homelife,'" he repeated, and the counselor was almost glad to hear something vaguely teenage come out of his mouth, so unnervingly mature did he appear. " 'What kind of a relationship do you have with your real father?' " Ari gave a scoffing exhale and looked around with an expression of barely veiled disgust. "Is this the kind of asinine nonsense they teach you at counselor school?"

The counselor laced his fingers together, realizing, with a dismaying jolt, that he had no idea what "asinine" meant. "I'm sensing a reluctance in you, Ari, a discomfort at being in this room."

"Well, then, your senses are finely tuned. I should be in double history now, preparing for my imminent and extremely important exams instead of in here answering simplistic questions about my family."

The counselor glanced down at the file, to glean some kind of insight into this boy. *Far and away the most intelligent pupil I have ever taught,* he sees, in a colleague's handwriting.

"Just to get back on track," the counselor said, "you haven't lived with your father—"

"Since I was little," Ari said quickly, too quickly, the words running into one another. "I don't see him and that's fine. He works incredibly hard and he's very committed to what he does. I have what you might call a father figure in my stepfather: I've lived with him since I was little. I accept the way things are. It's always been like that, and it's really no problem at all, so if you're trying to find a route to a source of trauma or stress in my life, I suggest you direct your attention elsewhere."

The counselor was thinking not so much about what Ari had said but the way in which he had said it. Those sudden breaks in the middle of words, the repetition of certain syllables. "Ari, have you ever had any counseling before?"

Ari shook his head.

"Any therapy? Of any description?"

Ari rubbed his forehead. "I think," he said, "what you're getting at now is-is-is"—he winced, turned his head one way and then the other, seemed to grip his hands into fists—"th-the way I speak. Yes?"

"Yes."

"I have a stammer," Ari said. "Had. Have. One of the two."

"But you're over it now?"

"You're never over it. There exists a theory in speech therapy," he spoke in a toneless voice, as if he'd explained this countless times, "that a stammer is like an iceberg."

"An iceberg?"

"Only a small part of it is visible, while under the water is a large, jagged, dangerous mass of ice."

The counselor smoothed the pages. "It interests me that you used the word 'dangerous.'"

"Does it?" Ari said. "I suppose you want me to ask why."

"Not necessarily. Does it interest you?"

"No." The boy sighed, placed his hands on his knees. "Look, why don't we get to the point? We both know why I'm here."

"Do we?"

"Yes. Because of Sophie."

The counselor leaned back in his chair. At the meeting he'd attended yesterday, the subject of Ari Lefevre Lindstrom Wells Sullivan and Sophie Bridges had been at the top of the agenda. They had been going out for a month or two, he'd been told, and several members of the teaching staff were uneasy about the relationship. The counselor had shifted in his seat, bracing himself for tales of trauma, unhappiness, victimhood, manipulation, abuse even. He was ready with numbers of helplines, with ways of handling parental input, with psychological support. But, no, the problem with Ari and Sophie was that they were too involved, too intense, too happy. They had stopped fraternizing with other students, the history teacher said. They spent breaks and weekends together in Ari's room, reading. They took walks, they listened to music, they sat together at meals. They had stopped sneaking out, like other sixth-formers, in the evening and instead were watching old movies on Ari's laptop. Sophie, who came from a good Home Counties family, had mentioned poststructuralism in class the other day. She had cut her sensible blond hair into a brunette bob. She wanted to do her course work on Simone de Beauvoir and her multimedia incarnations.

It didn't reflect well, the headmistress said, on the school or the pupils, this kind of adolescent intensity. We like our pupils to be healthy, outgoing team players.

"The pupils here," the counselor said to Ari in his office, "are encouraged to be healthy, outgoing team players. We emphasize—"

"The pupils here," Ari interrupted, "are brainless drones, encouraged to regurgitate prepared knowledge so that they can replicate the narrow, self-regarding, white middle-class lives of their parents."

"Well," said the counselor, "now, this is a viewpoint that—"

"The pupils here," Ari continued, "indulge in astonishing levels of drinking, drug taking, and promiscuity, to such a degree that you and your cohorts couldn't even imagine. But you don't choose to confront that, do you? You don't investigate that. You don't drag in those people selling weed and pills of questionable origin and purity. No, you choose to cast aspersions on two pupils who choose to step away from that kind of activity and form a relationship that is entirely—"

"I'm told you've been spending the night in her room."

Ari shrugged.

"Do you deny that?"

"No, I don't deny it. Sophie and I want to be together. You and your spies can't put a stop to that."

"It's against the rules, Ari."

"Well, it's a ridiculous rule."

"It's an important rule. It protects—"

"What about the rules of no drinking or no consuming drugs or no being a total and complete tedious idiot? Because everyone here is guilty of breaking those rules. Everyone."

"Everyone except you and Sophie?"

Ari got to his feet. He bent to pick up his newspaper. Straightening, he shook his head. "My mother was right," he muttered.

"Right about what?"

He looked the counselor in the eye. "School," he said, gesturing around him. "All this. You. Square pegs and round holes. The whole thing."

"Tell me about your mother," the counselor said.

Ari let out a short laugh. "No," he said. "I won't. I won't tell you about my mother."

"The staff say they've never met her, that she's never been here."

"She hasn't. So what?"

"Your teachers say they have spoken to her on the phone but it's only ever your stepfather who comes to the school, your uncle, and, once or twice, your grandmother."

Ari looked up at the ceiling and crossed his arms over his newspaper.

"Why doesn't your mother visit the school?"

Ari smirked. "At a wild guess, I'd say because she doesn't want to meet people like you."

"I've been told that you've been overheard having quite-heated phone calls with her in the last few days."

Ari shut his eyes and shook his head.

"You were heard speculating on the whereabouts of your stepfather."

The counselor left a pause for Ari to speak, which he didn't.

"Has your stepfather left? Is everything OK at home? Ari, does your mother suffer from depression?"

Ari looked at him and started to laugh. He laughed so much that he had to bend over and clutch his well-tailored knees.

"Why are you laughing, Ari? Depression is a serious thing but it can be treated. It can be—"

"I think what amazes me most," Ari said, "is how wrong you've got everything. You've clearly read my notes, researched what you can of me, but the result is a picture so skewed and erroneous it's really quite remarkable. I commend you for consistently getting the wrong end of every single stick, I really do. And now," Ari said, standing, "I think this interview is over. I'm heading back to my history class. *Adios.*"

The door slammed shut behind him. The counselor took a breath, a deep, cleansing breath that he hoped would clear this boy, his aggression, and his vocabulary out of his airspace.

He picked up his pen and inscribed the date in Ari's file. Then he stopped short, realizing he had absolutely no idea what to write next.

You Do What You Have to Do

DANIEL

Brooklyn, 1986

Daniel pushes at the door of the thrift store, knowing that the bell will leap on its spring, giving off that atonal two-note interval. He tries to cover his ears, but it's too late. The jangling bell has set up an answering tinnitus in his left ear, just as it always does.

It's made up of a repetitive baseline of a shurr-shurr sound, with the odd high clang or ting thrown in for good measure, as if someone is sweeping the floor near his head or going at their clothes with a brush, all the while wearing a cowbell around their neck. He shakes his head, like a dog trying to rid itself of excess water or unwanted scent, but the movement seems to unbalance him. The mat must be rucked under his feet or the door too narrow or the step too high. Either way, he is stumbling, the doorjamb lurching to meet him, his shoulder coming into painful contact with its sharp edge.

He is aware, as he rights himself, leaning heavily on a conveniently placed tapestry chair, that certain codes of behavior require him to nod at the ladies behind the counter, to bid them hello, but it seems too late, now that he's stumbled into their shop, now that he has dislodged a display of crystal animals from a small table with the tail of his coat.

The tiny glinting animals lie scattered about the carpet, like the victims of some terrible glass-based genocide. He sees an upturned squirrel, with one missing eye, a cat with ears of sharp glass, what is possibly a hippo.

It is important, he tells himself, to remain upright, to appear calm, collected, and, above all, sober. He picks his way through the fallen animals and moves toward the goods and wares, the racks and displays.

The rich, sour, yeasty smell of thrift stores the world over fills his nostrils, makes his throat ache and sting.

Sober, sober, sober, he is chanting to himself as he circles the aisles: racks of men's jackets, shiny at the elbows; a basket of woolen scarves, coiled like serpents; rows of lace-up shoes, rubber boots. The sad residue of human lives, washed up here to be resold, rehomed.

Sober, sober, calm, calm. The eyes of the ladies upon him, peering at him through their spectacles, muttering to one another, one of them over by the animals, replacing the crystal diorama. He has every right to be there: he would like to say this to them. Sober. How to achieve this when he hasn't slept in—how long?—two nights, maybe three, hasn't eaten since he can't remember when, hasn't been home for a long time, camping out at the apartments of aunts and uncles, on his youngest sister's sofa, when—

Daniel is brought to a halt by a box of trinkets, perched on top of a bookcase. A brooch in the shape of a terrier, a ring of adjustable circumference, a beribboned bangle, a lone earring. He reaches down and plucks out a hair comb. A curving band of clear turquoise plastic, radiating out from which is a row of long, sharp spines. A kind of flattened miniature porcupine. He holds it up to the light. One spine is half broken. Bubbles are trapped in the plastic, lenslike, tear shaped.

His mother had some of these. He knows she did. He has a distinct memory of her sitting in the kitchen, the newspaper open in front of her on the table, her hair held back at the sides by these plastic combs. Were they turquoise? Yes, he's positive they were.

He feels his pulse quicken, his lungs compress, as they always do when he finds something of Teresa's. He has three things now, no, four—the shoes, the silk scarf with blue swirls, that yellow cardigan, the gold bracelet—and this comb makes five. He clutches it in his hand, so hard that the teeth make a neat row of impressions on his palm, but it is a good kind of pain, a real kind of pain, the sort that feels clean and uncomplicated and purely physical. It is hers. It has to be. He lifts it to his face and sniffs it. Yes. It smells of her. It does. It really does.

"Can we help you with something?"

The question comes from close behind him and is not really a question at all, conveying as it does the exact opposite of its semantic implication. Does that, Daniel finds himself wondering before he turns around, count as a rhetorical question? Not really. It doesn't contain rhetoric, merely threat. There ought, he feels, to be a special linguistic coinage for this type of inquiry. One that purports to be helpful but is anything but. Maybe he will invent one. He could write a paper on it, perhaps, introduce the concept to the world, claim it as his own.

He turns, comb still in hand. The thrift-store ladies are upon him. Three of them. Weird sisters indeed. He bares his teeth in something he hopes passes for a grin. "I'm just browsing," he tells them, lifting the hand that holds the comb.

"Sir," the tallest one says, and Daniel laughs with delight at this appellation—to be called that while being thrown out of a shop is too much, too fantastic, the semantics too elastic to be believed. He should definitely do some research into this. "We need to ask you to leave."

"May I ask why?" Daniel says. He is keen to enter into and sustain this display of politeness-as-hostility.

That floors them. They exchange faltering glances; they lace and unlace their hands.

"I merely," he says, "wish to purchase this comb and then make a further perusal of your most interesting stock. Is that not what you philanthropic ladies are here for? To sell said stock to benefit the city's unfortunates?"

More exchanged glances. Shifting feet. The tallest lady, the one who called him sir, mutters something under her breath, then shuffles back to her position behind the till. Daniel is watching her progress, then contemplating an embroidered handkerchief folded on the counter next to her—familiar or not?—when he feels a hand on his arm.

"Did you find anything else of your mother's?"

Daniel looks down at the woman. She is, he would guess, older than his mother, in her late seventies or even early eighties. Whereas Teresa will never now see seventy. "How do you know about my mother?" he says to this woman, who mentions her so casually, so intimately, as if she knows him, knows them, knows all about it.

"You told me," the old lady in the glasses and string of beads says, a kind face she has, with rheumy eyes and cheeks that Daniel finds he would like to touch, slack and cushiony they would feel, he is sure, "about what your father did. When you were in here yesterday."

"I was in here yesterday?"

The lady nods. "And the day before. You come in every day, dear."

"I do?"

The lady smiles at him again, then nods toward the other woman at the till. "Don't mind her. You do what you have to do."

Teresa had been in the ground for three days when Daniel returned to the apartment to find that his father had cleared out everything that had belonged to her and taken it all to a thrift store. Her clothes, her jewelry, her books, her toiletries, her scarves, her gloves, her tins of toffee, even the cushion she liked to position behind her back as she read on the couch. Daniel had torn through the bedroom, the kitchen, the living room, searching for something, anything of hers, while his father had sat, arms folded, in a chair. If you think, his father said, when Daniel came to a standstill in front of him, that you can go off making a spectacle of yourself with your mother barely cold, you have another thing coming.

"What the fuck is wrong with you?" Daniel had screamed.

His father had leaped out of his chair. "My roof, my rules. I won't have that language here. It belongs in the gutter, along with the person who uttered it. Your sisters came and chose something to keep of your mother's, but you"—he jabbed Daniel in the chest—"you were off drinking yourself into oblivion, so you"—he jabbed him again—"get nothing."

Daniel had let out a mirthless laugh. "No, you're the one who gets nothing. Don't you see? You're a heartless bastard, always have been.

You kept her hobbled, financially and emotionally, and you can't even see where that leaves you, can you? You don't even recognize—"

His father had cuffed him then, twice, across the head, just as he always had done, behind the ear, and the noise inside his head was so familiar, so old—the hot, high pitch of ringing—that Daniel had wanted to laugh again. He hadn't, though. He had said, that is the last time you will ever hit me, and left, slamming the front door behind him. He hadn't been back since.

The thrift-store lady still has her hand on his arm. "It takes every-body in different ways."

Daniel stares down at her. "What does?"

"Grief." She shakes her head. "You never can tell how people will react. Remember that your dad is hurting too. He probably didn't mean to upset you."

Daniel is about to say, you don't know my dad, the man isn't capa-ble of feelings, when he is gripped by a sudden certainty that he will vomit. That rush of saliva, that heated pressure on the cranium, the heaving twist in the gut.

He pushes the lady aside—gently, he will hope later—and barges through the shop, through the racks of clothes that release the scent of a hundred empty wardrobes, past the books that have been read and reread or perhaps never picked up at all, past the rows of house-hold trinkets that were given in good faith or love or ill judgment, out through the door.

He is hit by a wall of icy air. Winter has come early in Brooklyn. The flat gray sky above him expresses a steady, peppering sleet. Daniel clutches his overcoat around himself, gulping at the air, steadying him-self against a streetlight.

He's going to puke, he can feel it coming. Whatever is in his stom-ach is going to make a reappearance, he knows it. What could it be anyway? No food, some whiskey maybe, or was there a vodka or two, from that place in Queens where he ended up last night? Whatever it is, it will not be pretty.

And, just as suddenly as it arrived, the urge is gone. It is not going to happen. Daniel screws up his eyes. He breathes deeply. He pushes himself upright. He is wondering what to do next, where to go—was there something he had planned today, something he had promised to somebody?—when he hears footsteps coming along behind him.

It is the purposeful tread of a woman. The stacked heel of a boot. Someone who has somewhere to be, someone pressed for time, someone who always knows what she is about.

The certainty that it is Nicola behind him is abrupt and powerful. Nicola, here, on this street in downtown Brooklyn, where he is standing in days-old clothes, a half bottle of whiskey in his pocket, a Baggie of dope and a hair comb that may or may not have belonged once to his mother, late of this parish, gripped in his hand.

Nicola has come. She is here. To save him, to forgive him, to take him into her arms, to enfold him within the drapes of her cloak.

Daniel turns. He swings himself around, heart pounding so hard that he's sure she will see it there in his chest, sure it will burst from him and lay itself at her feet.

But the woman is all wrong. She has hair spiked and stiff with gel, a fuzzy pink sweater, jeans, and hooped earrings, and Nicola would never wear such things, never. She isn't nearly as tall as she should be and her skin isn't clear and pale as milk, her eyes nowhere near large enough. She is all wrong. She gives him a strange look as she passes him, wrinkling her nose, curling her lip.

"You," Daniel hears himself roar, "you are all wrong. You know that?"

The woman whips her head around, eyes wide, then looks quickly away. She increases her pace in her heavy boots, the noise of which pierces Daniel through the chest in a way that feels entirely new and devastating, and then she breaks into a run.

"All wrong," he yells again, to her retreating back, to the cloud of pink emanating from her fuzzy sweater, to the way her strappy little shoulder bag bounces off her hip as she moves.

The faces of the thrift-store ladies float up toward the surface of the shopwindow, then recede.

I thought I saw you today.

The sentence cuts through his mind, like a scythe through grass. He puts a hand into his coat pocket and sifts through what he encounters there. The cold nub of a bottle top, some loose change, the Baggie, a subway token, half a shoelace, some curls of paper. He withdraws one of these and squints at it. Some kind of receipt—numbers in purplish ink, telling him that he spent exactly three dollars and fifty cents on something called sundries and received one dollar and fifty cents in change. Something is written across it in his handwriting: *The regret is crushing me. All I want to do is rewind time and do everything differently.*

He is composing a letter to Nicola. It is going to be a long letter and it is going to say everything he wants. Everything. Nothing will be left out. Which is why he must write these things down when they come to him, so that nothing is forgotten, so that he has them all there, when he finally comes to the moment and sits down, in front of some paper—beautiful paper it will be, he is going to buy some at a good stationery store, she appreciates that kind of thing—with a proper pen to write the whole thing from start to finish.

He turns over the piece of paper about crushing regret and, fishing for a pencil stub in his other pocket, starts to write *I thought I saw you today,* leaning on the streetlight. Lucky, he is thinking, that it's a bit of pencil he has on him because a pen wouldn't work at this angle, on this surface.

He is thinking about the word *angle* and how close it is to *angel* and he has gotten as far as the downstroke of *y* in "you" when he hears the gulp of a police siren, a block or so away. There it is again. The stuttering wail, the city's recurring riff. Daniel looks one way and sees the faces of the thrift-store ladies, still watching him. He looks the other, sees an alleyway, a befouled gap between buildings, and slips into it. He doesn't run; he doesn't move quickly; he doesn't attract attention. It's just a sideways slide to remove himself from view.

Once in the alley, he picks up speed. He is moving parallel to the river now; he has always oriented himself in Brooklyn according to the East River. Past a clutch of Dumpsters, an old mattress, a leaking gutter. The flank of a marmalade cat flashes ahead, disappearing over a wall. He pockets the piece of paper and the pencil and, as he does so, he feels the spikes of the comb. Was that it? Did they call the cops because he forgot to pay twenty cents for a shitty plastic comb? Those witches. He will, though, go back there tomorrow and give them the money. Because not to do so would be bad karma. Because he needs to keep going to the shop, in case anything else of his mother's turns up. Because that is what his mother would have said he should do.

I was not in my right mind. The words come from a place deep within him. He is not thinking them. They are not words of a cerebral, conscious nature. *Such an act would never have come from my heart. You must know that.*

That's a good one, but he hasn't time now to stop and write it down. He will remember it. He will.

Daniel reemerges on a different street, one thick with people, walking up and down, to and fro, going in and out of shops, calling to their children, lugging bags over their shoulders, going about their daily business. They are wearing coats, hats, mittens. Daniel doesn't know how winter could have come on so fast. It seems no time at all since he was in England, and it was summertime, and he and Nicola drove into the countryside, taking a rug and their books, and they sat beside a bend in a river, and when the heat became too much, Daniel dived into the water, which was cool and green and slow moving. When he emerged his naked body was streaked with slime, which made Nicola burst out laughing, her cigarette trembling at the end of her fingers. How can it now be winter and he is here in Brooklyn and everything is different? Nicola, the river, the summer, England, his mother—all of them gone.

Daniel heads into the wind, away from the river. He has no idea where he is going, but there is some urgency about the way he is moving, so he is just going to trust his instincts, his interior compass. Maybe his body knows something he doesn't. Taxis and cars and buses power past. A man with a scraggly beard thrusts a leaflet into Daniel's hand, without making eye contact, already turning away. Daniel passes a shop with a bank of pomegranates under a plastic sheet and he recalls his mother slicing one open in their kitchen. Him standing at her hip, just able to see over the counter's edge, the fruit's pale, lacquered skincase giving way to a jeweled interior—the scarlet, wet shock of it. Did she tell him then the story of the girl who ate six of those red seeds—such duality in them, that opulent, bursting flesh and that mean, hard little kernel—and was condemned to live underground for half her life, shackled to the king of the underworld?

Daniel thinks of wet, cloying earth, a vertical tunnel into the ground, a place sealed up, a place of no return. Wasn't it the mother who went down to the underworld to save her daughter, who took on the evil king, who ensured her child's safety for at least half the year? He shudders, groping again in his pockets, seeking something—the paper, the pencil, the comb, the bottle. No, not the bottle. Or, maybe, yes: the bottle.

He unscrews the cap, tilts it into his mouth, and the whiskey hits the back of his throat with a fiery fist. He swallows and waits for the drink to sink down through him, outlining his digestive tract, reassuring him of his physical presence, his continuing life.

An amount of time later—he isn't sure exactly how much—Daniel is walking in through the gates of the cemetery. He comes here at least once a day. It gives things an aim, a kind of routine. He makes his way along the graveled path, letting his eye rest on the hundreds and hundreds of gravestones, watching the way they pull themselves into diagonal columns as he passes, then unpeel themselves, then line up again. An endless process of arrangement and disarrangement.

He turns a corner, then another. He is aware of someone standing near his mother's grave, head bowed, hat held to chest, in the time-honored position decreed in cemeteries—Daniel has no idea why. They're all dead, he wants to shout to this man, in his camel coat, with his slickly combed silver hair. They can't see if you've got your hat off or not and, frankly, even if they could, do you think they would care?

He stumbles as he ascends the grassy slope, his feet tangling under him, his hand coming into contact with the wet grass, and he lets out a volley of curses—quietly, he believes, accidentally. The man turns and, for a moment, it looks to Daniel as though he has been standing, head bowed, at his mother's grave.

Daniel looks at him as he struggles upright. Does he know him? He doesn't think so. He examines the camel coat, the hat, fitted now back on the man's head, the trousers with perfect creases down their centers. There is nothing familiar about him at all.

Daniel moves in a possessive rush toward Teresa's grave. Who is this person who dares to stand there, looking down at his mother's grave, this person whom Daniel has never met? The man with the combed silver hair steps sideways, drawing on a pair of leather gloves.

He gives Daniel a sidelong glance, and Daniel can feel him, in his turn, taking in Daniel's stained coat, with the torn hem, his scuffed boots, the whiskey bottle, which for some reason he still has clutched in his hand, the general air of someone unkempt, unwashed, unslept.

My mother died, Daniel wants to say, OK? It wasn't my fault, it wasn't anyone's fault, but I'm having trouble keeping my head above water.

The man raises his eyes and, for a moment, their gazes lock, and it is not a look of opprobrium or disapproval or disgust, as Daniel might have expected. Daniel feels the lack of these judgments, feels it in the sudden shame of his appearance, the whiskey bottle. They seem to burn him, these failings. The man with the silver hair looks at Daniel with nothing but compassion. It is beatific, his gaze, ominiscient, almost priestlike. It is as if this man knows him, to his very core, knows every-thing about him. What else do you know about me? Daniel wants to blurt out, in fear, in fascination. What else do you see? But the gaze bestows understanding, absolution, and forgiveness, all at once. Daniel has not been looked at like that for what seems a long time, in such a way that says, you poor child, and also, all will be well. He hasn't, he realizes, been looked at like that since his mother passed away.

And then it is over, as quickly as it began. The man gives him a nod and moves off, his feet shushing through the grass. Daniel has an urge to run after him, to take him by the arm and say, who are you, what were you to my mother? But he doesn't. He leans, catching his breath, on her gravestone, that slab of blackish marble with letters cut into it that lies at a perpendicular angle to the length of her body, laid out as it is beneath his feet. Beloved wife and mother.

There is a sudden *dink* in his ear canal, followed by a *shurr-shurr.* It's the thrift-shop tinnitus. Daniel shakes his head, bangs his palm against his ear, but it comes again: *dink-dink-shurr.*

He pushes himself away from the gravestone—metallically cold today—and, stepping around where he estimates his mother's head and shoulders are, he makes off across the cemetery. He moves with speed and purpose now, along the gravel path, through the gates, just as the silver-haired man did, turning left along the road.

He has to go several blocks before he finds a working phone, one that hasn't had its cord cut, its mechanisms slashed free. This booth no longer has a door, but the phone itself appears to be fine. He snatches up the receiver, as if at any moment it might vanish from sight, leaning back to hurl the empty whiskey bottle into a trash can, followed by the dope, some tissues, a ring pull from a can. The pieces of paper with writing on them he carefully smooths and flattens with his palm and lays them out next to the phone, where he can see them. Then he slots in quarter after quarter. He has no idea how much money will be chewed up by a phone call to England, but he imagines it won't be cheap.

No matter. Just a short call will do. He is going to set a course for himself, the right course, the only course. His fingers fly over the buttons—he knows her number, of course, by heart, knows to add the international code, knows how to route this piece of electronic trickery so that any minute now the phone will ring on the wall in Nicola's house and they will be connected, he and she, and he will say all the things he wants to say. He will say: I can't be without you. He will say: Come. He will say: I'm sorry, I'm sorry, I'm sorry.

He hears the faint ringing and he is picturing the phone, the way it hangs next to the fridge, picturing Nicola crossing her hallway from her study, stretching out her arm and—

"Hello?"

It's a man's voice. Terse yet hesitant. Daniel listens for a moment, confounded. The man says it again: "Hello? Is there anybody there?"

Daniel replaces the receiver. Confusion buzzes through him as his coins are shucked and swallowed by the machine. He knows that voice. It was Todd. But what was Todd doing answering Nicola's phone? Why is Todd in Nicola's house?

Daniel stands for a moment, thinking. He must have misdialed. That was it. He must have called Todd's house by mistake, dialed that number, rather than Nicola's. He will call again, make sure he's getting the right number, then maybe he'll call Todd, to explain.

He's collecting his change, slotting it back into the machine and pressing down the numbers, when he hears a car door slam, some footsteps, then someone seizes him by both arms.

"Hey," he protests as the coins fall from his fingers. He twists in the person's grasp, catching a flash of uniform, a peaked cap. Then another cop is upon him and they have him spread-eagled against the roof of their car, his face jammed into its paintwork. He can see his curls of paper, with the things he needed to tell Nicola, scuttering all over the sidewalk. He can see the telephone receiver dangling loose in the breeze, see the tiny holes where, even now, Nicola's voice might be heard, might be answering, might be speaking. He is struggling, of course, because who wouldn't in his situation? But the cop has him in such a hold that he can't move, can't reach out and lift the phone to his ear and say, yes, here I am.

At the police station, he is allowed one call and he makes another attempt to reach Nicola, but the duty sergeant laughs at him, a scraping, jeering sound, and whips the phone out of his hand. You want to make long-distance calls, he says, you do it on your own dime.

It is several hours before he is brought up to the front desk and he is hoping against hope that it will be his youngest sister who has come to collect him. She is the most forgiving, the one least likely to tell their father that he was hauled off the street for stealing from a thrift store. But it's not her. His eldest sister is standing at the desk, leaning over to sign something the sergeant is holding. She has on a jacket over her pajamas, her face is drawn and creased, and Daniel feels bad because he knows she'll have to be up early to get her kids off to school.

As he walks toward her, she glances at him, then looks away, shoving her hands deep into her pockets. "Get in the car, Danny," is all she says.

When All the Tiny Lights
Begin to Be Extinguished

DANIEL

Paris, 2010

Here's a little-known fact about my wife: she is one of those people to whom it is impossible to lie. I don't know how she does it. She is able to sniff out an untruth, a vacillation, a cover-up, a white lie, a whopper, at twenty paces. The kids try it, I try it, on occasion, and we give up, defeated, every time: it never works. She has this way of staring at you, her eyes stretched and unblinking, while not saying anything at all, until you crack, until you cry out, OK, OK, it wasn't like that at all, I made it up.

Is it a form of telepathy? I have asked myself, never for a moment putting such abilities past her, or is it because she is herself so much practiced in the art that she knows each trick of the trade, as it were? We are, after all, dealing here with a woman who has more skeletons than the average graveyard in her closet.

So, with this ability of hers at the front of my mind, I am not, shall we say, in my most relaxed state as I get myself back down the hill, through all the gates, and off again to the airport, in slightly weary pursuit.

And where am I off to this time? Paris. Where else would Claudette run to?

My wife rarely travels—it is a major trauma for her to leave the valley, let alone Donegal—but she will go to Paris two or three times a year. She seems to feel an umbilical pull to the city of her birth. There is also an imperviousness, a self-containment, an incuriosity in the French national character that means she is not stared at, wondered about from afar. She can don a pair of sunglasses, a hat, and move around the city unbothered.

Also, I reasoned to myself as I checked my passport, swapped my travel-soiled clothes for clean ones, where else would you go? Whose company would you seek out if you were mad at your husband? The astringent Pascaline Lefevre, *naturellement.*

Winter is the best season to see Paris, I've always thought, when the pavements are sheer with frost, when the sun is low in the sky, when the Seine is swollen and brown, twisting fibrously beneath the bridges. In summer, to be frank, there are just too many people, too many of my goddamn compatriots, jostling around to get themselves photographed with some national monument or other in the background. But I'll take spring, when the pollarded fists of the plane trees are beginning to show green.

So I play my part. I get myself on a plane, for a criminal amount of money. On the road again. I touch down in Charles de Gaulle after midnight and decide that to announce myself at Pascaline's at that hour wouldn't exactly get me off on the right foot, so I get a taxi to a street where I know there is a string of hotels. I get a room, I take a shower, I fall into the bed, and I sleep, I sleep, I sleep, until I'm woken by some delivery vans banging shut their doors, the drivers swapping Gallic insults, and I realize I passed out for the whole night, that it's the next day already.

I call Pascaline's apartment and Claudette answers the phone and I ask her to come and meet me and, although she tells me to go fuck myself and that she'd rather chew off her own arm than be at what she terms my "beck and call," I hang up secure in the knowledge that I'll be seeing her—all limbs intact—and my children in the next few hours. The key to life with Claudette is knowing that her default setting is overreaction and outrage. If cornered, she will become livid. It's only when she calms down that she can think clearly and form an appropriate response. It's just a matter of sitting it out, waiting for the storm to pass. I've always figured that my predecessor, Timou, must never have worked this one out.

By lunchtime, I am waiting, as arranged, on the green-painted chairs that line the children's boating pond in the Jardin du Luxembourg. Will she come? Have I wasted my time? What will I do and where will I go if she doesn't turn up?

Kids lean on the circular wall of the pond, poking at their sailboats with sticks, watched over by tired *mamans* or authoritarian *grandmères*. I turn up my face toward the sun and bury my gloveless hands in the pockets of my overcoat. The ground is gritty beneath my feet. A couple of businessmen hurry past, pecking with their fingers at their phones, a walker with three ridiculous fluffy mammals that don't, in all conscience, deserve the appellation "dog." What is it with the Parisians and their miniature yappy canines? I've never understood it: they exercise such impeccable, flawless taste in all other areas but this.

Pigeons stalk and croon under the legs of the scattered chairs, searching for crumbs. I am rehearsing my lines, running through approaches in my head: an old girlfriend, a long time ago, something happened, I made a mistake, a—what is the phrase she uses with the children when they have done something wrong?—a choice, I made a poor choice. I have to get this right, I am telling myself. You get one shot and one shot only with Claudette.

A keen, chill breeze whips past and I am just watching the clouds scudding over me when my head turns.

I've heard them before I've seen them. Rounding the corner past the *palais* and the watery folly, where you can feed the ducks with a backdrop worthy of a gothic novel, or pull faces at the guards in their officious little uniforms, are my children. Some of my children.

Ari is pushing Calvin in his stroller, at a speed neither his mother nor I would permit. They veer and race along the path, Ari shouting or singing "La Marseillaise" at the top of his voice, Calvin emitting those deep baby belly laughs. Marithe is cantering beside them and appears to be whipping her big brother around the legs with a stick. My children, my children.

I stand and wave, like the idiot I am, yelling in my large American voice. Several people around me reel back in horror, but I don't care.

That I can see no sign of their mother doesn't dent my joy. I jump up and down on the spot, still waving, for Ari and I have a long tradition, a stupid joke, that if we see each other from far off, we will wave theatrically and expansively until we are right up close, pretending that we haven't grasped that the other person has seen us.

Ari is pushing the stroller so can't wave back, but Marithe takes up the family tradition and waves and waves, running toward me until she's about a foot away. Then she stops. She starts rooting around her pocket, as if she's forgotten I'm there. I don't care. I sweep her up and throw her into the air.

"Daddy, don't," she's saying. "I've got something to show you."

Ari and Calvin arrive. Ari is still singing, Calvin is shouting, "Bap, bap, bap!" over and over again. I embrace Ari with the hand that isn't engaged in holding Marithe; he ruffles my hair and pinches my cheek in the manner of an indulgent grandparent; I bend down to Calvin who shouts "Bap!" right in my ear and socks me in the jaw with a kick. Marithe is holding out her hand to me, in the palm of which is what is possibly a worm or perhaps an elastic band covered with mud and saying it's her friend and she loves it more than anything in the world, apart from Maman. I'm not taking this the wrong way when Marithe's shoe catches me painfully in the upper leg and I put her down.

"Where have you been, Daddy?" she says, accusingly, fixing me with a stare disconcertingly like one of her mother's. She's wearing overalls I've never seen before, decorated with embroidered rabbits, the tails of which are something that looks like sheep's wool. Claudette must have made them while I was away.

"Where have I been?" I repeat. "Everywhere. Over there and over here and then over that way." I pick her up again because I just need to, but she struggles to get free. "Did you know that, at one time, if Ari had sung that song here in Paris, he could have had his head chopped off?"

"Don't be silly, Daddy," Marithe says severely. "Nobody could chop off Ari's head. He's too tall."

She stalks off toward the boating pond, disgusted by my attempt at a history lesson.

"So," I say, looking back at my stepson, "where's your mother?"

Ari seats himself on one of the green chairs and gets something out of his pocket. "She's coming," he says. "She went back to change her shoes."

I sit down beside him. "And, er, what kind of mood is she in?"

Ari shakes his head. "Oh, boy."

"What do you mean?" I try to peer into his face, try to glean something of his mother's frame of mind from it, and what I see does nothing to ease the dart of fear that is now piercing my chest. Ari avoids my eye, gets up to fetch something from the hood of the stroller.

When he sits down again, he says, "You, my friend, are in so much trouble."

I swallow but my throat feels dry. "Really?"

Ari looks at me. "Oh, yes."

"No, come on, tell me what she said. Did she—" I stop. It has hit me that Ari is rolling a cigarette. To smoke, right here in front of me, involving the inhalation of carcinogens and addictive chemicals. "Hey!" I say, reaching for the tobacco tin, one of mine, I'm sure. "What the hell do you think you're doing?"

"Rolling a cigarette," my teenage stepson says, with infinite calm.

"You can't smoke! You're sixteen years old, for Chrissake. Are you crazy? Give me that."

Unperturbed, Ari turns away, out of my reach, strikes a match, inhales, and the craving for a drag of what he's got uncurls in my gut.

"You shouldn't be smoking." I make one last feeble stab at protest, before I say, "OK, let me have one and I won't tell your mother."

Ari blows out a ring of smoke, making a scoffing noise that means, you think she doesn't know?

I open the tin, roll myself one, light it, and inhale, a process that takes about two seconds. I've had a lot of practice. Marithe comes up to ask for some euros for a boat, which I give her. I turn Calvin around so he can watch his sister, and Ari and I sit side by side, smoking together.

A group of park workers in raincoats and waders arrive and start dipping large fishing nets into the pond. I don't know what they're looking for, but Marithe abandons her newly rented sailboat and goes over to watch. She's always loved a bit of filth: algae, mud, manure, anything will do. Beside me, Ari is removing his chestnut-leather gloves and laying them one by one across his leg. I've got to hand it to him: Ari is one stylish boy. I'm not sure quite how this happened: his mother scrubs up well, as we know, but most of the time she dresses like a maniac. The house looks like a garage sale crossed with the bottom of a birdcage and I struggle along sartorially. Somehow, from this messy brew, this tall, elegant child emerged, looking like a model for avant-garde tailoring. I sometimes wonder if it's his Scandinavian genes coming through: that pared-down aesthetic of his, the clean lines of him.

If there has been one bone of contention in my marriage with Claudette, it's that Ari has no contact with his father. It's against nature, it's wrong, and, unsurprisingly, it doesn't sit easily with me. The boy has a father, living and breathing, in Stockholm, and he doesn't see him. I've had this out with Claudette, time and time again, but she always says the same thing: He has no interest in Ari and we have to protect Ari from that.

You see, Claudette will cry, sitting up in bed, he knows that if he wants to see Ari all he has to do is get in touch with Lucas. He knows that. He'll get in touch when he's ready and apparently he isn't ready yet . . . I will usually interrupt at this point to say, but he ought to be given another chance, another opportunity, I don't think he'd give you away but he might want to see his son, he might just need us to reach out to him, and also Ari might want it but be afraid to suggest it.

Claudette won't be moved, and the few times I've approached Ari with the idea he has smiled his enigmatic smile and shaken his head.

It's nothing to do with you, Claudette says, if I raise the subject, and I have to admit she's mostly right. Drop it, she tells me. And so I do. Until the next time I can't keep it in.

"So," Ari says to me now, as we sit in the Jardin du Luxembourg, "what did you do?"

"What?" I say, startled. "Nothing."

"Yeah, right," Ari says. "That's why . . . that's why . . ." The utterance nose-dives off a cliff. Ari shakes back his bangs, passes his cigarette into the opposite hand, suddenly, childlike again. We both know his speech has closed up on him, like a trap.

"Tap it out," I murmur, keeping my eyes on the pond, on Marithe, who just might decide to vault over the wall and into the pond, if history is anything to go by. When Ari was a kid, I'd offer him my palm to use as a drum, a beating board, something to take it all out on. He would smack my hand with his fist, often painfully hard, until he could gain a rhythm that loosened the words so they could make their way out from wherever they'd been trapped. "Come on," I proffer my palm, for old times' sake. "Tap it out."

Ari ignores my hand. I see his ankle jiggling up and down and, in a moment or two, he's able to go on. "That's why we're in Paris, that's why Claudette is clearing out the cupboards—"

"Uh-oh," I say.

"Are you seeing someone else?"

"Ari," I say, hurt, "I would never—"

"That's what she thinks."

"I know she does. But she couldn't be more wrong. You have to believe me. It's just . . . it's hard to explain."

"Well," Ari stands, crushing his cigarette under his boot, "you'd better start trying because here she comes now."

Claudette is bearing down on us in a Paris park: hair tucked up into a felt hat with a wide brim, white-framed sunglasses with peaked corners, a silk kimono jacket. She carries some kind of tortoiseshell-clasped bag. I smile, despite everything. This is her idea of a disguise, her interpretation of incognito. She has no idea how startling, how eccentric, she appears. People see her, look, then look again, and it's hard to tell if they half recognize her or if they just need to get another look at the mad lady in the insane clothes.

I stand, I watch her, my wife, love of my life, as she comes toward me. I open my arms, I step toward her. Here she is, my beloved, my heart.

"Don't fucking kiss me," she says, serving me a blow in the center of my chest.

Ari chooses this moment to call to Marithe. His mother says something, fast, to him in French. Ari shrugs, says something back, and I curse myself, not for the first time, for not learning their secret language.

"Um," I say, "English, please?"

Claudette rounds on me. "You!" she cries. "You don't get to say what language we speak, we will speak in any way we bloody well like. You don't get to make any sort of demand around here at all. Understand?"

"Yes," I say meekly, thinking at the same time that I can tell she's been with her mother. She's been discussing me with Pascaline, who's never really liked me, who takes any opportunity to fill Claudette with all kinds of anti-male, anti-American, anti-Daniel propaganda. Claudette gets a certain look in her eye when she's been engaged in a mother-daughter marital dissection. It happens every time. It only takes me, what, a day or two to win her back.

Ari swivels the stroller toward the playground in the trees. He looks at me and winks. *"Bonne chance,"* he says.

That, I understand.

"Hey," I say to his back, the thought only occurring to me now, "how come you're not in school?" I turn to his mother. "How come he's not in school?"

Claudette removes her sunglasses, finds it too bright, replaces them. "Well, that would be because I signed him out."

"To come here?"

"To come here."

"Claude," I say, in a measured tone, "that's not a great idea. It's only a matter of weeks until—"

"Listen," and the glasses come off again, used this time to stab emphasis into each word she utters, "I will sign my son out of his school if and when I want to, without permission from his part-time so-called stepfather."

I sigh. "OK," I say. I sit myself down in a chair. "Maybe we should try to talk this out like adults."

My wife chooses that moment to turn her back on me and walk away, which I take as my cue to follow her.

· · ·

I catch up with her on a path winding under the gnarled, leafless branches of plane trees. We stand there together and I tell her everything.

Almost everything.

The other woman, for my sins, I leave out.

I tell her about hearing that radio program, my friendship with Todd, my relationship with Nicola, the bleak afternoon in a London clinic, the wedding party, the state of her, me taking off, the scramble to the airport, the return to Brooklyn, the letter I wrote and how I didn't hear anything back from her, how this broke my heart, how I schooled myself to discard my love for her, to dig it out of me, how I was so consumed, as if by fire, by the loss of my mother, the one person—until Claudette—who loved me with a ferocity so unquestioning, so complete, that after it had gone I felt unmoored, insubstantial, as if I myself had ceased to exist. Not, as I said to Claudette as we stood there, that this is any excuse. A girl died. And it was my fault.

It would return to me, every now and again, the sight of her there, lying on the ground in the cold air of the morning, the way Todd didn't look at me when he said: She's fine, go, Daniel, run. I carried the image within me, like a virus dormant in the bloodstream, and it would flare up at odd moments. I might be working, cooking, eating, driving, teaching, and I would suddenly be distracted by a flash of forest, a vision of the loch, firelight through trees. I would push it from me, tell myself that the woman had rejected me, hadn't wanted me, had disregarded my letter. I couldn't let any other interpretation in, you see. I couldn't let the possibility that I was at fault, that I had done something so wrong, intrude into the life I had found, the life I had chosen that day at the crossroads. I inoculated myself against all of it by marrying Claudette, by moving to Ireland, by having kids with her—or I'd thought I had. I'd thought I was safe from the fever, the spread of it. I'd thought I had it contained, thought I'd be able to protect them from it; I'd thought I could keep it from them, from our door. The mind is a powerful, persuasive tool: we all know that.

Claudette, love of my life, mother of my children, keeper of my house, listens. She turns her face, obscured by her ridiculous sunglasses, toward me. She shifts her tortoiseshell-handled bag from one arm to the other. When I have finished, she says nothing. She stands before me, the lenses of her sunglasses giving me back a doubled miniaturized, blackened version of myself. I have no idea, at this point, which way she will go, what will happen next. I don't think I breathe.

She murmurs my name, Daniel, almost to herself, and she lifts her arms, she puts them around me, and she holds me to her, in the middle of a path.

My relief at her touch verges on indescribable. I don't think our language contains a word with sufficient largesse or capacity to express the euphoria I feel as I bury my face in her hair, as I dive inside her coat and press her form to mine. What redemption there is in being loved: we are always our best selves when loved by another. Nothing can replace this.

"What a terrible story," she is saying. "Daniel, I can't believe you never told me that before. You didn't need to keep it to yourself."

"Well," I mumble into her coat collar, "it's never been something that I—"

"That poor girl," she exclaims, pulling away, her face creased with distress. "She died how long after you left?"

"A few months," I say. "Five, I think Todd said."

"And she'd been ill before, with anorexia?"

"Yes. When she was younger. She seemed fully recovered when I met her. I mean, you would never have known."

Claudette looks at me, her head to one side. "What I don't understand," she says, pushing her hands up inside their opposite sleeves, "is why you should feel such guilt, why it's thrown you into such crisis."

"Um," I say, casting my eyes up at the plane trees, "I don't know."

"I mean, you went back to the States because your mother was dying. It wasn't as if you were running away for nothing. Was it?"

"I guess."

"But you said"—Claudette frowns, perplexed—"it was your fault. Why? Why would you feel that? You wrote a letter. You tried. It wasn't your fault she never received it."

"No."

"It makes no sense that you should feel responsible, when you . . ."

Claudette trails away. She looks at me for a long moment. This woman knows me better than anyone else in the world. She can read every expression, every inflection, of my face.

"You and she had split up before you went away?"

"Uh-huh."

"After the abortion?"

"Yeah."

"Why?"

My mouth feels suddenly dry and I can't look her in the eye as I shrug. "It was a long time ago. I don't really . . ."

"You must remember."

I look about wildly, to find something that might distract her off this course. I take her arm. "Look," I say, "how about we walk to that bandstand?"

She allows me to fold my arm about her shoulders and we walk together along the path, but she cannot let this go. "Was it because of the abortion? Because you were angry she went ahead with it?" She steps to one side so that my arm falls away. She turns to face me. "Or was it something else?"

I sigh. I rub my palm against several days' worth of stubble. "Claude—"

"Daniel," she interrupts me, "why do I get the feeling that there is something about this you're not telling me?"

I see that evasion is useless, so I give her the missing piece of the jigsaw. What other choice do I have? I come clean about the other girl, the teacher-training student, about Nicola finding us the next morning. And then I brace myself for the onslaught because Claudette has never taken this kind of thing lightly.

But she doesn't say anything. She turns and walks up the steps of the bandstand, which is deserted, filled only with swirling leaves.

We sit on a bench. I am conscious of the wheels of Claudette's mind turning, forming connections, assumptions, slotting things into their places.

"So what you're saying, Daniel," she speaks slowly, "is that you took your girlfriend to get an abortion and then you came back home and slept with someone else?"

I grimace. I have never heard myself presented to myself in such a way. "Well . . . "

"Straightaway?" she persists. "The same night?"

I give something that is halfway between a nod and a shrug. "It might have been the following night. I don't remember exactly."

"That was your response to the termination of your girlfriend's pregnancy?"

"Listen, I was"—I scramble for words—"very young and . . . stupid and—"

"Twenty-four's not that young," she mutters.

She gets up, crosses to the other side of the bandstand, and leans on the railing, her back to me. I grip the bench in something close to terror, wanting to close my eyes but not being able to, wondering, as she stands there, looking toward the fountain, if I am witnessing the beginning of the end, if this is it, the tipping point we all dread. Am I living through the moment when all the tiny lights begin to be extinguished, when her love for me begins to falter, shrink, lose ground? I have been through the demise of enough relationships to know such moments arise, but would I know how to recognize it when it came? Is this it? What have I done?

I say her name—Claudette, Claudette—and my voice comes out as a hoarse, desperate murmur. She bows her head; she doesn't turn around.

It is possible, I think as I sit there on the cold wood of the bandstand bench, to see ailing marriages as brains that have undergone a stroke. Certain connections short-circuit, abilities are lost, cognition suffers, a thousand neural pathways close down forever. Some strokes are massive, seminal, unignorable; others imperceptible. I'm told it's perfectly possible to suffer one and not realize it until much later.

I won't have it. I tell myself this. Such things only happen if you let them. It is feasible, surely, to head them off at the pass.

I leap to my feet, I cross the bandstand in a few strides, I take hold of her from behind. She turns around inside my arms and I see that she will speak and, for a moment, I think she's about to ask me something else, some other piercing, reducing question, and I'm quailing because it isn't going to be a question to relish.

But she doesn't. Claudette is nothing if not unpredictable.

"I don't know what to say to you," she says, looking up at me, and her voice expresses a certain surprise, as if the sensation is entirely new to her.

No, I want to cry out, please know what to say to me, you always do.

"It's hard to believe," she says, with a devastating emphasis, "not only that you could do something like that but also that you never told me. You've never spoken of it, or her. You've carried this around inside you all this time. And you went running off like that because—"

"I didn't go running off," I cut in, tightening my hold on her. "I'm here. I'm right here."

"—you suddenly didn't know how to handle the guilt." She looks at me, her face more puzzled than shocked. "I don't know what to say," she says again.

Claudette walks away. She leaves. But I won't let her. She steps down from the bandstand in one jump and I'm right there with her. We make our way through the trees and I take her hand in mine, trying to communicate by touch alone that this is the way things are and will be, that we are together, that we are still the people we have always been.

As we emerge from the trees, I am thinking I will say something to this effect, to seal up or cauterize that moment in the bandstand, but suddenly the children are upon us and they are hungry, they are tired, they are wondering what is next on our Parisian itinerary and can they have a snack, a cake, a ride on the Métro, the loan of a phone, a box for their pet worm.

Down the Line

NICOLA AND DANIEL

London, 1986

Daniel sits opposite Nicola in a café. Separating her from him is a precarious obstacle course of teapots, milk jugs, cups, saucers, sugar bowls, spoons, napkins, teetering arrangements of sandwiches and scones, a vase in which a single plastic carnation slumps, exhausted, to one side.

He wants nothing more than to reach out and take her hand. She has painted her nails a purplish black, the color of the darkest grapes. He would like to touch that lacquer, tap his own nail against it, to press her fingers in his, to make her look at him, to say, is this what you want, are you sure, should we be doing this, it's not too late to change our minds.

Nicola has her face turned away from him, her chin propped in her palm. Her grape-skin nails click against the table in a descending rhythm. Her hair conceals one eye: how she stands it, Daniel has no idea. He couldn't bear it, would constantly shake it off his forehead, but it never seems to bother her.

"So how was the interview?" Daniel asks, and his voice feels strange in his mouth, labored, as if he hasn't spoken in a long while.

Nicola pulls her gaze away from the building across the street, where she has been watching a woman with a garbage bag circling an office, reaching out to empty each and every wastepaper basket. Not a single person looks up at her as she does this. Nicola allows herself to focus on the man opposite her.

Daniel is looking at her, a searching expression on his face. He wants to know something but she isn't sure what it is. Is she OK? Are they OK? Does she want milk with her tea, butter with her scone, jam with her butter? Any of the above could be spooling through his mind. Sometimes she thinks she can see the workings of Daniel's mind as if they were her own; other times he feels as alien to her as another species.

"The interview?" she repeats.

She has almost forgotten: she was at the BBC this morning, on live radio, a pair of earphones clipped over her head, her lips close to a preposterously large green-headed microphone, answering questions about gender bias in academia which were being filtered to her from somewhere, while people behind a glass screen adjusted dials and switches, transmitting her words into the radios of Britain.

It was only half an hour ago, but it feels as though it was something that took place in her distant past or possibly to someone else.

It had been her idea to pair these two activities on one day: the interview, which had been in her diary for weeks, and the abortion, which has been a recent and unexpected addition to her schedule. She is wondering now at the wisdom of this. She had not wanted to have what her GP delicately referred to as "the procedure" in the town where she worked and lived. She might bump into people she knew in the waiting room, her students, perhaps; the attending surgeon would probably be someone she studied with; it was all too close for comfort. This was not something she wanted ever to refer to or discuss again. So she had booked herself into a clinic in London, making the appointment just after her interview. It had seemed the obvious thing to do. She recalls feeling a rush of organizational pleasure as she noted it in her diary, the two appointments listed there together, before remembering exactly what the second would entail.

Daniel, of course, said he would come with her because that was the kind of man he was, she had discovered. When he had first come onto her radar, raising his hand to ask questions at the end of her seminars, appearing at her lectures, she had dismissed him as another introspective man-child. But she had, she is willing to admit, read him all wrong. There was something that set apart a man who had grown up among women—a strong mother and a clutch of sisters, in Daniel's case—from a man who hadn't. Men of this ilk were, in Nicola's opinion, much more evolved and therefore made much better lovers.

He had gone to a gallery while she did her interview. What he will do during her next appointment, she has no idea. She hasn't asked.

"It was fine," Nicola says. "It was all done down the line, which isn't my favorite way of doing it but, as the interviewee, one isn't really given the choice."

She sees, as she speaks, that Daniel doesn't know what "down the line" means. She also sees that he isn't going to ask for clarification.

"Hmm," he says, "good. When's it going out?"

He takes a sandwich from the plate between them and crams it whole into his mouth. Nicola watches him as he masticates, this man, her lover, who has come from nowhere and assumed a position of residence in her life, who has inadvertently impregnated her. Mostly, the five years' seniority she has over him doesn't make itself felt; other times, she finds him surprisingly, touchingly youthful.

Did she, she wonders, forget to take one of those little sugar-coated pills? Did she miss out some crucial day? Did her chemically stalled ovary see its chance and let slip a minuscule gamete into her waiting, pillowy, elastic-sided pouch? How else could this have happened?

"It's gone," she says.

Daniel stops, midchew. "Huh?"

"It's gone," she repeats, then realizes he has grasped the wrong end of the stick. "The interview," she clarifies. "It was live. All done and dusted."

"Oh." His face clears. "That's a shame. I won't get to hear it now."

Nicola shrugs. "It's nothing you haven't heard me say before."

Daniel swallows, leans forward, and seizes the teapot by its curved handle. "Still," he says, "I'd have liked to listen. You want some tea?"

He is brandishing the spout at her.

"No," she says, covering her cup with her hand—this varnish, she sees, was a mistake for today, arterial crimson, the color of the dark insides of things—and, shaking her head, "I'm not supposed to. You know. Before the . . ." She is left circling her other hand in the air. She doesn't know which word to choose. "Abortion" is so blunt, so devastating, so violent a term, with its emphatic "-tion" suffix, too close to "aversion" and "emotion" and "violation." But she can't say "procedure," can she? Not to this man, who has based whole papers on ownership of expression, on the importance of squaring up to semantics, to using the most perspicuous and apt word for something. And "appointment" is just dodging the whole issue, hiding behind a generalized umbrella term.

"The . . . the . . ." She's still there, trapped in her sentence, still trying to force herself over the top, and Daniel comes to her aid.

He reaches out and takes the flailing hand, the hand that seeks a word for what she is unable to utter, for what she is about to do, the word that expresses the inexpressible. He plucks the hand from the air, he presses it between both of his. He has to move his chair to do so because the table is piled high with things, things Daniel has ordered, things she can't eat or drink because she must have nothing in her stomach, nothing in her system, before she has the anesthetic before the procedure, the abortion, the termination, the intervention, the surgery, the end.

He places his chair next to hers and holds her hand, tight, and when she places her head on top of their combined hands, he puts his lips to her temple, to where the hair meets the skin, and she loves him for that, she does; she feels this for perhaps the first time, at the same time as knowing that this is not the moment to say it, not here, not yet, not today. And when he says what he says—*Do you think we're doing the right thing?*—whispers this, into the whorls of her ear, where each syllable is sent in reverberation along the chain of bones that form her aural canal, a part of her, a small part of her, wants to answer, *No.* No, this is not the right thing. This is absolutely the wrong thing. We must not do this. We must, above all other things, walk out of this café and away from this street. We must not keep that appointment. We must join hands, you and I, and leave together, as we are, intact.

He has managed to say it.

"Do you think we're doing the right thing?"

He has said it softly, into her hair, as she is curled there, on the table in front of him. So softly that, if she disagrees, if she's shocked or annoyed, he can pretend he wasn't serious, can laugh it off. He had to say it, had to let the words out, had to try to wedge open this discussion, as a burglar might force a door. For the idea of doing what they're about to do seems suddenly and glaringly monstrous to him, appalling, depraved. While she was at the BBC, he had found himself in a bookstore, found himself in the medical section, where he read, against all better judgment, a description of what they would do to her. Even now he cannot rid himself of certain words. "Probe" is one. "Products of conception" are some more. These words stick to the inside of his mind, like burrs.

Nicola doesn't say anything. He draws back to look at her. Her eyes are still closed, her cheek pressed to his hand. And Daniel feels his heart start to speed up as he sees what might be, just as it does before he needs to speak in public, or before he went into the confession box, a long time ago, when he still did such things. This is not, he has told himself, over and over again, a reluctance, a queasiness, born of that religion, the antediluvian set of values imposed on him by his parents, the rituals and murmurings, genuflections and icons, he was brought up with. It's not that which is causing him to feel as though he has wandered into a confusing and lethal maze, where at any point he might trip or stumble or bang headlong into a wall. It's not. It's something else. It's this: the curved fringe of lashes along Nicola's closed lids, the mapped waterways of veins in her neck, the way the cuticles lap over her fingernails. It's the precarious membrane between this, two people in a café, deciding their fate, and the beyond, the oblivion, the nothingness that they will all, in time, have to face.

"We don't have to, you know," he says. His voice is no longer a whisper. "We could keep it. You and I. We could."

Nicola is deep in a willed daze, her head on the table, but she hears this. *We could keep it.* She hears it and she receives it. She wants to smile but the effort that might require seems too great, especially if she is going to conserve her energy, her resources. That part of her, the small part that wants to answer, *Yes, we could,* seems to grow a little bit bigger.

She keeps her eyes closed. She keeps her cheek pressed to Daniel's hands.

There is also that other part of her. She knows this too. This Nicola is sitting at a distance, at the next table, perhaps. She is dressed in her favorite zipped boots, her legs crossed, her foot tapping up and down. The table is arranged with stacks of books and she is flicking through pages in her diary, a pen in one hand, a cigarette in the other. And what do you plan to live on? this Nicola is saying, without looking up. What about that sabbatical next year, the one in which you were planning to write your book? And does he have a salary? Does he have a visa? Isn't he only twenty-four?

But the small part of her feels the warmth of his chest as he curves himself around her, senses the drumbeat of his heart. She feels the ends of her hair catch in his stubble. This part of her murmurs to her as the other Nicola takes charge, makes her sit up, makes her push the chair back under the café table, pay the bill, walk through the streets, go through a pair of doors, give her name to a woman behind a reception desk, makes her nod to Daniel as he slumps into a chair, makes her gather up her things and walk down a corridor.

This part of her is still murmuring as she lies back on a gurney, as the nurse pulls a paper sheet over her, only it isn't a murmur now; it's a call, it's a shout. The other Nicola puts down her diary and lifts her head to listen.

"I think I've changed my mind," Nicola manages to say to the nurse.

"Don't you worry, dear," the nurse says, patting the sheet. "It will all be fine."

Nicola swivels her head to see a man—the anesthesiologist, the surgeon?—standing at her head, fiddling with something in a suspended bag.

"I've changed my mind," she says to him, struggling to sit upright.

"Count backward from ten," he tells her.

From the corners of the room, from under all the furniture, from the places where it has been waiting, the darkness swarms in.

And Who Are You?

NIALL

Donegal, 2013

Despite his fatigue, despite his thirst, Niall keeps on putting one foot in front of the other. The terrain is uneven and steep, the precipitation intense, but he is bound to continue. He has, for a number of reasons, gone too far with this escapade to turn back. No other option is available to him at this present time.

He pauses for a moment, listening to the tidal draw and suck of his breath. He checks the hand-drawn map once more, even though he doesn't need to. He has always had a photographic sense of such things, an ability to process the one-dimensional into the three.

He stands under the branches of a yew tree, which seems to hoard rainwater in its spiked, waxy leaves. He permits himself to register discomfort in the skin of his neck, his wrists, his left ankle: he recognizes the urge to scratch, to really tear into it; he breathes, he makes an attempt to push the urge from him, to stand apart from it. Just to be on the safe side, he bandaged himself—badly—on the arms and legs before he set off yesterday.

When Niall was a child, the ten-minute walk home from school began to take him twenty minutes, then thirty, then forty. He was arriving back more than an hour late before his mother noticed.

Why? she wanted to know. Why? his father asked him. Why? said his grandmother. Was he playing with other boys on the way? Was he going over to someone's house? Even at age six, it struck Niall as significant that neither of his parents asked him those questions. Other children had been noticeably absent in their theorizing.

The time of the walk crept above an hour, then to an hour and a half. After that, his father was waiting at the school gate for him: show me, he said, the route you walk. Niall showed him and they were home in ten minutes.

He didn't tell his father about the fear that had gripped him for some time, that when he got home, when he opened the door and stepped in over the threshold, his home might look completely different. The carpet in the hall, the one with the geometric pattern that linked up to itself in satisfying decimal blocks, wouldn't be there; the coatrack would be gone, the mirror with beveled edges, the yellow dish in which his parents put their car keys, their loose change, their pocket detritus. Something told him, every day, that while he was out at school his parents might have moved or vanished or been abducted and that an entirely different family would be living in his house. He would go into the kitchen and there would be another woman with a different face, a different voice, standing at the counter. Hello, she would say, and who are you?

Niall places the folded map carefully in his pocket, dabs the rain from his face with his bandaged hand, and continues up the track. There is, just as the map had led him to expect, a bend up ahead. He is expecting—hoping—to get some visual clue to his destination at that point.

The thought rises in him that the cure for that particular childhood anxiety was not his father's presence on the walk, not the cakes his mother would defrost for his return home—it was Phoebe.

On the track, Niall stops. There is the sensation that the ground might give way beneath him, the very bedrock collapsing, giving in to sudden erosion. The itch in his neck, in his left ankle, flares, crackles, sears, as if some internal thermostat has been turned up. He breathes once, twice. He bangs the ankle against the opposite foot, taps at his neck with the back of his hand.

Can he think about this? He finds himself constantly checking. Phoebe as a child is OK, he's found, but nothing beyond the age of around nine.

So it was Phoebe who cured him of the fear that his parents, his home, everything that was familiar and dear, would vanish. She was born around that time and her presence in the house somehow dispelled any threat of annihilation, of supernatural theft. He would get home and there she would be, on her play mat, her gaze wise and knowing, her fist outstretched to grip his hand, to hold him firm. And by the time she was up on her feet, she would run to meet him at the door. Make things with pipe cleaners was her take on solving life's worries, build me a fort of cardboard boxes, help me draw a unicorn, dig with me in the sandbox until we find treasure.

Niall rounds the corner and the rain suddenly clears. He takes in the sight of the house, which he'd known would be there. Is this the place? It is bigger than he was expecting, more substantial—more opulent, he supposes. He'd understood it was some kind of gatehouse, an outlying building of a Protestant mansion. This place looks like a small kind of mansion in its own right.

He proceeds, but with caution. It can't be the place. The map makes no hint at another house in the area, but that doesn't mean there isn't one. He is just about to get out the map again to have another look when a person appears from around the side of the barn and he knows instantly, without a shadow of doubt, that he is where he is meant to be.

The person is barefoot, an apple in one hand. She has a musical instrument—the name of which currently eludes Niall—slung on her front. She gnaws at the apple, once, twice, and flings it toward a tree trunk, where it shatters into white and falls to the ground. Then she sees Niall. She regards him for a moment, standing on one foot, wiping her mouth. "Are you lost?" she calls.

The piercing acuity of the question, coming from her mouth, floors Niall. He shakes his head. He doesn't, at this moment, trust himself to speak.

"The village is that way," she says, and points behind him, "the mountain over there." She sweeps her hand behind her.

"I know," he says. "I have a map."

"Oh," she says. "Good."

She puts the fingers of her right hand on the vertical keyboard of the musical instrument and presses a number of the keys, silently, squinting into the sudden sun to look at him.

That squint, that quizzical gaze, are so familiar to Niall it is as if someone is tunneling into his chest with a narrow flensing instrument. He has to look away, look down, shuffle his feet, quell the urge to scratch at his neck, his wrist. He never expected this.

He taps his bandaged fingers against his pulse point and, all of a sudden, the word comes to him: "accordion." The instrument is an accordion. He can see the page of an encyclopedia, summoned up from some distant afternoon, some hour between school and dinner, when he would lie on his stomach in his bedroom, committing the pages of information to memory, for want of anything better to do. Operated by a mechanism recalling that of bellows. Auditory changes effected by valves, opened and shut by the use of keys. Featured frequently in folk music of both Celtic and Eastern European origin.

Niall has to shake his head to rid himself of this shimmering textual visitation. "I'm ... ah ... ," he begins. How to say this? "I'm looking for Daniel Sullivan."

"That's my dad." The girl shrugs. "He doesn't live here anymore."

"Oh." Niall is taken aback. Some part of his mind is still running on accordions and supplies him helpfully with one further fact: often decorated with inlaid mother-of-pearl. He makes a supreme effort to return himself to the moment, to the here and now, to the fact that his father doesn't live where he'd said he did.

"I didn't know that," Niall manages to say.

"He lives in London, these days," the girl says, in her incongruous, singsong, almost-Irish accent, still regarding him with those unsettling eyes.

"OK. I'm sorry, I had no idea. He didn't tell me he'd ... moved. I would never have ... I'm sorry. Maybe I should ... ." Niall half turns, as if to go back, but stops, when he realizes there is nowhere to go.

"How do you know my dad?" the girl with the accordion is saying.

Niall gives in to the urge to scratch his wrist. He can't not do it—just for a moment, he has to, there's nothing to be done. "I ... er ..." He scratches, he drags his nails over the spot, and it is an exquisite, unbearable, temporary relief, he counts four, he counts five, he will stop at nine, yes, he will. "Well, he's my dad too."

Niall curses himself immediately. He shouldn't have said that. That was stupid. He hadn't meant to. If he hadn't been distracted by his skin, he would never have said it, he would never have given it away. He could have walked away from here unscathed, no harm done, back to the village, find a bed for the night, then back to the States, to his apartment, to everything over there.

"Really?" the girl says, standing straighter. "Wait a minute, are you ... what'shisname? From America?"

"Yes," Niall says. "I'm what'shisname from America." He has to take his nails away from his wrist, he has to, he knows this but he can't, he just can't. "Look," he says, "this feels like a mistake. I should have called first or written or something. Didn't mean to—"

"Wait here," she says, and runs into the house, the accordion wheezing as she goes.

Seconds later, the front door disgorges three or four dogs that surge around him, sniffing at his genital area and whining in high-pitched unison, and a Chinese girl in her teens. She is wearing a nightdress and possesses such startling, nascent beauty that Niall decides it's best not to look at her at all.

"Marithe says you're Daniel's son," she says, in an accent that is possibly English, Niall isn't sure. "Is that right?"

Niall always tells the truth: it's the way he's programmed. "Yes."

The young girl with the black hair and nightdress examines him carefully. He notices her taking in the backpack; he sees her eyes linger on the bandages around his wrist, one of which, he now sees, is showing a red bloom of blood. Her fine-hewn features carry the hint of suspicion, of disbelief, and who can blame her, really?

"I don't think we knew you were coming," she says, "did we? Daniel doesn't live here anymore."

A great weariness crests over Niall's head. "I know that now," he says, rubbing at his eyelid. "Marithe told me. Listen, I'm sorry for just turning up like this. Daniel told me . . . I thought . . . I just thought . . . I think I'm going to go. Sorry to disturb."

The girl seems uncertain how to proceed. She fiddles with the night-dress collar, clears her throat. "My aunt's not here at the moment. She's taken Calvin to the beach. She'll be back in an hour or so. If you . . . maybe give us your number? We could call you? Later on?"

Niall shakes his head. "Don't worry, er . . . sorry, you are . . . ?"

"Zhilan. I'm Marithe's cousin." She tilts her head, as if toward Britain. "From the other side of the family."

"I'll get in touch with my dad some other way. It was a—a spur-of-the-moment thing and . . . well, I'll take off."

He starts to back away. The dogs form a circle around him, as if to escort him from the property.

"He looks a bit . . . ," Zhilan murmurs, over her shoulder, and from behind her steps out the girl, Marithe, this time minus her accordion, and her reappearance shocks Niall all over again, like an electrode applied to a temple, shocks him to his marrow: the length of red-gold hair over the shoulder, the milk-white skin, those wide-spaced eyes, the angle of the nose. It is joyful and exhilarating and excruciating to look at this girl, all at once. It feels like the thing he most wants and the thing he is least able to bear.

He thinks of his grief over his sister as an entity that is horribly and painfully attached to him, the way a jellyfish might adhere to your skin or a goiter or an abscess. He pictures it as viscid, amorphous, spiked, hideous to behold. He finds it unbelievable that no one else can see it. Don't mind that, he would say, it's just my grief. Please ignore it and carry on with what you were saying.

Behind him, as he moves away, he can hear the cousins whispering, conferring: "Is he crying?" one of them says.

Is he? He's aware that he's moving unsteadily, that the ground is bucking beneath him. I am sleep deprived, he wants to say, I am dehydrated, I am not myself, I am somewhat out of sorts, and four months ago my sister was in a drugstore with her friend when a masked teenager burst through the door and waved a gun in the air and told them all to get down on the floor and Phoebe, my sister, took longer to do this than everybody else because she had this problem with her back, so the kid shot her. He shot her through her head, her beautiful, clever head. And now her head doesn't exist anymore and neither does her back and neither does she.

He seems to have made contact with the ground. He can feel stones pushing up through the knees of his jeans, can smell the wet-earth scent of them. It seems to make sense to him. To be here, on the ground, in the rain.

They were buying lip gloss. This fact still makes him angry; it makes him furious. His sister died because she wanted some fucking lip gloss. Last week he went into the drugstore and stood in the place she'd died—he'd asked the police to show him exactly where—and then after a while he filled a basket with every tube of lip gloss they had and took them to the counter and paid for them, and then he had lit a fire in the sink at his apartment and thrown them in, one by one. He'd gone back the next day and done the same, and then on the third day the security guard had barred his way and said he was not permitted entry. There had been a scene of sorts, with the police and then the head of his department and his mother was there too. So Niall had gotten out the piece of paper his father had given him at the funeral and booked a flight.

When things become clear again, it strikes him that he has never been in a room of this color. He isn't quite sure what color it is: midway between green and blue and gray. It's all three at once and yet none of them exactly. The ceiling has gold stars stuck to it. He is sitting in an enormous, sagging chair that seems to embrace him on three sides. Over his legs is a patchwork quilt: tessellated fabric hexagons of varying patterns but uniform size. There is a stove, and next to it a nest of kittens stir and sigh around their striped-browed mother, who regards Niall with incurious yellow eyes.

A woman is moving around at the other end of the room, arranging logs in a basket, pushing books into place on the shelves, setting the table, lifting a kettle from the range. Niall looks at the line of her jaw, the set of her hands, the braid of hair hanging down her back. She is dressed in a man's shirt with a cardigan over it, a pair of reading glasses pushed to the top of her head. Even though he has known for some time whom his father married, it is quite something to see her here in the flesh, no longer young, but still unmistakably her, still unmistakably in existence.

"It's the invisible woman," he says.

She turns her head to look at him. After a moment, she smiles. She picks up a tray and comes toward him. Really, it's uncanny, seeing her like this. Niall saw one of her films only a few months ago: he had streamed it to his laptop, one rainy Sunday afternoon when nothing much was happening, in that strange, distant, inaccessible time before life caved in on him.

She sets down the tray and hands him a cup. "Apple tea," she says. She gives him a plate. "Drop scone."

Niall holds these things in his hands for a moment, transfixed by their ordinariness and simultaneous strangeness. Who has plates with the faint outlines of unicorns and dragons just discernible along their chipped edges? Is it possible to drink something as ordinary as tea from a cup that looks as though it belongs in a museum, with a gilded edge, a delicate handle in the shape of a peacock's tail? What is a drop scone, anyway?

Then he gulps down the tea, as if it is the first thing he's drunk all day. Which, he reflects, it might be. She lifts the cup from his hand and refills it.

"I'm sorry," he says while chewing the drop scone, which turns out to be a kind of smallish pancake with butter on it. "I don't really know what I'm doing here. My dad told me at the funeral that if I was ever in trouble, I should come here, I should just show up and—"

"I'm glad he did."

"—he drew me a map and everything. I had no idea you and he weren't together anymore. He never said. I would never have come. I mean, I have no right, under the circumstances, really, I just—"

"Shhh," Claudette Wells says. "Eat."

"I didn't mean to frighten your daughter, or your niece. I only—"

She shakes her head, cutting him off. "It takes a lot more than that to frighten Marithe and Zhilan. They are both made of fairly stern stuff."

"The thing is . . . the thing is . . . she . . . Marithe, I mean . . . she looks so like . . ." Niall finds he can't go on.

"I know," she says. "I know she does." She puts down her own cup—a thing of turquoise china with interlocking green leaves—and leans forward. "Niall, I am so sorry about what happened to your sister. I can't imagine what you must be going through. How much you must miss her."

Niall cannot open his mouth, he cannot trust himself to speak. He finds he is weeping, which is strange, because he very rarely weeps. His mother always said that he was a freakishly silent baby, that he never cried. The number of times he's cried in his life could be counted on his fingers. He didn't even cry at Phoebe's funeral, which is odd, really, but then Niall has always known he was odd, in many ways.

Claudette has taken his hand in hers; she has her fingers wrapped around his bandages. "Stay," she is saying, "for as long as you need. You are very welcome here."

Niall looks out of the window and sees the side of a mountain. He can read rock formations the way some people can read text at a glance, and he knows just by looking at it that it is quartzite. At the base of this mountain, he can see children, his half-siblings among them, and their cousin, running back and forth with sticks. There must be some point, some edict, to the game, but Niall cannot, for the moment, see what it is. There are children, there is yelling, there are sticks, and there is a ball, or perhaps two. They run, oblivious to the rain, from one tree to the next, and their cries stretch out to him, sitting in the gray-green room, as if on elastic.

Niall does what he always does in times of stress: he enumerates known elements of his situation, concrete facts. One: he is sitting in a room in a house that doesn't even have a street address, surrounded by people he has never met. Two: there is an incomprehensible game going on beyond the window, played by children with whom he shares DNA. Three: his father, both hero and demon of his life, has done another of his Houdini escapes. Here is another house in which his father, Daniel, is absent yet present. That coat behind the door, those linguistics and psychology books on the shelves, those auburn-haired children through the window. Four: he has no return flight to the States, as he'd had insufficient funds in his checking account for anything other than a one-way ticket. He could, he had reasoned at the ticket desk, sort something out later. Five: he knows precisely no one in this country, now that he has learned that his father no longer lives here. Six: a vanished movie star sits beside him, holding his hand.

Niall inclines his head at the woman and the movement causes the plate in his lap to slide to one side. The dragons and unicorns tilt into the light, they are suddenly illuminated with sun, their worn edges flaring, sparking, lit into life, like phosphorescence, like magic.

Absolutely the Right Tree

CLAUDETTE AND DANIEL

Donegal and London, 2013

Claudette stands in the window of her bedroom, looking down at the gravel where the car is usually parked.

She is looking without seeing. She doesn't see the tire swing, oscillating by a quarter circle and back; she doesn't see the surface of the pond, broken here and there by alabaster spikes of water lilies; she doesn't see the jay fling itself from lawn to sky.

The morning is cool, with mist hanging low over the valley, but the sun may break through the moisture later. It may. Even now it will be shining down on the clouds; it may come streaming through toward the earth at any minute.

Claudette is thinking of many things as she stands at her window. Some are mundane: that the bed needs making, the kitchen tidying, the dogs walking, the wood chopping. Other threads weaving through her head are more abstract: that time in Kerala, when she bought those leather slippers she used to love, how hot it was, what damp heat, how vibrant the colors of the spices along that street, kept there in burlap sacks, great heaps of saffron and cumin and turmeric, the air heavy with their scent. And: Will the weather where the children are be wet like this or will it be warm? Hard to know. And: That shirt of Daniel's, the one he had when she first knew him, the same blue of the walls of the spice street in Kerala, a denser blue than that of a cloudless sky, the faded fabric at the neck, at his cuffs, the way he always—

Claudette twists away from the window, sets herself in motion, picks up clothes from the floor of her bedroom blindly, tossing them to the bedstead, not even caring when they slide once more to the floor-boards. She seizes a hairbrush from her dressing table and, dragging it downward through her hair, sets off for the stairs.

It's the first time the children have been away, she's telling herself as she goes down, the first time you've ever been without them. The hairbrush catches on a snarl and she winces. The first time. It's bound to feel strange.

Hundreds of miles southwest, in London, at exactly the same moment, Daniel is lying on his side, in bed. He is watching the red digital num-bers of his alarm clock mutate into their successors: 5 gains an extra descender on its lower-left corner to become 6; to become 7, the 6 must lose almost all of itself, all its left-hand side, all its lower and middle strokes; the only consolation, he tells the 6-soon-to-be-7, is that you'll get them all back for the full house that is 8.

He watches the numbers tot themselves up, then spill over into another hour: oo shows itself in the minute section, which is Daniel's least-favorite digital configuration, and the radio sparks into life. A voice is telling him that it's 7:00 a.m. exactly and that he is about to hear the news. There are the chimes of Big Ben, there are the weird beeps—"the pips," Claudette taught him to call them, which always made him think of the interior of apples, those mahogany-shiny seeds—and so begins another morning in London, another working day.

Not, however, Daniel thinks, as he turns over, pulling the covers over his head, for him.

.　.　.

In the living room, Claudette searches for a box of matches with which to light the stove, running her hand along the mantelpiece.

She hadn't been sure it was the right thing to do, to allow Niall to take Marithe and Calvin to see the Giant's Causeway. Was Calvin too young to be away from home and was Niall up to the sole charge of his two energetic half-siblings and would Marithe get carsick? Last night, though, on the phone, they had sounded buoyant, excited, thrilled with the youth hostel and its bunks, its strict mealtimes, its lists of rules; Niall had said everything was fine, everyone was doing great, she mustn't worry.

She comes upon the matches, hidden beneath a book, and is just sliding them into her dressing-gown pocket when she is hit by a thought. Is this the first time she has ever spent a night alone in this house? Could it be? She stares at the windows, the walls, the chinoiserie curtains with the lonely woman on her bridge, forever waiting for her man to turn up.

It must be. In all the permutations of people who have lived in the house, in her time, not once has she been here alone. First, there was her and Ari, then her and Ari and Daniel, then Marithe arrived, then Calvin, then Ari left for school, then university. And then—Claudette makes herself think this, it is good for her, part of the process of facing up to what happened, to accepting it, to moving on—and then, of course, Daniel left. The house lost Daniel.

Claudette crams kindling and firewood into the mouth of the stove, shoves them all in together, in a haphazard, disordered heap, seeing her life stream before her as a series of mathematical formulas. Her + Timou = Ari. Her + Daniel = Marithe + Calvin. Her − Daniel = this. Whatever this is. Being solitary, in a state of undress, making a mess of lighting a fire.

She slams the stove door shut, furious with herself, with the tears that are inexplicably stinging her eyes, furious with the stove, which is refusing to catch, furious with everything, furious with her husband, estranged husband, former husband, whatever he is, who lost his way in life so badly that the only option for them was to—

Claudette refuses to allow herself to finish that thought. Why today, of all days, is Daniel invading her head? It's been almost two years, for God's sake, since he left, which is surely more than enough time to get over a man.

The next thing to happen, in the mathematical scheme of things, she supposes, as she fumbles to light another match, is that Marithe and Calvin will leave. They will grow up, they will go, and then what will happen? Will she live here, at the top of the valley, alone? The children will visit, of course, but how will she survive, on her own, in this place?

Claudette, with a kind of growl, flings the box of matches across the room. She kicks the door of the stove shut—who needs a fire anyway?—and stomps toward the kitchen.

She opens and shuts cupboards at random. You need, she tells herself, to stop this. Enough. What is wrong with you? You're alone in the house, for God's sake. It's not the end of the world—why can't you just make the most of it?

Claudette takes the lid off the kettle, carries it to the sink, but leaves it there without filling it.

In the bathroom, Daniel avoids his eye in the mirror. He spends a great deal of time avoiding mirrors. Overrated things at the best of times.

Only when he has swung open the bathroom cabinet does he look up. His fingers stray through the contents of the shelves. Soaps, shampoos, shaving gear, medication—some over the counter, some prescription—deodorant, mouthwash, and right at the back he finds a small, amber-colored bottle. Daniel lifts it out and considers it, frowning. It's some miscellaneous homeopathic stuff and he has no idea how it got there because it isn't the kind of thing he pisses away his money on. It must, he thinks, date from Claudette's time. He should get around to chucking it out one of these days: hadn't he told her often enough that homeopathy was a shameful scam? Not that she'd ever listened, of course.

Daniel presses two painkillers from their foil into his palm and swings the cabinet shut. A momentary flash of a grizzled, semi-bearded, whey-faced ogre passes over his vision, but he closes his eyes just in time. What in the world is that monster doing in his bathroom, and when will that guy take his leave?

He gropes, eyes still closed, for the tap and turns it on. He tosses the painkillers to the back of his tongue and bends to suck water from the tap. It hits his lips and teeth with an icy punch.

"Urgh," he hears himself say. "Aaaah."

Wiping his mouth on the back of his sleeve, Daniel makes his way along the corridor and into the living room. He sits himself carefully on the couch. A headache like this requires gentle handling, special treatment. Sudden movements are out of the question, as are loud noises, even speech. The pain, which began life in the cerebellum area, is now spreading its fingers along the sides of his skull to press at his temples.

He directs his gaze out of the window where, over the leafless bushes of the communal mansion-block garden, he can see windows identical to his, all stacked on top of one another. That was what he had found most unsettling about London when he moved here—how crammed in everyone was, the lack of room between living spaces, the airlessness, the feeling that always, wherever you were, whatever you were doing, someone was watching you with detached, impersonal eyes. And him a New Yorker! He had chided himself for feeling such claustrophobia, for the loss of his city legs. Those years of living in the wilds of Donegal had done him in, ruined him, spoiled him, in perhaps more ways than one.

His gaze drops to the wall and to his photographs of Phoebe. He is collating them, collecting them, trying to find at least one for each year she was alive, which is no mean feat given that he didn't see her between the ages of six and sixteen, and how that lost decade gnaws at him, enrages him, especially in the dead of night.

He sees, as he looks at them, that the photograph of her, aged eight, given to him by Niall, has slipped slightly.

Daniel is out of his seat and across the room in seconds, easing the picture off the wall, finding a length of fresh tape, affixing it back to its rightful place, between a shot of her aged seven, with a gap-toothed smile and too-short bangs, and one aged nine, where she is gravely holding a resigned-looking rabbit in the backyard.

He retreats to the sofa, sits down. He allows himself to run the thought *My daughter is dead* through his head. He has to block images of drugstores, of youths in masks, of injuries, of his angel child sprawled across the floor. These are things he must not think about. He becomes conscious, as he concentrates on not picturing the moment of Phoebe's death, of something digging into his side, so he puts his hand in his pocket and pulls out the bottle of homeopathic medicine. He doesn't remember putting it into his pocket, but he must have. How else could it have gotten there?

How come, Claudette thinks, there is nothing to eat in the whole house? How can this be? She extracts a box of muesli, contemplates the picture of a man gazing joyfully at a china bowl, puts it back. She picks up a loaf of bread. She puts it down. She yanks open the fridge to find an etiolated carrot, a hunk of spore-covered cheese, some curdled milk. How can there be nothing? Or nothing she feels like eating?

She pulls open a drawer, finds a collection of corn-on-the-cob holders, most of them broken, and tries to shut it again but finds that it is jammed. She shoves at it with her hip but something at the back is catching, preventing it from closing. She jiggles it toward her, but it is now refusing to open, so she snakes her hand into the hollow space to try to release whatever it is.

She feels a solid, squarish package, clipped at the top, cool to the touch. What could it be? She reaches for it with the very tips of her fingers but, again and again, it slips from her grasp.

"Goddamnit," she mutters, trying to ease the thing toward her, "just behave, will you?"

With the oldest, marmalade cat watching from the sideboard with inscrutable interest, Claudette contorts herself so that her shoulder is hunched, her back arched, and her hand palm up, and manages to grasp the thing. She has it. She grins triumphantly at the cat, who gives her a slow, impassive blink. She wriggles her wrist free. It is out. Here it is.

Claudette looks down at the thing in her hand. She turns it one way and the other.

It is a packet of Italian coffee, half used, left behind. Innocuous enough in itself, but in Claudette's hands, this particular morning, it is as dangerous as cyanide.

She isn't going to sniff it, no, she isn't. She wouldn't be stupid enough to attempt such a thing. Just a whiff of those smoky, dark, aromatic granules—heated up, they always were, at length, lovingly, every morning in this kitchen, for all the years he lived here, the way he would stand waiting for them to brew, looking out of that window, that robe of his loose over his pajamas, a child, usually, on his shoulder or his arm—would be enough to tip her over the edge. She isn't going to do it. Certainly not.

Then she does, of course. She removes the clip, she places it on the counter, she parts the top of the silver-and-red packet, and she brings it to her face and she inhales, she inhales, she inhales.

Minutes later, the cat makes its sinuous way down off the sideboard and across the floor and toward the woman of the house who, the cat observes, is inexplicably slumped on the floor, hands covering her face. The cat rubs its head against her legs, once, twice, and waits for a response. Nothing. The woman still sits there. The cat winds its way through her ankles. It wonders when the woman might get up and what the meaning is of this odd behavior and how long it will be before she recalls that the cat has still not had its breakfast.

Daniel takes two of the homeopathic pills. He has no idea what they are. The label, being made of organic paper or some such, is so worn and faded it's impossible to make out the name of the medicine.

Do you, in fact, call it medicine? Wasn't there some other word for it? He is sure there is. Cure? No. Something else more obfuscatory.

The pills—he remembers you're meant to call them pilules, which he always found a most unpleasant neologism—are minuscule and sweet. He rolls them around his tongue until they dissolve into a kind of sugary fairy dust. Delicious. No wonder the kids never minded taking this stuff.

He takes two more. Holds the bottle up to the light. Hundreds of the little things, all perfectly round and uniform. IGNATIA, the label reads, he now sees, in faint, rubbed-away ink, and he is struck with the sudden recollection of Claudette giving these to him as she left this very flat, after she had brought him back from Phoebe's funeral. They had been separated for almost a year but she still came, when she heard, deposited the kids with Lucas, took a train to London, got him on a plane, held his hand on the flight, drove him to the funeral, picked him up afterward, watched him get drunk in a hotel that night, escorted him to his room, gently disengaged his hands when he made a clumsy pass at her, then brought him back to London. He remembers her putting this bottle into his outstretched hand, here in this room, then turning away, and he hadn't been reaching for fucking homeopathic remedies, that's for sure, but that was what she had given him. Ignatia. For grief, she'd had the gall to say. Do you think, he had roared at her, this pointless bullshit placebo is going to bring back my daughter? Is it going to make losing you OK? Is that what you think? That this will in any way help?

Daniel shuts down the memory. He doesn't want to think about her leaving that day, walking away from him down the corridor. He did not follow her out into the lobby, he did not. He did not yell at her all the way to the curb, to the cab door. He did not then switch to pleading and try to grab hold of her coat, her arm, her bag, whatever he could reach. He is sure of that.

He takes another two pills, then another. Is it possible to overdose on these things? Daniel lets out a bark of a laugh. What a turn-up for the books that would be. Death by placebo.

He could phone Claudette and ask her. He could pick up the phone and dial and be put through to that house, their house, her house. What would he say? Hey, honey, I might have exceeded the recommended dose for ignatia. Does this mean that I'll die? Or that I'll be happy forever?

Daniel tosses the bottle aside. He picks up a newspaper, reads the headline, registers that it's over a week old and that he's read it before, cover to cover, but still carries on running his eyes along the lines of words.

Without taking his eyes off the page, he reaches out for the little amber bottle and tucks it back into his pocket.

.   .   .

This is better, Claudette thinks, as she walks along the strand, her coat buttoned against the cold. She is out, she is doing something active, she is coping—more than coping. What was all that in the kitchen, anyway? It was nothing. She's fine. Crying over some coffee, indeed. What in the world is wrong with her? She's just feeling a bit down today, that's all. Who needs a husband when they have all that she has?

She turns to face the water: layers of turquoise under a piled, gray-blue sky, the lace of the surf edging the slick-wet sand. The dogs are dark arrows, far in the distance, circling each other, paws kicking up the spray. She whistles to them and they rear their heads, ears turning in the breeze.

She called Niall, just after she parked the car. They were out on the causeway and Niall had said something about basalt and polygonal columns, which had made her smile, and he had handed over the phone to Marithe who had talked very fast about geological hammers and the legend of the giant, and Calvin, when he got his turn on the phone, asked if they could get a new puppy, and could they call it Finn?

Yes, she had found herself saying, yes.

In less than twenty-four hours they will be back and life will return to normal and the house will be full of voices and footfalls, just the way she likes it.

Daniel circles the aisles of a supermarket in Belsize Park. He has gotten himself dressed, after a fashion, and has walked all the way up the hill with the express purpose of coming here and buying some food of a nutritious content. Ari came to see him two, maybe three, weeks ago and cooked him dinner. After that, he cleaned the kitchen and filled—Daniel squirms to think of it—the fridge and stuck a note to it, saying EAT SOMETHING. Like Alice in Wonderland, Daniel thought afterward. He could visit again, at any time, and Daniel wants to show him that he doesn't need to worry about him, that he has his head above water, that he's fine. It's not that he wants this message to filter back to Claudette, no, not in the least: he just wants the boy to stop thinking he's in any way responsible for the welfare of his feckless stepfather. God knows Ari has enough responsibilities of his own.

Daniel wanders up an aisle filled with seventeen different types of diaper. He hates this supermarket, he remembers now. It has a particularly low ceiling and very little natural light, and the tills are arranged in a maddening nonlinear way so that queues of people waiting to pay snake back through the aisles.

Coming across one of those wheeled stools that supermarket workers use to stack the shelves, Daniel sits down. Just for a moment. To take the weight off his feet, to nurse his head, which is throbbing in sympathy with the Muzak filtering into the shop air.

He looks down into his basket. A can of tuna, a bottle of vodka, and a single apple.

The problem is, he thinks, that there seems to be nothing to buy. The shelves are crammed but there is nothing he wants to pick up and take home.

He watches a couple about his age coming toward him. The woman pushes a shopping cart, which is filled with sparkling water and eggplants and French cheeses and star fruit, and the man walks beside her. They stop at a display of crispbreads and study them with serious absorption. The man places a hand on his wife's back and Daniel has to look away, has to take another couple of the homeopathic pills and grind them between his molars.

When he considers the end of his marriage, there is one moment in particular that haunts him, especially in those sleepless hours before dawn. He is often awake, addressing the ceiling above his bed, redrafting this moment, rewriting it, reediting it to his satisfaction. (To no avail, of course: the woman for whom these alterations are intended is a thousand silent leagues away.) It was early morning, a few months after they had come back from Paris, and Claudette had been in bed beside him, regarding him from her pillow. Daniel had been sitting up, smoking, unshaved, unslept, and he was reading an old academic textbook that contained a paper by Nicola. He was ignoring Claudette, his wife, the living and breathing woman in bed beside him. He was pretending he didn't know she was awake because some conversations are too difficult for first thing in the morning, because he didn't feel like having another dissection of his failings and shortcomings, because he was, in short, an idiot. If he met the man he was that morning, Daniel wants to say to the couple by the crispbreads, you know what he would do? He would take him by the shoulders and shake him and say, get it together. Do you see this woman, this room, this house? You're about to lose it all. The whole kit and caboodle. So put that fucking book down and turn toward your wife and get a good grip on her and hold on as tightly as you can.

But there was no future self in the room that morning, so Daniel carried on reading, carried on smoking, carried on ignoring. And then, beside him, Claudette took a breath.

"Do you think, Daniel," she said to him, rolling over onto her back so that she was able to look out of the window while she spoke, "that we might have reached the end of our story?"

Such a Claudette way to put it.

Claudette treads her way up and over a headland and down into a smaller beach where the cliffs curve protectively around the sand. She realizes too late that she has arrived at the exact spot where she had first brought Daniel, after she and Ari had met him that day at the crossroads, when they had almost said goodbye forever, almost missed each other, until Ari said, will you come to the beach with us? and Daniel had said yes, and they had driven him north, along the coast, to here.

Claudette sighs. She considers turning back, not walking the sand where once, a decade and a half ago, a small Ari had stripped off his clothes and run naked in the shallows, shrieking and kicking, and Daniel had been a hulking stranger, dropped into their lives from nowhere, who had made a pile of flattened stones there on the strand and said to Ari that they weren't going to leave this beach until he had learned to skim stones.

She walks on, grimly. She will not turn back. She will not let him ruin this place for her. Everywhere has echoes of Daniel. If she tried to avoid everything that reminded her of him, then she'd have to dig a hole in the ground and live in that.

So he and Ari had stood at the waves and he had adjusted Ari's stance, the angle of his arm, and it had taken what seemed like hours. But there he had stood, next to her son, again and again saying, Like this, good job, try again, one more time. And by the end of the after-noon, Ari could make his stone bounce three, four, five times on the surface of the sea.

It is possible, Claudette thinks, that she decided she wanted him there and then. Or was it later, when she dropped him back at the cross-roads, where they had left his car, and he'd said, in a garbled rush, that he wasn't leaving Donegal anytime soon, that he had some work to do "in the area," that he'd be here for a while and could he take her to dinner, no, not dinner, who would babysit the kid, how about lunch or maybe a walk or could he cook for her or maybe she and Ari would like to go visit a castle the next day or farther up the coast or maybe a holy well, if she wasn't busy?

She picks up a length of driftwood and throws it for the dogs, who both hare after it, jostling and shoving each other.

It didn't take long, that much she knows. She'd thought it was pretty clear to both of them where they were heading, but when she touched him for the first time, when she held him in her hallway and pressed her lips to his, she was amazed to find that he was shaking, that he had been under the impression that she wasn't interested, that he was bark-ing up the wrong tree. No, she'd said, putting her arms around his neck, the right tree, absolutely the right tree.

Claudette sinks onto a rock. What is she doing? How did she get to this place, crying as she walks along a beach? How did everything go so wrong?

She pulls out her phone and looks at it. She has banned herself from calling Daniel; it is not allowed, it is not right, it is not fair to him. They are separated; it is over. This she must accept.

She presses the button that lights up the phone. There is, she is both annoyed and elated to see, a signal. A faint one, but a signal all the same.

Daniel takes a right off Haverstock Hill. There is a library down here that he likes, an old-school place with kids' story times and stern librar-ians and clanking radiators and ancient computers and geriatrics doz-ing at tables.

He has left the supermarket, abandoned his shopping basket right there in the aisle. He considered taking the vodka, just slipping it into his coat pocket, but good sense prevailed, just in time.

He walks down the side street, past lines of parked cars, past wrought-iron gates, past cats sitting on doorsteps, past windows that give views of sofas, dining tables, kitchen cupboards, lit rooms, where other lives are being lived out.

Sometimes he wonders what the hell he is doing here, in this city, where he has no connections, no history, no contacts, other than his stepson, who is a student at the university. He had a job here, of course, for a while, but not at the moment. Compassionate leave, they called it.

The thing was, Daniel thinks as he gazes into a house where he can see a child, juice box in hand, staring into a television screen, he had believed his move here to be temporary, a marital blip. He had no idea his split with Claudette would turn out to be permanent. Isn't that often the way of these things? Shortly after the conversation in the bedroom that morning, he had taken himself (in a state of injured, wronged rage) to London, for a while, he had thought. He would take the six-month contract he'd been offered and serve her right. He was entirely of the opinion that he could talk her around, when he was good and ready, when she'd had time to see sense. He'd thought he could get her back, fool that he was, but first—*first*—he had to sort out the Nicola issue.

How do you absorb the idea that you've killed someone into your ordinary life? How do you go about the minutiae of the everyday when you know that, because of you, a girl is dead? It's impossible. The specter of the girl lying in the woods, the girl in a hospital bed, haunted the rooms of his flat, his new, diminished life in London. She lurked around corners at the university; she hung about on Underground stairwells; she sat in the empty place opposite him at his tiny dining table.

Then he'd gotten a call on his cell phone in the middle of the night and he'd seen it was Niall and he remembers being pleased—alone, as he was, in a flat in London, away from everyone he loved. He remembers snatching it up eagerly and saying, hey, how are you?

You know what his immediate thought was, on being told that his daughter had been shot dead in a drugstore? That it was his fault. That it was karma, it was comeuppance, it was punishment for him running away from that forest and not going back. An eye for an eye, a girl for a girl.

Even now, almost a year on, he cannot shake that conviction. He knows it was somehow down to him.

Daniel climbs the steps to the library, holds the door for a woman with a double stroller, and seats himself in the travel guides and nonfiction section, grabbing a selection of books at random.

He opens something called *The Big Book of Facts: Everything You Need to Know About Everything,* questioning the wisdom of repeating "everything" in the title, which is a pretty ugly and prosaic word, when you think about it. Here is a page with graphs of world grain consumption per continent, America coming out top of all grain guzzlers. A diagram of the rate of polar ice melting. A league table of land animals and their respective speeds in kilometers per hour.

Daniel flips the pages and finds himself looking at pie charts of gun crimes.

He shuts the book with a snap. He lays his head on the table, on top of the cover, and the word "everything" stretches away from his eyes, the wrong way around, in vast, unavoidable letters.

"*Maman?*" Claudette says into her phone. "*C'est moi.*"

During the ensuing pause on the line, it hits Claudette with a plummeting sensation that she should never have rung Pascaline. What was she thinking? She'd only done it to stop herself from calling Daniel. Can she hang up, before it's too late, pretend that her phone ran out of charge, that she lost the signal? Her mother possesses an unnerving ability to decode her moods immediately and she doesn't want to talk about how she's feeling right now, not at all.

Claudette tries valiantly to inject an upbeat tone into her voice: "*Ça va?*"

"What's wrong?" Pascaline replies, in English, which she reserves for interrogation purposes. "You sound terrible."

"No, I don't," Claudette says. "I'm fine. How are you?"

Pascaline ignores the question for a second time. "Where are you?" she asks. "Who is with you?"

Claudette takes a deep breath. "No one," she says, and bursts into tears.

The dogs find a length of bladder wrack to squabble halfheartedly over, the clouds move along the coast in a stately procession, the tide pulls off the strand, leaving furrows and ridges in the sand, and Claudette must listen to her mother's theories as to why her marriage broke down.

"The point is, my darling," Pascaline is saying as her daughter hurls stone after stone into a nearby rockpool, "that his behavior had nothing to do with you. Nothing at all."

"I don't know about that. It's not as if I—"

"None of it was your fault."

Claudette sighs. "You don't think perhaps you're a little bit biased?" She squeezes her eyes shut. "You know, I really don't want to talk about this anymore." But then she finds that, in fact, she does. "I just wonder," she says to her mother as she sits on the beach, "whether I did the right thing. Maybe I shouldn't have asked him to leave. I thought that maybe some time apart might give him the jolt he needed. But now everything is so much worse with him, of course, and I still wonder if—"

"He needs to get well," Pascaline interrupts, "before you can even consider—"

"I know that," Claudette says irritably, "you don't need to tell me that. But maybe he can't get better on his own in London. Maybe he needs to be here, with us, with—"

"The man is an alcoholic," Pascaline says bluntly. "That would not be easy for you, for the children. You want to know what I think?"

"Not really," Claudette mutters.

"I think that the person you are missing today is the old Daniel. Not the current one. Yes?"

Claudette moves her feet in semicircles around herself. Could this be true or is it just more of her mother's intrusive psychobabble? She presses her hand to her eyes. She can't tell anymore. She can no longer think clearly about Daniel.

The dogs come and stare at her, martyred, affronted at this hiatus in their walk, as Pascaline offers more ideas as to why Daniel went off the deep end and a list of reasons why Claudette should sell the Donegal house and move to Paris.

Daniel sits on a bench next to the duck pond. Dusk gathers itself around him, spreading out from the branches of the trees. He shivers inside his coat. There are footsteps from the path behind him, people going to and fro, back from work, back from school, on their way home. In front of him, across the pond, lights come on in the windows of the big houses.

In one hand, he holds a bottle of whiskey and a joint, in the other the little amber bottle. The tip of the joint glows orange, and its smoke drifts sideways in the evening breeze.

He is alternating, one toke on the joint, one sip of the whiskey, one pill from the bottle (he refuses to say "pilule").

It is proving to be an interesting combination.

The ducks draw silver lines after themselves over the surface of the pond. A siren sounds from the north, getting closer and then veering away. Somewhere to his left, a horse-chestnut tree is dropping its fruit: conkers land every few minutes with a cracking thud, green, spiked cases splitting open, the polished seeds rolling free. None of it matters. Nothing matters. His daughter is dead and nothing can bring her back.

Claudette moves through the house, pen and paper in her hand. *Paint bathroom,* she writes, underneath *Reseal windows Ari's room* and *Stair carpet?*

She needs to give this place a revamp, a new life. Out with the old, in with the new. All this gloom today is caused by an uncertain feeling that life is moving on, the children getting older, and maybe—just maybe—the idea of being alone is a disquieting one.

Because, Claudette thinks as she sits down on the top stair, how likely is it that she will meet someone else? She will stay in this house, despite Pascaline's exhortations to move to Paris, and realistically how many potential husbands will come wandering up her track, carrying the ashes of their grandparent in a box?

Claudette looks down the curve of the stairs and up at the skylight, which is turning a deep, inked blue. "The witching hour," Daniel always called this time of day. He used to go out in it, every evening, and have a last cigarette as he walked the perimeter of the garden. He liked the moment, he said, when it was neither day nor night, but indefinably both.

She puts down her pen; she puts down her list. She picks up her phone. Everything, she sees, has been leading to this. She was always going to call Daniel today: that much was clear from when she got up. It was written into the weft of the day: Claudette will call Daniel.

She presses the buttons. She waits for the ring. She wants to hear his voice. She wants to say hello. She wants to say, I am sitting at the top of the stairs and it is halfway between day and night. And: our children are with your son, on a causeway made by a giant. And: I am thinking of you. And: do you still think of me?

Daniel walks through the lobby to his flat, registering, as he always does, its unpleasantly high temperature compared with the sharp air outside. Another thing living in that house in Ireland has done to him is that he cannot stand central heating anymore. He keeps his flat at arctic levels, much to Ari's amusement.

At his door, he can't find his keys. He feels in his coat pockets, but they contain only the empty amber bottle and conkers, handfuls of them.

He tries his trouser pockets, hearing now that the telephone inside his flat is ringing. Who might it be? Ari? One of his sisters, calling with unwanted advice, numbers of grief counselors, offers of visits?

Still no keys. Is it possible he left them behind? Has he locked himself out?

The phone continues to ring. Daniel tries his coat pockets again, his shirt pocket—nothing. He jumps up and down on the spot, hearing the unmistakable jangle of his keys. Still, the phone rings.

He pats himself all over. There. They're in the top pocket of his coat. He remembers now transferring them when he was bending to collect the conkers.

He yanks them out, he slots one into the door, he unlocks it, he steps through, and, as he does so, the phone falls silent.

Daniel stands for a moment in his hallway. The flat breathes its emptiness at him. He hangs up his coat. He makes his way to bed, flicking off the lights, one by one.

An Unexpected Outcome

Transcript of Interview Between Timou Lindstrom and a Journalist for the *London Courier*

Dalsland, Sweden, 2014

LC: Testing, testing. [*Background noise, some shuffling, throat clearing, the machine switched off, then on again, the cry of a bird.*] So, I am sitting here with Timou Lindstrom, by the side of a lake in Dals . . . how do you say it? . . . Dalsland?

TL: [*Correcting him.*] *Dals*land.

LC: Dalsland.

TL: [*Correcting him again.*] *Dals*land.

LC: [*Laughs.*] OK. Well, moving on. Is it OK if I record this interview?

TL: Of course.

LC: Great. So, Timou, we are in what I would call the middle of nowhere. We're surrounded by forests, birds, lakes. We're sitting outside a small wooden shack. It's taken me almost two days to reach you. This is where you live now? How come you chose somewhere so remote?

TL: No, I don't live here. I live in Stockholm. This is my *sommarstuga,* my—

LC: Your what?

TL: *Sommarstuga.* A summer cabin. Swedish people like to go to a cabin in the woods for the summer.

LC: Why?

TL: Why do you think? To be with nature, to get away from the city, the everyday life, to reflect.

LC: And what are you reflecting on?

TL: Me? I'm not really reflecting right now. I'm working.

LC: On what?

TL: A new script.

LC: You're writing a script?

TL: Yeah.

LC: A film script or a—

TL: A film script.

LC: Can we talk a little bit about your return to directing?

TL: Sure. What would you like to know?

LC: Well, you've been— how would you put it?—out of the game for a while, haven't you?

TL: No.

LC: Your last film came out almost twenty years ago. I'd call that a while, wouldn't you?

TL: My last film was eleven years ago. It was called—

LC: The Unanswered Question, yes. That was self-financed, I believe? It didn't get a screen release.

TL: It did in Sweden. It was—

LC: OK, so your last major release was almost twenty years ago and since then you have made a self-financed—

TL: A low budget indie.

LC: Right. A low-budget indie. But recently you've been working on a TV series that has won lots of awards here in Sweden, and it's about to be shown in the UK and the States. You must be really pleased about that. How did you feel when you got the call, asking you to direct this series?

TL: I was cautious, at first. I'd never worked in the medium of TV, never been involved in such a corporation like that, and I've been used to working with my own material, in my own way. I'd also never been a fan of the crime genre—

LC: How come?

TL: It can be too prescriptive, too formulaic. You know—a body is found, a detective is assigned, lots of danger and peril ensue, then at last a criminal is apprehended. I prefer to work with a looser structure, you know, an unexpected outcome. Ideally, I would—

LC: But for you, getting that call, inviting you to direct this series, must have been a relief.

TL: A relief?

LC: Well, you had effectively been out of work for—

TL: I have never been out of work. I've been working all this time.

LC: You have?

TL: Yes.

LC: On what?

TL: Many different things.

LC: Would you be able to expand on that?

TL: Not really. You will see.

LC: I will see? These things you have been working on will see the light of day, they will be released?

TL: Yes, I believe so. What you see from the outside is perhaps a career break, but for me it has felt like lying in wait. I had to look at the rules I laid down for myself. I had to rethink their parameters for a changing world. I needed to regroup, to reassess after—

LC: After Claudette Wells left you?

[*Pause.*]

TL: She didn't leave me.

LC: She didn't?

TL: No. She left you.

LC: Me?

TL: Not you personally but what you stand for. You are the synecdoche for what she ran away from.

[*A pause. TL can be heard disappearing into the undergrowth and fossicking around.*]

LC: What are you looking for?

TL: [*Distant.*] It's ... [*inaudible*] ... many of them ... chan ... possible to collect them and ...

LC: What?

TL: Mushrooms. Chanterelles. They grow this time of year in ... [*inaudible*] ... fry them ... [*inaudible*] ... grouped like this ... damp places ...

LC: Oh.

[*More distant sounds of cracking and branches, then the sound of TL returning.*]

LC: Wow. That's a lot. Are you going to eat them?

TL: We are going to eat them. You and me.

LC: [*Anxious.*] Um. Are you sure they're safe?

TL: Of course.

LC: Because I've read that—

TL: Don't worry. I've been doing this all my life. What do you think, that I might poison you? [*Laughs.*]

LC: [*Clears throat.*] So, we were talking about Claudette Wells.

TL: No, we weren't

LC: You were saying that she didn't leave you, that she was running from ... the media? Is that what you meant?

TL: [*Sighs.*] Do we really have to do this?

LC: You don't want to talk about Claudette?

TL: Of course not.

LC: Why not? Is it painful for you still?

TL: No, it's not painful, it's just ... Can you imagine how many fucking times I've been asked these questions, over the years?

LC: I imagine it's a lot.

TL: A hell of a lot.

[*Pause.*]

LC: You seem angry.

TL: [*Something inaudible.*]

LC: Are you angry with her?

TL: Come on. Let's not talk about this. OK?

LC: You'd have a perfect right to be angry with her.

TL: [*Something in Swedish.*]

LC: She did walk out on what was to be your biggest film, which effectively put you out of work for two decades. Do you blame her entirely for your lack of output?

TL: Listen, I was a filmmaker before I ever met her. I never needed her. She was nothing—she was an actor and actors are always replaceable, always—

LC: That's not quite what she was, though, is it? She acted on other films but with you it was different. She cowrote and codirected your most successful, most experimental films, didn't she, as well as appearing in them?

TL: [*Mutters.*] Up to a point.

LC: Up to a point? You're saying it isn't true? That those films were entirely your work? *When the Rain Didn't Fall* was just you? And *A Manual for Living*? It wasn't with her input?

TL: No, I'm not saying that. I'm actually not saying anything. I do not want to discuss this. Ask me something else. Let's talk about the TV series.

[*Pause.*]

LC: Did she tell you she was going to go? Did you know she was planning to disappear?

[*Silence.*]

LC: When she vanished, off the coast of Stockholm, did you know she was leaving?

TL: [*Mutters.*] Of course I knew.

LC: You did? She told you?

TL: Not in so many words. But I knew. She was my partner, my almost-wife. You can't live with somebody for as long as Claudette and I lived together and not know the workings of their mind. I knew she would do it, that she would ... dematerialize, disappear herself. I knew it was a matter of time. I think ... I think I just hoped she might finish that film first. It would have been our masterpiece, our best work. But she couldn't do it. She had to go.

[*Silence.*]

LC: You've never said this before.

[*Silence.*]

LC: Are you in touch with her?

[*Silence.*]

LC: Timou, are you in touch with Claudette?

[*Silence.*]

LC: You shrugged just then. Was that a yes or a no?
TL: It was a no comment.
LC: How about the son you had together? Are you in touch with him?

[*Silence.*]

LC: Was that another no comment?
TL: It was.
LC: Timou, do you know where Claudette is?

[*Silence.*]

LC: Timou?

[*Silence.*]

LC: Is she even alive, do you know?

[*Silence.*]

LC: You have no idea where she is? None at all? Is she . . . could she be . . . nearby?

TL: What—here? In Dalsland? You think I'm hiding her in the out-house over there? In the attic? In the woodshed?

LC: Are you?

TL: [*Laughs.*] Yeah, sure, why not? You've hit the nail on the head. [*Pretending to shout.*] Claudette! Time to come out! The game is up! There's a journalist here who wants to talk to you!

[*Pause.*]

LC: Do you know where she is?

TL: [*Mutters something.*]

LC: What was that?

TL: I said, yes, OK?

LC: You do? You know where she is?

TL: Of course.

LC: You know where Claudette Wells is? You can confirm she is alive?

TL: I confirm nothing.

LC: [*Excited but trying not to show it.*] But you're saying you know her whereabouts?

TL: I do. I have always known. Like I said, she was my almost-wife. We were each other's worlds, for a time. I knew everything about her. She knew everything about me.

LC: Can you tell us where she is?

TL: What do you think?

LC: I think that maybe—

TL: You think I'm going to keep it a secret for all this time and then suddenly one day I will just tell it to some journalist who turns up at my *sommarstuga*?

LC: Well—

TL: You think I will do that? Tell it to a complete stranger?

LC: I don't know, I—

TL: This is ridiculous.

[*Pause.*]

LC: Do you think she will ever come back? Do you think you'll ever work together again? Timou? Will Claudette ever come back?

[*Silence. TL reaches over and pulls out the microphone. He walks away. Interview ends.*]

To Hang On, to Never Let Go

LUCAS

London, 2014

Lucas taps with his knuckles on the door of the flat, once, twice, three times.

Nothing, just the roiling swell of television noise, coming from behind him, and the whirring sound of the lift, ascending in its shaft elsewhere in the building.

He knocks again, louder. "Daniel? It's me. Lucas. Are you in there?"

He emailed Daniel a week earlier to say that he'd be in London and would like to meet; he'd suggested a café around the corner from the flat where Daniel was now living, in a brick mansion block near Chalk Farm tube station. He'd got no reply, but from what Ari had told him about Daniel's current state, this wasn't exactly a surprise.

Lucas steps back and leans against the wall. What should he do? Stay or go? He could try Daniel's mobile, but Ari said that Daniel never answers it or never keeps it charged. One of the two.

He should go, he decides, but then just as swiftly is sure that he should stick it out.

The corridor of the mansion block has a distracting hum. Either the lighting or the heating has a defect somewhere, a loose connection, which is vibrating at wasp pitch. Lucas is examining the ceiling out of habit, looking for an ailing lightbulb, a fuse about to blow, a short-circuiting security camera, when something about Daniel's door catches his eye.

At the pinhole center of the tiny spyhole drilled through the door, Lucas detects a movement. A flicker, nothing more, a heartbeat of motion in the stillness beyond.

Lucas pushes himself off the wall and taps his knuckles against the thickly painted door. "Daniel, I'd really like to talk to you. Could you open the door?"

Still nothing, but Lucas is sure he hears the soft scrape of a foot sole against the floor.

"We could go out for coffee, if you'd rather not invite me in. I found a good place around the corner. I'm sure you know it."

Lucas puts both hands against the door frame and leans into it.

"Daniel, I just want to talk. Nothing more. Claudette says—"

"Is she with you?"

The voice, muffled, still distinctly Brooklyn, comes through the cracks at the edges. Lucas allows himself a small smile. From the years in his former job as a social worker, he knows that any kind of dialogue is the first step to communication, to establishing trust. Or reestablishing, in this case.

"Is she here?" Daniel is asking from behind the door.

Lucas shuffles rapidly through possible replies, trying to calibrate the least-damaging response. Would Daniel want her to be here? Or not want her? Hard to say.

"She's with the children, in Ireland," he says eventually.

Lucas hears Daniel sigh. "So," comes the laconic voice, "I've got the monkey, not the organ-grinder."

Lucas puts his hand in his pocket, feels the sharp corners of the papers Claudette gave him. "I suppose we could look at it like that," he says. "Do you fancy a coffee with this particular monkey?"

There is a silence from behind the door. Lucas sees the spyhole darken, the bright dot at its center become eclipsed, and he knows that Daniel is looking out at him. He tries to arrange his features into a friendly, unthreatening expression.

"What did you . . . ," Daniel begins indistinctly, and the rest of the sentence is inaudible.

"What was that?" Lucas leans close to the door. "I didn't hear you."

"I said, what in God's name did you do to your hair?"

"My hair?" Lucas puts up a hand to his head. "Nothing, I think."

"Was it always so . . . long?"

"Maybe not," Lucas says. "I don't remember. Perhaps it's time for a cut."

"I'll say."

The spyhole returns to its bright pinprick and Lucas hears the sliding, clunking sound of locks. The door swings open.

The light in the mansion-block corridor is so glaring that, for a moment, Daniel is just a dark silhouette, swaying slightly in his doorway.

"You want to go out," Lucas says, "or . . . ?"

Daniel steps back and Lucas sees his face for the first time. He is careful not to betray any kind of shock, but Daniel's appearance is rather worse than he'd been expecting. A gray pallor to the skin, several days' worth of unshaved beard, eyes carrying a yellowish tinge, a frame several pounds lighter than it ought to be, a bathrobe worn over some crumpled clothes. Lucas sees it all. Hair standing on end. Fingertips stained ocher. The skin around his lips chapped and split.

The two men consider each other for a moment, then Daniel turns and disappears into his flat.

"I'll come in, then," Lucas says to the retreating figure.

Daniel doesn't answer and, after a moment, Lucas steps over the threshold and follows him down a short passageway into a room, where Daniel has thrown himself onto a sofa.

The living room of Daniel's flat is strewn with papers, a desiccated houseplant or two, discarded clothing, and books—books, everywhere. Lined up on shelves, stacked on the floor, tipping sideways on the windowsill, splayed facedown on the coffee table. No sign of bottles, empty or otherwise, Lucas finds himself noting, no drug paraphernalia. A hand-rolled cigarette smolders in an ashtray, a line of smoke rising in

such a straight line that, for a moment, it seems to Lucas to be performing some kind of optical illusion, as if the cigarette is suspended from
the ceiling by a thread of smoke.

"So," Daniel's voice interrupts his reverie, "what's the verdict?"

"What do you mean?"

"I saw you," Daniel points the edge of a book in Lucas's direction,
"casting your professional eye over the place. Casing the joint. I was just
wondering what conclusion you'd come to. Drug den? Alcoholic's lair?
Depressive's hangout?"

Lucas shakes his head. "Daniel, come on, I just wanted to see how
you were doing, how—"

Daniel waves this sentence away with a dismissive gesture. "Lucas,"
he says, "I've always had a lot of time for you. You and you alone
remain the only in-law of mine that I have ever liked, but I would bet
my last dollar that you have something intended for me in one of those
zipped-up, all-weather pockets of yours."

Lucas swallows and says nothing. He takes a step sideways and sits
down in a chair opposite Daniel.

"Am I right," Daniel says, folding his arms over his bathrobe, a wolf-
ish scowl on his face, "or am I right?"

Lucas crosses his legs, leans on the arm of his chair. "I don't know
what you mean."

"Sure you do." Daniel nods at him. "Take a look. Go on. Open up
your pockets, empty them out. What will we find? Could it be a set of
divorce papers, just for me?"

"I came because I was in London and I wanted to see you, OK?
Don't try and twist this. I thought we could—"

Daniel holds up a finger. "Cut the crap. Tell me yes or no. Do you
have divorce papers on you?"

"Daniel, when did you last eat? Have you—"

"Yes or no, Lucas."

Lucas sighs. "Yes."

There is a short silence in the room. Daniel sits back, tightens the
fold of his arms. A muscle to the side of his jaw clenches and something
like a shiver runs over him. Lucas finds he himself is barely breathing.
He tries and tries to meet Daniel's eyes but he can't. Why, he wants to

yell, did he accept this mission? What was he thinking? He had told Claudette it was a terrible idea, him delivering these horrible papers, but she had begged and pleaded until he had given in; Maeve had left the room, shaking her head.

Daniel scrubs at his face with his sleeve, scuffs a foot against a stack of newspapers on the floor. "So," he says, "she's decided to go the whole hog, has she? Nice of her to let me know. I mean, she could have discussed this with me, at the very least, or—"

"She's tried," Lucas says. "You must know that. I think she just needs some closure on this. She says she's emailed you several times and written you a letter. We even asked our lawyer to get in touch. But you didn't respond, you didn't—"

"Well," Daniel snaps, "I've kind of had a lot on my mind."

Another silence. Lucas thinks he should probably just go. This is not working. He had pictured himself and Daniel going out for coffee, sitting opposite each other in a bright, noisy café somewhere. He would hand over the papers, sliding them across the table toward his brother-in-law, and Daniel would take them quickly, wordlessly, tucking them away without discussion. But, then, has Daniel ever done anything without discussion? How did Lucas forget that about him?

Lucas will leave. He would almost rather be anywhere than this dim, airless room. How can Daniel stand it, day after day? How can he live like this? The debris all over the table, the laurel leaves pressing themselves in at the windows, the fug of cigarette smoke. He will get up and leave the papers on this table right here. He could tell Claudette that he did as she'd requested and that she can never, ever ask such a thing of him again.

Daniel is speaking. "Well, I guess now we know where we stand. Now we've established why you're really here."

"Can I say one thing?" Lucas asks, standing up.

"I don't know." Daniel squints up at him. "Is it more lies, more dissembling, or is it something that resembles the truth?"

"I was coming to London and I told her I would be seeing you. Or that I would at least try. And she asked me to bring the papers. So the seeing-you came first, do you understand? I'm going now, but I want you to know that I came here with good intentions. It was always—"

"Here's a question," Daniel says, ignoring his imminent departure, sounding for all the world like the professor he so recently was. "Don't you ever get tired of being her messenger boy?"

Lucas leans one hand against the wall. "I'm not sure I know what you mean."

"I often used to wonder," Daniel says, his gaze directed out of the window to the communal garden with, uneven paving and overgrown shrubs, "how you stood it."

"Stood what?"

Daniel swings his head around and looks him right in the eye. Lucas has forgotten the penetration of that blue gaze. "Lucas, buy this house for me. Lucas, call my lawyer for me. Lucas, get in touch with my ex. Lucas, go to Ari's sports day. Lucas, get Daniel to sign these divorce papers. Lucas, enable my whole insane lifestyle."

Lucas clears his throat. "You know, you do a pretty good imitation of her voice. I never knew you could—"

Daniel leans forward and jabs his finger at him. "Aren't you ever tempted to tell her to just fuck off?"

"Well, I—"

"Not even once? Not ever? You realize, don't you, that her whole existence is entirely predicated on your assistance, your collusion? Without you, her cover would be—" Daniel makes a gesture like a firework going off. "She'd be outed. She'd be busted. She wouldn't last a week without you. You know that? She'd have to come down off that mountain and face the bloody music. And yet she treats you like shit, like a PA, like an unpaid lackey, like a bodyguard, like a—"

"Daniel," Lucas cuts him off in a steady voice, he is not going to let this get to him, he is not, "you need to stop. You're out of line, OK?"

"I am? But who else is going to tell you this, Lucas? I worry about you, I really do. I kept my counsel while I was married to your sister—well, I guess I still am married to her, until I sign those papers in your pocket, which, by the way, will be never, you can tell her from me—but no one should have to put up with the amount of crap she heaps on you. No one. It's not fair, it's not right, it's—"

"Look," Lucas interjects, "I don't want to get into this, but we both know that Claudette's is a pretty unusual situation. I can assure you that I am not being taken advantage of. That just doesn't come into it. She's my sister. I'd do anything for her and I know she'd do anything for me. She has, in fact, many times, and—"

"Oh, yeah, I forgot." Daniel places first one foot, then the other on the littered coffee table. "She paid for your whole fertility roller coaster, didn't she?"

Lucas narrows his eyes. After a moment, he nods. "That's right."

"And she footed the bill for the adoption."

He nods, once more. "She did." He refuses to let Daniel rile him; he will not give him the satisfaction.

"So, in effect, she bought you off by procuring you a child. Your own little orphan from China, in exchange for a lifetime of servitude. Wasn't that nice of her?"

"Fuck you, Daniel." The words have flown from his mouth before he is even aware of thinking them. His hand is slamming itself against the wall and he is shouting. "How dare you? I don't want to hear you speak of my family in that way again, ever." Lucas feels himself shaking, feels adrenaline firing through him. "That's my daughter you're talking about. My child. I know you're going through a really hard time at the moment—we all know—but to bring Zhilan into this is low. Lower than low. I will not have it."

Lucas reaches the end of this speech. His throat feels raw and scraped. He has no idea what will happen next. Will Daniel yell back? Or worse? How, he is asking himself, will he explain to Claudette and Maeve that he managed to get into a brawl with Daniel?

But as Lucas is readying himself, steeling himself, curling his hands into fists, Daniel does nothing. He seems to be contemplating the lacing of his shoes. Lucas is wondering whether the best thing now would be for him to just turn around and leave, when Daniel says something so quiet Lucas can't make it out.

"What was that?" Lucas says, straining forward.

"I said you're right," Daniel mutters, raising his eyes to look at him. "I'm sorry, man. I'm really sorry. I don't know what came over . . . I just . . . Seeing you, you know, brings it all back and . . . I thought for a minute there when I heard you at the door that . . . well, that she had come too and that maybe . . . I don't know . . . I don't know . . . I just . . . I don't know anything anymore."

He puts his hands over his face and sits like that, on his sofa. After a moment, Lucas moves toward him, cautiously at first. Then he sits next to him. He puts a tentative hand on Daniel's shoulder. "Listen, it's OK."

"I'm sorry," Daniel keeps muttering into his hands. "I'm so sorry."

"It's really OK. We both lost it a bit there. I know you didn't mean those things. I know you love Zhilan. You're her favorite uncle. She's always saying that."

"Oh, Jesus," Daniel says, lifting his head, rubbing at his face with the flat of his hands. "That makes me feel like shit. Kick a man while he's down, why don't you?"

"It's a good thing, a nice thing, being someone's favorite uncle." Lucas gives him a clap on the shoulder. "You should be proud."

Daniel pushes himself upright, sniffing. "Proud I am most definitely not right now." He moves around the coffee table and out of the room. "Can I get you something? You want a drink?"

Lucas hesitates. "A drink? You mean—"

"I mean a drink," Daniel calls from the kitchen. "A beverage. Of a hot temperature and a nonalcoholic nature. PG-rated liquid in a mug."

Lucas smiles. "Then, yes. Please. That would be great." He gets up and goes to the window. He takes a deep, uneven breath, then another. What a weird thing that was. How did everything get so scrambled so fast? Would he really have punched Daniel back there? What a strange thought.

He lifts his shoulders and lets them fall. Things are back on track now. This is good. Things are looking up. They have made a break-through of sorts. The dilapidated concrete courtyard that passes for a garden in Daniel's block of flats has taken on a less gloomy aspect. Lucas is sure, fairly sure, that he can make out the green spears of cro-cuses pushing up from the ashy soil under a tree. A bird alights on a branch for a moment—Lucas sees the flash of a pink-brown underside, a chaffinch, perhaps—and then is gone. He feels himself expanding with relief, feels the earlier adrenaline dispersing. He will be able to tell Claudette that Daniel is, if not exactly well, then showing signs of recovery. He is not painfully thin, as he was a few months ago; he is not too jaundiced. The flat isn't completely chaotic; it could be rated, in his opinion, as the dwelling of someone who is making progress. Claudette worries about Daniel constantly, is consumed with concern for him, despite how difficult he has made—

Lucas catches sight of something on the wall. A photograph of Marithe, tacked above a desk. He ducks his head to look at it, as it isn't one he can recall seeing before. In it, Marithe is wearing a denim jacket and she smiles at the camera, her mouth laced with braces. Lucas frowns. Marithe has never, to his knowledge, worn braces: Claudette loathes them, calls orthodontics "child abuse." Then the realization hits him. It's not Marithe. Of course it's not Marithe. It's Phoebe. How could he have been so stupid? Lucas looks at her, at Phoebe, the lost daughter, looks right into her eyes, which are crinkled, as she must have been facing into the sun, and he gets the urge to reach his hand into the frame of the photograph, to push through its celluloid surface and take hold of her as she was on that day, far away, across the Atlantic, to grasp that sunburned wrist and to hang on, to never let go.

He allows his eyes to drift sideways, along the wall above Daniel's desk. Another picture of Phoebe, older in this one, with her arm around Daniel, Niall standing behind them both. A couple of Calvin and Marithe, one with Ari, in the garden in Donegal. There are several of Claudette, Lucas notes with a grimace, some recent, one of her pregnant, possibly with Marithe, one of her beside a beach campfire, an old publicity shot of her wearing a negligee and a peculiar hat, hair draped over her shoulder. Lucas looks away from this, at a map tacked to the wall. It appears to be the Scottish Borders, with Xs marked in red ink, like a child plotting treasure. A murky, worn photograph of a woman with sharp features, wearing a black cloak, the kind of thing you might put on at Halloween, standing under a crenellated archway, eyeing the camera with a taut, appraising glance.

"You sure you've seen everything?"

Lucas whips around. Daniel is standing in the doorway, two mugs held in his hands.

"There isn't anything you missed?" Daniel's voice is low with menace, and Lucas can see that the other Daniel, the Daniel they all know and love, who reappeared for a moment there, has been subsumed by this other, frightening, furious alter ego. "Are you sure you committed it all to memory?" He strides across the room and Lucas can't help himself—he takes a step back. Daniel puts down the mugs on the desk edge. "Did you see this?" He yanks the map of the borders from the wall and hurls it toward Lucas. "And this?" The photo of the woman in the cloak. "How about this? And this?" Pages, letters, photographs, are ripped out of drawers and files and hurled into the space between the two men and still Daniel keeps talking. "Make sure you tell her that, yes, I was fired. My compassionate leave magically morphed into a termination of employment. Don't leave out that I've got a restraining order on me, from my friend Todd. Be sure to say that I'm still fixating—her word—on my ex-girlfriend, the one who killed herself. Or did I kill her? I never can work that one out. One of the two, anyway. Maybe you'd like copies of all these. I'll make you copies. So you can go back to your sister and give her the ammunition she needs, so she can put in a claim that I am unfit, unworthy, that I mustn't see my children, that they must be kept from me, but you tell her"—Daniel is yelling now, at the top of his voice—"you tell her I won't have it. I won't take it lying down. I won't have anyone do that to me again. I will see those kids, I will. She can send whoever she likes with whatever fucking papers she likes, but nobody—*nobody*—is going to take my kids away from me."

"Daniel, listen," Lucas says. He is near the exit. He has made sure of this. Three steps, maybe four, and he would be at the flat's door, the one that would lead him out into the corridor and then the lobby. "Claudette has no intention of stopping you seeing the children. You know that. She wants you to see them. She would do anything to make that happen."

Daniel is still ranting: "She's even got Niall there now, telling him God knows what, getting him on her side. I don't know how she does it, how she exerts this power over—"

"It was you who sent Niall to her. Remember? You even drew him a map so he could find the house. And you know what? It was exactly the right thing to do. Niall is doing really well, he's—"

"He is?"

From across the littered room, Daniel looks at him, chest heaving.

Lucas nods. "I was there two weeks ago. Niall is in good form."

"Really?"

"Yes. Claudette has him out in the greenhouse, tending her cour-gette plants. He's teaching the kids geology. They go off on walks together with these little hammer things. Calvin has a rock collection now. Niall's helping him label and classify it." Lucas pauses. "She wants to be fair to you. She wants it to be amicable. She says she'll give you however much you—"

"I don't want her goddamn money," Daniel snaps. "She knows that."

"Well, either way, she wants you to see the kids. She just doesn't want them to see you like this."

Daniel glowers at him, fists clenched.

"Can you understand that? She wants more than anything for you to be a father to them, but, Daniel, think about it. Would you want Marithe to see you in this state? Would you want her to come to this flat, to spend the night? Can you picture her and Calvin here, as it is right now?"

Daniel drops his gaze.

"You need to find a way through this," Lucas says. "You need to get yourself together. Do you think you can do that? Daniel? Do you?"

Always to Be Losing Things

ROSALIND

Bolivia, 2015

When the driver comes, stumping wordlessly out of the hut, laden with sacks of food and flagons of water, and flings open the doors of the truck, the group of waiting people seems to hesitate, hang back, to gaze up at the sky or glance at their watches or make some final adjustments to their backpacks.

Nobody, Rosalind sees, wants to get in first. Nobody wants the back-seat.

Suppressing a teacherly sigh (because, really, isn't this the kind of behavior more suited to children on a school trip?), she steps forward, places her bag on the dirt track, and climbs in.

The interior of the truck, van, whatever you want to call it—it resembles most a Land Rover her uncle used to drive, a lifetime ago in Suffolk—is airless, musky, and smells vaguely moldy. A fecund, lichen-ous, hothouse scent. Rosalind seats herself in the farthest corner, by the window: she isn't prepared to forgo that privilege.

She and this group of people, none of whom she has ever met

before, are to spend the next few days making their way by truck to the Salar de Uyuni, a salt desert in the Bolivian Altiplano.

When she booked her place, the man in the little adobe house that served as the tour office had looked at her doubtfully, taking in her silk shirt, her sleek white hair, held back in a velvet band, her gold earrings, her pigskin document case. It is, madam, he had said, in halting, formal English, very rough. No hotel room. Dormitory only. She had replied, in her flawless Spanish, honed from three decades of living in South America: *No me importa.* It doesn't matter. Nothing, you see, she had to stop herself saying to him, matters anymore.

Rosalind directs her gaze at their destination, but the periphery of her vision takes in her fellow passengers as they clamber in. What the backseat may lack in comfort is made up for in vantage point.

The large, bespectacled man is the first to board, just as she'd somehow suspected—he is closest in age to her, albeit younger by a couple of decades—folding up his considerable height to fit through the door. He is succeeded by the Swiss couple, a boy with a grimy tracksuit top, half a beard, and his bafflingly beautiful girlfriend. The boy puts out his cigarette before he gets onboard, Rosalind is pleased to see, but throws the butt on the ground. They, with the self-assurance peculiar to youth, slide themselves onto the front seat, beside the driver, thereby securing themselves the best view. The lone man in his late twenties, who has not yet spoken a word, climbs in last. He makes no eye contact with any of them and sits in the middle row before proceeding to unpack some kind of equipment, possibly photographic, piece by piece.

"Mind if I sit here?" the tall man is asking, in an American accent, indicating the seat beside her, stooping in the confined space, grimacing slightly, as if the movement gives him pain.

Rosalind gestures assent with an open palm and he sits down with a crash, causing her to ricochet upward, once, twice.

She has never been substantial of physique. Like a bird, her lacrosse teacher at school used to say, but a quick one. Nightingale, her husband had called her, in the early days of their marriage. "Spry" is the word used for people of her age, isn't it? Horrible word, Rosalind reflects, like a mixture of "spray" and "why."

She turns her face toward the window, just as her seat companion speaks: "So, you're going on the trek?"

I would have thought that was fairly obvious, she wants to reply, but has had experience with Americans taking this kind of dry British remark the wrong way, so keeps it to herself, merely nodding and saying, "Yes." She then feels that the single word might come across as rather reserved, so adds: "I'm very much looking forward to it."

The bespectacled American is expending a great deal of effort patting his pockets, leaning forward and back, delving into his jacket, inside and out.

"Have you lost something?" Rosalind inquires.

"No . . . It's just . . . I thought I had . . ." He twists around to find his bag, twists back, then yanks his passport out of it. "Oh. There it is."

Rosalind bestows upon him one of her understanding yet distant smiles: the ones she used to use for the servants, for her husband's secretaries, for wait staff at receptions and parties. The smile that says, while I am fully appraised of and sympathetic to your plight, I do not wish to involve myself further. The last thing she needs on this trip is to take charge, to feel responsible for a disorganized male.

Two months ago—can it really have only been that long?—she had been going through the contents of the high cupboards in their bedroom, with a view to what she should take, what she should leave for the servants, what she should throw away. Her husband had been a foreign correspondent in Chile for thirty years, and they had lived all that time in a house high up in the Santiago hills, with its terrace hung with bougainvillea, the parrots that screeched in the mornings, its irrigation pipes of verdigrised copper. And now they were leaving: her husband was retiring, and they were going to live in a cottage in Dorset, near where he had grown up. She had seen photographs of the cottage: it had a blue door and red splashes of hollyhocks growing up the walls and windows latticed with lead. There was a kitchen with an electric cooker: she would have to learn to cook again. She used to know, a long time ago; she was sure she would remember. There they would be, in bucolic retired bliss, with the hollyhocks and the electric cooker, forever, or for at least as long as they wanted.

But the problem was these papers. These lists of figures. These columns of debit, these total amounts now due, these receipts of payment sent. There were bills for in-college dining, for extracurricular sports, for chess club. There were charges for bedding, for heating, for textbooks.

Rosalind had gone through them all, one by one. She had arranged them chronologically, as was her wont, the most recent on top. She had the urge to find a file for them. She even thought about clipping them together.

They were from a college in Canada: that much she could comprehend. But it was the name that was bothering her. Samuel Reeves. Samuel L. Reeves. Samuel Lionel Reeves.

"Lionel" she recognized: it was her husband's name. "Reeves" she recognized: again, it was her husband's and it had been hers for forty-five years. But "Samuel" she did not recognize. She didn't know anyone of that name and, she was quite sure, neither did her husband.

But it seems he did. It seems he knew this boy, this chess-playing, rock-climbing, chemistry-major boy, who required heating and bedding and food, who needed books and sports jackets and extra tuition in something listed as statistical analysis. It seems he knew him very well. Well enough to pay for his college education, for his rent and bills, books and tuition. Which must, she reasoned, as she sat on the bed, mean he knew him very well indeed.

The truck starts up and Rosalind feels a dart of excitement. She sits forward, gripping the seat in front. They are off! She feels as she had when the train that would whisk her off to boarding school had started: ahead of her was potential, was life, was, above all, release.

Someone on a boat in Patagonia had told her about these trucks that took travelers across the salt flats: a German man with a ponytail and a lisp. You should see it, he had said, and swung his head from side to side. It is like nowhere else you've ever been, like nowhere else you've ever seen.

The concept, as much as the inadvertent rhyming couplet, had appealed to her.

In the last two months, Rosalind has climbed Machu Picchu with some gap-year kids. She has been to the Atacama Desert, visited a witches' market in La Paz. She has swum in a thermal pool, been massaged with volcanic mud, and hiked through an araucaria forest. She declined to go white-water rafting on account of her contact lenses, but she did cycle along the world's most dangerous road, which was overhung with waterfalls and pitted with crosses marking places where people had died, at the end of which was just a town with a square and an ice-cream shop and a hotel with a murky pool and soporific fish and a DVD player and a stack of dubbed Hollywood movies. She wanted nothing more than to go somewhere that was like nowhere else she'd ever been: that was, in a nutshell, exactly what she wanted.

So here she was. Off in a vibrating, rattling van, her backpack lashed to the roof, her walking boots and sunscreen at the ready, in search of an ancient prehistoric lake, dried out by the sun, in search of a place where the white desert meets the blue sky.

Without warning, the hitherto silent lone man on the seat in front of her utters the word "Dad?"

Rosalind could not have been more surprised, until the American answers "Yeah?" without looking up from his guidebook.

Rosalind watches, fascinated. These two know each other? They are father and son? They had all been in that hut, waiting for the truck to arrive, for over two hours, and neither of them had given the slightest sign that they were together. They had sat, she remembers now, on opposite sides of the hut, each looking out of the window. (The Swiss couple had pawed each other briefly, then settled down to gaze at photographs of themselves on their phones.)

Stupid of her, really, she thinks, as she covertly glances from one man to the other. They actually look very alike.

"Can you hold this for a second?" the son is saying.

The American puts out his hand, still without looking up, and the other man, the son, places into it a piece of machinery. Some kind of dial with wires trailing from it.

"What is that?" Rosalind asks. She can't help herself.

The father glances at her, then back at his book. He has startlingly blue eyes, an unusual blue, not pale, not dark, but somewhere in between, and a heavy, emphatic brow. "It's part of a seismograph," he says, "a machine that measures—"

"I know what a seismograph is."

"You do?"

"Of course." She rearranges the bag on her lap. Men could be so arrogant. "I've just never seen one before."

"Well, OK." He inserts a finger into his book, to mark his place. "You'll see one later today. Niall is going to take some readings."

They both regard the back of the son's head. He doesn't turn around but continues working on his machinery, fitting one part of it into another, straightening a wire, lifting a valve of some sort to his mouth and blowing away the dust.

"Of the Salar de Uyuni?" Rosalind asks the back of his head. "What for?"

They leave a pause for the son to answer, which he doesn't.

"He's a scientist," the father says, as if this explains everything.

"Here in Bolivia?"

"No, New York."

"I see," Rosalind says. She switches to her drawing-men-out mode. She prides herself on being adept at this. "The two of you work together? A father and son seismology team? How very unusual."

"No"—he shakes his head—"we don't work together. Niall is the seismologist but I'm just . . ." He hesitates. "I was . . . I'm not working at the moment. I . . . "

He grinds to a halt. A terrible crevasse has somehow opened up in the conversation. Rosalind can almost see it there in the truck as it speeds through scenery that isn't yet spectacular, just generic South American plain—scrubby cacti, a few haughty-faced llamas, graveled verges—as the Swiss couple settles down for a conjoined nap. She seems to have stumbled on the one thing this man does not want to talk about, perhaps what he has come here precisely to avoid. It is clear to her that this man, these two men, have undergone some terrible personal trauma. She has seen this before, the taut-eyed expression of despair, felt the atmosphere of silent, gagged tension: it will mean a breach, a loss, an inconsolable termination of some sort. Something has happened, something has ended, something has been wrenched from them. Rosalind sees this. Something has derailed these two men, and here they are, as she is, in the Bolivian Altiplano.

"I'm not ... I'm ..." The man is trying again, his hands holding the pages of the guidebook are trembling, with grief or illness or both, Rosalind doesn't know, doesn't want to know.

"You're taking a break," she finishes for him quietly, before turning back to the window, signaling that she will press him no further, that the conversation may cease, if he so wishes.

And he does wish. For the next hour or so, the only sound is that of the wind rushing past the windows and the tip-tip-a-tap of the seismograph vibrating as the truck navigates rougher and rougher ground.

The problem was, Rosalind thinks, as they speed into desert— an ocher place of streaked sand and strange wind-blown rock formations—that Lionel had been so appallingly unapologetic. He thought, or seemed to think, that having a son he'd kept from her for twenty years was not something that necessitated any kind of excuse or regret. Worse, he seemed to think it was none of her business. When she'd confronted him with the bills and invoices he'd sat for a moment at his desk, his head lowered, buried in his hands, and she'd thought he was grappling with feelings of guilt and remorse so strong that he couldn't meet her eye. She, his wife, who had stood by him, who had remained at his side, for three decades in this country, who had supported and aided and eased his career at every turn, lunching and dining and entertaining God knows which dignitary or politician he would turn up next, ensuring he had a pressed silk square in his breast pocket every single morning, slotting a boutonniere into his jacket, fitting a hat to his balding crown before he headed out into the sweltering city. But when he raised his head, his expression hadn't been as she'd expected—ashamed or furtive or even placatory. On the contrary, he'd looked irritated and weary, as if she was bothering him with some trifling matter, or had taken it upon herself to meddle in something that shouldn't concern her.

He had taken off his glasses and pinched the skin of his nose and rubbed at his forehead, all the while telling her about how he'd started "seeing"—as if it was just a matter of eyes, of vision, something that involved the engagement of a single sense—a woman a long time ago, while she, Rosalind, had spent those months back in England.

He made it sound, she thinks now, as she sits in the truck, as she feels every knock and bump and rock in the road travel up through the wheels and axles and suspension of the truck into the scantily padded seat and up into her spine, as if it had been a holiday. As if she were lounging about, living it up there in England for that year, reading magazines and seeing friends, when in fact she had been helping her sister with the early arrival of her second set of twins.

So while she was teaching the older children to sit on the potty or helping bathe the tiny babies or pegging out endless laundry or getting up in the night to prepare bottles or negotiating with the health visitor for extra orange juice or mopping up her sister's copious tears, her own husband was at home in their Santiago house "seeing" another woman.

Rosalind has no idea what this "seeing" entails. She has vague images of evenings spent in restaurants or nightclubs, dancing in half-light to a swing band, clandestine meetings in hotel rooms, glasses of wine, presents, perhaps, from that jeweler's with the green leather boxes.

The woman, he'd said, was no one she knew. A Toronto journalist, in Santiago for a few months. There had, he'd said, in a monotone, apparently weary of the conversation, been a child. ("A resulting child," was his exact phrase, as if the boy was the residue of some chemistry experiment, some kind of statistic, to be recorded on a graph or logged in a column.)

He had, he'd said, felt he needed to "do the right thing by them" and provide the boy with an education.

Something had happened then: the phone had rung or one of the servants had come through a door with tea on a tray to be drunk, post to be opened and read. He had turned away from her to deal with whatever it was, as if that was an end to the matter. So Rosalind had walked away, through the rooms and corridors of their house, and she had been thinking of all the questions she hadn't put to him: did he still see the woman, had he loved her, did he see the boy, how often and when, what did he look like, did he look like him, and what about her, Rosalind, his wife of forty-five years, what was she supposed to make of this information, what about doing the right thing by her, and what on earth would that right thing have been?

She wasn't thinking of her sister, in the first few weeks of the babies' lives, how she had sat in her nursing chair with her head in her hands, saying, how will I cope, how will we manage, I can't do it, Rosie, I just can't, you take one, please, take both. She hadn't, of course, even though she would have loved nothing more than to bundle one—or even both—of those little pink babies under her arm and trot off back to South America. She didn't think about how, when she next visited England, two years later, none of the children had any memory of her, even though she had fed them, changed them, sung to them, lulled them off to sleep, wiped their bottoms, mashed up their first foods. She didn't think about whether Lionel had had the woman there, whether they had been together in these rooms, whether the servants had known, had known all this time, all these years, whether everyone knew, except her.

What she did think about was the children she and Lionel had never had. The ones who didn't make it, the ones who were but then not quite. There had been three—what a number, astonishing to think!—until Lionel had said, enough; until Lionel had said, no more. We're fine as we are, he said. Just us. Rosalind pictured them, those three, as she often did: sitting in the chairs of her drawing room, loitering in the hall, waiting for her on the treads of the stair, their little chins resting on their knees, although, of course, they would have been quite grown-up by now. She thought, too, about how she'd read somewhere that the only language that had a word for existences, lives such as theirs, was Romany. *Detlene,* they called them. The wandering souls of miscarried or stillborn children. Those who had undeniably lived but only within their mother.

In the truck, she is suddenly conscious that the American man is glancing over at her. She puts up a hand to her lips. Had they been moving? Had she been murmuring to herself, as she knows she does sometimes, had she said *detlene* aloud? (A strange comfort it had been, to find a word for the very thing that lies in the core of your being, in the most secret alleyway of the heart.)

She wills herself not to meet the inquiring gaze of the man beside her. She does not want to look into his bluntly direct gaze. None of his business and, anyway, it's highly unlikely anyone would know such a term. Unless, she reflects, the man is Romany. Which she is fairly confident he is not.

·   ·   ·

The doubting travel agent in the adobe hut had not been wrong about the beds, Rosalind reflects, as she tries to find a comfortable position for her neck. The pillow, such as it is, seems to be filled with some kind of grain. Millet, perhaps, or amaranth. It is rock hard, either way, and makes a disquieting crunching sound when she moves her head, not unlike footsteps on gravel.

They are in a room about the size of the second-best guest bathroom in her house. But there the resemblance ends: no gold taps here, or glazed tiles, underfloor heating or piles of towels. The walls are of compacted mud, the floor grit; the low ceiling releases wisps of what looks like straw or dried grass from the depths of its weave. No lights: they must all use a flashlight. No windows. The door is a tacked length of sacking, which inflates and deflates in the breeze.

Five camp beds are arranged in a line, all of which have an iron bar running down their length. She is right in the middle of the row, the filling in the sandwich. The couple has pushed theirs together, naturally, and have gone to sleep rather sweetly holding hands. The Americans are on her right, the father hunched inside his sleeping bag, the son finally settled, after performing some intricate ritual with lotions and bandaging. The poor soul has the most appalling skin condition: she glances over for long enough to register scarlet swarms and welts on his back, his arms, his legs, before turning quickly away. Everyone, she knows, deserves their privacy, even on a trip like this, where they are housed together in unprecedented proximity, like animals in a rescue kennel.

Rosalind shifts her socked feet so that they are both curled against her water bottle, which the American father filled with boiling water and wrapped in a towel (an old scout trick, he said, giving her a wink that could almost be said to border, disconcertingly, on flirtatious). The air temperature is a marvel: Rosalind can see her breath condensing before her as she lies there, arms crossed over her chest, like a church tomb effigy. It was scorching all day and then, by evening, the chill descended and took hold. She can feel, already, the effects of the altitude. A slight slowing of the body's movement, a pressure on the forehead, an urge to take deeper breaths. They had, the driver said, to expect symptoms to get worse tomorrow.

The truck had climbed and climbed. Oh, the things they had seen! Rosalind feels herself tremble with the pleasure of it all. They had passed lakes of startling, unreal cerulean ("It's the minerals," the scientist boy had explained, squinting through binoculars), geysers belching sulfurous steam, flocks of cerise flamingos, fastidiously high stepping through the algae. Such things! Rosalind wants to hoard each and every one in her mind, placing them carefully on a shelf to be looked at, marveled over in the days and weeks and months to come.

Which is possibly why sleep is eluding her. She is tired, down to her bones, soaked right through, like a rag, with exhaustion but she is simultaneously filled with an effervescent glee, an irrepressible thrill. She is doing this, she is really doing it: everyone said she was crazy, she was out of her mind. Her friends in Santiago and her sister over the phone from London exclaimed in horror when she told them she was leaving Lionel and going traveling, on her own, for two months, maybe three, or perhaps even close to a year. She would be mugged, she would be murdered, she should come back home to England, she must have taken leave of her senses, it must be the shock, she must get Lionel to apologize, was it really worth throwing away a good marriage, she shouldn't rock the boat, she must let things lie, she mustn't do anything in haste.

But the haste, it seemed, had appealed to her, for once. She who had never done anything without careful, detailed consideration; she who had taken eight weeks to decide whether or not she wanted to accept Lionel's offer of marriage; she who took days and several visits to a shop before she could commit to buying a new dress. She had packed a single portmanteau, she had extracted her passport from the bureau where all her and Lionel's documents were kept—their marriage certificate, their visas, their vaccination cards, their insurance—she had tipped the servants, embracing some of them, she had written Lionel a note, three sentences in total, and off she went.

With a trumpety-trump, Rosalind thinks and has to press a hand over her mouth so as not to let out a giggle.

A movement on the other side of the hut makes her turn her head.

One of the Americans is sitting up, unzipping his sleeping bag. The father. Rosalind sees him, through the thick dark, putting on his glasses, rifling through his pockets, his pack. Is it another passport panic? Is he always going to be losing things? She is about to call to him, to ask him, would he like her to switch on her flashlight, when she hears the crackle of something like foil or plastic, and sees him stumbling for the door.

He pushes aside the sacking, ducks down through the door frame, and is swallowed by the gloom.

After a moment, Rosalind unzips her own sleeping bag, swings out her legs and follows him.

The cold outside is static, polar. There is no wind and the thinnest of frosts gilds the ground. The coin of a moon dangles low in a punctured, glittering sky. The sight of it arrests Rosalind on the threshold. She looks up and up. It is the biggest sky she has ever seen, dark lapis in color, so big that it feels almost possible to discern the curvature of the earth beneath it.

"Quite something, huh?"

The American is a little way off, in the lee of the outhouse wall. She can see his outline, the jut of his profile, the fiery tip of a cigarette, moving up toward his mouth, moving down. It reminds her of a satellite, circling in its own lonely orbit.

"It is indeed," she says.

"Niall says," the man begins, blowing out a lungful of smoke; it drifts into Rosalind's face, "that this place is the purest on earth. You can believe it, can't you, when you see it like this?"

She has to struggle not to cough; she has never tolerated smoke well. "Purest in what sense?"

"Something to do with the elements. Chemical elements. They are the purest you can find, because this place was under a sea that was cut off in prehistoric times. So the sodium, the lithium, the magnesium, here are ... "

"Unadulterated?"

"Exactly." He shrugs. "I'm probably explaining it badly. You'd have to ask Niall."

"I might," she says, "if I didn't worry that his answer might be somewhat over my head."

The man nods. "There's always that danger. Niall is a man of few words and those he does say are mostly incomprehensible."

"Was he always like that? A child genius?"

He takes another draw of his cigarette. "He was, I guess. But to me, he's always been just himself."

"Unadulterated," she says, and he turns toward her and she can feel that he is smiling.

"Exactly. Niall is the Salar de Uyuni of the human race." He is still looking at her, tugging the ear flaps of his hat farther down. "So, tell me, Rosalind," he says, "what's your story?"

"My story?"

He shrugs. "What brings you here? I mean, you have a perfect right to be here, of course, but you're hardly the average backpacker. You're, what, sixty years old?"

"Sixty-eight."

"Sixty-eight! Your accent is straight off the pages of an Evelyn Waugh novel, you're all the way out in South America, alone, you speak perfect Spanish. I'm intrigued. What are you doing here?"

She decides to deliberately misunderstand him. "Talking to you."

There is a pause. The man—Daniel, he is called, she now remembers, he'd told her earlier today—looks at her, then away.

"OK," he says. "We can carry on talking about elements and prehistory, if you like."

Rosalind nods. "That would be preferable."

He begins yet another of his searches through his pockets. First the side pockets, then the chest, then the inside ones, then the ones in his trousers.

"Do you ever think," Rosalind asks, "you'd be better buying clothes with fewer pockets?"

Daniel laughs, properly, and for the first time. "My wife says that." He then amends this to, "My ex-wife."

"Well, the woman has a point. It's merely a question of probability," she continues. "If you limited yourself to one or two pockets, you would avoid this matter of constantly misplacing—"

"Aha!" He cuts across her, triumphantly holding aloft a small bottle. "You see? Not too many pockets at all."

He proceeds to shake out a pill from the bottle and gulp it down, without water.

"I don't suppose you could spare me one of those?" Rosalind asks.

"One of these?" He seems amused. "Are you in the habit of asking strange men for prescription medication?"

"No, I—"

"Do you even know what they are?"

"I assumed they were sleeping pills but—"

He shakes his head. "These aren't sleeping pills."

"Oh."

"They're—" and he says a word she doesn't recognize.

"I don't know what that is."

"Then you have led an upright life in the company of decent people." He gives her a pained, abashed glance through the dark. "They're for alcoholics. They make you violently ill if you so much as touch a drink."

"I see," Rosalind says. She turns her head from left to right. "And you're worried about running into a bar around here?"

He recaps the bottle and pushes it into one of his pockets, buttoning down the flap. "No, it's not that. I've made a promise—to Niall and my wife, ex-wife, I should say—to take one every day." He waves a hand through the air. "Niall lived with her for a while there and the two of them got together and formulated this plan. If I take them, she'll let me see the kids and Niall will let me live with him. If I don't, I'm out on my ear. No place to live, no contact with the children."

"That sounds rather harsh."

"Harsh but fair. The signature stamp of my spouse. Former spouse."

"She seems to be a woman of strong opinions."

"You, Rosalind, have hit the nail on the head. She also has the annoying habit of being right, most of the time." He shifts from foot to foot, hands deep in his pockets, then says, in an altered, expressionless voice, "She kicked me out, you see, three years ago. I don't blame her. I was not in a good state and kids shouldn't grow up around that. I'm doing the Twelve Steps now. For my sins."

"How are you finding it?"

"Terrible," he says cheerfully. "I hate it. It's a toxic mixture of pious

344

and dull. And the people you meet are so ... I don't know ... mono-maniacal. There's no one more joyless than a drinkless drunk."

"What step are you on?"

"Two." He grins at her. "It's the third time I've done it. Niall calls them the Thirty-Six Steps. So maybe I should take the optimistic view and say I'm on step twenty-six."

Rosalind shivers. The cold has crept up on her, sliding its fingers along her skin.

"Come on," he says, noticing. "We should get some sleep. May I escort you back to the penthouse suite?"

"You may," she says, and takes the proffered arm.

Daniel insists that Rosalind sit in the front seat, next to the driver. When she demurs, he divests her of her coat and her small bag and stows them in the footwell, so she really has no choice other than to climb in with them. It is, she learns, as soon as they set off, the most comfortable place in the truck. Which isn't saying much, but there is a modicum more padding here than in the back and she can see the whole wide vista of the windshield.

In the back, the Swiss couple bickers in their seesawing language; Niall sits with a notebook open on his lap, marking something down in it; his father sits beside him, eyes hidden behind dark glasses.

Rosalind attempts to engage the driver in some small talk but doesn't get very far. He is called Carlos, he lives in Potosí and has four children. And that, it seems, is that. Carlos, Rosalind would venture to guess, is not a man who derives a great deal of satisfaction from his job.

They reach the salt pan by midday.

Rosalind must have been dozing because she comes to in a place so dazzlingly light that, for a moment, she cannot see. She had been dreaming of the veranda that adjoined her house in Santiago: the suc-culents with symmetrical faces, bedded in gravel, the spike-fingered yuccas, the moist-petaled orchids perspiring in their mossy peat.

She wakes with a small cry. She knows this because she hears it reverberating in her ears. She sits herself straight, clears her throat, clutches at the bag on her lap, avoids the eyes of those around her.

Will they have heard her? What would they make of it? Will they say anything?

Then she stops thinking these thoughts. She stops thinking anything at all.

The world around her is startling, unaccountable. While she has been sleeping, the truck has pulled into a place like no other. She has never seen anything like it before.

The windows are filled with a relentless, merciless magnesium-white glare. She has to hold her hands over her eyes and open her fingers just a crack. Her neck and forehead throb with a bright, sharp pain—either the altitude or the retinal shock.

Everyone in the truck is silent, motionless. Nobody speaks.

When she is able to remove her hands, she sees that the oblong of the windshield is bisected by a thin, hazy, bichromial line: blue meets white. That is all. Salt topped by sky. Pure, twinned color.

Someone in the seats behind lets out a low whistle and this seems to break the spell. The door is clicked open and there is the sound of footsteps, of scrambling, of exclamations.

Rosalind gathers up her hat, puts on her sunglasses, and releases the catch to her door. Her boots crunch as she steps down. She looks at the white at micro-level: minute crystals of salt. She turns around: white, white, white, salt, salt, salt, as far as her sight will stretch.

She turns 360 degrees, her hand shading her eyes. It is, she thinks, quite unbelievable. Her eye searches for an irregularity, a seam, a trick, a flaw, but there is none. Salt reaches up to meet the horizon and then there is a cloudless expanse of sky. Blue matched by white, one reflecting off the other.

The effect is somehow celestial. It is as if she has woken in the afterlife, and heaven is a place of purity, clarity, and two colors. And completely, unutterably empty.

Or not quite. Some way off are the tiny pegs of figures. She can hear the fetch and fall of voices. The Swiss couple is photographing each other. Rosalind watches, impassive, as the boy sheds his clothing, his equipment bouncing up and down as he struggles with his last remaining sock. The girl's laughter rolls along the salt toward her, like a bright, shining ball.

"I hope he's got sunblock on that."

Rosalind turns to see the scientist beside her. He is disheveled in a misbuttoned shirt, a blue hat, sunglasses, and a cream so thick it renders his face a ghastly pallid hue.

"Shall we ask him?" Rosalind says, watching as the Swiss boy performs naked cartwheels, his girlfriend running after him with the camera.

The scientist, Niall, pulls a face. "No, thanks." He turns his attention to some monitor that he's carrying. "He needs to be careful, though. This place has the most intense level of ultraviolet light anywhere in the world."

"Does it?" Rosalind asks and, aware that he'll know the answer, says, "Why?" She never shirks the opportunity to gain knowledge, to add a fact to her store.

"Because the rays come from above," Niall points up, "and reflect back off that." He points to the glistening white ground, flat as a mirror. "You know anywhere else in the world where you need to apply sunblock to the underside of your chin?"

With that, he walks off, leaving Rosalind alone. She reaches for her camera, Lionel's camera, raises it to her eye. She turns the lens left, she turns it right, scrolling over the landscape. She positions the horizon line halfway up the viewfinder, she shifts it down. Then she lets her hands fall. She replaces the lens cap.

Within the camera, the salt desert looks faked, tricked up, the brain-child of some filmmaker or optical illusionist. No one would believe these photographs. No one would look at them and gain even a fraction of the awe, the surreality, the—here, she thinks of the scientist, twenty feet or so from her, staring up at the sky, his head on one side—*purity*.

Overreacting. That was what Lionel had charged her with. Over-reacting. Emoting. Crying. He had never expressed that he felt hers was a peculiarly female response but the implication was there. The correct response, he seemed to be thinking, the male response, would be rationality, calm, order.

"It happened so long ago" was the other thing he said, over and over again. It was years ago. As if this would take the sting out of it.

And yet, there was this person, this boy, this man. The resulting child. Evidence, living and breathing, of what had taken place while she was thousands of miles away.

Rosalind has only ever known the body of one person, in that way. She has only, in all her sixty-eight years, had intercourse with one man: her husband, Lionel. She had believed, for her entire marriage, that it had been the same for him, that their aging bodies had known only each other, enjoyed only each other, responded only within their exclusive, private pairing.

Now, though, she cannot think these things, she can no longer rely on them. Now she sometimes feels regret that she hadn't taken the many opportunities that had come her way—because they had, in her twenties, her thirties, sometimes even her forties. There were men, always, who had signaled to her, overtly or otherwise, that they would have been pleased to share her bed. But she had always rebuffed them, always lowered her eyes, always eased away a hand she found on her knee, her waist, her shoulder blade.

Too late, now, of course. Rosalind adjusts her sunglasses, dabs at the beads of sweat collecting along her hairline. She will be seventy, in the blink of an eye, and somehow she finds herself adrift, homeless, husbandless, childless, grandchildless.

It is not what she had expected of life.

She walks over the crisp skin of the salt. She tries to picture this place, filled as it would have been with water, with tides, with raging, restless seas. What a transformation has been here!

The problem is, she thinks, as she comes to a standstill beside a peaked stalagmite of salt (like a sculpture or a vase, perhaps), that she doesn't know where to be. How to live. Where to put herself. She is English: she sounds English, her passport is English, all her relatives are English. And yet she hasn't lived in England nearly half her life. She has been moored here, in South America, for so long that she thinks in Spanish, she dreams in Spanish, she pictures the globe oriented so that the dagger shape of South America stabs proudly down the middle, Europe, Africa, and Australasia somewhere off at the periphery.

The idea of going back to England, she reflects, as she rubs her fingers over the crusted, desiccated skin of the stalagmite, is alien to her. Where would she go? Where would she live? Going back with Lionel seemed somehow less strange, as if he carried an element of South America within him, a necessary portion. Without him, it simply doesn't compute.

Could she live in a little London flat? Rosalind forces herself to envisage sitting at a desk, writing letters, perhaps, in a bay window painted white, veiled in net curtains, somewhere in Maida Vale or St. John's Wood.

What, she wonders, would she do all day? Could she grow succulents along the sills? Would bougainvillea take in a pot? Could she be bothered to cook, to feed herself, in a narrow galley kitchen? Would Lionel try to see her, assuming he goes back to England, to the cottage, as planned? Would she let him?

The altitude is making itself known, she realizes. To put one foot in front of another takes a supreme effort, a laboring of the lungs. She can feel her heart knocking away, in its reliable, responsive way, but clearly confused, wondering what on earth is going on.

She needs a moment of shade. She turns back toward the van. She will, she decides, sit in it, with the doors open, to catch whatever breeze comes her way.

She finds the American, Daniel, already there, blowing smoke out of an open window.

"Does it seem sacrilegious to you?" he says, indicating the cigarette. "In this place?"

"Not particularly." Rosalind climbs into the seat next to him and unbuckles her bag, searching for her tube of sunscreen. "I've been chatting to your son."

"Oh, yeah? What about?"

"Sunburned genitalia."

Daniel, in the act of tapping ash into a can, stops. "Excuse me?"

She gives a short laugh, smearing cream from her chin to her neck. "Never mind. Doesn't matter."

They look together at Niall, who is bent double, scraping at the salt with some kind of knife or scalpel. Beyond them, the Swiss couple are putting on their clothes, picking up empty shirts and shorts and handing them to each other. Niall ignores them with a determined, stolid air.

"He is so like you," Rosalind says, "and yet so different."

If it weren't for the boy, she thinks, it might have been all right. I might have been able to forgive, to overlook. But the child, the boy, the student, bothers her, devastates her, in a way so visceral, so elemental, she cannot find a way around it. She will not live in that cottage with Lionel. She will not. But will she stay here or will she go to London and live near her sister, her nieces and nephews?

"Yup," Daniel says. "He's different from me in all the right ways. My wife's theory about Niall, my ex-wife, I mean, is that—"

"Did you know," Rosalind interrupts, turning to him, "you do that every time you mention her?"

"What?"

"Call her your wife, then correct yourself to 'ex-wife.'"

Daniel stares at her, ash collecting at the end of his cigarette. "I do?"

Rosalind nods. "Every time."

Daniel stubs out his cigarette with exacting care and drops it into the can. "Huh," he says, after a moment. "I didn't know that."

"Is it a case of forgetting?" she says, because she doesn't see the point in dissembling, not at her age, not after what she's been through, not with this man whom she will probably never see again. "Because it's so recent? Or is it a case of not wanting to believe it?"

"Um." Daniel scratches his head, takes off his sunglasses to wipe at his brow. He laughs. "You ask very penetrating questions, don't you? Well," he clears his throat, "it would be the latter, I guess."

Rosalind nods. "It's none of my business—"

"You're going to say 'but' now, aren't you?"

"Yes," she says, "I am. It's none of my business *but* if you want her back, if—"

"If?" He sighs, with all the longing and regret of a much-younger man, as if he's only just realized, as if he's only now willing to admit it.

"—then you must get her back. Or, at the very least, try." Rosalind taps him on the arm with her camera strap. "Life comes to us but once, Daniel."

"Tell me about it," he murmurs.

Niall appears at the open door. He hurls a backpack onto the seat in front of them, followed by his sun hat, followed by some kind of tripod.

"What are you two talking about?" he says, without looking at them.

"Claudette," Daniel says.

This makes Niall stare, first at his father, then at Rosalind, his eyebrows raised. "Really?" he says.

"Rosalind here was giving me some advice. The female perspective."

"Nonsense," Rosalind chides. "Being female has nothing to do with it. It's a simple case of following through."

"Following through?"

"You must take your pills," Rosalind says to him, "as promised. You must get yourself back on your feet, prove to the world that you've changed. Am I right?"

Daniel shrugs. "Maybe."

"And then—and only then—you must go to this Colette or Claudette or whatever she's called and you make sure that she sees you, in your new, revised state. Lie across her front doorstep, if necessary. Don't leave until you have her attention. And when you do, you tell her."

"I tell her what?"

"Whatever it is you wish you'd said to her years ago, when you were still together. I have a theory," she says, looking far ahead, at where salt meets sky, "that marriages end not because of something you did say but because of something you didn't. All you have to do now is work out what it is."

Rosalind tears her gaze away from the blue, the white, and she looks at the two men in the truck, who are staring back at her.

"That's it?" Daniel says.

"Were you not listening?" Rosalind says. "It's not exactly straightforward. It's going to require fortitude and courage, determination and insight. It will be difficult, it will be a struggle. But," she says, snapping shut the clasp on her bag, "I have no doubt you can pull it off."

Daniel responds by rubbing at his eyes, wearily, resignedly, as if to contain all they have seen. "I don't know," he murmurs. "Claudette isn't exactly a pushover."

"Well, of course she isn't," Rosalind says. "She wouldn't be worth it if she was. Would she?"

She sees that Niall, for the first time, is smiling. A lopsided half smile but a smile nonetheless.

"Anyway," says Daniel, raising his head, "what about you, Rosalind?"

"What about me?"

"What are you going to do?"

"That," she says, as the truck's engine starts beneath them, "is another story."

Gold-Hatted, High-Bouncing Lover

ARI, CALVIN, AND MARITHE

Belfast, 2016

The cheetah paces to the end of its compound and turns, walking straight toward them, toward the glass where Zoë and Ari are standing. Ari can't help it: he pulls Zoë back by the wool of her hood, away from the animal, its gliding flank, its muscled golden fur, its baleful ocher eyes, its maddened face, streaked by twin tracks, as if it has wept black tears and scored itself forever.

"Daddy." Zoë objects mildly to the manhandling, freeing her hood from his grasp, without taking her eyes off the animal.

"Sorry," mutters Ari, who is checking his watch with one hand and his phone with the other. It's about the right time but there's still no text from Daniel, so perhaps it isn't going to happen after all. After the weeks and months of Ari's clandestine engineering and planning and arranging and persuading, the idea that this might not come off gives him the urge to bang his head against something. Hard.

He slides the phone into his pocket, then finds himself looking into the curious eyes of the woman next to him—a cookie-cutter middle-class mother with blond highlights and two kids in a double stroller. Ari holds her gaze, registering and challenging her surprise, until she looks away.

He's used to people thinking he is Zoë's older brother or male nanny or kindly cousin. Twenty-two-year-old dads of five-year-olds are apparently not something you see every day.

The cheetah treads its path to the compound wall where it turns, just as before, and heads back toward them. Ari tells himself he mustn't pull Zoë back: the animal is behind reinforced glass, it can't reach her, it can't harm her. But as it nears them—again, the beautiful terror of its markings, so close he can see the irregularities in the pattern—he has to put out his hand to touch her hair, still infant-soft, where it gathers and flows into a hair clip.

He feels the eyes of the woman on him once more. He turns to see her staring at him; when their eyes lock she tries to turn her stare into a smile but he knows. He knows she's thinking, how can that boy be that child's father? What is the world coming to?

Ari wants to turn to her and say, I knocked up a girl at school, OK? A condom split on us, bad luck, chance in a million, could happen to anyone: fill in whichever cliché you like. The girl was Catholic—one of the posh ones you get in England—so she wouldn't have an abortion and here we are. Do you want to take a picture or what?

The mother senses some of his ire, Ari is sure, because she pushes down on the handle of the stroller and swings it around, away from the cheetah.

Zoë wants to see the cheetah every time he brings her to visit his family in Ireland. She will ask about it on the plane, ask again when Claudette picks them up, ask every morning until they agree that, yes, they will take her to the zoo. It's not as if, Ari said to Claudette yesterday, we don't take her to the zoo in London. He and Sophie are always getting the bus with her to Regent's Park and spending hours in front of the cheetah compound.

Claudette had shrugged. So she loves cheetahs, she said. It's an excellent thing to have passions. It's a good sign. We'll go to the zoo tomorrow, she said to Zoë.

So while Sophie will be at a lecture and his colleagues will still be in bed, sleeping off a hangover or a late night, Ari has been up since dawn, as he always is on days when he and Zoë are in Donegal. She can't sleep, she says, because she doesn't want to miss a thing.

Zoë likes the cheetah but not the lions. She likes the lizards but not the penguins. She hates the monkeys, she hates the grin-toothed piranhas. She likes the parrots and the meerkats and the sun bears. She will not go anywhere near the giraffes ("too tall") or the llamas ("I don't like their nostrils").

"Is the cheetah happy?" Zoë asks, twisting her head around.

Ari, caught in the act of checking his phone again, looks at her, appalled. Of all the times they have stood here, she has never once asked this. He has often wondered what she is thinking as she stares at the circling animal, as it wears deeper and deeper grooves in the mud of its cage.

"Um," he says, hating the weak tone of his voice, "I don't know. What do you think?"

Zoë narrows her eyes—she has Claudette's eyes, pale green with darker edges, but Ari's thick, dark hair and her mother's long nose—and says, "What do *you* think?"

Ari sees he can't sidestep this. "I think," he says carefully, "that perhaps the cheetah would like a bit more space."

"To walk around in?"

"Yes."

Zoë considers this, looking back at the cheetah, which has stopped by its bare, muddy branch, from which hangs the skinned carcass of some small mammal: white ribs, sawn off, protrude from the marbled flesh, like piano keys. The cheetah stares past them, a simmering, sour expression on its face, at something only it can see: the vestigial memory of a grassland, perhaps, with wide-leafed trees and leaping gazelles. "I think the cheetah is sad," she says.

"Really?"

"Because it doesn't get to see me every day," says Zoë, with the myopia of a five-year-old, lacing her fingers together and pressing her forehead into the glass.

"Well, perhaps he—"

Ari is interrupted by someone barging into him, pushing him so that he nearly drops his phone. He staggers forward, toward the cheetah, which is now on the other side of the glass. He turns to see Marithe, who is dressed in peculiar shredded trousers and a black hoodie, earphones in.

"Urgh," she says, holding her nose. "What's that stink?"

"It's the cheetah," Zoë explains, putting her arms around the legs of her aunt. "He does poos in there but he can't help it because he doesn't have anywhere else."

Marithe looks down at Zoë, momentarily speechless. Then she says, "Gross." Then she turns to Ari. "Have you got any food? I'm starving."

"People in refugee camps are starving, Marithe," Ari says. "You are merely hungry and probably only because you didn't bother to eat any breakfast."

Marithe rolls her eyes. "Who made you minister for food?" She takes Zoë's hand and tugs on it. "Come on, Zo-zo. Let's go and hit up Grandmère for a fiver and we'll get ourselves some chips."

They find Claudette at a picnic table beside the trampolines, where Calvin is bouncing around inside a net. Zoë runs toward her and Claudette envelops her small form in a sweeping hug.

"Did you see the cheetah?" his mother is saying to Zoë, as Ari approaches. "Is he as beautiful as ever?"

Zoë is nodding, thumb in, head inclined against Claudette's shoulder.

"And was he walking his walk? Did he look at you and smile?"

Calvin sees his family as a blur: smears of color in the hinterland beyond the net encircling the trampoline. Snatched syllables reach him. An "erp" in his mother's husky tones; a "tting" from Zoë. A rumble of an "aah" from his brother. Marithe, he knows, will be mostly silent from the outside but inside—inside!—her world will be one of aural color, music, beat, lyrics filling her skull, a private stream of sound from her earbuds. She lets him listen sometimes, if he asks her nicely, in the back of the car: she will hand him one earbud, which he will insert, and they will listen together, caught as a pair in the eddying world of her music.

Right now, he can hear the hammering of his heart, the rush of blood in his ears, the rhythmic thunk of his feet against the webbed elastic surface of the trampoline. He is pure sensation, pure motion. The sky reaches down and smacks the top of his head, again and again, the trees lurch their branches toward him, like Baba Yaga's forest, but the rest of the world is gone—his family, the crowds, the walls of the aquarium, the chip stand.

He is bouncing higher, higher, trying to remember the rhyme his mother says sometimes, about a gold-hatted, high-bouncing lover, which ends with an emphatic *I must have you,* at which she would always scoop him off his feet into a flailing, tangled hug, when he was little, when they were on the trampoline at home together. He is getting his vision above the top of the net: he can see the monkey enclosure, the tops of buses on the roads outside the zoo, and the entrance gate, which is why he is the first to see his father.

Daniel is walking toward them: he appears to Calvin in stop-motion, his progress across the zoo punctuated by the trampoline net, but he's getting closer with each bounce. He has on a gray overcoat, one Calvin hasn't seen before, and a paisley scarf around his neck.

"Hey," Calvin yells, breathless, his legs buckling under him so that he falls to his side, dizzy and disoriented by the sudden return to static life. "It's Dad!"

Claudette, in the middle of drawing a picture with Zoë, looks around at Calvin, crayon in hand, as if to admonish him for yelling such outrageous untruths. Ari, who is texting Sophie with a photo of Zoë and the cheetah, looks up from his phone, which is just this minute receiving a message from Daniel: *I'm here. Where are you?* Marithe does nothing. She's wired up to her music and so has no idea that her father, who lives these days in New York, whom she hasn't seen for a month and a half, is coming up behind her.

"Oh," Ari says, flushing, turning to his mother, aware all of a sudden that his stammer might make an unwelcome appearance. "I . . . I . . . I m-meant to say. He mentioned . . . ages ago that he . . . he might be in town and I just—I just—I just thought—"

His mother is staring him down. She raises her eyebrows at him, then reaches for her sunglasses, on the table in front of her, and puts them on. "I see," she says.

"I'm sorry," Ari says, trying to motion to Marithe to take off her earphones: he could do with her help here, but she is miles, oceans, time zones away, "I thought I'd said . . . ," he lies. "M-m-maybe it slipped my mind."

Claudette is smoothing Zoë's hair with a stiff hand. "Well," she says, "he's here now."

And indeed he is. Daniel reaches their group, a huge grin on his face, overcoat flapping open. "Hey!" he booms, and Ari smiles, despite himself, despite the awkwardness swirling around him, despite the incriminating messages on his phone, which his mother must never, ever find. Daniel's voice has always carried a head-turning volume, more than he himself is perhaps aware.

"What's with you all?" he yells, then seizes a surprised Marithe off her seat, bear-hugs Calvin, hurls Zoë into the air, and slaps Ari across the shoulders. When all this is done, he stands in front of his ex-wife. Ari is finding it hard to breathe; he is trying not to look at them yet is unable to tear away his gaze. Claudette and Daniel haven't, as far as he's aware, clapped eyes on each other for three, maybe four, years. In that time, Daniel has moved back to the States, been to rehab, taken up running, got himself a new teaching post, seen the children every six weeks, and has started a charitable trust for elective mutes. He is, in short, a different man from the one Claudette kicked out four years ago.

Daniel waits, Claudette seated before him. He lifts his palms into the air, as if to say, and?

Claudette fiddles with the cuff of her glove, then extends her hand. "Hello, Daniel," she says.

Daniel looks down at Claudette's hand. He lets out a laugh. Marithe looks at Ari and grimaces.

"Seriously?" Daniel is saying. "You want me to shake hands with you?"

Behind her sunglasses, Claudette gives one of her shrugs, learned at the feet of the master of Gallic *froideur* (Pascaline).

"Come on," Daniel says and, pushing aside the gloved hand, he leans in, cups the face of his ex-wife, and kisses her on the cheek, for perhaps only a fraction too long.

Daniel seats himself, without looking at Claudette, and pulls Zoë onto his knee, asking her what she's seen at the zoo, this cheetah he's been hearing so much about. Ari sits at the neighboring table, under the guise of watching his daughter but actually keeping an eye on Claudette and Daniel. He has invested too much time and effort in this meeting to abandon them, unsupervised, so soon. He is interested to see how his little experiment will progress. Calvin resumes bouncing, working up to being able to see over the net once more. Marithe is asking Claudette, then Daniel, for some money so she can buy snacks, bringing Zoë onside for leverage, and Daniel is saying, I've been here for two minutes and already you're asking me for cash?

"Nice picture," Daniel says to Claudette as an aside, nodding at a crayoned drawing of a monkey.

"Thanks," she says.

"Did you do it all by yourself?"

Ari sees his mother frown, trying to be cross but actually battling amusement. He wants to punch the air. The minute she smiles, he knows that Daniel will have won a significant victory. Daniel was always so good at puncturing her hoity-toity tendencies with humor.

"So," Daniel says as Zoë clambers over his head and onto his back.

"What?" Claudette says.

"How come you're being all . . . "

"All what?"

"I don't know." He rubs a hand over his stubble—should he have shaved perhaps? Ari wonders. "All Pascaline Lefevre."

"What do you mean?" Claudette demands.

"You know."

"I don't know."

"Yeah, you do. All," Daniel waves a hand in the air, "chilly and elegant and disapproving."

"Is that what you've come here for? To insult my mother?"

"No, never. I was in Ireland for . . . a conference and thought I might come and pick up those things of mine still at the house and I heard you guys were going to be at the zoo today so I came to see my kids. Our kids."

"Hmm."

"And since when," he says, "has 'elegant' been an insult?"

Marithe stands among the iron picnic tables, unsure what to do, where to go. Calvin is back on the trampoline, singing now, something about camels and deserts and moving shapes. He's learning it on the guitar at home. Ari is accepting Zoë onto his knee; they have their dark heads bent together; Zoë has her thumb in and her feet dangle down almost to the ground. How can she have grown so much? She's a proper child now, Marithe suddenly sees, not at all a baby, her face no longer round and squishable. At the next table, amazingly, sit her mother and her father. Together. In one place, at the same time. She could almost use the word "parents," something which, she now thinks, has slipped from her vocabulary.

She stands facing these people, her family, uncertain to whom she should attach herself. Ari cradles Zoë on his lap, saying something into her ear: there seems no requirement for a third person there. Perhaps she should go to her parents, to smooth things over, to ensure they don't start a row.

She assesses them from between her narrowed lashes. They don't, she knows, look like other people's parents. Daniel is larger, louder, more expressive than other dads. He waves his arms in the air. His hair is wilder, his shirts more elaborate, his coats scruffier. He picks up on the things people say, the way people say them: he is obsessed with the words people choose and why, with accent, with inflection, with why you say what you say, whom you're copying when you say something in a certain way, with the differences in what he calls regional vocabulary. Marithe realized a year or so ago that not everyone's fathers do this.

It seems to Marithe that her life has undergone two changes: one, when her father left. And two, when she turned thirteen, when her life and the way she felt about it and the way she viewed it suddenly tilted, like the deck of a ship in a storm.

At first it seemed to her that her house, her family, her dogs, her accordion, her books, her room with its geology samples, its display of feathers, its pictures of foxes and wolves, all took on an unreal aspect. Everything felt like a stage set: she kept viewing herself as if from the outside. Instead of just acting, just doing, just running or speaking or playing or collecting, she would feel this sense of externalization: And so, a voice inside her head would comment, you are running. Do you need to run? Where are you going? You're picking up that rock but do you want it, do you really need it, are you going to carry it home?

Certain things she'd always loved, like lighting the dinner-table candles or stirring a cake mix alongside her mother or sitting up on the roof to play her accordion or decorating the Christmas tree or collecting the eggs in the morning, felt suddenly hollow, distant, staged. It was as if someone had dimmed the lights, as if she was viewing her existence from behind a glass wall.

And her body! Some mornings she woke and it was as if lead weights had been attached to her limbs by some ill-meaning fairy. Even if she had the urge to walk across the paddock to feed the neighbors' horses—which she hardly ever did anymore, she didn't know why—she wouldn't have the energy, the sap in her, to do it.

She wanted it returned to her, Marithe did, that sense of security in her life, of certainty, of knowing who she was and what she was about. Would it ever come back?

She had asked her mother this one night, lying on the sofa, looking up at the gold stars they had cut out and stuck up there once, a long time ago, her mother teetering at the top of a ladder, which had made Daniel shout, later, when he found out, because she was pregnant with Calvin and Daniel said Claudette must be "out of her mind" to be climbing up stepladders. Marithe had looked at her, at the zone around her head, and wondered what it would be like to be outside her mind, where it would be, what it would feel like to be caught, luxuriating, hanging around in all that hair.

Anyway, the older, longer, sluggish Marithe had looked up at the stars and asked her mother, who was sitting in the chair opposite, whether it would come back, this sense of being inside your life, not outside it.

Claudette had put down her book and thought for a moment. And then she had said something that made Marithe cry. She'd said: probably not, my darling girl, because what you're describing comes of growing up, but you get something else instead. You get wisdom, you get experience. Which could be seen as a compensation, could it not?

Marithe felt those tears pricking at her eyelids now. To never feel that again, that idea of yourself as one unified being, not two or three splintered selves who observed and commented on each other. To never be that person again.

For Calvin, she feels a simultaneous jealousy and pity. He still has it, that wholeness, that verve. There he is, on the trampoline, completely on the trampoline, not worrying about anything, not thinking, But now what? Or: What if? Pity, because she knows now he'll go through it. He'll have to lose several skins; he'll wake up one day wearing new, invisible glasses.

And where does she even start with her mother? When she was a child, her mother had been her mother, but Marithe is aware that most children don't grow up in a house like hers, most people are not taught at home instead of going to school, that what she has is not normal or ordinary, that people sometimes stare at them, then look quickly away.

The last time Ari came to stay, Marithe had seen a line of light under his door late one night. She'd knocked, then tiptoed in. Ari had been sitting up in his bed, his laptop open in front of him, working, she supposed. He had set up some website in London with friends of his; they took tourists on guided walks through the city, telling them about places that appeared in films or books or plays. He'd explained it all to her before.

She'd sat herself down on his bed, and he had smiled at her in a way that meant he didn't mind her interrupting, but he might have to go on working anyway.

"Can't sleep?" he'd said absently, his eyes still on his screen.

And Marithe had taken a deep breath. Why, she'd said, do we live here? And why won't Mum go anywhere and why are we homeschooled and what is it, what is the thing that everybody knows and I don't? I know there is something.

Ari had looked at her then. He'd looked at her for a long time. She could see him weighing up answers in his head, see him trying to decide what to say, how much to tell her. Then he'd bitten his lip and said, "You should really ask Mum."

Marithe had banged him on the leg. "I have asked her," she'd said. "She just smiles and shakes her head."

Ari looked up at the ceiling and sighed. "She'll kill me if I tell you," and Marithe felt blood rushing through her chest, thick and fast. She felt that she was close to something she'd almost always known, something that had been on the other side of a curtain, all her life, and Ari had the power to whisk the curtain away. She was close, she was so close. "Tell me," she urged. "Please."

"You have to promise not to let on that you know. You have to swear."

"I promise."

"I mean it, Marithe. You have to swear on . . . the donkey's life."

Marithe squeezed her eyes shut, tried not to picture the donkey, whom she loved more than any other animal in the world, ever, and said, "I swear."

Then Ari did something surprising. Instead of speaking, he typed something quickly on his keyboard, hit return, then swirled the laptop around so that Marithe could see the screen.

"There," he said.

Marithe looked at the screen. She couldn't comprehend what was appearing there. She glanced at her brother, who was sitting up in bed, arms folded. Image after image of Claudette, much younger, materialized on the screen: her on a flight of stone steps, standing in a lake in a white shirt, in an embrace with a man Marithe didn't recognize, on a stage in a red dress that trailed on the ground, close to the camera, far away. "What," she'd said, "are these?"

Ari had explained the unbelievable. That Claudette, their mother, had been an actress and a filmmaker, a famous one, a very famous one, a long time ago, when he was just a baby.

"You can find her films just about anywhere," he'd said. "People still watch them. They're classics." Then he'd shut the laptop with a snap, his face twisted in a way that was very familiar to Marithe.

"What?" she'd demanded. "What is it?"

"Nothing."

"There's more," she'd cried. "I know it! I can tell by the way you're pressing your lips together."

So Ari sighed and they argued and wrangled for a bit longer and Marithe had to promise she wouldn't tell Calvin and that she'd never let on to Claudette that Ari had told her, and that if Claudette ever did tell her, Marithe had to pretend she didn't know.

Eventually, Ari reopened his laptop and typed in something else. He hit return. He frowned. He clicked a few times and then he turned the screen back.

It was an article from a newspaper, dated several years before Marithe was even born. Marithe read the headline; she read the words.

She looked at the accompanying picture of her mother, grainy, in black and white, standing at a window, holding a dark-haired toddler.

When she looked up, her brother was regarding her with an expression of concern, of sympathy.

"I don't . . . ," she began, trying to master her thoughts.

"You don't what?" Ari said, after a moment.

"I don't get it."

"What don't you get?"

"Any of it!" Marithe rubbed her eyes; she suddenly felt incredibly tired, almost tearful. "It says she disappeared. It says they think she might have drowned. It says you, too, but . . . but how can they say that . . . when"—she was crying now, tears coming hot and fast down her cheeks—"when we know it isn't true, when I can see you right here in front of me?"

"Marithe—"

"It doesn't make any sense. How can it be written in a newspaper that you and Mum might have drowned in Sweden when—"

"She made it look like that."

"Deliberately?"

Ari nods. "She had to put them off the scent, to give us time to get away."

"But that's an awful thing to do, to make people think you've died, to lead them to believe—"

"Listen, everyone realized very soon afterward that we hadn't died, that she'd staged the whole thing. They traced us through several airports. She'd used our French passports, which put off the police a bit longer, as they were searching for our British ones. My father, Timou, gave an interview about it at some point—there's a picture of him with our other passports." Ari looked at Marithe. "I only know all this because I've researched it online. She won't talk about it to me either."

Marithe stared at her brother. Ari was biting his lip, clicking his pen on and off. "But why would she go to those lengths? What was she trying to get away from?"

"I don't know exactly," Ari said, reaching for his cigarettes, "but whatever it was it must have been pretty bad for her to do something as drastic as that. Don't you think?"

Marithe stands in the zoo and this knowledge rests on her, like a coat with stone-loaded pockets. Most of the time she can be as she always was with her mother: they drive to the beach, they walk to pick up the milk from the farm, they study together, they chat as they dig the garden, they make dinner, they chop wood. Other times, often when her mother is engaged in some task, shelling beans or straining cheese or patching Calvin's trousers, she finds herself staring at Claudette and turning over the facts, quickly and stealthily, like the pages of a forbidden book: a famous actress, a disappearance, the waters surrounding the city of Stockholm, only the rowboat was found, leaving Ari's father behind, suspected sightings but none of them confirmed. She will look at her mother's hands and think, she lifted Ari into the rowboat. She will look at her mother's face and think, she acted in films, she wrote films. She will cast her eyes over her mother's shoulders, bent over an atlas with Calvin, and think, you were so unhappy that you ran, you escaped, you hid yourself away.

She hates that this now sits between them, that this gully has appeared: she knows but can't tell Claudette that she knows. She twists her fingers into the wires of her headphones, until their tips turn magenta vivid.

She shuts her eyes, trying to blind herself to everything she knows, trying to unknow it. She hears Calvin's breathing, she hears Zoë's voice, asking Ari if he will draw her a hopscotch when they get home, she hears her father talking to her mother, not what he is saying, just the rumbling timbre of his voice.

She opens her eyes and finds her mother is looking at her in that way she has sometimes: motionless, penetrating, unblinking. Marithe cannot tear her gaze away. Her father and mother are holding hands. A strange shoot of hope unfurls somewhere in her and she feels again the wrongness, the disjointedness, of them no longer living together. Oh, she wants to say, do you think you might, would it be possible?

Then she sees they aren't holding hands after all. Her father has his hand pushed toward Claudette, but Claudette's fingers are curled around the purse on the table in front of her.

Claudette looks at Marithe, and Marithe looks back, and the sense that her mother knows it all floods through her. She knows what

Marithe was just thinking; she knows that Marithe knows about everything. Relief and fear compete within her, but her mother blinks, then smiles at her. She raises her hand in a gesture that might be an indication to come forward and might be a sign to say, all will be well; everything is going to be all right.

For Dear Life

DANIEL

Donegal, 2016

You know what's strange about having kids over the age of ten?

They don't go to bed.

Time was, you could put them in the bath at 7:00 p.m., stick them in their pajamas, read them a story, and by eight o'clock they'd be asleep: job done. You and your spouse could lift your heads and look at each other for the first time all day. You'd have two or three clear hours in which to do whatever you liked. Talk to each other, read a book, something a little more horizontal, or just revel in the idea that no one would tug on your sleeve and make strange demands of you. (I once wrote down my favorite of these: "Daddy, while you're cooking dinner, can you make me a puppet theater?" Marithe, aged four.)

But the over-tens, now, that's a whole other matter. They hang around. They refuse to be compliant about bathing. They wolf down their dinner, then require further sustenance. They want entertainment, conversation, help with suddenly remembered projects, debates over pocket money, holiday destinations, choice of available beverages. You might try to slope off somewhere, to some armchair in a quiet corner of the house, to open a book, when in bursts a teenager, incandescent with rage because the laces have broken on a particular pair of sneakers.

It is, in some ways, harder than all the cajoling and soothing and settling you have to do with the under-fives, and I thought, at the time, it couldn't get harder than that.

So, anyway, here I am, having inveigled my way into the house of my ex-wife, formerly my house, where I lived for almost ten years. It looks remarkably like it always did, except that she's repainted everything, but that doesn't in the least bit surprise me. Claudette has an internal engine that moves at a speed faster than that of any other human I have ever known. She cannot stand still, cannot sit, of an evening, on a sofa and just contemplate her house, her rooms, her home, the way it is. No, she must get on, she must work, she must change things, always. It's nothing short of a compulsion. She doesn't see a room, an alcove, a wall, a piece of flooring: she sees a work in progress, a project just waiting to be embarked upon.

The sitting room is still smoky blue, however, I'm happy to see, and the gold stars are still in place and I am, for the first time, pleased to look at them. Whenever I caught sight of them, in the time I used to live here, all I could think about was how Claudette had scaled a ladder while six months pregnant to stick them up. My fury about that used to kind of take the edge off my appreciation. But now? Now I can see their appeal, their idiosyncratic genius.

I am sitting in one of the leather armchairs by the stove, trying to stop myself from wondering who might have advised her about that mud-spattered four-wheel-drive vehicle parked in front of the house. Claudette has less-than-zero interest in cars, so somebody must have helped her buy it. Of course, my mind is galloping ahead, whisking me toward disaster: another man, another marriage, has my place been taken so soon?

It's past ten o'clock. Ari has put Zoë to bed and has shut himself away upstairs to catch up on some work, or so he said. Calvin is in bed, although not asleep, judging by the plaintive requests for drinks from his room, and Marithe is slumped on the couch, like a felled tree.

Claudette is moving around the house, clattering dishes in the kitchen, flitting past the door with armfuls of laundry, picking dead leaves out of a plant, straightening the books on the shelf. This is silent Claudette-speak for *Time to leave, Daniel.* I know this, she knows this, but I'm not ready, not quite.

On the sofa, my daughter, my only living daughter, yawns, her mouth opening pink, like a cat.

"Sleepy, honey?" I say, ever hopeful.

"Nnnn," Marithe says, through another yawn. She turns over onto her side, rubbing her eye, and her face is soft and blurry, like it was when she was a baby. "Dad?"

"Yes?"

"Are we still coming to New York next month? Me and Calvin?"

"Certainly."

"Even though you came to Ireland?"

"You bet. I booked all the tickets. Your mom's got them. I'll be there to fetch you from the airport, like always."

"Can we go to that place again?"

"Which place?"

"The one with the train tracks and the ice lollies."

I'm mystified by this description. "Train tracks? You mean the subway?"

Marithe shakes her head and strands of hair fall over her eyes. "Nah." She raises her arm above her head. "Up high. Like, a park."

"Oh, you mean the High Line."

She smiles, under her hair. "The High Line," she whispers, half to herself.

"You want to go there? Sure, we can go there."

"Can Niall come, like last time?"

"We can ask him. I'm sure he'll come if he's not busy." I go over to the sofa and take her by the hand. "Come on, sweetheart. Time for bed, I think."

Marithe stumbles to a standing position, leaning on my arm as we move up the stairs. "Does Niall still live with you?" she asks.

"No, not anymore. He has his own place now."

"Have I been there?"

"No."

"Can we go?"

"Sure."

At the bathroom door, she turns to look at me. "Is he still sad?" she asks.

I reach out my hand to brush the hair off her face. "Niall is a lot better. You mustn't worry about him. It's nice that you do, but Niall is OK."

My daughter looks me in the eye and says, devastatingly, "Are you still sad?"

I swallow. "Am I still sad . . . about . . . Phoebe?"

She frowns, concerned, and nods. And I look at her, this perfect being, her skin so vital, so pale that you can see the lifeblood coursing beneath it. I am beset by twin sensations: that I am lucky, the luckiest man in the world, to have this daughter, these children, and that I would kill, maim, destroy, any person who tried to harm them.

"I will always be sad about Phoebe," I say, with an effort to keep my voice even, "and so will Niall. But what happens is that, after a few years, you slowly realize it's OK to be happy too."

She looks at me for a moment longer, as if checking the veracity of this idea. Then she turns and goes into the bathroom.

"I'll come tuck you in," I say as I walk away.

I go back along the corridor, down the stairs, across the hallway, and into the sitting room, where the heat from the woodstove hits me in the face as soon as I open the door. There is no one there.

I move back into the hallway. "Claude?" I say, softly.

No reply. I try the front room—where I discover the addition of a somewhat-dilapidated chandelier since my time—and the scullery, where all the laundry is done, in a soap-and-steam–scented haze. She's not there either. Just some piles of clothing, in varying states of cleanliness, and some bottles of something labeled as plant-based, detergent-free laundry liquid.

I ascend the stairs, halfway. "Claudette?" I call again, louder this time, tilting my head, straining my ears.

I hear an answering "Yes?" coming from somewhere, a muffled, indistinct noise. Was it upstairs or down?

"Claude?" I try again.

"I'm here," she replies.

"Where?" I ask, baffled. I'm wandering now, down the corridor, into the sitting room, out again, seeking the source of her voice, a person engaged in a treasure hunt, desperate for clues.

"Here," she says again.

"I'm going to need a little more detail on that."

"In the—" and she says something incomprehensible.

"The what?"

"The Time Capsule," she replies.

I stand for a moment, my hand on the newel post where, a long time ago, Marithe, sent out here for throwing her dinner at the wall, carved several nicks in the wood with a penknife left carelessly on the stairs.

I had forgotten all about the Time Capsule. That was what Claudette always called a small wedge-shaped space leading off the front room. None of us quite knew what it was for, awkwardly and inexplicably attached to the main room, shelved in marble, with a miniature fireplace set into the wall, where you could have burned—at most—one or two twigs at a time. She never did anything with it: she kept it exactly as it had been when she'd found the house, so the walls were streaked with verdure and the fireplace was eaten by rust. Hence the name: the Time Capsule.

She liked to throw open the door sometimes and gleefully declare to whoever was listening—me, the kids, her mother, the dogs—this was how the house was when I found it. It was her testament, her monument, to her and the house, how far they had come together.

I find my way there now, through the front room, which, by the looks of it, is still used pretty much by Calvin and Marithe for knocking about on days too wet and cold to go out.

The Time Capsule door always was a little stiff, so I put my whole weight behind it, but it seems it must have been planed or rehung because it opens easily and I fly through it, arriving in the cramped space more precipitously than planned.

My ex-wife is crouched on the floor, her ass toward me. I land almost on her—I have to grip a marble shelf so as not to fall right on top of her.

"Jesus, Daniel," she is saying, putting up her hands to protect herself, at the same time as I am saying "Oh" and "Sorry" and "My goodness."

It takes us a moment to recover from this. We need to avoid eye contact, brush down our clothes, resettle our nerves.

She has changed into overalls and appears to be in the middle of peeling up the carpet, ripping it from the tacks that hold it in place. The walls have been scrubbed clean, the fireplace scoured, and some tiles decorated with butterflies have emerged from the decay.

"So," I say, after a moment, "you decided to fix this place up."

"I did," she says, turning back to her work. "I just thought, you know, why not?"

"Why not indeed?" I say, and wonder why I'm being so agreeable, so fucking hearty. What is going on with me? I need to find the right tone for what I'm hoping I'll find the guts to say; I need to locate the proper register.

Claudette wrestles a claw hammer into place by the baseboard and pulls down on it. "I met a woman in the village," she says as she strains against the handle, "whose mother used to work up here as a house-maid. So I asked her about this room."

"Oh, yeah?"

"You know what she said? She said"—Claudette waggles the hammer back and forth, her bottom lip held between her teeth—"that this was the flower-arranging room."

"The what?" I say, and look around at the walls, the shelves. "You've got to be kidding me. They had a room just to arrange their flowers in?"

Claudette gives a wry grimace. "Apparently so."

"Because everyone needs one, right? A dedicated flower space. I can't believe I don't have one. I'm going straight back to New York to put that right."

"Well, good luck with that."

"I hope that's what you're going to be doing in here. I can see you now, with your vases and your secateurs and the world's smallest fire roaring away in the world's smallest grate."

Claudette smiles and rips up a section of carpet.

I lean against the doorjamb (in itself a work in progress, I notice, with half the paint scored off and several test strips of color painted on its edge), fold my arms, and watch her, this woman I was married to for almost ten years.

What can I say about the end of our marriage? That I lost my way and she her patience. That it was, without doubt, the most ill-judged misstep I ever took. That I still wake, four years on, stunned that I ever let her slip out of reach.

That at my lowest ebb, she dispatched my son Niall to my flat in London. That this saved my life. He was fresh from Donegal, from this house. I could almost smell it on him when I opened the door and found him standing there: the air of this place, the valley, the trees, these rooms. He told me in his perspicuous and unadorned way that I had the choice between an early death or getting myself together. So he and I moved back to the States, two lame ducks together, and I checked myself into rehab and my son looked after me, cooked my meals, did my laundry, housed me, and basically did the things that I should have done for him all those years ago when he was growing up.

So here I am. Still alive, by the skin of my teeth.

Claudette yanks at the carpet and a section comes away with a violent ripping sound.

"If I had to place a bet," I say behind her, "you or the carpet, my money would be on you. That hairy old thing doesn't stand a chance."

She turns and I see that her mouth is filled with tacks.

"Have you thought about seeing a dentist?" I say.

Claudette rocks back on her heels and takes the tacks from her mouth, one by one, and lays them carefully on the shelf above her.

"You look . . ." She stops, considering me, her head to one side.

"I look what?"

"Different. Healthy."

"Oh," I say. "I was hoping for 'manly' or 'incredible.'"

She rolls her eyes, passing her claw hammer from one hand to the other.

"But I'll settle for 'healthy,'" I say, crossing the room, fetching a chair and settling myself in the doorway.

She looks at me; she looks at the chair. "You're leaving tonight?" she says—somewhat pointedly, I feel.

"I am. I gave a paper at the conference this morning and now I'm done."

"What time is your flight?"

I shrug. "I still have a couple of hours. I thought I'd take a look through those boxes in the barn, sort out the things I want to keep from the things I can chuck, then I'll arrange for them to be sent to the States. If that's OK with you."

She nods and turns her head away, back to her carpet. "I think Marithe is waiting for you to say goodbye," she says indistinctly as she bends back over her work.

I kiss Marithe, who is already mostly asleep. I straighten the comforter over Calvin. I look in on Ari and Zoë, who are both fast asleep. I visit the bathroom; I put my briefcase and overcoat by the front door. I do all the things one is meant to do before departing for the airport.

Then I come back into the Time Capsule, or the Flower Room, as it should now perhaps be called. Claudette has half the carpet up. She is surrounded by rolls of old matting and underlay. She has her hair tied back and her sweater off. I look at her bare arms, her shoulders, the nape of her neck, and I am struck by how the familiar can sometimes look so ineffably strange. I think about the four women I've slept with since her and how none of them came anywhere near her. But, then, how could they?

"Wasn't it Cleopatra who rolled herself up in a carpet so she could visit Mark Antony?" I say as I get hold of another, smaller, claw hammer from the heap of tools on the shelf.

Claudette fixes me with a stare that I recognize the way I recognize my own reflection in the mirror: assessing, evaluating, not fooled by anything.

"Caesar," she says eventually. "Julius."

I kneel, my left knee complaining only a little. I catch the edge of the carpet tucked in around the fireplace with the spikes of the hammer. We are, she and I, wedged into this wedge-shaped room, like cats in a basket.

"As opposed to?" I say as I tug.

"Octavius or Augustus." She points to my hand, to the hammer. "You need to waggle it back and forth."

I do just that as I say, "I never knew you were such an expert on ancient Rome."

She shrugs. "I did the play."

"And you were Caesar, Julius?"

She turns to give me a look. "No, I bloody wasn't. I was Cleopatra."

"Of course you were." I turn to face her and we regard each other at our new proximity. "Now that's what I call typecasting."

She narrows her eyes at me and is just about to utter a riposte when the nails suddenly give way, the underlay tears, and we stagger backward holding a large section of old carpet between us.

"Want to be rolled up in this," I say, when we've regained our balance, "for old times' sake?"

She lets go of her end, pulling her best hoydenish face. "No, thanks. And that bit doesn't appear in the play," she says, "actually."

"Well," I say, tossing aside the carpet, "it should. Shakespeare missed a dramatic trick there."

She kicks some underlay into a rough pile, picks up a saw, puts it down. "So," she says abruptly, without looking at me, "how is life with you, these days? I hear you have a new apartment."

She is making a great show of examining the window frame, running her fingers along the sash mechanism, picking at the peeling paint, the crumbling putty.

I think about her as she is in front of me, in her weird overalls and woolen socks and fancy leather slippers. I wonder if she still wears that Indian shawl around the house, if she still drinks hot water with a spoonful of some honey that she claims has miraculous, antiviral, immortality-giving properties, whether she still plays the piano late at night and insists on cooking pasta in not-quite-boiling water because she's too impatient to wait. I wonder whether she still crashes the gears on the car as she's driving but denies all knowledge of this. I wonder if there is anything of mine that she's kept, any shirts, any books, any letters. I wonder if she still walks in her sleep and whether there is anybody there to get up, follow her, and lead her back to bed.

And then I think about the earth in the Borders of Scotland. Niall told me once, when I asked him, that it would be made up of soft sedimentary strata. I picture this earth as dark, near black, and moist, riddled with tree roots, with knotted tubers, the slow leaf-rich paths of worms. Soil is memory made flesh, is past and present combined: nothing goes away. I think about a night I spent there, sleeping on its surface, its crust, with that dense matter teeming beneath me. I think about a moment across a café table in Bloomsbury, when I could have changed things, could have laid my hand down and said, no, this must not be. I think about how Nicola and I might have come back together but in all probability not for long: we were too young, too different, we were straining in opposing directions. There might have been another Sullivan child—Niall would not have been my firstborn but my second—but otherwise I might still have ended up at a crossroads in Donegal, finding a woman and a boy sitting on the roof of their car, looking up at two hawks and a buzzard. Claudette would still have happened, either way. I think about this, how she is my unavoidable constant. And I think about an afternoon in a drugstore where I might have put myself between my child and that boy, absorbed that bullet into my own guts, my own head. How different it all might have been, how minuscule the causes and how devastating their effects.

"Yeah," I say. "I do have a new place. I figured it was finally time for me to fly the nest. It's really not that dignified to be living in your son's guest room at my age."

This, I want to communicate to her. I choose this. The here and now. I almost gesture around me, at her, the mysterious room, the floor above, where our children lie sleeping, but manage to stop myself. We must pursue what's in front of us, not what we can't have or what we have lost. We must grasp what we can reach and hold on, fast.

My fingers grip the fabric of my shirt cuffs, as if to underline this point to myself.

"And . . . how about the drink?"

I grin at her. "Sober as a nun. Haven't touched a drop for nearly two years," I release my hold on my cuffs and cross myself with an ironic flourish, "so help me, God."

She doesn't say anything but sidesteps me and slips out of the door. I hear her making her way through the front room, under the chandelier, and out into the hallway. There is something about this departure of hers that feels definitive to me, final, in a way nothing else ever has. I find myself standing in the confines of the Flower Room, devastation sweeping through me. Can she really have walked out, just like that? Is there really no hope for us at all?

After a moment or two, I go and find her. She is pulling a jacket around her shoulders, an old corduroy one of mine that I had forgotten about. "Shall I," she says, "show you where those boxes are?"

I look at her, I meet those green eyes, and we stand in the hallway of the house, she and I, and we look at each other. Her gaze is uncertain, wary, a crease between her brows. I think again of the first day I came here, the state of the place, Ari as a speechless six-year-old, the holes in the floorboards, which later I would mend, cover up, hammer down. I realize we are standing in the exact place where we first touched, first laid hands on each other—or, rather, she laid hands on me because I, uncharacteristically, couldn't bring myself to do it, to pull it off, to reach out for her. This is Claudette Wells, I kept telling myself as she cooked dinner for me for the third time that week, as we settled Ari to sleep together, as we sat on her couch, finishing a bottle of wine. You can't possibly make a move, are you crazy, get yourself out of here without making an idiot of yourself. So she went for it first: the one and only time in my life that this has ever happened. I think she must have sensed my predicament. I was saying good night and thank you for dinner; I was heading back to my B and B for the night; I was going in for the single peck on the cheek when I felt her grip the lapel of my jacket, felt her other arm curling behind my head, and I remember it was the first time that I had ever felt faint, felt consciousness waver, so great was the rush of blood shot out of my heart.

"The boxes," I say to her now, standing there in her Wellingtons. "Yes. That would be great."

We step through the front door, down the steps. The night is crisp, cloudless, the trees black and still against the glimmering sky.

Next to me, she shivers. "Feels like frost," she says, "doesn't it?"

We crunch our way across the gravel, past the car (whose provenance I would still be interested to know), and over the path to the barn.

"Watch your step," she says to me, as if I don't know this terrain, as if it wasn't me who laid these flags, as if I don't think about this place, these paths, these borders, this sky, every day, as if I don't map this place in my head every night as I am falling asleep in Manhattan.

In the barn, which smells as it always has, of dust and hay and bicycle oil, she waves an arm in a curve. "There," she says.

We are facing an entire wall of boxes, of tea chests, of suitcases, one of which I recognize as the holdall I brought with me on spring break all those years ago. Is it possible that it still holds the ashes of Grandpa? Eminently so.

"My God," I say.

"I know."

"I had no idea how much I left here, how much I—"

"I tried to tell you."

I turn away and see, behind me, a tangled mass of children's vehicles. There is the tiny blue-framed trike Ari used to circle the house on, when I first got here. There is the yellow bicycle I taught Marithe to ride, holding the back of the seat, until I felt the surety of her balance and was able to let go. An old stroller of Calvin's, covered with thick layers of dust.

"You know," I say suddenly to Claudette, and I need to make my apology, I need to look her in the eye and say sorry, but what comes out is something quite different. "You have done such an amazing job with them. You really have. They are so lucky to have you."

These words have an unaccountable effect on Claudette. She looks astonished, then confused, then floored. Then her eyes brim with tears, which spill from her lashes, down her cheeks. I reach out and, with the very tips of my thumbs, I brush the tears away.

"Oh," she whispers, bowing her head, "why do you always do that?"

"Do what?" I say, and I step toward her, closing the gap between us.

"It drives me crazy."

"What does?"

"Your ability to . . . to . . . say the thing I least expect you to say." She tosses her hair back off her face and glares at me. "It's—it's very disconcerting . . . I mean, I get myself to a place where I know how I feel about you and then"—she is shouting now—"then you turn up, out of the bloody blue, looking all . . . all . . ." She gestures at me with a violent shoveling motion.

"All what?"

"All nothing!" she yells, and gives me a shove in the chest, which makes her, not me, stagger backward toward the bike-and-scooter tangle. "And then you go and say something like that."

"Why shouldn't I tell you what an incredible mother you've been? Those kids wouldn't have had a chance without you, without your—"

"Stop it!" She puts her hands over her ears. "Just stop it. I don't want to hear it."

"OK," I say. "I won't breathe another word about your mothering skills."

"Good."

"Superlative as they are."

"Daniel—"

"Can I say one more thing? If I'm allowed?"

She shuts her eyes. "If this is about Marithe going to school, then I refuse to—"

"It's not about Marithe going to school."

"Oh. What is it, then?"

I take in a lungful of the barn's dusty, chill air and I think about the glistening white of the salt desert, the way the lakes threw back images only of the sky above, how the landscape still held the form of its aquatic prehistory. "I owe you an apology," I say. "I'm sorry for everything," I say. "I'm sorry for going off the deep end, for leaving you to cope with everything, for dropping out of your lives for a while there."

She regards me from across the barn throughout the length of this speech, her fists buried in her jacket pockets.

"Most of all," I say, "I am sorry for being cavalier with our marriage. I regret that more . . . more than I can say. I am so sorry." I open my hands to her, as if the apology is an object that could be contained within them.

Claudette looks at me for a moment longer. Then she gives a short nod, the kind you might give to an acquaintance seen from across a street. Then she turns and, for the second time that evening, my ex-wife walks out on me.

She leaves the bikes, she leaves the barn, she leaves me, sliding through the gap in the doorway, her footfalls biting down into the gravel as she goes.

It won't surprise you to hear that it takes me a while to collect myself. I look at the bikes, the scooters, the handles of Calvin's stroller, where patches were worn bare by the grip of our hands. I cast my eye over the cliff face of boxes. I fiddle for a moment with the latch of the barn door.

When I finally do step outside, the night has changed, moved on. Clouds have blown across the moon, obliterating its shadowy light, and a breeze is gusting in the tops of the trees, so I don't see Claudette until I almost trip over her.

She is sitting on the front steps of the house, a hood covering her head, her jacket wrapped around her.

"I don't suppose," she says in a low voice, "you have a cigarette, do you?"

Despite myself, despite everything, I laugh. "You're asking me for a cigarette? You?"

She shrugs. "I just had this strange urge for one and I thought maybe—"

"I'm afraid not," I say, and I lower myself down to sit next to her. "I don't smoke."

It is her turn to laugh. "Really?"

I shake my head. "Nope."

She is still laughing. "You gave it up?"

"I did."

"Completely?"

"One hundred percent."

"I can't believe it," she says.

"Neither can I, sometimes." I sigh, button up my coat, look at my watch. "Well, I should probably—"

"I've been thinking," she interrupts, in a rushed voice.

"Oh, yeah?"

"About the boxes."

There is a pause. She stretches out her fingers, laces them together, clears her throat.

"There are rather a lot of them," she says.

"That's true."

"It occurred to me that it might ... take you a bit longer than we thought. To sort through."

"It might."

"Maybe ... ," she begins, then stops.

"Go on," I say.

"Well, I don't want to ... I mean, I know you're busy ... you probably need to get back to New York quite soon ... "

"Not particularly," I say.

"Well, it's just an idea, but you could, if you wanted to ... if you felt like it ... change your flight."

I half turn to look at her, but she bows her head so that her hair forms a curtain around her face.

"My flight?" I say.

"Just so you have time to go through all that stuff properly. A day or two."

I make a show of considering this idea but in truth my head is filled with a tornado of sound, of confusion. "It's a possibility," I manage to get out.

"The kids would like it," she continues. "Having you around for a while."

"I guess."

"You could ... stay in the village, I suppose ... in—"

"A B and B?"

"Yes. Or maybe it makes more sense to ... "

"To what?" I say, and it's taking all my willpower not to reach out and seize her, to grab her arm and say, really? This is happening? Are you saying what I think you're saying?

"Stay here."

"Here?" I almost bark.

"In the house. There's plenty of room, of course, and ... "

"And?"

"Well, you could get on with the boxes more easily, couldn't you?"

"Oh, the boxes, yes. I suppose I could."

I make a show of looking at my watch, trying to ignore my heart, which is pulsing at such a rate that I'm sure she will be able to hear it.

"It is getting kind of late," I say, in a thoughtful tone.

"It is," she says, without looking at me. "Maybe you should call the airline."

"Maybe I will."

We sit side by side, our hands in our laps, and the mountain is one side of us, a dark, protective shape, and the village is far below us, pinpricks of light glittering and fracturing through the night. Somewhere behind us, an owl sends out its lilting, voweled cry. Claudette shivers. "I'm going in," she says, standing up, the hem of her coat brushing against my face. "Are you coming?"

"Yes," I say. "I am."

Acknowledgments

Thank you, Mary-Anne Harrington.

Thank you, Jordan Pavlin.

Thank you, Victoria Hobbs.

Thank you, Christy Fletcher.

Thank you, Jane Morpeth, Hazel Orme, Georgina Moore, Yeti Lambregts, Vicky Palmer, Barbara Ronan, Amy Perkins, Cathie Arrington, Laura Esslemont, Kate Truman, and all at Headline.

Thank you, Ruth Metzstein, for being my final reader; Simon Vickers, for guiding me through the mysterious world of auction catalogues; Dan Friedman, for transatlantic support; Morag McRae, for the loan of the headless lady; Louise Brady, for patience and kindness; Moira Little, for reasons she will know; Daisy Donovan, for always being ready to answer peculiar questions; Sarah Urwin Jones, for tea and encouragement; B. Marguin, for French-dialogue consultancy; and Katharine Hamnett, for her generosity over the gray dress.

Thank you to Falko Konditorei, for putting up with me for long periods of time.

Thank you, Rob and Janet, of Lancrigg, Grasmere, for providing me with a haven, yet again.

Thank you, Juno.

Thank you, Iris.

Thank you, Saul.

And thank you, Will.

I also owe an enormous debt, in more ways than one, to Antonia and colleagues at the Dermatology Daycare Unit in Lauriston Place, Edinburgh, who help people like Niall every day of the week.

A NOTE ABOUT THE AUTHOR

Maggie O'Farrell is the author of six previous novels: *After You'd Gone; My Lover's Lover; The Distance Between Us,* which won a Somerset Maugham Award; *The Vanishing Act of Esme Lennox; The Hand That First Held Mine,* which won the Costa Book Award for best novel; and *Instructions for a Heatwave,* which was shortlisted for the Costa Book Award. She lives in Edinburgh.

A NOTE ON THE TYPE

This book was set in Celeste, a typeface created in 1994 by the designer Chris Burke (b. 1967). He describes it as a modern, humanistic face having less contrast between thick and thin strokes than other modern types such as Bodoni, Didot, and Walbaum. Tempered by some old-style traits and with a contemporary, slightly modular letterspacing, Celeste is highly readable and especially adapted for current digital printing processes which render an increasingly exacting letterform.

Composed by North Market Street Graphics,
Lancaster, Pennsylvania
Printed and bound by Berryville Graphics,
Berryville, Virginia
Designed by Soonyoung Kwon